PRAISE FOR INTERFACE: BOOK ONE: CONNECTIONS

5 stars **Very Pleased with This Book!**

This was an excellent read for me. I usually avoid dystopian fiction, but I'm pleased I got this one. Wonderful character growth can be seen in Emerson, Quinn, and Ana. The most striking realization was how much I related to and cared about their plight. It's obvious that the author places a premium on strong female characters, and these three are no exception. The author's worldbuilding struck me as both intricate and credible. When I finished a book, I found myself wondering about the characters long after I had put it down. The following chapter has my full attention.

5 stars **A Sci-Fi Master Class**

Interface is a master class on how to write a great sci-fi novel. It has great characters, and original story, and a powerful message about our planet and how we are treating her. Interface takes place in the beginnings of a post-apocalyptic world. It is not quite at the point of no return yet, but if the people are not careful, it could be the end of humanity. The warring sides mirror ideas that we see in our own world. This could very much be an allegory for how we operate in our own time. After you are done reading, you will come away with new ideas of what we need to do in our own world to avoid ending up in a world like the one in the book.

5 stars **Challenges Our Trust in Technological Solutions**

Interface, Book One: Connection is a compelling and thought-provoking work. Hillhouse has crafted a universe that is both interesting and entertaining, leaving readers yearning for more. If you're seeking for a book to keep you interested and stimulate your mind, pick this one up.

5 stars **Loads of Fun**

This is a good book, plain and simple. The story grabbed me very quickly and I managed to read it in one sitting at the weekend. Not often that that happens and I think that says it all, no?

5 stars **Sci-fi Grounded in Stewardship**

The writing style is easy to follow, with pros that are engaging with relatable dialogue. Main characters have a sense of heart that is seemingly absent in so many modern sci-fi novels, which was appreciated. Looking forward to future installments

5 stars **Incredible World Build!**

I greatly enjoyed this read, enough to turn around and re-read it again after finishing the first time. If you have a taste for post-apocalyptic stories with one foot planted firmly in speculative fiction and the other in your backyard, you will absolutely enjoy this. Can't wait for the next installment!

5 stars **Very Captivating!**

This book is a captivating tale of a post-apocalyptic world where hope and freedom are scarce commodities. The characters are well-developed, and the story is engrossing, with enough twists and turns to keep the reader engaged. The author skillfully explores themes of power, corruption, and the struggle for independence in a world where those in charge are not always benevolent.

5 stars **Creative!**

A creative use of today's climate crisis and projecting into the future it's aftermath. I enjoyed the science that was based on factual interpolation.

5 stars **Great Book!**

"Interface" is a fascinating and introspective read about the protagonist's fight for freedom from an evil government and the post-apocalyptic world, with well-developed and believable characters and impressive world-building. I strongly recommend it!

5 stars **A Great Adventure!**

I really loved this book! Although I'm not a big fan of dystopian novels, I'm really glad I read this one. The character development of Emerson, Quinn, and Ana is wonderful. More importantly, I found that I really empathized and cared about them. It's clear that the author is invested in strong women, and the three here are exceptional.

I love experiencing the alternative worlds of this kind of writing from the imaginations of the most creative individuals. Interface is exceptional. It ties you to the present with descriptions of life outside the city, and, for better or worse, brings you to the future with the Interface. A fascinating read. The title says, "Book One". I am ready for more.

5 stars **Modern Lit with Classical Depths**

As I began to read, I was pleased by the depths of the story-telling, character building, and thought provoking plot-lines. I glanced at the bio of the author to actually find that the name is a pen name for two people who are well read and educated. This book was definitely well put together.

5 stars **Amazing!**

This story got my attention from the first until the las page. Especially the characters are very interesting.

I am definitely gonna read it again.

5 stars **Fresh and Hopeful**

The main characters are developed and approachable. This take on a post-apocalyptic world steps way beyond your average zombie/mutant genre and goes so far as to educate the reader to environmental issues going on today and how they could play out in the not too distant future. The description and dialog are very rich and layered in a way that while painting visuals never before seen............create a familiarity that makes you want to stay.

5 stars **Great Classic Sci-Fi**

This book reminded me of great sci-fi from the past, Heinlen, Asimov and others. It posits an imaginable dystopian future resulting from known issues currently being ignored or disregarded. The science makes sense. The future makes sense. The triumph of a free thinker unencumbered by the double speak and programming reinforces my understanding that knowledge is the most important thing to hand down to our children.
It was a great read.

5 stars **Get Comfortable**

I think you're going to enjoy this book! I had a hard time putting it down, real page turner. I'd start reading and next thing I know its been 2 hours. Totally worth the lack of sleep this past week. To me, the details and descriptions were incredible. I can't wait to read the next one! I'm already recommending it to my friends.

5 stars **Powerful. Worth the Read!**

I was swept away. The descriptions of food and sex were great. This is a new author to watch. This novel should be a movie or a Netflix series. I can't wait for the next book!

5 stars **Palette Cleanser**

Lovely world building with interesting character dynamics. I greatly enjoyed this read. If you have a preference for post apoc novels you will like this installment

5 stars **Deeply Sympathetic to the Injuries to Our Planet Wrapped in a Very Cool Storyline.**

The author is a good writer. Easy to sink into the story. Reminds me of early Stephen King in his prose and ability to capture the ordinary and mix it with the dramatic.

5 stars **Thoughtful**

A well-imagined yarn of the not-too-distant future. A vision that seems sadly possible, considering the steady creep of climate change and general technological hubris. And an awful end-state for today's digital divide: the wealthy and well-connected can get "Interface" implants that let them control the world's increasingly complex technologies. The poor are left behind.

Loved the characters, both the good ones and the bad ones. Also, the ones who are not technically human. Most of all, I liked the sense of hope that pervades the story, even in its darkest moments. I'm interested to see that story play out in the next installment

5 stars **Good Read**

I highly recommend this book to anyone who enjoys a well-written and engaging story. The author has done an excellent job of creating characters that are both relatable and interesting, and the plot is full of twists and turns that keep you guessing until the very end. If you're looking for a book that you won't be able to put down, this is definitely one to check out.

5 stars **A Story About Image, Power and Truth**

If this book is not about us, the current state of our collective political will, technology that is threatening to spiral out of hand and earth that promises disaster to come, then I don't know what to tell you. Very interesting way of telling the story of the human race and it's probable ending as most think. For transparence, I got the ARC of this book.

5 stars **Great Book**

It is hopeful, realistic and instructive in its reverence for the planet.

5 stars **Grab a Tea or Coffee and Travel Through This Great Read!**

I love this book and can't wait for the next in line. This is a great read, one you will find hard to put down. I don't write spoilers so you will have to enter the journey on your own, but it will be worth every minute!

5 stars **Realistic and Instructive in its Reverence for the Planet.**

Interface: Book One: Connection is a science fiction novel that explores the potential consequences of advanced technologies and their impact on society.

The author's ability to create a believable and compelling world is fantastic. I appreciate the book's fast-paced plot, engaging characters, and thought-provoking themes.

If you enjoy science fiction and are interested in exploring the potential consequences of advanced technologies, Interface: Book One: Connection may be a book worth checking out. I really enjoyed reading this!

5 stars **Beautifully Written with a Deserving Hero.**

The cover hooked me right away, but I stayed because Emerson Lloyd, the main character, felt so real it was as if I knew him. It is a well-paced, quick read that will keep you cheering for Emerson as he finds his way in a post-apocalyptic world filled with both wonderful and terrible people. I loved the tech in the simulation used as Emerson learned to fly. It was just the right amount of sci-fi, believable but not quite realized from what we know now. And the entire book gave me memories of *Ender's Game*, which was one of my all-time favs as a kid.

Really fun read with a powerful message that sounds almost too close to home right now. Bravo. Can't wait for more books from the author.

5 stars **Great Read!**

From the first paragraph you're in; brought into a world that is both simple and complex. Varied societies have sprung up as humans have learned to adapt from the loss of advanced civilization. All depend in some way on artifacts from the past. Nature has adapted too. An intuitive read. There's no need for long-winded character introductions or verbose world descriptions. You effortlessly form a relationship with the characters as you travel through their world with them. This clever story connects its post-apocalyptic world to our present-day mistakes, making clear credible links to our possible future. A compelling story that has as much to say about us today as it does about the world you are transported to.

INTERFACE

BOOK TWO: CROW CITY

R. K. HILLHOUSE

Cover designer: Iram shahzadi: aaniyah.ahmed@99designs.com

Publishing Services provided by Paper Raven Books LLC

Printed in the United States of America

First Printing, 2024

Paperback ISBN: 978-0-9909387-9-8
Hardback ISBN: 979-8-9878816-0-6
eBook ISBN: 979-8-9878816-1-3

INTERFACE

PART ONE

THE CHANDLER CUBE

Chandler didn't age. There was no reason he should. But every time Emerson entered the simulation, he was surprised by his grandfather's youthful appearance. The fact that Chandler had made the sim cube a few years before he'd died didn't enter Emerson's thoughts until after the disorientation of being in the sim wore off a few minutes into the session. There was something about the Interface's neural implant that interfered with his cognitive speed until his brain adjusted to being connected to the expansive worlds inside the computing device. And Chandler was a master programmer. His artificial realities were indistinguishable from life by most people.

Emerson took a moment to absorb the simulation. Chandler sat in his chair, one of the first he'd built out of bent oak and tanned elk skin. Standing, he was six foot four with long, white, wispy hair and brooding dark blue eyes that twinkled when he broke into a smile.

Chandler said, "Hello, boy, good to see you. When are you going to bring my great-granddaughter to meet me?"

Emerson was thinking about the room. Chandler made everything he saw, called it the homeplace. It was the house Emerson had grown up in. The same house that he watched be devoured with Quinn, Ana, and Elli by the biggest tornado he'd even heard of.

Emerson was sitting in the great room of that house, in front of a warm fire, sipping a cup of sassafras tea sweetened with his grandfather's disgusting stevia leaves. Chandler was in the chair beside him. Emerson grinned at his grandfather. He had to strain to remember that he was actually sitting in the cockpit of The Black Mariah, a modified executive-class shuttle he'd taken from The City and painted with flat black stealth paint.

As many times as he entered the sim, he still resisted letting go of the truth, that Chandler was gone. It didn't seem right, somehow, like a betrayal to the real Chandler. Of course, he was in an extremely high-resolution, Interface-connected, simulated reality, and his "grandfather" was merely a very detailed construct programmed by the old man when he was alive. The intelligence that was running the sim knew all of Emerson's thoughts almost before he recognized them. Thus was the two-way nature of the Interface.

Chandler said, "Emerson. I'm all that's left of Chandler now. There ain't no one to betray."

He got up and hugged Emerson fiercely. When he pulled back, there were tears on his deeply lined cheeks. He'd wet the younger man's shirt collar. He smiled and said, "It's me, Emmer. You can be here with me."

It felt real. And it felt good. A tiny part of his cynical self, ironically, the part that was most like Chandler, stood off to the side, frowning and shaking his head. It was dizzying. While he tried to regain his balance, Chandler said, "Now, what about my great-granddaughter? When are you going to bring her to meet me?"

"I don't know. Quinn doesn't want to implant Marya even if she did turn six last week."

"I'm *aware* of her age and Quinn's *opinions*." He snorted.

In some ways, the Chandler in the sim was easier to handle than his grandfather ever was when he was alive. He was always focused on Emerson and his family. When Emerson was growing up, Chandler was busy. Busy and grouchy most of the time. Now that he lived only in the simulation, Emerson could be the center of his attention. In other ways the sim pushed Chandler's feelings of superiority to the surface. While it was true that he knew everything that anyone inside the sim knew, he never seemed to tire of making the fact known.

Chandler went on, "So put an external one on her. You remember. Eggert put one on you when he gave your entrance exam."

Emerson had forgotten. "Yeah, but we don't have anything like that here."

"So? Get that genius girlfriend of yours to make one; I'm sure Anastacia could adapt an implant."

Emerson said, "Yeah. That sounds like a good idea..." A signal came through a separate channel on his communicator. Ana was calling him. He opened the call.

She said, "Someone is here."

"Someone? Who?" he asked.

"Someone you should meet. Where are you?"

"In the Chandler Cube. On The Black."

"Say 'hi' for me. Tell him I want to bring Little Chandler to meet him as soon as he's old enough." Little Chandler or LC was Ana and Emerson's son. He was a year younger than Marya.

"We were just talking about that."

Chandler said, "I heard that. Hi, Ana. How's my namesake?"

"He wants to do everything, all at once, and he's frustrated that his little body can't do it yet."

"Just like me. Hell, just like his father."

Ana was distracted. "Okay," she said, "I have to go, Grandpa. Emerson, you should come out now." She disconnected. Anastacia was an orphan and never knew her own grandfather. Emerson was happy she felt like a part of his family. The old man loved her, and she was an Interface programming savant. She often entered the sim to work on engineering problems with him. Simulation Chandler treated her like the daughter he'd wished Emerson's mom, Deborah Soo, was. But Soo was never interested in anything Chandler thought or did.

Emerson closed the sim and opened the hatch. The day was warm and sunny with almost no wind. The weather on the beach was like this most of the time. Emerson thought it felt amazing for February, having grown up in the southeast with its unpredictable weather. When the rains came, they were light. The air was almost never humid even with the constant breeze that came off the ocean. It seemed like the weather patterns had stabilized here.

The hatch stair retracted as Emerson stepped on to the sand. A movement caught his peripheral vision, and he turned. A strangely colored fox sat calmly at the base of the rocks that formed the natural wall behind their camp.

"Hey, what are you doing here, little one?" Emerson asked.

His Interface connection pulled up data on the fox's odd coat. He rolled the term, *melanistic fox*, over his tongue. They were typically orange and black. This one looked both diabolical and regal at the same time. She was a female, her eyes hazel: the same as Emerson's.

The fox whined and cowered, rolling over on her back and exposing the snare wrapped around her hind quarter, digging into her swollen flank, the fur completely rubbed away. Her flesh looked hot and angry.

Emerson approached. The fox did not move, but panted rapidly, making little squeaking noises. The snare was a braided sinew cord, obviously manmade. It had cinched so tight the circulation in the animal's limb was nearly cut off. The leg was shriveled and crooked. The cord had been there a while. The pads of her foot were cracked and bloody.

He bent and with a single move slipped his knife between the lash and the animal and sliced the cord, freeing her. The fox leapt away, scampering up the rocks. She avoided the leg; he hoped it would heal. But he had done all he could. She turned to look at him once and disappeared behind a bush.

Ana and Quinn stood 100 meters away, near the gate of lashed driftwood, blocking the path up and out of their protected beach camp. A tall stranger stood facing the women. Quinn and Ana each had a child on their hip. A plasma rifle hung from Ana's shoulder. Quinn's hand rested on the hilt of a large, sheathed knife tucked in her belt. Marya dropped to the sand and ran to Emerson, reaching to be picked up. Emerson scooped her off her feet as he approached and said, "Hey, Monkey!"

The visitor wore a close-fitting skin vest and leggings. A small bag and a cap made of the same tanned skin hung at her hip. She didn't look armed. Her posture was neutral.

Ana said, "This is Saą."

Little Chandler said, "Saą." Emerson bent forward and kissed him quickly. LC and Marya laughed.

Emerson turned back to Saą and extended his open hand, palm up. "Greetings."

She had umber-colored eyes. Her hair was so black it appeared blue in the sun, and her skin was the color of wet terracotta. Marya's face was brought close when Emerson leaned in, and she stared directly into Saą's eyes for a moment before the older woman turned her attention away.

Saą lifted her chin and looked directly into Emerson's eyes without blinking. "Greetings," she said, "I was traveling to the ocean for kelp, and I smelled your camp. I come from a settlement a few days' hike away, in the mountains." She pointed over her shoulder to the northeast. "We are a peaceful people and live with a minimal dependence on electricity. I am a healer." She had an accent Emerson had never heard.

Marya said, "Your skin looks like clay pots."

Saą smiled at her. Marya couldn't help but smile back.

Emerson noticed a hunting sling tucked into the waistband of her leggings. She saw him looking at it and added, "Small game." He nodded.

Marya squirmed to be let down and walked a few meters where she dropped down and began digging in the sand. The child looked like a miniature version of her mother with Quinn's straight black hair and long bones. Little Chandler stretched to go with his half-sister.

Quinn, suspicious of the newcomer, said, "We don't see many people. As a matter of fact, in close to six years, we have never seen or heard anyone." Quinn was thin. Her arms and legs, even her neck, were long. She tucked a strand of her shoulder-length hair behind her ear. Her violet eyes assessed the stranger. The silver ring in her right ear caught the afternoon sun as she turned her head.

Saą said, "My family keeps to themselves. You would never see us if we didn't want you to see us."

Ana said, "Where are your people? We've been flying all over this area and never saw any sign." She shifted her stout frame. Her adopted mother back in Blue Hole called her "big-boned," but there wasn't an ounce of fat on her. She put her hands on her prodigious hips. Her wavy auburn hair, braided in colorful ribbons, lifted in a puff of breeze, blowing into her eyes. Saą noted her emerald-green eyes and the opal stud in her left nostril. The three tiny gold rings along the edge of her right ear tinkled against each other as she tossed her head to clear her vision.

Saą looked at Ana for a long moment, formulating her words. "Your presence is pretty obvious," she went on. "I *have* seen your *shuttle*, as you call it. It is the sort of electronic technology that my people avoid. It will be a challenge to overcome when you meet them."

Quinn stood up straighter and said, "We're not going anywhere. What are you suggesting?"

Emerson resisted the urge to put his hand on her arm. Quinn responded angrily when he advised caution with that particular gesture. Instead, he said, "Why do your people avoid *electronic technology*, as you call it, Saą?"

Saą said, "Excuse my bad word choice. I only meant that interacting with my family, should you ever meet them, would be a challenge because of your use of *electronic technology*, as I call it." She smiled widely. "I carry no biases; I am a human first and then a healer. That is enough to fill up anyone's mind."

"I'd like to know more about your family. Would you share a meal with us? We could talk," said Emerson.

Marya had collected a few shells and was arranging them in the sand, pretending they were buildings. She was talking to herself in low murmurs.

Saą said, "I must be going soon, but a meal would be acceptable." They walked down the beach toward the encampment.

Emerson called to Marya, and when the girl did not come, he went back to retrieve her.

Saą continued, "I actually came to warn you."

"Warn us of what?" Ana asked.

"The earthquake. It will happen soon."

◆ ◆ ◆

SHIP AHOY

Elli had spent the morning near the shore where the freshwater stream ended its snaking trail and emptied into the ocean. The rocks at the shoreline were a perfect home to the small freshwater crayfish that she and Mule, an oversized housecat who shared a deep psychic bond to Emerson, collected in reed baskets.

Well, Mule didn't. She watched from a safe distance. Those little lobsters had proven painful when she put her nose too close for investigation.

Elli talked to Mule as if she was able to answer her. The woman wouldn't have been surprised if the big cat did. Mule seemed to speak directly into her mind, at times, but that was usually during some sort of crisis where everyone had to think fast—when there wasn't time to question. After the fact, Elli was never sure if it was the cat or just some part of herself that spoke.

"I think we got enough here, baby." They were back at the communal table setting out plates when the others arrived. The water on the fire was nearly boiling.

Emerson introduced Saą. Elli nodded and poured the crayfish in. She didn't speak or look at the stranger.

The oversized langostinos were the only one of Emerson's favorites. Elli put out a dish of whipped oil, which was as close to butter as any of the other crew had ever tasted. Emerson's granddad had stored a crock of butter in the cold storage. But they didn't eat any sort of dairy on a regular basis. Chandler only brought it out on special occasions. Emerson never did find out what sort of cream he'd had made it from. Before it was gone, the flavor had become as cultured as sharp cheese. When it ran out, Chandler had not replaced it.

Before eating, Saą bowed her head in a silent thank you. She said, "We make butter from milk fat where I live. We have a small herd of bovines." Ana passed the serving bowl.

Emerson said, "Cows?"

"I thought they were extinct," said Ana.

Elli snorted and broke open a shell with her teeth, sucking out the meat and reaching for another of the steamed, pink creatures. "You people. You think you've seen everything. If flying across the continent taught me a thing, it's that I haven't seen anything, yet." She laughed.

Elli had grown into an athletic young woman with bright red hair which became especially curly. It refused to stay contained in any weather. Her eyes were a striking ice-blue, and her skin was as pale as skim milk. At twenty-five, the spray of tiny freckles across her cheeks and the bridge of her nose had nearly faded away. She looked like a ghost next to Saą.

Saą said, "I agree with you, Elli. There really is more to the world than most believe. And yes, cows and most bovines were susceptible to the virus. But as with people, they weren't completely wiped out. Mother tells me that some bred with animals closest to their genetic relatives, and, because of the weakness of the originals, genetic abnormalities took over and became a new species."

She dipped a crayfish into the oil and ate it whole, wiping the corner of her mouth with the back of her hand. She continued, "Our cows are smaller and wider. They have thick, curly hair, but their faces look more like deer than buffalo. And they are docile. We let them wander free, but they come in for milking. The milkers, who are usually children, have a song. I don't profess to having a milker's voice, but I can carry a tune."

She pushed herself back from the table: a long, low workbench where the crew cooked and ate and built things. She stood and closed her eyes, tipping her head back. Her hands hung at her sides.

The melody quietly rose followed by several dips, building to the crescendo note. She repeated the phrase several times, smiled, and opened her eyes.

Her song lingered in the air like cleansing smoke. Ana found herself humming it. Elli caught herself grinning and quickly frowned, looking down at her pile of crayfish shells. She licked her finger. "That was beautiful," she said.

Mule appeared and leaned into Saą's shoulder.

Quinn said, "Where's Marya? She was here a second ago."

Emerson stood as he said, "She knows not to go near the water, and we are pretty well contained here." He called, "Marya!"

The others were standing now too.

Emerson said, "Ana, go up the beach, okay? Quinn and I will loop around behind the shuttle and scan from the rocks. Saą and Elli, go directly to the water."

"She knows not to go down there," Elli said.

"Go anyway. We should be sure."

Five minutes later, Quinn pointed and yelled, "Up there," and sprinted ahead. Emerson arrived soon after. Marya hung, unconscious, ten meters up the cliff face. Her ankle was caught between two boulders. The color drained from Quinn's face.

She and Emerson scrambled up the crumbling dirt, panting, out of breath. They reached their unconscious daughter and lifted her up, unpinning her foot from the rocks. Quinn gripped the limp, almost-six-year-old to her chest, tears streaking her face. She leaned on Emerson, his jaw clenched as he picked his way down ahead of her.

When they were halfway, Ana said, "Why would she go up there?"

Emerson stopped and looked out across the water. He could see the entire inlet from that point and scanned the horizon. It was probably ten minutes before sunset. A flash of light from far out to sea paralyzed him. Quinn bumped his rear.

She said, "Hey, let's move."

"Wait a second," he replied, taking the Interface-enabled optical sighting device from a loop on his belt. Ana had helped him craft it from a cannibalized helmet. He connected to it and scanned the horizon. A red blinking square surrounded a tiny black dot. With a thought, he zoomed in, and the image filled his vision. It was a tanker. Rusted orange and listing badly starboard. The stacks belched black smoke. He said, "This is bad, very bad."

They put Marya on the table. Elli looked in her eye with a light. Her pupils were fixed and dilated. "She must have hit her head."

Quinn felt Marya's skull. "Yes, she has a lump."

"Turn her."

They parted the child's dark hair. A lump covered the back of her skull near her neck. It was already turning purple. Elli felt it.

The color drained from Quinn's face. Emerson stepped forward. He put his arm around her.

Saą said, "I am a guest, so I do not presume anything. But I am an experienced healer. If you consent, I may be able to help."

Emerson moved himself and Quinn away. Quinn frowned. Saą put her hands on the girl's head and closed her eyes. She stayed that way for a moment and then sighed. "Roll her over. Put something soft under her neck." Ana rolled up her coat.

Saą put her lips to Marya's forehead and hummed a few notes. She took the girl's pulse and repeated the gestures, humming a little higher. After two more tests, she said, "Mother says the girl will be fine. But we may need to feed her while her nerves heal. She may be asleep for a while."

Quinn broke away from Emerson and said, "How long will she sleep?"

Saą said, "It's hard to say. As long as her body needs."

"That's not good enough for me. How do I know she isn't dying in there, unable to speak? What if she has a bruise on her brain? What if we need to ease the swelling? You want me to just wait? Fuck you." She went to Marya's side and looked at the child for a long moment, like she was trying to decide if she should take the girl and fly the shuttle back to the doctors in The City.

After a tense moment, she strode away up the beach. Ana said, "I'll go make sure she's alright."

Saą said, "Mother is never wrong. Why do you not believe her?"

Elli said, "We don't know you, for one, and we don't know your *mother*, for another."

Saą said, "She is not *my* Mother, Elli Moon. She is *The* Mother. *The Mother* of us all."

Emerson said, "I don't have any reason to doubt your mother, Saą. But until we have proof, I am going to do whatever I can. Help me bring her to bed. It will be full dark soon, and the temperature is already dropping."

Mule would not leave Marya's room. Emerson left a lamp burning low and the door open.

Emerson's house had only three rooms for sleeping and talking. They used stones for a foundation and salvaged timber and windows for the structures. All four houses in the encampment were small but snug, built in a semicircle around a large wooden table. Food preparation was done under the awning at the communal kitchen area, and everyone went into The Black Mariah when it was stormy or cold.

Quinn arrived back with Ana near midnight. She went to see her daughter. Saą squatted in the corner with her eyes closed near Marya's bed. After staring at her sleeping child for a long minute, Quinn sighed and left.

Emerson went to the girl and felt her forehead. He said, "Elli, can you sit with Marya for now? The rest of us should talk together in the shuttle."

She said, "Yeah, no. I don't mind being left out of everything." She grinned and waved for them to go. Emerson heard her sarcasm and reminded himself, again, to give his people the space to make their own decisions. It was hard to remember, especially when order went to shit, and he felt he had to act in a crisis. Someone needed to stay by Marya.

Quinn told him to lighten up. She'd said, "You don't always have to be the one in charge. The rest of us are more than capable, and you know it." He did. But knowing and doing were two different things. He opened a channel so Elli could participate.

He thought about including Chandler in the meeting, but it would exclude Saą. And even if she could join them, he wanted to keep the full powers of the Interface a secret until he was sure he could trust her.

They sat around the mess table in the rear quadrant of The Black Mariah. Quinn was distracted, unable to get comfortable. He changed the ceiling lights to a soft blue. The sound of the surf was amplified through the ship's speakers. Emerson didn't wait until everyone sat. As soon as they were all in the room, he said, "I don't know why Marya was going up on the rocks. But there is a tanker coming straight at us."

Ana said, "I thought there were no more tankers."

Saą said, "Yes, I have heard this story before. But it is false. Shipping was crippled and reduced, but not eliminated, run by a navy of slaves. Which, after the Interface, was most everyone."

"So, are they coming here?" Ana asked Emerson, but she knew he didn't know.

Saą said, "If the ship is a listing tanker, I would bet it is going to end up wrecked on the coast somewhere."

Quinn said, "But what can we do about Marya?"

Emerson held her hand. "We just have to wait, I guess."

Ana said, "What about this earthquake?"

"You said soon. What does that mean?" Emerson asked Saą.

Saą sighed. "There are signs. You are not seeing them."

Emerson said, "Show me, then."

Saą made a sound like air escaping a balloon. "It takes time. You have to put the clues together."

"I'm a quick study."

"We don't have the time."

Elli came in then, holding Marya on her hip. Quinn and Emerson stood.

Marya reached for him and said, "Daddy."

Saą said, "If you have ice in this boat, you should put some on the back of the child's neck and make sure she takes it easy. I must leave in the morning."

◆◆

Later before dawn, after everyone was still asleep, Emerson went down to the ocean. It was a tonic for insomniacs. He found Saą on the bench he'd built there. She was waiting for him.

"I knew you would come, Emerson."

"That's funny. I didn't know myself."

"It was inevitable."

They peered into the black sea where it met the slightly lighter grey at the pre-dawn horizon. There were so many stars; they looked like paint splatter. He took out his optical scope and sighted the ship.

He gave it to Saą and said, "It's a monocular that we've modified to the Interface. But you can see through it like a regular scope." She was looking, holding the scope in her lap. He went on. "Look for the smoke blotting out the stars. Once you find that…"

"Found it."

"You'll see the ship beneath, though it's faint."

"No lights."

"Yeah. Probably no people. But it's heading toward the shoreline."

She was still looking. "You can see by the angle that it's full of something. Either oil or water."

"Or a bad combination. Hey, you can see that? You must have amazing eyesight."

She handed him the scope. "I don't have to look with my eyes, Emerson Lloyde."

He looked back at her, not sure what to make of the information. It was hard not to fixate on. *Seeing without your eyes, without the help of the Interface.*

She continued, capturing him from his thoughts. "If it's oil, it will be a disaster for the coastline. You know the ocean is finally coming back. That is if the climate doesn't keep changing."

He said, "It's a disaster no matter what is inside it."

"The question is—can we do anything to make it *less* of a disaster? You and your crew and your flying technology."

The sky behind them began to lighten. Before long, the first beams of sunlight stretched out on the sand leaving the camp in the jagged shadow of the cliff-edge but lighting their backs and the glowing space before them to the ocean's lapping edge. They stood and turned back, walking together.

◆ ◆ ◆

THE PLATES WILL SLIDE

They sat around the long wooden table. Ana had pulled the overhead tarp tight to shield them from the mist that began falling soon after dawn. Quinn and Emerson had cups of steaming coffee they'd salvaged, and Ana sipped tea brewed from raspberry leaves sweetened with wild honey she and Elli harvested last summer. She had scars from that escapade.

Quinn was in a dark mood. She stared sullenly into the mist covering the ocean. It had been six years since she and Marya had escaped. Elli Rattlesnake Quinn was part of the aristocracy of The City, the only daughter of Boston Quinn, one of the original founders' families. It was his father, Mangrove Quinn, who brought the founders together to build The City when the world was nearing collapse—even before the virus. He knew what was coming. There were rumors that he had hastened its arrival. The secret story that floated around when she was a teen was that Mangrove released the virus selectively so he and his oligarch friends could take power over what was left.

Her father and the other lords called it a conspiracy theory—a transparent technique from the early twenty-first used to discount the truth by acting as if it were ridiculous. She and her friends never found any real evidence of that level of evil from her great-grandfather. But it didn't keep the rumor from circulating and growing wilder with every telling.

The fact was Elli Rattlesnake Quinn was not a rugged outdoor woman. She grew up with a personal maid, Tanya, who came to live with Quinn when both girls were just twelve. She had a private apartment at the top of Founder's Quarter with a secret entrance. She and her friends, other founder family children, grew up as royalty. She used her privilege whenever possible on whoever she needed to move.

True, since leaving The City, she fought in a war and became a refugee, learned to shoot a plasma gun and fly a shuttle. She mourned the death of her closest friend, Max Hamp; she still wore his stretch hat. But living out of a shack on the beach and sleeping in a shuttle cot or on a hard bed was getting stale. She hated her father and couldn't imagine going back to her other life. But Quinn was tired of adventure. She just wanted to go home and sleep in her feather bed. She was hardly listening to Emerson.

Saą added, "When the earthquake comes, it will compound the eventual situation with the tanker, wherever it makes landfall."

"So when are we going?" Ana asked.

Quinn said, "I can see that's the plan, but can we roll back a few meters here? This earthquake. How do we know about that? I haven't felt anything."

Saą said, "I'd like to say trust me, because you should, but this morning, Emerson and I were on the beach at sunup. I pointed to a school of fish swimming erratically and too close to shore. And then there were the northern geese. It's winter. They should be bedded down for the season. But instead, just this morning, we saw a V-formation, confused and flying out to sea."

Elli said, "What does that mean?"

"It means the electromagnetic forces that the animals use for navigation are fluctuating. I've felt it for weeks. A huge geological shift is building up. When the tectonic plates slip, the ground is going to move. It is only a matter of time."

"But how long?" Quinn asked. Little Chandler pulled his mouth from Ana's breast and burped. Everyone laughed.

"Soon. A few weeks, maybe. Not more than a month."

Elli said, "So what's the plan with this tanker? Is anyone on it?"

Emerson said, "We don't think so, but we can't be sure. There are no lights."

"We should fly out there and look around." Elli was always ready.

◆ ◆ ◆

ATTACK OF THE FROGMEN

Emerson was nervous about flying over so much water. The trauma lurked in his bones. When he was a toddler, his mother and father were killed aboard a boat in the middle of a lake at night. He drifted in the half-sunken vessel with the corpses until he was picked up and brought to his grandfather. He didn't talk about it, but Quinn, Ana, and Elli knew his history.

Saą was apprehensive about riding in the shuttle at all. But her curiosity overrode her concerns. Quinn showed her how to strap into the harnesses. Ana stayed behind with the babies. Marya seemed unfazed by her coma, but Emerson and Quinn were cautious about the potential catastrophic effects the pressures of flying in higher altitudes might have on her delicate cerebral blood vessels. Ana preferred working in the lab to the field. She used the time to research navigational systems in tankers from the late twentieth century while the kids went down for their nap.

She'd be able to zero in once they radio her with the ship's name and registration number. That was if the printing on the hull was still legible after more than half a century at sea. It only took ten minutes for them to reach the ship, which was listing terribly; the starboard side rail was nearly in the water. Inky-black smoke seeped from the stacks, and a trail of greasy, rainbow-colored film coated the water behind the nearly crippled vessel. The oil made a brown foamy churn in its wake.

Emerson said, "I can't make out the name on the bow. We'll fly around back to see if the stern printing is any clearer."

Elli said, "*Barrique.* That's an odd name."

Ana radioed back, "It means little oak barrel of wine, Bordeaux to be precise."

"What's a Bordeaux?" Elli asked.

Quinn said, "It was a region in the country of France—also the name of a robust red wine."

Elli said, "You would know that." Quinn ignored her.

Ana said, "It's not in the registry. I have no clue."

"We can't land on that angle, and I am uncomfortable with landing on the ocean—too much chop. But I want to go down to look around," Emerson said.

"I'll go," Elli offered.

"Don't leave me up in the air," Saą said.

Emerson put his hand on her arm. "I'll bring The Black down close to the ship and set the autopilot to stay locked hovering over the deck."

"I'm going with you," Saą said.

"Suit yourself."

When he opened the hatch, The Black Mariah was a couple of meters off the deck, but the tanker tilted so badly, they couldn't stand without gripping the rail. With the hatch open, the noise of the tanker's deteriorating engines was loud even over The Black Mariah's reactors.

Emerson shouted, "I need to check the bridge, but I don't feel hopeful. And it sounds like the mechanics of this boat are about to self-destruct. I can't believe the bearings haven't exploded yet."

Ana radioed, "If that's what you are hearing, I'd say you only have a short time before it fails, and considering how big it is and how fast it is moving, I expect that failure to include explosions and large metal parts bursting through the hull. It will probably sink quickly."

"Yeah," he replied, "We need to get off this disaster before that happens."

Saą said, "I'll check the hold to see how much oil is still in there."

"What do you intend to do about it?" Emerson asked.

"There are remedial mycelium strains that will neutralize the hydrocarbons. But we would have to make sure the hold was sealed before we introduced them. We might not have time."

"Can you find the right strains quickly?" Quinn asked.

Saą replied, "We can use almost any mushroom to break it down. But the mutant bearded oyster mushrooms are the fastest. I have seen them in the pine forest to the east. Plus, there are ways to speed propagation."

"We won't know what we are up against until I see," Emerson said, "But walking around on this thing is impossible."

Saą said, "I know how to find the correct strain, but I'll have to hunt for it."

"Is there a way to shut this thing down?" Elli asked.

"That's why I need to get to the bridge."

"Right." Elli scaled the steps to the control room, climbing freehand. She was long-bodied and toned, scampering up the rusting metal ladders and rails. All arms and legs, Chandler would have said. She could barely see through the filthy window.

She texted Emerson:

```
There are no controls. This is an Inter-
            face-controlled ship.
```

Emerson wrote back:

```
I can't connect. You are going to have to
              plug in direct.
```

She climbed back down. Emerson gave her a portable power supply cube. Once she got up to the door, she texted back:

```
It's rusted shut. I can't open it. I'll cut
                a hole.
```

She reset the power and used her plasma rifle to free the door. They had all become very accurate with the weapons. Elli cut a line in the door, severing the lock. The line glowed orange for a moment before swinging loose.

Every surface on the bridge was covered with rust. The only light that penetrated the grimy, mold-covered glass was milky green. The captain's and first mate's chairs were spring skeletons covered by scraps of moldy leather. The floor was scattered with powdery foam rubber. Elli used her knife to scrape corrosion from the access panel and pried open the twenty-centimeter-wide door. The inside was covered with white corrosion, but she was able to chip enough off to plug the cube in.

An instrument array lit up on the blank screen just above her brows, inside her skull. It was a confusing, multi-layer set of menus written in Cyrillic and Chinese logograms.

Emerson called on his communicator, "Pass me control."

"That's it. You're in," she replied.

Emerson said, "Leave the remote cube in the control room and come back."

He had been a highly trained pilot for The City's Enforcer corps, and he was familiar enough with Interface instruments to be able to patch a translation onto some of the tags. He sent images to Ana, who helped translate the rest. Within twenty minutes, the engines went silent. Emerson found the ballast pumps and tried to right the ship. The pumps failed with a terrifying screech before it was completely level, but at least they could walk on the decks.

Emerson said, "We are too far out to drop anchor. I'll stay with the tanker while Saą goes back to the shore to collect the oil-eating fungus. I'll keep it in more or less the same position with what power I have left. Quinn can fly The Black. Elli and I will explore the hold to see if it can contain the oil." He took a case of drones.

After Quinn flew away, Emerson and Elli were left standing on the upper deck.

"I hear something," she said.

"There are several processes that are still running in the background," Emerson said, "The engines are nuclear, and the diagnostics say the reactors are within spec, but the mechanics are worn beyond use. They aren't going to last much longer."

He used the front turbines to push back against the current, which was drawing them toward the shore. The bearings were so badly damaged that it sounded like the death of Chandler's salvaged diesel semi engine. The old man had repurposed it as a generator, but it was ancient and worn out, besides being far too big for their meager needs. One summer at dawn, a cam-shaft bearing disintegrated, and the thing self-destructed in a wrenching howl that had Chandler outside and naked, gripping his double-barrel Mossman shotgun. Until then, Emerson didn't know he slept with it.

The ship shuddered but seemed to be stationary. He and Elli went in search of the tank hatches.

"What do you think happened to the crew?" she asked.

"No telling, there's no sign of anyone. They probably died from the virus."

"This ship couldn't have been floating around the world aimlessly for fifty years. Something isn't right here."

They went to the main deck, and Emerson sent commands to open the hatches. He dropped an Interface-enabled drone into the first hole and shared the feed with Ana. The tank was nearly empty. Judging from the worn numbers on the wall, there were less than a thousand gallons.

They checked the remaining tanks. Ana used an X-ray filter to analyze the surfaces. The whole process took hours. Quinn arrived back on the tanker near sundown. She landed on the main deck this time and joined Emerson and Elli at the stern. Ana was just finishing up the final scan.

She said, "You can see the readouts. The walls are breached in several places. But emergency patches will seal most of it. Saą estimates that the oil can be absorbed and changed into a benign slurry of carbon nitrogen and sulfur. We need to give the mushroom a base on which to propagate. She says we can use wood chips, soil, compost, and leaf litter as a medium to grow them. We inoculate it and put it in the tanks. The fungus will do the rest. Once the oil is neutralized, we can decide the best way to dispose of the ship. I'd be able to sink it remotely."

Saą set to work making fruiting baskets for the fungi. Emerson, Quinn, and Elli located the worst breaches in the tanks and set the drone up to apply the patches. The first one was done and they were moving to the next when the tanker hit something in the water. The sound reverberated through the metal hull. In the distraction, Emerson slammed the drone into the bulkhead, knocking it into the oily muck. Quinn said, "What do you think that sound was?"

"There's so much trash in the oceans. You can never tell. Probably a shipping container. We have a couple more of these drones."

The second drone had patched tanks two, three, and six when Elli, who had gone back to the shuttle for a drink, sent a strange message to Emerson.

It said:

      Comenow.

Quinn said, "I'll go. You finish up here."

Emerson was frustrated. The hole he was patching was larger than the patch, and the metal of the rotting hull was crumbling beneath it. He said, "Yeah, yeah," only half hearing.

Quinn walked across the deck to the shuttle. The drone sealed the final patch, but dipped into the murky sludge enough to short out and sank, immediately leaving a couple stray bubbles. A moment later, a sound shocked Emerson out of his concentration. *Plasma rifle!* he thought.

◆ ◆

The blast Emerson heard was Quinn's rifle burning a hole through the six-centimeter-thick steel panel beside a man's head. It threw glowing red embers onto his wet suit, melting the neoprene onto the skin of his neck and shoulder. He screamed like he was being burned alive.

Quinn had already turned to the other man. Her Interface calmly informed her that military men in wetsuits used to be called frogmen. It was useless trivia considering the situation. Number Two was gripping Elli by the back of her neck. At the first man's scream, Elli's captor turned toward his partner, raising a sixteen-centimeter blade. Quinn adjusted the power of her rifle and removed two fingers from his hand. The knife clattered on the metal deck; he released Elli to grab the stump of his mutilated palm and howled. Elli twisted away and produced her hunting knife, also six inches, but wider and sharper than the frogman's.

Emerson rounded the corner and yelled, "Elli, no!" He was still several meters away.

The red-headed woman sliced a second mouth in Frogman Two's throat; it grinned at her as he crumpled to the deck.

Quinn pressed her rifle against the chest of the screaming man and said, "Stop or I'll stop you." He went silent. Emerson arrived. Elli wiped her knife on the dead man's wetsuit.

◆ ◆ ◆

YOU CALL THAT A PLAN?

"Who are you?" Elli asked.

She removed his mask and peeled away the head covering from his suit. The bald man didn't speak; he looked for an escape, but Quinn poked her rifle in his face.

Emerson said, "That's less important than what you are doing here. Are there more of you coming?"

Emerson used his Interface to text Elli and Quinn:

```
Now that you've killed one of them, we can't
let this one go. But I need to find out where
                 he came from.
```

He was talking more to Elli than Quinn. Emerson didn't want her killing this man before he questioned him. Chandler had drilled him on this sort of situation while they had walked in the woods.

When he was fifteen, Chandler had asked his grandson, "An armed stranger surprises you. What do you do?"

Emerson was used to his grandpa's teaching style and answered quickly without thinking, "If he was threatening me? I'd kill him."

Chandler said, "Wrong. Chances are good he's not alone. What happens when his friends find out you killed him?"

Young Emerson was silent, absorbing the direction things would go because of his actions.

Chandler continued, "Then you have a war. And what if these people could have offered you something you need or value? Most people can. That's the point of people—we help each other. You just ended any possibility of that. But at a more basic level, son, you should never kill unless there is simply no other way. How do you think the person's mother or brother would feel if you killed them?"

Emerson had imagined what he would feel like if someone killed his grandfather. And now that Chandler was really gone, he understood the lesson at a deeper level.

Elli texted him:

```
Sorry, Dad.
```

She would tell anyone that Emerson was not her father. He looked over at her, but she was looking away.

Quinn texted:

```
Isn't there some other option?
```

Emerson did not reply. He spoke to the frogman, "I know you can understand me. You must know that I can't let you live. But if you tell me where you come from and if you have friends nearby, I can at least kill you quickly."

The frogman's face was blank. He looked from Quinn to Emerson quickly, calculating his options. Emerson looked at Elli and nodded. She drew her knife and stepped toward him.

He blurted, "I can tell you where they are if you let me live. Otherwise, you will be at their mercy."

Emerson stopped Elli with a gesture. "Who was he to you?" He nodded at the dead frogman.

Number One had a slight stutter. "Another s-s-soldier. A nobody l-l-like me."

"Where do you come from?"

"We've been trailing this crippled tanker for weeks hoping someone would try to salvage it. Our boat is tied up on the port side near the bow."

"You're pirates."

"We have a beacon on our b-b-boat. They track our position. They know where your camp is. It's clear at night; you're the only light on the shore."

"How many are you?"

"Sixty, maybe. We live on an island south of here. I-I-I can show you."

"Why would you give up your friends?"

"They're no f-f-friends of mine. I was captured, see…" He pulled down the neck of his wetsuit, revealing a silver collar. "If I get too far away or try to escape: Zap! The shock will knock me out. Then they come find me. Punish me."

Emerson said, "So what are you proposing? If there is a way to free enslaved people, we are obligated to consider it."

He looked at Emerson and Quinn and then said, "I take one of you prisoner. The others follow at a safe altitude in your airship. When we get to the island, you help me kill my captors, and we go our separate ways."

"Why the fuck should we trust you?" Quinn asked.

"Your other choice is suicide. At least this way you get them first."

"That's if you are telling the truth, which I doubt," Elli replied.

Froggy shrugged. "Your risk, either way."

"Okay," Emerson said. "You can take me."

"No. I need a woman. If I bring back a man, they will know something is wrong. I'm only supposed to bring back women. They kill the men."

Emerson said, "That's bullshit."

"I'll go," Elli offered.

"You are who I'd pick," the frogman said. "You scare the shit out of me."

◆ ◆ ◆

A SILVER INTERFACE COLLAR

The surviving frogman's name was Paxon. The skin on his face was scarred from a childhood chickenpox infection. His cheeks were darkened with a shadow beard, and the burn on his neck oozed.

They agreed to follow his plan. He gave Elli a silver collar like his and showed her how to snap it on her neck.

"Once it's on, you can only remove it with a key. The bosses have them," he said.

Elli backed a step away. "Nah, I don't think so."

"They will know you are not collared and kill us both. Believe me, these fuckers don't mess around."

Emerson said, "Let me see that." He used a magnifying setting on his scope to inspect the small seams in the collar.

He sent Elli a text:

```
Interface-controlled. You can unlock this
              anytime you want.
```

She replied, I could unlock his too, right?

He shot her a look and wrote,

Not yet.

She snapped the collar around her neck. Three LEDs in the seam flashed red for three pulses, and the lock snapped closed. The lights turned to a single emerald green and faded out.

"They know I have her; I need to head back now," Paxon said.

Emerson gave Elli a ten-millimeter-wide, silver cube, about the size of a six-sided die. He said, "Keep this close. I can track you with it." Elli knew that the cube was also an Interface computer which would enable Emerson to remote control and monitor other Interface-controlled machines from The Black Mariah. She would keep it hidden.

As they climbed down onto the frogman's boat, Emerson called, "Paxon, if I suspect that you are double-crossing me, I will let Quinn here kill you. That plasma rifle will cut through anything. The range is a half kilometer. Don't fuck with *me*."

◆ ◆

They waited until the boat was 100 meters from the tanker before charging the turbines on The Black Mariah. He switched to silent mode and rose to 4,000 meters. Then he messaged Elli to tell her he had her in sight and not to worry. She sent him back a poop emoji.

Quinn communicated the plan to Ana. She and Saą began setting up the inoculation pouches for the remedial mycelium. They were linked into the tanker and monitored its position.

Then Quinn spoke to Marya on a handheld communicator, "Hey, hon. How's your head, baby?"

The girl was used to the handheld; she called it her talky. "I got a headache, Mama. Ana massaged my neck, and it got better, but I'm tired, like my brain is too big."

Quinn frowned. "We'll be back soon. You do what your aunty tells you and don't wander away. She has enough to worry about with your half-brother."

Marya said, "I love you, Mama. Tell Daddy I love him, too."

Quinn turned to Emerson and said, "That worries me. I wish we could perform a CAT or an MRI. Doctor Sailor has scanners. My father is an ass, but he listened to her when she told him to find all that advanced imaging. We should have that too. We need it, Emerson."

Distracted, Emerson said, "Right. I hear you. As soon as we get free of this bullshit."

Quinn grabbed his hand and said, "Hey, I'm talking about our daughter, Emerson."

He turned and hugged her, whispering in her ear, "I'm sorry, Quinn. Too much is happening at one time here."

◆ ◆

They tracked Paxon's forty-three-foot Chris-Craft Roamer from an altitude of 4,000 meters. He routed the sound feed from the cube Elli carried to The Black Mariah's cockpit speakers.

Paxon said, "You have really unique features. What did you say your name was?"

"Oh shit…" Quinn said.

Elli replied, "I didn't."

The sound of the boat's diesel engine glugged in the background for a long minute.

Emerson said, "He has no idea…"

Paxon said, "Anyone ever tell you, you got pretty eyes?"

Emerson texted Elli:

```
Ignore him. Don't hurt him.
```

Elli said, "What, Paxon? You think you want some of this?"

Emerson moaned. He knew that Elli was showing him her ass.

Paxon said, "Oooh. Nice. What's that tat mean?"

"It means that if you come near me, I'll pop your eyeballs out of your head with my thumbs. FUCK OFF, SHITHEAD."

Emerson imagined Paxon warding her away with raised hands.

Paxon said, "Okay, okay. Don't have a hemorrhage. Sheesh!"

Both Quinn and Emerson laughed.

◆ ◆

Emerson saw the island on the map overlay. The actual land came into view a moment later. He told Elli her ETA was twenty. He sped up and flew over the island at 20,000 meters, then doubled back and hovered at high altitude in stealth mode, ready to dive in if necessary. He routed the scope camera feed to the main display. The resolution was high enough to see the blackheads on Paxon's nose.

When the Chris-Craft entered the bay, two skiffs with outboards closed and chained the underwater gates behind him. No vessel could enter or leave. They brought the boat to the pier and cut the engine.

A paunchy, bald man in a silk kimono, flanked by two huge, broad-shouldered guards, strolled onto the pier. Paxon brought Elli up out of the boat, gripping her arm. She let him push her around. When they were standing on the splintered wood, the man in the kimono said, "Where's Mack?"

Paxon looked at the boards and mumbled, "He didn't make it."

Kimono grunted. "This is all? Were there any others?"

"All dead. This was the only cunt."

Kimono grinned. "Is that what it is?"

Elli struggled against Paxon's arm. She put on a good show. Emerson had trained her. He knew she could kill all three of them before they saw her move.

Kimono suddenly clapped his hands like a happy child and said, "Goody goody! Clean her up and dress, er, undress her. Put her with the rest." Elli heard him suck the saliva back into his mouth. He was actually drooling,

One of the burly guards took Elli by the arm and led her away. She resisted enough to make it look like she was trying and then submitted. As they crossed a lawn, she noticed everyone except Baldy the kimono man wore a silver collar. They entered a building that looked like it was once a marina. The far end had caved in. There were weathered patches on the main roof where the shingles had blown away. The wood was rotted out, leaving several large holes. Sunlight shone through.

Emerson and Quinn tracked her on their internal displays. He said, "We need to know where the people are."

"Right. And where their computers are," Quinn added.

Emerson said, "We'll disable their Interface ability and any data stores. That should give them something to worry about besides us."

Elli sent him a text:

```
I'm with the women now. Going to have a bath
and get changed. Holy shit, they have fruit!
```

Emerson asked for more, but Elli didn't respond.
Ana texted him:

```
I found some details about this island they
are on. Seems it was privately owned. There
is a big house and several outbuildings. The
people who lived here were like some kind of
royalty. They were well supplied, like they
          expected the collapse.
```

Quinn said, "Several of the families that got together after the collapse and formed The City came from private sanctuaries like this. Most of them were too isolated to survive on their own. I bet this island was the home of someone like that. I might even know their kids."

```
   I sent you the plans I have, Ana replied. The
    buildings are probably falling down. But
  there is a system of connecting tunnels that
   the servants and staff used. That may be of
                  some help.
```

The sun was setting. From the front windshield of The Black Mariah, it looked like a 360-degree rainbow circling the shuttle. A flock of birds passed beneath them, flying in formation. Suddenly, the group scattered, coming together again in several smaller groups, each heading a different way. Emerson looked at a compass—the needle jumped, returning to north but drifting past it slowly before snapping back again. The ship's diagnostics flashed an orange warning.

He said, "There's something to Saą's earthquake prediction."

He looked at the birds. They had reassembled into their original formation. "It is going to be a while, Quinn. We shouldn't try to go in until an hour or so before dawn. Let's get some rest. This has been a crazy day. The Black Mariah will wake us in a few hours. Autopilot will keep us hovering in position."

They went to the captain's cabin and cuddled together on the single cot. Sleep came quickly. Soon after, another electromagnetic wave disrupted The Black Mariah's chronological processor. As a result, comms went offline while the system attempted to diagnose the gyroscopes.

◆ ◆ ◆

ORANGES AND CONCUBINES

"Where did this come from?" Elli sucked on an orange slice, sitting waist deep in a brass bathtub filled with scented water. A woman in a mauve, silk sari was brushing her short hair with a hard bristle brush. Other women were padding silently around the low-ceilinged room, moving from place to place, carrying books, pillows, trays filled with fruits, and pitchers of drinks. The walls were hung with tapestries; thick pile rugs were scattered underfoot. Each woman had a silver collar. Some were naked, but most wore a strange array of costumes.

Elli shifted the silver cube from one side of her mouth to the other. *I hope they give me something with a pocket*, she thought. When she realized they were taking her clothes, she had few places to hide the Interface cube. It was a struggle to eat around. She contemplated other locations she might have to stash it and shuddered.

The sari woman said, "There is an orange grove on the island." She sighed. "I have never seen such fine red hair. Many would kill for your hair." She glanced at Elli's thighs. "And naturally red. You, my new friend, are a very rare treat. The bosses are going to cover you with affection." She raised her eyebrows. Elli got the impression that *affection* was code for something other than praise.

Elli was an abandoned orphan raised by Michel as a branded pleasure girl. He was a sadistic asshole and put her to work on the streets when she was twelve. He called her Mew Mew and marked her with a dark blue tattoo on the back of her hip, a triangle pointing down with a red dot in the center. After her village was leveled by Boston Quinn's Enforcers, Emerson found her in the rubble, filthy and mute, and gave her clothing and named her Elli after Elli Rattlesnake Quinn. He brought her to Blue Hole where she met Ana and the rest of the juice hackers, and, eventually, she began to trust him and relax a little.

Her past life was a fading nightmare. Elli found new purpose in firearms. She owned several weapons in addition to her beloved plasma rifle. She was a natural markswoman, and her accuracy was nothing short of astounding. But she knew nothing of her ancestors. The void was like a thorn in her brain. And since there was no one to ask, she would always be disconnected from her history, not knowing where her true talents and attractions were rooted.

Elli stood at the sari woman's gesture, and two younger girls rubbed her body dry with large plush bath sheets. The towels were thicker and softer than any Elli had ever felt. The girls giggled and ran away laughing.

The sari woman said, "They have never seen red hair on a girl's head or… elsewhere. All the women here are shaved."

Elli sniffed. She never went near a razor, and she didn't intend to. "Huh," she said.

The other woman tipped her head. "You'll see. We do things the way the bosses say here." She tapped her silver collar with one long red fingernail.

They dressed Elli in a green sari. It was really just a long swath of silk, tied around her waist and over her shoulder. It had no pockets.

Another girl arrived. She was dressed in silk balloon pants and a red velvet jacket with large silver buttons that matched the combs holding her black hair away from either side of her face. She whispered something to the sari woman who said, "It's time to meet your master!"

Elli texted Emerson:

Please get here soon. I may have to kill
someone if you don't.

The girl with the velvet jacket led Elli into a cathedral-ceilinged banquet room. At first, she thought the roof was glass, but looking again, she realized that the frame was all that remained—there was no glass. After that, she noticed the signs of damage. The carpets were rotting. The tables were warped and delaminating. The upholstery was torn and threadbare. Stuffing spilled from the chairs.

Scented water had been sprayed around, but Elli could smell the greasy-sweet odor of mildew and rot. The bald-headed kimono man stood before the table with his arms out in a welcoming gesture. A group of five similarly dressed men, some with huge beards and long hair, others skinny, hairless, and bent, stood behind him. Many wore sunglasses; their skin was pale and blotchy. The sari woman and the other women began to file into the room. All of them were naked, their bodies hairless.

Baldy dropped his kimono and turned to the other men, who were also now naked and in various stages of arousal. The men were not shaved. The velvet-jacketed girl disappeared. Elli couldn't recognize anyone. She saw a black velvet clutch in a pile of clothes and snatched it up, slipping the strap over her head.

The women began circulating through the men's group, taking them by the hand and leading them to couches at the edges of the candle lit room. The shadows flickered over the patterns in the decomposing rugs. The unattached women began pleasuring each other, kissing and rolling around on the rugs. Elli put the Interface cube into the purse and snapped it closed.

She supposed she was expected to shed her clothes and pair off with one of these groups for sex. Elli was momentarily concerned that they would find her hairy body revolting. But she pushed the fear from her mind. *Fuck that shit*, she thought and used her Interface to unlock her silver collar.

She texted Emerson:

YOU BETTER COME NOW. THIS IS YOUR FUCKING
SIGNAL.

When he didn't respond immediately, she decided to unlock every collar on the island. *That should stir things up*, she thought.

She spotted Paxon looking miserable, holding a large silver vase. A naked man was pissing into it while two of the concubines nibbled his ears and pressed their breasts onto him. All three giggled. When the locks released, every collar on the island clattered to the floor. The music, which Elli hadn't noticed before, coming from an ensemble of naked women, also stopped. The hand drums, finger cymbals, and flutes went silent. The room froze for what felt like a solid minute, though it was only seconds.

Then all hell broke loose.

◆ ◆ ◆

WHO YOU GONNA GET TO DO THE DIRTY WORK?

Emerson woke up startled. In his dream the ground had been moving. As his consciousness rose out of the murky depths, he received Elli's second text. He read the first which woke him up immediately. A moment later, The Black Mariah was in a powered dive toward the main house on the island. Before slowing, he noted the reactor was in silent mode and looked at the fuel gauge, cloaking the reactor's wasted fuel. And since they didn't have a ready source for concentrated hydrogen pellets, it stressed him. He texted Elli:

```
Coming.
```

"'Bout fuckin' time!" she said quietly to herself.

Quinn woke up pressed uncomfortably against the bunk straps. "Thanks for the warning," she choked.

Emerson explained the situation to her. He cloaked The Black Mariah. Between the paint and the darkness, it would be nearly impossible to see them without infrared. They landed fifty meters from the back of the building.

When he opened the hatch, they heard the chaos from inside. Emerson saw that the dome in the center of the building was missing most of its glass, and the frame that remained was twisted and corroded. The lack of a roof made the ballroom into an amphitheater; it was as loud outside as inside. Flickering lights shone on the underside of the surrounding trees.

At first, Quinn thought the multitude of voices were laughing, but a moment later, she realized that they were screaming. Screams of rage, screams of terror.

Elli texted back:

They seem to be occupied. Where are you?

Leaving the building, Paxon saw Elli. He advanced from the shadows; she turned to face him. He whispered, "Thank you. Can you take us away from here?"

"Us?"

Two of the women, one dressed only in torn shreds of cloth, appeared out of the same shadow. One was the girl who'd bathed Elli, and the other was the woman in the velvet jacket. Both had lost all of their other clothes. They were dazed, maybe drugged.

"Not my call," Elli said. "Follow me."

Quinn nearly incinerated them when Elli opened the hatch. "What the hell is going on in there? And who are they?" She pointed at the women.

Paxon said, "These people are freed slaves. We need to help them."

Emerson arrived from the shuttle. "What about everyone else?"

Elli answered, "They seem to be able to take care of themselves. I unlocked everyone's collar. I wasn't very important after that."

"If we can help, we have to. You know that," Emerson said.

Quinn said to the women, "Find some clothes. Hide until we get back."

The commotion inside the building calmed. Emerson looked in a window. Quinn and Elli followed, leaving the women behind at shuttle. Twenty or more newly freed slave women and men surrounded the six bosses who were now the only people completely without clothing. One was on his knees, pleading for his life. The others were backed against a wood-paneled wall. The mob taunted them with knives and clubs. One woman had a chair leg on her shoulder.

As Emerson weighed his options, the ex-frogman, still dressed in his moth-eaten tuxedo, joined him. "Paxon, you know these people, right? Can you talk to them?"

Paxon said, "I wouldn't. They're out for blood."

"Where are the computers?" Quinn asked.

"I'll show you. This is about to get ugly." As they followed Paxon, they heard a grunt and a roar as the crowd advanced on the bosses.

◆ ◆

The computer room was a cluttered office with an ancient Dell desktop attached to a cracked flatscreen monitor. A plastic oscillating fan spun sluggishly. Quinn tore the cover off and used her rifle to melt the processor and hard drives. Without a base processor, none of the Interface-enabled security systems would function. They would have to rebuild the system if they could find the right components. To be sure they would be disabled, Emerson put a small thermal charge next to the generator. He set it for thirty minutes.

He told Elli and Quinn, "We'd better get out of here."

When they got to the shuttle, many of the freed people were milling around outside. Elli recognized one bulked-up man as a guard from the dock. He called to Paxon. Elli, Emerson, and Quinn stood together. The shuttle was cloaked. Paxon's female friends were hiding behind it.

"Hey, Pax. Who are your friends?" It was one of the guards from the dock.

"You can thank this one for freeing us. Brunt, meet Elli. I don't know anyone else's name."

Brunt extended a hand. "Thank you, Elli." Her hand looked like a doll's next to Brunt's.

She said, "This is Emerson and Quinn."

"How did you get here?" Brunt asked.

Emerson cut in, "That's a long story. Look, if there is anyone who wants to get off this island, we have some room. But we can't take everyone."

"Now that we've eliminated the bosses, this is a great place to live," Brunt said.

"Until you run out of food and fuel," added Paxon. "I want to get back to the mainland. I'm anxious to get up into the mountains and away from all these crazies."

Brunt said, "I hadn't thought of that… Maybe I should come with you?"

By that point no one was listening to him.

Ana texted Emerson:

```
I have control of the tanker. And the grow-
ing medium is inoculated. We should seed the
                  tanks tomorrow.
```

Emerson said, "We'll be leaving as soon as everyone was asleep."

"Or so drunk they wouldn't notice," Elli said. She relayed the message to Ana.

The thermal charge went off, but no one seemed to hear it. They were celebrating. People laughed and talked to each other animatedly in little clots around the outside of the ballroom. No one seemed concerned that they had just murdered six men by stabbing and beating them to death.

Brunt, Paxon, and the two women, Sandra and Anoush, were coming with them. The island was quiet by two a.m. The Black Mariah lifted off silently at three fifteen.

♦ ♦ ♦

ESCAPE

The four freed people had never flown before. Brunt, surprisingly, for his size and bulk, spent the first twenty minutes in the head, emptying his considerably large stomach. The women sat together. Anoush wore her unbuttoned red velvet jacket; the silver combs were missing. It was large on her slight frame and reached almost to her knees, giving the appearance of a thick skirt. Beneath it she wore faded Levis and a threadbare pair of pink Hokas. Anoush had wide hips and large, brown, almond-shaped eyes. Her waist was small and her breasts large. She'd found a blouse. But it strained the buttons and made her cleavage bulge.

She said, "The bosses sent their mercenaries to raid other settlements, making sex slaves, cooks, and cleaners of the women and killing the men once they had enough guards. They stole everything of value and brought it to the island. There is an underground storage locker filled with stuff." Emerson noticed her exceptionally long lashes. She noticed him looking and smiled at him.

The other woman, Sandra, added, "That's where most of our clothing came from." She had found a t-shirt and a baggy pair of chinos. She was only a scant 150 centimeters, six-and-a-half stones. She had stringy, blonde hair and a sharp nose. Her fingers were freakishly long. She kept her mouth closed in a coy smile, covering her crooked teeth. Sandra hardly spoke above a whisper.

She said, "And canned food. They gathered up loads of canned food. We tended the groves when we weren't tending the *bosses*." She looked at Paxon. "I hear you guys beat them to death." She nodded to Brunt, who was returning from the toilet. His face, behind the black beard, was pale as milk. He nodded, burped, and sat alone, away from everyone else.

Paxon sat in the cockpit with Emerson. He said, "I knew they were controlling the collars somehow. We heard stories about the Interface when we were kids, but I never met a user."

Emerson said, "They didn't really know how to use the Interface tools. The server was old and stuck together out of spare parts. This shuttle, The Black Mariah, is an Interface-only craft. All functions are managed by Interface control. Before the collapse, over fifty years ago, the world was split into Interface users and everyone else. The users had technology, and everyone else was demoted to persona non grata: non-human.

"There would have been a mass uprising if not for the virus. By the fifth wave, over 80 percent of the population was dead. Almost nobody had access to the Interface or the education to use it. I grew up in the shadow of The City, a walled enclave to the east, where everyone is implanted, and the Interface runs everything and everyone except the highest elites."

"You escaped The City?" Sandra asked.

"It's complicated. Like I said, my grandfather raised me outside The City. When he died, I went there and learned to fly. I met Elli Rattlesnake Quinn, who is High Lord Boston's daughter. We have a daughter, Marya. We escaped to a small village called Blue Hole, but Lord Quinn eradicated it trying to capture us. We left the east and have been living on the coast for the past six years." He looked at Elli, and she shook her head. They didn't need to know everything.

Paxon said, "That's an amazing story. I am just a wandering laborer. I've worked around all my life; got no family anymore. The bosses captured me a couple years ago. Before that, I never came to the ocean. If I never see it again, it would be fine by me."

Anoush said, "On the island, the bosses had all this power for decades. It went to their heads. They made us do these huge orgies, but the old farts couldn't get 'em up. If it weren't for the collars, we would have killed them long ago." She had moved close to Emerson and was leaning against his arm. He glanced at her naked breast which had escaped the constraints of her shirt. She looked at him and smiled, pulling the coat open, exposing a dark nipple.

Sandra nodded. "I grew up in a village up the coast. The men in wetsuits came in the night and killed almost everybody. My people were fighters, but the attack surprised us. There were only a few younger men. My brother was one of them. The other girl kidnapped with me jumped overboard on the way to the island. I think the collar must have knocked her out. Her limp body disappeared in the surf."

Elli moved away from the women and sat by herself with her plasma rifle across her knees. Quinn noticed, but she let Elli have her space. The younger woman was never fond of human conversation.

Brunt was one of the men who was ordered to put on a wetsuit and raid other settlements. He was part of the raid that killed Sandra's people. He still felt queasy and couldn't seem to look anyone in the eye. His face was laced with regret, as if he wished he hadn't left the island. When the shuttle began its descent, his stomach flipped over, and he ran to the head.

Emerson notified Ana that he was making his final approach. The shuttle set down in the dock they'd built for it. The sunrise was only a rumor, a glow on the east horizon. It would not be up for another hour. Emerson was exhausted and looked forward to passing out in his cabin. When he opened the hatch, Ana was there with both babies. Marya reached out to him and said, "Daddy!"

He wasn't as tired anymore.

♦ ♦ ♦

MULE KNOWS IT!

Saą and Ana had created a growing medium from the pine needle litter they collected at a nearby logging re-plant. The trees were planted more than fifty years ago, and the forest of mature timber was cool and alive with plant and animal life.

Saą was an experienced mushroom hunter. The first day, she returned at sunset with a basketful. She and Ana used clean silicone dishes to collect the spores tapped off the open gills. They introduced them to sterile sawdust and let them rest in a warm dark corner of a cabin after she pre-inoculated the growing medium with mycelial accelerant.

She explained, "This strain propagates quickly and reliably. We can put the inoculated medium in the oil and leave it. No need to wait."

When he returned, she showed Emerson their progress.

Ana was able to access all levels of the tanker's control systems via remote Interface. The vessel's ballast tanks could be filled and emptied. Ana calculated that once the oil was neutralized, explosive charges set between the ballast and storage tanks would sink the tanker while it was still away from the shallows running along to the coast.

Saą said, "The magnetic fields are more erratic now. The wildlife has mostly left the area. I will be leaving tomorrow. You have this under control. You should follow."

Emerson noted the coordinates for her settlement and assured her that they would leave as soon as the tanker was taken care of.

The group came together for a midday meal. Ana had a stew going, and Marya and Elli had collected a wide array of wild greens, scallions, and carrots. Emerson's field of buckwheat didn't do as well in the sandy soil of the west coast as it did in the river-rich land near the homeplace where he grew up. But it yielded enough grain for the little community to have groats and to make bread in low-temp fired clay pots, buried in hot coals. The grains made a perfect complement to Ana's slow-cooked root veggies and rabbit.

"Where do you get the yeast?" Sandra asked.

Emerson said, "Yeast is everywhere. We leave a paste of buckwheat flour in a bowl overnight, and the next day it's bubbling with yeast—sourdough."

Anoush said, "I have never had bread like this. It's nutty and delicious."

Elli blurted, "They gave me actual oranges."

"Yes," she continued. "We grow them on the island. There are gardens of berries and melons. The bosses didn't eat meat, so we only had what we could scrounge, occasionally rats and raccoons."

After the meal, over cups of warm tea, Emerson explained the plan. "Ana and Saą put together a pretty good chipper from salvaged parts. We have enough bedding ready to go. We make an island on the surface of the oil with chips and needles. Then we'll take the baskets of inoculated growing medium and lower them into the tanks. A drone will stay with one basket so we can monitor growth remotely. We'll set the charges to sink the ship before we leave. When we have determined that the oil is neutralized, Ana will detonate the charges, which will flood the ballasts and oil tanks. And that will sink the ship."

Quinn said, "How long will it take for the mushrooms to consume the oil?"

Saą said, "The fungus will consume the hydrocarbons and other toxins over the next few months. But the earth will move long before that time."

"Earthquake? What earthquake?" Brunt asked.

Saą said, "Yes, an earthquake is coming. The animals know it." Mule, Emerson's oversized feline, leaned against her thigh, nearly knocking her off the bench. She laughed, "Mule knows it."

"If there is an earthquake and we leave the area," Ana said, "I'll still be able to monitor the drones from The Black Mariah as far away as 300 kilometers. As long as the Van Allen belt is still working, that is. And I can control the tanker too."

Brunt said, "I didn't sign up for no earthquake. I've seen what the last one did to Beso Muerte. Not interested, man."

Emerson said, "Beso Muerte? Kiss of Death? Where's this?"

Saą answered, "It is a monstrous, crumbling city in the south. In another life, it was known as Las Alas, but no one lives there now."

Ana said, "The home of Interface Industries. I'd like to mine their servers for code."

◆ ◆

That night, Quinn stayed with Emerson rather than going back to her own cabin. Ana often spent the night with Elli, who slept outdoors on the ridge. LC was with his mom. He had a bed in Marya's room too. They set up a tent for the newcomers to sleep in.

It was dark inside the houses, except for a trickle of light coming from the waxing gibbous moon, which only rose an hour prior so it was still low in the sky. Later, it would look brighter than an overcast day. The night was warm, and Quinn slept naked. She and Emerson lay on top of the sheets, their skin washed in silver light. She turned to Emerson. Her lavender eyes were startlingly bright.

She said, "If Saą is right, we should be preparing to move."

"Amazing," Emerson murmured.

"Huh?"

"It's like your eyes have lights behind them, like a cat. Damn, babe, you look… demonic." He lunged at her side, digging his fingertips into the soft flesh above her hips, Quinn's ticklish spot.

She screamed. Her body spasmed, and her knees came up involuntarily, kicking Emerson's hands away. "Stop it! You bastard," she said through her laughter. "You'll wake Marya."

"That child would sleep through a bomb blast."

She lay back, grinning a toothy smile. Emerson remembered the first time he'd seen her with her graceful neck and straight white teeth. Signs of health and strength he'd seldom seen in the citizens of The City. *The Middles*, he reminded himself. Emerson leaned over and kissed her. He began pulling away, but she followed him, so he lingered. She pressed her body into him. They hugged each other tighter. She said over his shoulder, "I think she's right. Mule seems to trust her."

He fell back on the bed and sighed. "Yeah. I suppose. It's just so damned inconvenient."

"Well, dealing with Boston killing Max and my mom and wiping out Blue Hole was pretty fucking inconvenient, too, Emerson."

"Yeah, The Death was pretty fucking inconvenient, now that you mention it." He paused and said, "But I like it here."

She leaned over and kissed him on the lips. "Stop whining, Tiger. I guess we aren't home yet. I have to admit, I need something more substantial than a driftwood shack, Emmer. I've always thought of myself as a flexible girl, but I think I'm straining my limit."

"Yeah, I didn't really think we were staying. I was hopeful, but yeah. We need something more permanent. Tomorrow, I'll tell everyone to start packing."

The next morning, Saą met them as they were leaving the cabin. Just before she opened her mouth, they felt a small vibration deep in the ground. The wind picked up and died down. "I'm going now. You are welcome to follow me," she said.

Emerson replied, "Yes, we are packing up and leaving tomorrow after we plant the fungus."

"I wouldn't wait—I'm not going to wait. And Mule is coming with me."

Emerson had no control over what Mule did. He trusted the big cat. He was actually happy Saą wouldn't be alone. He liked her. She was a non-tech person interested in technology. They had a lot in common.

Emerson shut down the tide-based generator. It was an experiment of his and Chandler's. They'd used salvaged rubber balls as floats with a simple gear box and a small motor. They'd transferred the rise and fall of the tides as well as the natural ebb and flow of the ocean into current that was regulated by the same circuits that the wind and solar power ran through. Later, he and Chandler had decided the trial was successful, and they drew up plans for a scalable generation system for coastal villages. That project would be on hold for a while.

Brunt slipped out while everyone else was asleep. He took a plasma rifle and a pound of preserved day rations. When Elli discovered his departure and theft, she muttered, "Good fucking riddance."

The morning was spent ferrying the forest floor out to the tanker. Ana brought the tanker in closer; by noon, they had inoculated the tanks and turned their attention to packing. Near three, Marya tugged on Quinn's pant leg and said, "Mama, I'm really sleepy."

She brought her daughter to her room and laid her down for a nap. At dinnertime, Elli went to get her. She came back alone. "I can't wake her up, Quinn."

They tried several ways to revive the girl. She was breathing deeply like normal sleep, but she didn't even respond to ammonia held beneath her nose.

Elli said, "She's lapsed into a coma again. I can't feel what the problem is, but I'll bet it has something to do with her hitting her head."

"She was fine the whole time you were gone," Ana replied.

Quinn said, "Do you think there is a hospital in this crumbling city?"

"Interface Industries was in Mount Sinai, the location of the biggest, most modern hospital in the world," Ana said.

Emerson nodded. "If any place will have the diagnostic tools we need, they would."

"If the building is still there," added Elli.

Emerson, Ana, and Quinn made ready to go. Elli stayed behind with the children and the newcomers. They packed what they could back into the holding crates from The Black Mariah. Emerson piloted The Black Mariah into the pre-dawn of the next day.

◆ ◆ ◆

YOU LIKE MACHINES, RIGHT?

Cybernetic Soldier 105.34 heard it first. The aircraft came into his viewfinder a moment later. It was an air shuttle. He hadn't seen or heard one in several decades. The unidentified craft entered firing range. He had it sighted for evaporation, ready to fire as soon as he received the go-code. But he knew the order would not come. He hadn't received such orders since the collapse, over sixty years ago. A cybernetic was not able to fire a weapon or endanger another being's life without explicit orders to engage from a trusted authority. He shut down his weapon systems.

The human part of him, the part that used to be Charles Plummer, felt a pain in his chest. *Heartache*, he thought. *Ironic, isn't it? I have neither a heart nor a chest, but I still feel the pain just the same.*

The flying machine was a corporate-class shuttle, typical transport for Interface Industries' bigwigs and high-ranking lawyers, accountants, and executive assistants. Seeing it was disorienting. Even for his enhanced computing abilities, it took a moment to realize the shuttle couldn't be new. For a millisecond, his fifty-year nightmare had not been real. But C-105.34 righted his perceptions. He remembered how long it had been. Ecclesia Mortis was gone; the inhabitants of this craft were *new*. He reassured himself that he was sound even though his processors had been failing for the past decade.

The shuttle was painted with a black, light-absorbing paint. If C-105.34 didn't have infrared and ultraviolet optics, he wouldn't have seen it at all. As it was, when the craft touched down, some kind of cloaking rose up. After that, he could only see a shifting fractal when he looked at it peripherally. No Interface Industries shuttle was ever cloaked or painted black.

It landed a few hundred meters away from the loading docks, near the wing of the ruined hospital he'd been living in since the collapse. He needed to be close to the operating room with its robotic surgery and monitoring instruments. Also, the roof didn't leak here. Radiology and Imaging were just down the hall. He reasoned an 80 percent chance that the visitors were headed there.

C-105.34 pressed himself into the shadows and shut down everything but essential functions. Three humans entered the hallway. The two women, one with shoulder-length auburn hair and the other with a worn stretch hat pulled over her black pageboy, carried what he identified as Interface-controlled, mid-twenty-first-century plasma weapons.

Interface users, he thought. He hadn't seen another Interface user since the last soldier in his platoon died. The man was dressed in an old, military-issue, button-front coat. He held no apparent weapons, but his Interface-controlled helmet scanned for movement with a sweeping infrared beam.

◆ ◆

C-105.34 fell into a memory. Remembering bathed his nervous system in endorphins, even though the release trigger was a mechanical injection rather than actual brain chemistry secretion. His brain had been floating in a tank of nutritional gel inside his torso for three decades.

The first time he'd seen such a shuttle was during his initial training. He was mostly man then, having only had minor eye implants and, of course, the Interface implant under the skin below his ear. The commanding officer and his assistant arrived in a small shuttle on his first day of training.

The company had jacked up his hormonal levels, especially his testosterone, in preparation for the rigors of training. At the end of the ten-week intensive, C-105.34, who was still mostly Charles Plummer at that point, was given his processor and the programs he needed to become active. The terms and conditions of his employment demanded he surrender his Rights of Sovereignty, making him the legal property of Interface Industries. Any enhanced mercenary had to give up his human rights. The sort of surgical changes they made were illegal. At least they were at that moment in history; things changed lightning-fast near the end. Most human rights laws were rescinded by the World Government when the virus became a global crisis. But what did laws mean in a world without people?

Before Charles could be deployed, the fifth wave infected everyone in his division, including the other seven cybernetic soldiers from his platoon. The virus attacked the brain and interrupted life support. After the second wave, it mutated and learned to keep its host alive longer, but the infected were essentially braindead and never regained consciousness.

His platoon-mates each had different enhancements. Because of his size when he was human, he was originally outfitted with assists on his arms and legs in addition to his processing and vision tools. Fellow platoon member Kyle Bossart, AKA C-105.40, had microscopic manipulation capability; his fingers contained a set of nano-wires that could be sent two meters into a tight place, through nearly any material. The tech havoc he could have caused was monumental, not to mention his ability to kill with those things.

But the virus was not choosy. It attacked everyone, even the biological remnants of Charles. He didn't know why it didn't kill him, but it didn't. It left him alive to witness his cohorts in various stages of paralysis. The disease infected living tissue, but depending upon what cybernetic enhancements had been done, it was only able to partially disable many of them at first. The horror of those times changed him. He would spend decades rewriting his own programming. But first, he had to unlock the security systems that prevented access to his own processor.

Charles was not a programmer, but his processor enhanced his deductive reasoning, and he had a talent with mechanical things. His cybernetic hardware and software were designed and fabricated at the headquarters of Interface Industries, right here in the same building as the newest wing of the hospital, several floors above.

He was in the largest city on the continent. In the past half-decade, nomads referred to it as Beso Muerte, the kiss of death. But until it began to deteriorate, the city and surrounding region was powered by a grid of solar panels and vast wind farms in the deserts to the east. After the collapse, the electricity remained on for years.

C-105.34 poked around and learned as he went. He found a complete set of Interface tutorials in the library on the twenty-sixth floor. He also discovered the office of the lead cybernetics designer: Ito Jones. Research and development labs were on the twelfth floor. He scoured Jones's office and laptop. Not only did the engineer have a password spreadsheet; he had editable ghost images of the entire platoon's processors. Each of them could be run in a virtual machine and tested, altered, and resaved. Jones's laptop contained everything he needed. He just had to learn how to use it. Time was not a problem.

C-105.34 used the laptop to create a new image for himself. He was also able to create other cyborgs using wild animals as hosts. For twenty years, C-105.34 was busy. His programming prowess increased, often through terrible errors. As he gained mastery, he began thinking of himself as C. PLUMMER again. The one routine that eluded his interruption was FSX7, commonly known as the Kill Switch: a program that was hard-coded into his core circuitry.

The Kill Switch was the program that prevented Interface Industries Cybernetic Enforcers, or IICEs, from harming themselves or others. It was not created by Ito Jones or his team. It was mandated by the World Government just prior to the collapse. WG engineers wrote the routine to appease fears that an army of IICE would be an uncontrollable threat to humans. Though C. PLUMMER was able to rewrite his programming and break his servitude to a company that had turned to dust over half a century ago, he was not free. If he was, he would have killed himself decades ago.

◆ ◆

Emerson, Ana, and Quinn sought the most advanced diagnostic tech available. Marya's life depended upon it.

"I want to check out the server room," Ana said. "The newest hardware and software of the day was created here."

Quinn said, "Let's stay together until we have confirmed that no one else is here. This place looks too clean and orderly for me. It should be covered with fifty years of filth."

Emerson didn't speak; he was listening. As his grandfather would say, "Animals activate their cannabinoid system when they require intense concentration. We humans have access to it, too, but we're all too fucking numb from having everything handed to us nice and easy, see."

As a boy, Emerson often didn't know what his grandpa was talking about. But on the eve of Emerson's sixteenth birthday, Chandler had opened an antique, tin cigar box, packed a sixteen-centimeter-long glass smoking pipe with a dried herb, and handed it to him. He had lit his laser fire starter and said, "Take one big pull. Hold it in your lungs. Don't pass out."

Emerson had sucked on the glass tube. The taste was strong, musky, and complex like roasted coffee or skunk spray. He could only hold his breath for a second and coughed ferociously. When he'd quieted, it took a moment for the drug to hit his bloodstream. When it did, his viewpoint left his body and had floated up toward the ceiling. Chandler's voice had sounded distant, like he was underwater. "Concentrate, boy. Make your chatterbox brain shut up for a second. Breathe slow; in… and out… in… and out…"

The experience had changed him. With practice, Emerson learned to find the calm, expansive awareness even after the drug wore off. When he found it, time slowed, and the dark outline between objects clarified. Over the years that followed, he learned how to bring that same calm awareness to his hunting. Combined with the enhancing capabilities of the Interface and his shuttle helmet, Emerson possessed truly superhuman observational skills.

He would have noticed Plummer in the next second if the cyborg hadn't involuntarily moved toward the door.

Plummer's self-preservation programming required him to move into the sunlight and recharge each day. It also required him to consume water and living material in order to fuel his nutritional gel. If he did not initiate these actions willingly, the program initiated itself. Plummer often neglected the responsibility and allowed the routine to take care of it. Living alone for so many years, he chose to forget about it.

The humans were halfway to the first operating suite when Plummer's survival program suddenly kicked in and transported him toward his required hour in the sun. The movement startled the shuttle team. Quinn, the least weapon-savvy of the three, nearly vaporized him.

Emerson yelled, "Wait!"

Quinn and the cyborg froze.

Plummer vocalized. It was the first time he'd spoken in decades. His voice sounded foreign to him. "I am not a threat. Don't shoot."

"How do we know? What *are* you?" Emerson asked.

Plummer said, "I'm C. Plummer, a cybernetically enhanced human, but my programming requires that I move into the sun to recharge. Please don't shoot me. FSX7 makes me harmless." He rolled away down the cluttered hall toward the dock on dual roller tracks.

Quinn, Ana, and Emerson stood stunned for a moment.

Emerson said, "Ana, you can go look for the server room. Quinn and I will see what's up with Plummer, whatever he is."

They met the cyborg outside. He'd crossed what used to be a parking lot and was now standing in a field of waist-tall scrub grass and pigweed. They walked the narrow trail Plummer's treads made by taking this trip every day. His solar collector was open, which made him look like an oversized, metal, neck lizard with an erect hood. A haphazardly patched, once army-issued, green shirt hung in tatters from his shoulders. The nametag on the left breast read C. PLUMMER.

His four arms, which looked like miniature segmented cranes made of erector-set parts, hung limp at his sides. His head was tipped back as though he were under a tanning light, but the paint on his resin-cast face had mostly flaked off, leaving worn, rash-like patches on his cheek and temple. The colors were bleached and pale.

"Can you speak while you're recharging?" Emerson asked.

He said, "Uh-huh. What can I tell you? I've been here so long I don't know where to begin."

"I'm Emerson Lloyde, this is Elli Rattlesnake Quinn, and Ana is inside looking for the server room."

Quinn inspected his body. While she was looking, two rats scurried out of the weeds. She jumped back, startled.

Plummer said, "They are harmless. Meet Rat One and Rat Two."

Quinn squinted. "They don't look like rats. They're too big."

Plummer replied, "They were rats when I found them. But I fixed them. Now they are *my* rats."

Emerson knelt down and let Rat One smell his extended hand. It stood up on its hind legs, and he saw the second set of arms constructed out of similar, smaller, erector-set parts tucked into its sides. The animal held out its actual right paw and nodded.

Emerson said, "It wants to shake my hand?"

Rat Two sat down by Quinn's foot and retied her shoe. "Shit!" She nearly pulled her foot away. "It has too many arms. You designed and built these?"

Rat Two sat on her haunches and looked up at Quinn and said, "Rat One actually helped build me." Her voice was soft and exaggeratedly feminine.

Quinn said reflexively, "Why do you speak like that?"

Plummer answered, "They are my assistants. I needed to create programmable cybernetic creatures to help me rebuild my own body. After the virus, I was slowly decomposing. I learned the hard way I had to replace my dying parts. The rest of my cohort expired in gruesome, drawn-out deaths. Rats were the smartest animals left. They speak like that so I can tell them apart. They are Interface only. Non-implanted people cannot hear them."

"Don't blame me," Rat Two said, tipping her head to one side. "He made me this way."

Ana had come outside when she couldn't locate the server room. She'd heard Plummer's last comment and said, "You made these things, and they helped remake you? That's amazing."

Plummer retracted his solar collector and looked at Ana for a long minute. He had no facial expressions, so it was impossible to know what he was thinking. Finally, he said, "After the collapse, people blamed everything on technology. Many survivors joined the radical anti-technology church: Ecclesia Mortis. It gathered lots of angry humans with nothing left to lose and no one alive to blame for their misery. They attacked and destroyed every machine they found, sentient or otherwise—piled it all in huge pyramids, doused it with the worthless petroleum that had murdered the planet, and let the fires burn until they went out. Sometimes for years.

"Disciples believed the reeking mountains were holy ground and fought each other for the privilege of dwelling near them. The smoldering ruins belched poisonous chemicals into the air and leaked toxic sludge into the sewers, killing most of the remaining population. The few survivors called it cursed and scattered. One of the biggest is just down the street. You should go see it before you leave!"

He barked a strange noise that sounded like something between a seal and a myna bird, thinking it sounded like a laugh. "The machines will outlive us all in the end. Ecclesia Mortis's hatred for technology defined the struggle between science and ignorance for the next hundred years. I barricaded the hospital; they got in anyway. I had to defend myself."

Emerson said, "I thought you were harmless."

"I can't hurt anyone or myself. Waiting passively to be murdered is suicide. I am prevented. I tried not to hurt anyone too badly, but I…"

After waiting a long half-minute, looking from Ana to Quinn, Emerson said, "Plummer?"

The cyborg did not move or speak. Emerson could hear his gel churning and a faint, purring electric motor. Quinn shrugged.

Ana said, "Did he go offline?"

Before anyone moved, Plummer continued as if he hadn't paused. "…am very strong. That's the way I was designed."

Emerson glanced around but didn't speak.

Ana said, "That's terrible. You seem like a gentle being. It's a tragedy that they came after you like that."

He went on, "I can't blame them; the world ended. They'd believed it would continue forever. Anger is irrational. In the absence of an enemy, they lashed out at what appeared to be the cause."

"Yes," Ana said, "but they were wrong. It's unjust."

Plummer made another sound which his processor must have cataloged as laughter. It sounded more like a donkey braying. Emerson smiled and Ana continued, "What? What's funny?"

Plummer said quietly, "You have an innocent idea of justice."

Quinn changed the subject. "You have lived here alone all this time?"

Plummer rolled closer to Ana, flexing his optical array level with her breast, which had leaked, darkening the fabric of her shirt. LC was still nursing. But he was hundreds of miles away with Elli. Oblivious to how inappropriate his actions were, Plummer said, "I have my rats. But yes, all alone. There are several other beings, but no other sentient biological life."

Ana said, "I can't imagine." She stepped away, shivered, and turned her back to him, searching the overgrown roofs of the surrounding buildings.

Plummer turned to Quinn and said, "You like machines, right?"

She smiled, glanced at Ana, and said, "Most of the time. I certainly don't blame machines for the evils that men program into them."

Emerson said, "We believe in appropriate technology use. In my opinion you should never have been created. But now that you are here, we will treat you with the respect any living being deserves."

Plummer replied, "You came here for medical equipment, correct? Please, let me help you. As I said, I am very strong. And I know where everything is in this building. I have been living here for a long time." He rolled off in the direction of Radiology.

Quinn side-eyed Emerson at Plummer's swift change in subject, but she said nothing.

Ana told Plummer what she was looking for, and then Emerson explained about the MRI and X-ray machines. "And we can also use pharmaceuticals, surgical tools, bandages, skin knitters, surgical glue…"

Plummer stood motionless.

"Are you hearing this?" Emerson asked.

Plummer said, "Yes. Why?"

"Because when you stand still and all I hear is your fluids sloshing around, I'm not sure if you can hear me."

An annoyed tone shaded his machine-generated voice. "Right. You *do* know that I'm mostly a machine, right?" He went on after a slight pause. "I hear and record everything." He played the recording back: "`I hear and record everything`. If I say I am listening, I am. I cannot lie."

Emerson said, "Sorry, I didn't mean to doubt you…"

"Well, there you go again. I am not seeking an apology; I am stating facts with the intention of improving our communications in the future. However, the small but significant part of me that's still human thanks you for your concern."

Emerson suspected Plummer's instability, but he nodded and said, "Okay then. Imagine you are starting a colony, and you want to make sure to bring anything of relevance. Tell me what it is and where we can find it."

◆ ◆ ◆

SOMETIMES IT SEEMS LIKE YOU'VE LIVED TOO LONG

Plummer led Emerson to Radiology. The ceiling tiles had rotted away, exposing the pipes and wires above the grid. They kicked up a thick dust as they went. Glass and plastic detritus crunched under Plummer's treads. Rats One and Two scampered after them, sometimes swinging from the naked drop-ceiling grids like spider monkeys. The humans wrapped filter masks around their faces, a material that Emerson's grandfather invented.

Ana said, "Plummer, how did you end up surviving The Death and becoming a cyborg of all things?"

"I was drafted."

After waiting a while for a story that never came, she said, "Okay, your automated voice, is that what you sounded like, or is it just a randomly generated machine voice?"

In Blue Hole, where she grew up, Ana was a juice hacker: a group of Interface programmers operating outside the restrictions of The City. She had genuine interest in Plummer's programming. A being like him was capable of many things that humans were not, besides the fact that he was a goldmine of data on advanced cybernetics. The implications for medicine were overwhelming. Understandably for Plummer, value was an idea he had long since forgotten. Over the past several years, he had given up on the idea of being useful.

"Strangely enough," he said, "it is as close an approximation of my voice as was possible. My processor had plenty of recordings from which to create a profile. So, when we removed my lungs and larynx, that profile was the basis of my artificial voice. But I don't think it sounds like me."

◆ ◆

Later, when, they were back at the shuttle, Quinn said, "Something seems off about our favorite cyborg."

Ana replied, "He has glitches, if you know what I mean. I tried to run a diagnostic on him, but he locked me out. He said," she did a poor imitation of the cyborg's electronic voice, "'I run mah own diagnostics, thank you very much.' It's hard to tell if he is a machine or a man. It's like he evolved with the worst attributes of both."

Quinn said, "If we can get him to open up his processor, I bet Chandler could reprogram him."

"That's a big if." Ana shook her head.

◆ ◆

At Radiology they found the equipment they sought. Quinn, Emerson, and Ana disconnected components, and Plummer carried the parts to the dock. On his final trip, he offered to show Ana to the server room and opened the locked steel door. But after she entered the room and ignited her halogen lantern, he sealed the door behind her.

"Plummer!" she yelled and pounded on the door, but it was solid. The room was a Faraday cage; her comms were useless. She didn't know why the cyborg locked her in, but it was the place she was seeking. She put her concerns on hold and set to work rigging a temporary power supply and switching on a bank of computers.

Fifty racks filled with multithread processing servers sprang to life; power lights flashed from yellow to orange, eventually turning green moments later. She used her Interface to find a login point and cracked the password, which was poorly encrypted by her twenty-second-century standards. Ana forgot where she was for the next hour as she searched storage abstracts and copied code.

◆ ◆

After Plummer locked Ana in the server room, he rolled back to Quinn and Emerson, who were filling a cart with drugs and paraphernalia. Plummer offered to bring it to the shuttle.

Emerson asked, "Where's Ana?"

Plummer said, "In the server room."

"Where's that?"

Plummer didn't answer.

Emerson stopped loading and stared at the cyborg. "Plummer, where is she?"

Plummer backed against the wall and made a sound like gas escaping a tire.

Emerson said, "Well?"

"She's fine. I, I locked her in." He paused again. Just before Emerson replied he said, "Please, I don't want you to go."

Plummer went on, "The plan is companionship. Female companionship. No offense, Emerson, but I never developed much of a taste for men."

"We have a family, Charles. We can't stay here. We have to go back."

Emerson said, "You could come with us. Your needs could be met by coming to live with us. That way, we could all benefit from your cybernetic expertise, and you wouldn't be forced to live alone any longer."

Plummer was silent for a long minute. His nutritional gel gurgled. Quinn began to wonder if he'd hit a glitch again. Maybe he'd blown a fuse. Suddenly, he replied, "You'll take me flying? Up in the shuttle?"

◆ ◆ ◆

BRINGING HOME STRAYS

Ana was nearly finished copying programs when the server room door opened, when Quinn and Emerson entered with Plummer. "I got what I came for," Ana said.

Quinn added, "We are taking Plummer and the rats back to the beach with us."

The floor trembled. Dust leaked out of the ceilings. Some sort of metal fell, rattling to the floor in another room. Everybody froze.

Plummer said nonchalantly, "Oh yes, I'm expecting a big one. I was hoping it would drop the hospital on me unexpectedly, but if we are going to go, I suggest we hurry."

Quinn said, "Get ready to take off."

◆ ◆

The shuttle door was too short for Plummer. He had to disconnect his head to get in, and once it was back on his shoulders, he continually scraped the ceiling. After a considerable effort, the cyborg, his assistants, and the equipment were on board with the rest of the crew. Launch disoriented him; he had never planned for rapid acceleration, and his nutritional gel sloshed around. He had to shut down sensory inputs to keep from reacting, unsure if it was fear or excitement; he hadn't felt anything so strongly in a half-century. It felt like running into a bitter old friend.

They were cruising at 4,000 meters. Emerson was in the cockpit.

Plummer brought himself back online and said, "I've heard that there's no time like the present, but I believe it's more like no time *but* the present… Either way, the time is now."

Quinn said, "What are you talking about?"

He said, "I've thought about your offer, and I decline. Living any longer when there is a possibility that I might have a way out is unacceptable."

"So, what are you saying?" Ana asked.

He replied, "You have provided a way out. That's all I really wanted."

Emerson arrived from the cockpit. The Black was on autopilot. "What's going on?"

Plummer said, "You are going to help me terminate my miserable existence."

"What?" Emerson said. He suppressed the urge to yell. It made him sweat. "I thought we worked this out."

He was surprised by Plummer's reversal, which made him sound indignant and didn't make anyone feel any calmer. Quinn said, "That wasn't the agreement, Plummer. You were coming back home with us."

"Yeah, it was an enticing offer," said Plummer, "but I realized that being up in the sky could afford me an opportunity I'd never even thought of before. I can use a manual override and disengage my driveshaft. If I reset my system, it shuts down the Kill Switch. In the thirteen seconds it takes for my processor to reboot, I can kill myself before it can stop me. You just have to open the door, and I'll do the reset. You tip the shuttle, and I'll roll out the door. By the time my program recognizes what has happened, it will be too late to do anything about it."

Quinn said, "I could have just vaporized you if all you wanted was to die."

"The program wouldn't allow it. Protection systems are always active against weapons fire. They do not reset. I'd have killed you before you pulled the trigger."

Emerson said, "I refused to be a party to your suicide. There has to be another way."

"Tough titty said the kitty. My mind is made up. You have no idea what half a century alone can do to a man's mind."

They stood frozen for a brief moment. Plummer continued, "I can do quite a lot of damage in thirteen seconds. And I still might be able to make it out the door."

◆ ◆

Emerson brought the shuttle down to a manageable 4,500 meters.

Plummer said, "Thank you for granting a dying man's last wish. Well, one of them, anyway."

Emerson said, "It's possible that we could correct your degradation, you know. If you'd give us a chance."

Plummer ignored him and continued, "And thanks to all of you for the part you have played in my escape from a lifetime of bondage. I would hug each of you, but my form makes that uncomfortable."

They stood around silently. Finally, Plummer said, "Please open the door before I lose my nerve."

Emerson slowed the shuttle down to just above drop speed and opened the door. Plummer shut down. The wind streamed in. Vast fields of windmills, some still spinning, but most collapsed, rusted, and broken off like rotting teeth, drifted by below. They crossed a superhighway, clogged with cars, frozen in time, bricked and VIN-locked where they were when the radio frequency monitoring systems failed.

Ana and Quinn were so mesmerized by the landscape that they were shocked when Emerson tipped the shuttle and Plummer rolled out of sight.

Emerson initiated the door close. Just before it sealed, one of Plummer's claw hands gripped on to the bottom ledge. Ana yelled, "Stop,

Emerson. He's changed his mind." But the door continued, severing four of Plummer's metal fingers. Rat One scampered up and collected them, slipping them into a pouch on her belly. Rat Two joined her. They turned to face the humans together and bowed. They scampered off again into the bowels of the ship.

Emerson said, "That was completely bizarre."

Ana barked a nervous laugh. They heard a sudden pounding on the outside of the ship.

Plummer's body appeared at the main hatch window; his artificial head had blown away. He banged and yelled. The sound vibrated through The Black Mariah's hull, making it sound like his artificial voice was coming from everywhere.

"Open the door. Let me in. It didn't work. I guess I'm coming with you."

When they landed back at the beach and Elli met Plummer, Rat One, and Rat Two, she said, "Damn, Emerson, you are always bringing home strays."

◆ ◆ ◆ ◆

END OF PART ONE

INTERFACE

PART TWO

LORD QUINN

In the six years since Elli Rattlesnake Quinn and Emerson Lloyde escaped from The City, Boston Quinn, Elli's father, named himself High Lord of The City, and his mental state steadily declined. Boston always fancied himself as the top elite—but with his increasing age came heightened paranoia. It didn't happen all at once.

Since his mind unraveled slowly, his measures seemed to escalate steadily from the time his daughter defied him and ran away. But it wasn't really an escalation. Like the typical crazy man in a long line of leaders who had lost their minds while in power, Boston Quinn had no one around him to temper his extremism. But because Boston had an IQ of 120, which even in his great-grandfather's time was rare, he also believed himself exceptional. He really was smart enough to prevent most people from challenging him.

He locked down the wall and stopped most of the trade with surrounding villages. Citizens were subjected to increasingly stringent restrictions on what they could do or say. Anyone who objected was corrected through their Interface implant.

The result was a festering but vague dissatisfaction with life, which infected everyone but the elites. And because dissent was discouraged—read: prevented—the people had no way to process what they felt. As a result, they retreated further into the hundreds of multiplayer experiences afforded to them through the Interface. New ones seemed to spring up overnight.

Lord Quinn had always used every citizen's mandatory Interface connection to keep peace and neutralize threats. But like all control mechanisms, justification came easily when you became afraid that someone, or some *group*, was interfering with your plans. Especially when you held all the power. Boston was suspicious of the other lords. The City was always a basilisk's nest of ambition and political savagery.

Eventually, he gave up any pretense of respecting freedom and declared a City-wide emergency. He fabricated a threat from within: a fascist group calling themselves The Protectors, which was dedicated to destroying their "peaceful" way of life. He claimed, "It's all-out war!" Even though there was no evidence. Lord Quinn's extreme crisis called for extreme measures.

The Authority began monitoring and modifying the behavior of any person suspected of insurrection, which in Lord Quinn's dictionary meant disagreement. Since every citizen was implanted and only very few were privileged enough to have their implants locked, Lord Quinn's emergency measures gave him near total control. It made him feel safe—for a while.

Everyone, including the other elites and their families, were required to address him as High Lord Quinn. They were not pleased. Even though their Interface connections locked out the sort of abusive influence that the Middles were subjected to, the weight of Lord Quinn's authoritarianism was a constant burden. Most lived in fear for their lives. He controlled the Enforcer Corps. His threats of retaliation were veiled, but everyone knew he was comfortable with murder. His wife, Lucia, was the last of an elite family. Everyone knew he killed her in a rage.

It was common knowledge that he had obliterated Blue Hole, mainly because the juice hackers threatened his supremacy over everyone: the outsiders and the citizens inside the wall as well. Boston knew his power was based in the Interface and that he was vulnerable to anyone smart enough to hack it. And it didn't figure in his calculations that the people in the shantytown of Terminus, who were scratching out their survival, couldn't even use the Interface to keep a fire lit, let alone attack him. Nobody in Terminus was thinking about Lord Quinn. Still, he fretted and worried, locked in his guarded private apartments, behind the second protective barrier in a high-walled city.

Lord Quinn worried that the wealth he had amassed would run out. The fear of it ate at him. He had planned to leave the ruling power to his daughter and her child, but that was before Emerson Lloyde.

"Fucking Chandler Estes," he muttered about his granddaughter's other great-grandsire. "I should have had him assassinated when his wife, Ciara Coke, died." He spat on the floor.

A servant, assigned to follow and clean up after High Lord Quinn, wiped the floor slates with a rag and scurried away before the demented autocrat could cuff him.

Quinn yelled for the Secretary General of the Enforcers, Marchal Corbet. He could have easily opened a communication line through his Interface implant, but that would not have reinforced his authority sufficiently. When Corbet didn't materialize before him, he shouted louder.

"CORBET, HERE, NOW!"

A short man with a mop of messy black hair burst into the chamber, pulling his coat over his shoulders. The High Lord required all his secretaries to wear black, thigh-length, crushed-velvet military dress jackets in his presence. Improper dress brought demerits. Too many demerits warranted dismissal. And since military positions were high-security positions, dismissal required a mind-lock. You didn't retire from the High Lord's service. You *were* retired.

Corbet had witnessed the aftermath of an Interface mind-lock. The prior Secretary General, Sarah Morton, spent her remaining days in a padded room with a caretaker feeding her though a straw. They said she was neurologically restrained twenty-four-seven to keep from harming herself. Corbet believed it was to keep her from harming Lord Quinn.

To say Boston Quinn had become capricious and arbitrary would be like calling an angry rhino unpredictable. He was as violent as a wounded boar. But like everything in High Lord Quinn's purview, he ratcheted his behavior up to unheard-of heights. His private physician, Dr. Stephany Sailor, was sure he was in the early stages of dementia. The condition was increasingly prevalent in all the lords.

Elites had privileged access to processed foods from past civilization—foods loaded with carcinogens, endocrine disruptors, mercury, and other neural toxins. Shit, most of it was made from fungicide-soaked corn, embedded with poisons, stored for decades so the chemicals could concentrate in the fats. The irony was that they were some of the few people left on the planet who had access to fresh, real foods, but they preferred to eat the over-salted, over-sweetened, over-processed leftovers from a collapsed society. The foods that they identified with for their status were the very foods that contributed to the collapse. They were locked into the habit and appearance, having mistakenly come to believe it was their culture.

Sailor tried to explain this to Boston, but he ignored her. More now than in years past. He felt betrayed by her for helping Elli Rattlesnake get away with that Lloyde character. Elli took his granddaughter and heir. He would have executed anyone else, but he needed Marya Rattlesnake Lloyde, so he let them live. *No matter,* he thought. His people were closing in. He'd find them. He would bring her back, with or without her mother, and then all his plans would be set right.

He needed spies in that shantytown, Terminus, where the last dregs of the Blue Hole juice hackers were hiding. They undoubtedly knew where to find his traitorous daughter and her renegade lover. The idea of Lloyde impregnating his child made him spit on the stone tiles again. Corbet, who was standing close, jumped out of the way. The phlegm narrowly missed the hapless servant trying to anticipate the High Lord's expectoration.

Lord Quinn kicked at him but missed, then said, "Corbet, send a team to Terminus to collect anyone who knew my daughter and her annoying pet penis. Bring them to me. Then level the place. I have tolerated their insubordination long enough."

Corbet attempted to defuse the High Lord's anger. "But the people in Terminus live outside the wall, my High Lord. Outside your control. I fail to see how they are insubordinate—they do not recognize your authority and—"

"Whose side are you on, Corbet? I am the High Lord. Everyone is my subject. Fuck what they recognize. Bring me those people. Now git." He threw a pewter plate at the secretary's head; it missed and clattered on the tiles.

Corbet backed out of the chamber, bowing as he went. High Lord Quinn mandated his servants to be obsequious. The secretary was relieved that he hadn't been mind-locked already.

He muttered, "As you wish, Lord."

Lord Quinn yelled, "Wine and meat, goddammit. Bring me food and drink, I'm parched and starved." When his personal maid arrived a half-minute later, he said, "And where the fuck is Corbet? I have a mission for him. Tell him to get his lazy ass in here, STAT!" Corbet had passed her in the doorway as she came in. She didn't dare mention it.

◆ ◆ ◆

TERMINUS STATION

Eric Eggert was a balding ex-Enforcer. His close-set, pale blue eyes were often squinting, especially when he smiled, which was most of the time. He had a gap between his top front teeth, traces of a grey goatee, and a crooked nose from having it broken in several bar fights throughout his thirty-some years in service. He was trying to be retired. He and his mate, Margaret, spent their days tending their garden, and occasionally helping the villagers.

Maggie brought him his meals and spent time with him every day while he was detained in Blue Hole. Eventually, Eggert realized there was no lock on the door and decided to stay. Life in Blue Hole was luxurious compared to his time in the Enforcers. Margaret stayed with him. She had curly grey hair, apple-red cheeks, and a small, rounded chin. Her arms were thin but strong. She looked younger than her fifty-eight years. And she was a good listener, a perfect complement to Eggert with his affinity for soapbox rants.

Actually, Terminus needed Little Wing, his personal-class shuttle, and Eggert was the only pilot, so retirement would have to remain a dream for the immediate future, not that that bothered Eggert. He wouldn't know how to actually relax anyway.

When Boston Quinn sent his army to destroy the juice hackers, Eggert was a key player in relocating the people to Terminus. He and Rosco, the lead juice hacker from Blue Hole, rebuilt the governance systems for what was left of the population. Though it was still a refugee outpost, at least there was a council, and everyone had a roof.

They'd held their first settlement-wide election for speaker the past year, and, surprisingly, a young woman named Laith won. Though she was only eighteen, her passion and charisma made her the number-one choice. The people of Terminus trusted Laith. They smiled when they met her. She stood tall and strong in the face of near destitution. She was smart and organized, but the main attribute she brought was hope. She gave the people hope. Over the past ten months, she took over managing most of the day-to-day business of the village.

The refugees' time was still mostly spent taking care of essentials: heat, food, water, shelter. Eric, Rosco, and his mate Grendel, along with Doctor Pamela P, had written the basic by-laws which set up a government. They established weekly meetings to hear and rectify grievances, form committees to do research, and assign projects to the engineers. Since Laith's election, the elders took on more of an advising position. She chose a handful of trusted advisors and secretaries that helped her. But after hunting and food and tending to the old and sick, there was little time for much else.

The first winter they'd lost nearly half of their population. Doctor Pamela P had a few women helping her, but there were almost no drugs, and her diagnostic tools were destroyed in Blue Hole. She and her nurses mainly made the dying comfortable. She'd gotten a bad cold herself and spent a week in bed with a fever. It seemed to come back every winter now. She was tired most of the time and leaned heavily on her assistants. Pam, as she preferred to be called, didn't think about her own frailty; she knew she had cancer. But the people needed her, and so her own needs would wait.

Secretary Corbet sent a four-person team to Terminus Station to, as he worded it, "infiltrate and gather intelligence." They were to take no action. Corbet was a cautious man. He would act, but only if he was sure. The team was well trained and loyal to The Authority. Corbet had no reason to believe the mission could create a problem. But upon leaving Interface range, the team passed beyond the reach of The City's control systems, and Corbet had underestimated the deleterious effects of High Lord Quinn's behavior modification programs.

Consequently, the men, Parker and Smith, and women, Felice and Murman, grew more and more critical of the Lords and The Authority the further they walked from the wall. By the time they were climbing the last hill overlooking Terminus, the intent of their mission had changed drastically.

They'd followed the railroad tracks out of the wasteland of Blue Hole. It took them a day to cross it. The tracks and ties just materialized at the boundary of the blast, growing out of the featureless dust. During the siege, the Enforcer army set mass wave generators to level the village once they had evacuated, but Elli Quinn's oldest friend, Maxamillion Hamp, attempted to disarm them and ended up vaporized with the last of the Enforcers. All that was left of the village was a circle of devastation twenty kilometers wide. Nothing but rolling hills covered by fine grey sand.

As they trudged through the featureless wasteland, Parker said, "See? See what he's done? I mean, in a world where people are nearly extinct, how can he justify wiping out an entire village like this? It's monstrous, inhumane, horrifying…"

Murman said, "I heard there were hot springs here. And the people had personal heat and hot water and gardens with real food. It sounded like a paradise." People in The City ate replicator food—a 3D representation made from a fungus base where all taste and texture were delivered via Interface. Emerson once described the taste as mildewed carboard when his Interface was shut down.

"You can understand why Lord Quinn felt threatened, eh?" Smith added and snickered.

Murman said, "I heard that the pilot, Emerson Lloyde, went rogue and kidnapped Lord Quinn's daughter and granddaughter."

Felice said, "Yeah, but the child is Lloyde and Rattlesnake's. Now there's a rumor that Emerson was the grandson of Lord Coke's only daughter, Ciara. If I could have a daughter, I would move the world to protect her." She stood facing into the breeze, sniffed, and pointed to the south. "Terminus is there. You can smell the wood smoke."

"Shit, I smell the latrine." Parker spat.

They crested the hill. Terminus Station appeared as a collection of muddy pathways between rough wooden shacks, each with a fire burning out front or inside. Smoke twisted from hundreds of mud-brick chimneys and rusty metal smoke pipes.

Smith said, "We have to go back to The City, you know. What if Quinn sends out another search team? Maybe Blue Hole was a paradise. But this," he indicated the sprawling camp, "this is no alternative."

Murman, never one to waste a breath on emotions of any sort, said, "Fuck you, Smith. Living in a cave is better than letting Lord Quinn live in my head. I say we warn the refugees and head west. Fighting children, the old, and the sick ain't part of my contract."

They walked on toward the gate, which was a twelve-meter-high structure made of eight-centimeter thick Bodock limbs strapped together with sinew laces. Before they got within twenty meters, a guard carrying a plasma rifle yelled for them to stop. He sent a runner to warn Rosco and the Council.

Parker raised his hands. The others stood fingering their crossbows. He said, "We come from The City with a message. We seek no harm, only to talk."

Rosco and Eggert arrived in moments.

Smith said, "You're Eric Eggert. We heard you died a hero's death in the siege against the juice hackers."

Eggert sucked his teeth and said, "Whatever they told you, it's a lie. That's what the Lords do. Don't believe a word."

The guard, a tall, heavy woman nicknamed Crusher, said, "Drop your weapons. If you move funny, I'll reduce you to a bubbling puddle of goo."

The four didn't hesitate.

Rosco had a big belly, a black beard, and black eyes deep-set into his polished bronze face. He was usually quiet but quick to smile. The legal and constitutional systems in Blue Hole and Terminus owed their design to him. He said, "Who are you and what do you want?"

Parker spoke, "The High Lord wants any friends of Emerson Lloyde and his daughter, Elli Rattlesnake Quinn. He is intent on finding his granddaughter and obliterating all traces of this settlement."

"I figured he'd get around to that eventually," Rosco replied.

"The Lord has lost his mind," Murman said. "He has The Authority monitoring everyone and manipulating personal behaviors without consent. It's gotten out of control. Lord Quinn needs to be stopped."

"The High Lord is a danger to everyone," added Felice.

Rosco said, "I am going to have to take you into custody until I can verify you are telling the truth."

Murman laughed. "You don't have the luxury of time. Lord Quinn's got screws lose. He won't wait for us. When we don't return, he'll send an army to repeat what he did to Blue Hole. Let us go. Evacuate as many as you can. They are coming. They might already be on the way."

Rosco said, "Nevertheless, you need to come with me. We can get you some food and let you clean up. I have to discuss the rest with the council."

◆ ◆

When Lord Quinn's advance team was securely housed in the meeting hall, which was just a longer shack, Rosco, Grendel, and Eggert met with Pam.

Grendel was Rosco's life partner. She wore her grey dreadlocks loosely tied behind her head like a bundle of snakes. In middle age she'd grown round. Her sepia-colored skin was always as soft as warm butter. She walked with a limp, which was deceptive. Grendel would wrestle a lion to protect her clan if there were any left. She compound-fractured her leg trying to save her stepfather during the bombing of Blue Hole. The bones had healed, but the effects lingered.

Eggert began, "I know what he is capable of, and I say we get out."

Pam said, "Besides that, there is nowhere *to* go. How do you propose we deal with all of our people? Most are underfed. We have children and infirm elders. We hardly make it through the winter every year, and we are just setting the foundation we'll require for a functioning society."

Eggert sucked his teeth again, and said, "Solid foundations won't be much good to the dead."

Grendel said, "Call Emerson, Rosco. If there was ever a time that we needed his help, it's now."

Rosco knew it was true. But asking Emerson and Quinn to come back now was inviting them into the mouth of the beast. There were no good choices. He sent an alarm text through the satphone. It pinged the network, which meant the system was functioning. But he had no way to know if Emerson received the call. He would have to wait for a reply.

"In the meantime," Pam said, "I will start figuring out who can move and who can't."

Eggert nodded. "We need supplies and weapons. If the Enforcers want to take Terminus, there is currently nothing we can do to stop them."

Rosco said, "At least they used all their missiles on the last attack."

"Yes." Eggert sucked his teeth. "Unless they found more. The only way to avoid another bloodbath is to leave before they get here."

Rosco asked, "Yeah, but where?"

Pam said, "What are we going to do with the spies? They did warn us."

"Not sure we can trust them." Rosco scratched his beard.

"Not sure we have much choice," Eggert said. "We need their help. The citizens are overwhelmed just helping their families survive."

Rosco said, "I suppose going anyplace will be better than standing still. Here we are just a target for the next wave of Enforcers to aim at."

◆ ◆ ◆

A WAVE OF EARTH

When Emerson, Quinn, and Ana arrived back at the encampment with Plummer and the medical equipment, they found Marya still asleep. All of the encampment's supplies that could be fit into The Black Mariah were crated and labeled. Paxon was pretty organized, and both Anoush and Sandra were happily carrying their own weight. Emerson wasn't certain about Anoush. She was polite, but he felt like she was keeping something a secret. Besides that, whenever they happened to be alone, she always found some excuse to touch him.

Emerson didn't know what was done to the women on the island, but he guessed it left scars. He had to give Elli time, and, like her, when Anoush decided to speak, he would listen. And if she didn't, it was her burden. He didn't presume to know better than her. He made a mental note to talk to Chandler about his concerns the next time he was with him in the sim cube. He owed his understanding of boundaries to his grandfather. The old man made his share of mistakes raising him, but as an adult Emerson recognized the man's wisdom daily.

He wished Saą was still there. At least she offered encouragement about Marya's injuries. He tried to show a confident face to Quinn and the others, but his doubts made holding on to all his other responsibilities much harder.

Elli interrupted his thoughts. "There were tremors this morning. I think that's what they're called. The ground vibrated. It was weird."

Emerson was considering setting up the magnetic resonance imager. But if an earthquake was imminent, they needed to load the ship. Elli was a step ahead of him. She went on, "I can see you need rest. We'll get the shuttle loaded; go and see Marya."

As she was turning, he said, "Watch out for Anoush. There's something going on there."

Elli knew what he meant. She'd seen it. She nodded and left. Emerson met Quinn in her cabin. They sat on the bed next to their unconscious daughter. Quinn hugged her limp body. Emerson put his hand on her arm. Her color looked good, and she was breathing regularly. When Quinn looked inside her lower eyelid, it was not bloodshot, and her circulation seemed fine. Emerson listened to her heart and nodded. It seemed that all they could do was wait. It was nearing noon, but he couldn't stay awake any longer. Just before he drifted off, he said, "We'll set up the MRI as soon as we get inland."

◆ ◆

Plummer and Ana met with Elli after she left Emerson. The cyborg loaded crates into the rear cargo hold of The Black Mariah. Ana had fashioned a head out of a pillow, tying it onto the lugs his poly-cast skull used to be attached to. She resisted drawing a face on it. The thought made her giggle. Rat One looked up at her inquisitively.

Plummer said, "Ana is doing me a kindness. We shouldn't be vain at a time like this." He sounded like he was teaching a child.

The rats disappeared. Ana explained the cyborg to Elli as they packed the last of the lab and cooking equipment. In the middle of the second run, Plummer entered his recharge cycle. He and Elli talked while Ana went and checked on Quinn, LC, and Marya.

Elli said, "I'm not sure I can trust you, Plummer. How do I know you won't, like, try and blow us up in order to kill yourself? Having you around seems like a liability unless, of course, you discount that with your value as a self-directing tractor."

Plummer let out one of his strange mis-approximations of a laugh that Ana already had plans to reprogram. He said, "Hey, that's not a bad idea."

Elli smiled her wryest and said, "I'm getting to like you, Plummer. What else can you do besides carry around boxes that are three times your weight?"

"I used to be able to cook a mean Texas chili back when I still had a stomach and intestines."

"You know that's gross, right?"

"But that's what you love about me, isn't it, Elli Moon?" She snorted. He went on, "We'd need to find some tomatoes first—or grow them."

"Are you any good at that?" She was inspecting the wielding work on his upper torso; it was impeccable.

He whispered, "No. I wouldn't know the first thing about planting seeds. However, I can make miniature cybernetic animals from live ones."

Elli stepped back. "Ew, man. That's really gross."

Rat One appeared by her leg and gave her pants a tug.

Rat Two stood on his hind legs and shielded his eyes from the sun reflecting off the bare metal of Plummer's arm plates.

Rat One said, "Hi, Elli. Am I disgusting?"

Rat Two added, "How about me? You like my welding, right?"

Elli looked at Plummer and said, "You made these?"

"Well, Rat One helped build Rat Two, but, yeah."

"How do you make them talk? Do they have voice boxes like you?"

"Actually, you are only hearing them because you are implanted. Communication with my rats is Interface only."

"We should get the last of this stowed. I don't want to be here when the earth begins to quake."

"Have you ever been in an earthquake before?"

"No."

"You are right, Elli Moon. You don't want to be here."

• •

Ana arrived with Quinn and Emerson. Marya was limp in her arms. Quinn said to Plummer, "Nice head."

"Ana made it for me."

Ana said, "It was creeping me out that he had no head. It was either that or draw eyes and a smile on his chest."

"Wait, is that my pillow?" asked Quinn.

"It was the only one that wasn't stowed."

At that moment, a flock of at least 100 starlings swooped into the camp and abruptly changed direction twice while flying a few meters above the sand. Then, the entire flock flew straight up into the sky, turning 180 degrees at about 300 meters, and dove directly into the ocean. Each of the small birds made a tiny splash as it burrowed its bullet-like body into the sea in a machine-gun blast of rapid-fire drops.

Everyone including Anoush and Sandra gaped at the spectacle. Emerson broke the silence first.

"Get in the shuttle! NOW, NOW, NOW, NOW!"

They ran. The sand of the encampment began to dance. It seemed that the waves weren't ending at the shoreline any longer but continuing up the beach. Amid the rumbling, which was growing louder by the second, chips of the cliffs above began breaking off and raining to the ground around them. The sand rolled, knocking them down and showering them in dust and debris.

Emerson sprang to his feet and pulled Quinn up. She was still clutching Marya, slung over her shoulder. Plummer had not fallen. His treads spread wider, giving him more stability in the rolling sand. He reached out to the others and yelled, "Grip my arms. I will pull you." They all made it to the hatchway just as the shaking stopped.

Emerson scrambled into the cockpit and initiated the reactors. Ana strapped Little Chandler into a seat and helped Sandra, Anoush, and Paxon get buckled. She grabbed Plummer's pillow and threw it to Quinn so she could strap the unconscious Marya into two seats. Ana shut the door, put a tether strap on Plummer, and went to the cockpit to sit with Elli and Emerson. The entire shuttle vibrated. Rocks rained down on them.

Emerson shouted, "We're out of here!"

The Black Mariah lifted off the sand, angling backward away from the cliff wall and out over the ocean.

As soon as he'd hovered up to 100 meters, the reactor signaled a fully charged state, and Emerson opened the throttles. Every passenger on board was pressed deep into their seats and could not move for a solid minute as the shuttle gained altitude. Rat One and Two gripped the back of a seat, their bodies pulled horizontal by the force of acceleration. Anoush gasped when she saw them.

Emerson routed the lower outside cameras to the screens in the cabin and cockpit. The scene was unbelievable. They were high enough now to see several hundred kilometers up and down the coast. The ground rippled. Waves undulated beneath the tree-covered soil. Sharp rocks poked through the surface at odd angles, like Poseidon rose under the land and stabbed his trident up through the earth. Except the earth wasn't solid anymore. It seemed more like water or sand, shifting and churning, swallowing the surface and vomiting up a new world. A horrible new world.

◆ ◆ ◆

A LONE WOMAN AND HER LARGE CAT

Saą was followed. She not only heard Brunt; she smelled him. His fear was acrid and greasy. He was less than a day behind her, followed by a pack of coywolves. They knew he was starving, so, they hung back, giving him time to weaken before finishing him off.

Mule sat in the middle of the trail at the top of the ridge they had just climbed, looking back at the path. They were out of the earthquake's direct range, but Saą still felt signs. At least the animals acted normally here. She expected to reach her people's lands in three days. As long as she could keep moving.

Brunt wasn't just tired, hungry, and scared—he was hurt. The first morning out of Emerson's camp, he'd slipped on loose rock and tumbled down a 200-foot embankment. Nothing was broken, but his head was bruised, and he was pretty sure his shoulder had dislocated and snapped back in before he'd come to rest in a pile at the bottom. The burly man still looked like a black bear, but he couldn't raise his left arm away from his side without excruciating pain.

When he'd stood, he realized his right ankle was twisted too. He tore his shirt into strips to tie a stick pushed into his boot for a splint. He was able to walk, but had to rest often. It took the rest of the day to climb back up to the trail. He didn't think about what he'd do when he caught up to her, but she was his only way to survive. He was a mile from the bank where he fell when he realized that he'd lost all the rations.

The coywolf pack began trailing him near sunset the first day. They watched silently from a distance. Brunt saw them and tried to use the rifle, but he wasn't implanted and knew nothing of Interface-enabled weapons. He threw it into a bush in frustrated disgust. He didn't have flint or matches; he wouldn't have known how to make a fire if he had. The wind up on the ridge was too strong for a flame anyway, and there was little wood up this high. He felt tremors the next morning. They woke him at dawn. He was almost too stiff to stand and found a rotted branch to use as a walking stick. The wood was riddled with poison ants which crawled over the hapless traveler's hands, arms, and neck before he realized what was happening. The acid from their skin burned intensely.

Brunt screamed and tore off what was left of his shirt. He rolled in scrubby dirt and was twice as miserable for the rest of the day. The wolves heard him and wondered what his calls meant. He was acting like an animal with a sickness. It excited them. He would be an easy catch.

He didn't notice the lake through the trees as he left the hillside. A quick bath might have cleared his head enough to save him. It would have definitely relieved some of the torture. He found a field of blackberry bushes and ate until he was stuffed. The water he drank out of a depression in a rock was growing a nasty strain of E. coli. The resultant diarrhea caused him to soil his clothes and further dehydrated him.

The coywolves knew he was struggling. They became excited and almost broke into a full howling chorus when the moon rose that night. Brunt had a low-grade fever. His ant burns had turned into tiny, itchy, pus-filled pimples. If he inadvertently scratched one, the subsequent burn would spread to all the other pimples like a chain of fire. It brought tears to his eyes. He fell asleep on his back, uncovered, thinking about his life on the island before Emerson Lloyde *saved* him.

Fucking hero! he thought.

◆ ◆

The morning of the third day, Mule went to check on the man following them. Saą knew better than to try and change her mind and continued on. *The big cat will catch up,* she thought. She felt the earthquake in her heart. The land cried out in pain as the old was eaten and the new was born. She could only bear witness and keep her heart and mind open to the ways she could help.

Saą placed her hands on the ground and felt for the tickle of intelligence that she associated with The Mother. She stayed that way, in a meditative state, drinking in the power, beauty, and balance of the natural world until she felt clear and strong. Mule would be fine; she knew these mountains and woods better than she.

Saą had mixed feelings for the man. Part of her was sad for his impending death. All people were children of The Mother. She grieved all death, even as she required it for all life. The larger part of Saą was satisfied that the forest would take care of him in whatever way was best for all. The wolves were hungry in this season; everyone needed to eat. She walked on, expecting to reach the outer boundaries of her family's lands before sunset. By tomorrow she would be with her people, and the prospect lightened her mood.

Mule found Brunt before noon. He was straining his bowels near a pine tree. The cat recognized the hairy poison oak vines twisting around the trunk which the man was leaning on. Cats like Mule didn't get dermatitis from plants like the oak or the ivy. But she'd seen the result on the children. But there was no way for the cat to warn the man. She stayed out of sight.

The coywolves had dwindled to a pack of three over the winter. The deer were gone, and the elk which migrated south dwindled. The mutant animals were surviving mostly on mice and berries. The prospect of Brunt's meaty body had them salivating and biting each other in anticipation. Mule heard them; they smelled the blood in Brunt's stool. It drove them crazy with lust.

When the burly man finished and pulled up his pants, the pack came out of the brush, snarling and whining. Humans were an easy mark unless they carried weapons. But there was always a chance of death in any hunt, so they were erratically bold and cautious. Their fear mixed with excitement and hunger. The larger female, one who looked like she might have had a German Shepard somewhere in her ancestry, lunged at Brunt. He screamed, covering his face, and fell back against the tree, hitting his head.

Mule stepped out from behind a scrub oak in between the coywolves and Brunt. The female stopped. Mule growled low in her throat. She was easily twice as heavy as the wolf. The fur on Mule's back stood up; her tail lashed menacingly. The growl slid lower, making them tense. The other wolves looked at each other and at their leader. They took a step back. Mule jumped toward them, and the female stepped back, signaling Mule to finish them. Mule leapt at the female's face, opening a large red gash on the coywolf's nose. The canine yipped and turned. All three ran into the brush.

Mule turned back to Brunt, who had lost control of his bladder and was blubbering with his face in his hands. She strode to the trembling man and sniffed him, squatted, and peed on his boot.

◆ ◆

Emerson got the alarm notice from Rosco while they were cresting the highest peak of the first mountain range to the east. The sat network had degraded since the last time he and Quinn had used it. It was a miracle that it still worked at all after fifty-plus years of neglect. He guessed that one or more of the satellites in the system had stopped working or fallen out of orbit. If he waited, the remaining parts of the network should move into position and allow the call. He checked periodically over the next hour, expecting Rosco's phone to become available. His guess proved right. The call went through.

"Hey, what's up? It's been a while. Is everyone okay?"

Rosco said, "The system is really degrading, I can hardly hear you. How's the weather on the west cost? Yeah, everyone's okay. For now."

"For now?"

"That's why I called. High Lord Quinn is gunning for us. We gotta run. Can you help?"

Emerson thought about the cargo they were carrying. "You're timing is either great or shit, brother. We are running away from an earthquake right now."

"You should get out more, Emerson. You are going to die of boredom, boy. We want to transport people to safety, but Grendel, Eggert, Pam, and I need to get away from them. We endanger everyone by being here. Where are you going? Eggert can fly us there in Little Wing."

Emerson thought of Saą and her people. They avoided electronic technology. Rosco was one of the original juice hackers. Emerson remembered him saying, "The code is my blood." He knew bringing them uninvited would create a problem. But there didn't seem to be any other choice.

Rosco said, "I'm losing signal here, Em. When you figure out where you're going, send us coordinates. We'll have to make it work until then."

The connection ended before Emerson could respond.

◆ ◆ ◆

A LAND RULED BY CROWS

Saą arrived at the boundary of her village that evening just after sunset. She was met by a young woman she'd known since she was a child. They were like sisters. She and Kim embraced in the middle of the trail. When the younger woman released her from the hug, Mule was standing with her head nearly touching Saą's elbow.

Kim stepped back, startled. "Who's your friend? Introduce us?"

Kim bent, and Mule touched her nose with hers. A moment later, they pressed their foreheads together. The big cat sat. Kim said, "Good to meet you, Mule. Welcome to The Land Ruled by Crows. The crows are mostly gone now, but the name remains."

To Saą, she said, "Come. We'll have a meal, and you can tell us about your adventures." They walked down the hill into the village together greeting those they met and enjoying the warmth of the day rising up from the ground.

Saą's parents were killed when she was young. She was the last person in her line. But being dedicated to The Mother, she could choose not to have children, which she knew was essential if the race was to survive. Because of her dedication, she could stay at the village, and the people would care for her needs, or she could wander. She was a healer, after all. But Saą had not decided the nature of her contribution. She was dedicated, yes, but the way she served The Mother would be her choice and hers alone. She wasn't ready to make it yet.

And there was something about Emerson and his crew. Mother urged her to stay close to them. Mule knew they were coming; the big cat showed no anxiety. Saą expected them soon. Before she was finished bathing and combing her short hair, the tables were set, torches were lit, and platters of steaming meats, vegetables, and grains rested on the serving board. Her adoptive family put together a feast in her honor.

The assembled group applauded when she emerged from Kim's house. She blushed, never wanting to be at the center of attention. The crowd quieted, looking at her intently. Shocked, she realized they wanted a speech. *Oh, Mother, why me?* She raised her hand. "No, sorry. Not tonight."

Tri, a teenage girl, brought Saą a mug of kiras, an effervescent, alcoholic brew made from honey and herbs. One sip reminded her how strong it was. She needed to pace herself, or she'd black out. The others around the table were drinking and talking. Conversation got loud as the diners became more and more inebriated.

Saą told Kim about Emerson and his tribe. She carefully avoided saying anything about their use of electronic tech. Her friends were excited to meet new people and planned to have a celebration in their honor when they arrived. Saą hinted at their flying machine, but did not give much detail, only saying that they would cover the distance between the ocean and the village faster than she could walk it.

She didn't mention Brunt at all, unsure if he would make it and positive that she could handle him by herself. After she'd eaten and passed Mule a haunch of venison, she apologized for her exhaustion, excused herself, and left. Mule followed, trotting close by her side. The big cat's head was nearly as tall as Saą's shoulder.

She said, "I wish to be home until I get here. Then I realize I crave solitude. I love my family, but I can't take much of them." The cat rubbed against Saą's hip as if to agree. They walked into the woods, and she sat against a tree looking at the sky until midnight.

Coming back into the house, she found Kim sitting in front of the hearth spinning yarn on a large pedal wheel; a cup of birch bark tea steamed on the low table next to her. She said, "I can only sleep a few hours a night. Want a cup?"

Saą said, "Sure," and picked up a small stoneware goddess from the ledge above the fireplace, kissed it, and put it down. Each house had a massive clay wood-burning oven. They were used for cooking and heat. A small fire always burned, even when the weather was warm. Since the stoves were constructed out of hundreds of kilograms of grass-reinforced clay, they emitted heat long after the fires burned down. The finished stoves looked like a smooth rounded mound with a small mouth facing the room and a ledge-like hearth beneath. Everyone's main room had one. Kim's had a dark wooden board embedded above the opening that served as a warming tray, a knickknack shelf, and an altar.

Each additional room of the houses was built off the central section in spokes. Inhabitants spent most of their time outdoors or in the common room; the spoke rooms were mainly for personal solitude and possessions. Handmade rope rugs, woven from yarn or grass, lay scattered on the polished clay and blood-cured floors. The houses had several thick glass windows that could be closed with wooden shutters. At night, they were illuminated with oil lamps, but the wicks were made of woven grasses specially imbedded with carbon that burned as bright as a full-spectrum LED and emitted no smoke.

Many of the windows could be tipped out to open, allowing the free flow of air to keep the temperature at a constant, and allow precise regulation. The settlement was high in the mountains, so even in the hottest part of the summer, the evenings were cool. At the high elevation, the humidity was usually low, and the sun particularly intense. The thatched roofs were pitched at the perfect angle and overhung the exterior walls enough to provide summer shade but admit direct sun in the winter months, assisting in the passive solar design.

Saą said, "Mother calls me to do things, Kim. Things that our people believe are wrong. I need to reconcile these feelings, or I will have to leave. And I am attracted to Emerson, a man from a technologically dependent society. His people are implanted with the Interface. I am honestly interested in trying it. I am afraid that our leadership will try to exclude them, and they are not even here yet. If they go, I must go with them because Mother says there is something I need to do, but she is tight-lipped on the details. I ask and get nothing. I need to go into deep contemplation to hear her counsel."

Mule scratched at the door. Kim let her in. "You are a big girl." She scratched the cat behind an ear. "Saą, do you know where she comes from? Are there others like her?"

"Emerson told me she had a litter of cubs years ago, in the east, but he's never seen another adult like her."

Mule curled up next to the stove, tucked her nose beneath her tail, and sighed. She stayed that way until dawn when Saą rose, and they walked to the ridge beyond the western boundary. She sensed that Emerson would arrive soon. The Black Mariah descended silently from the clouds a half hour later. Emerson had set the reactors to stealth so as not to alarm people. But the craft was seen, and word spread like a late summer fire.

Within an hour, a group of representatives from the people's leadership council arrived. India Tarn, a copper-skinned woman with black dreadlocks twisted into a bundle at the back of her head, wore the standard dress of the people: a close-fitting tanned-skin vest with leggings that reached just below her knee. The seams were so tight and the sewing so meticulous that Emerson could hardly make out how the garments were assembled. India held a black, polished, wooden walking staff with a smooth round stone set into the top. It was taller than her by at least a head.

"Greetings, Emerson Lloyde," she said, her bottle-green eyes glinting in the morning sun, "your reputation precedes you."

"All good things, I hope."

"No, actually. We do not use the electronic technology that you are dependent upon. You may enter The Land of the Crows, but you cannot stay within the village boundary overnight. You must return to your encampment outside the border to sleep. You must swear to our laws and customs before you can move about without a guide."

Saą said, "I will make sure my guests understand our ways, India. I believe that Emerson and his family have much to offer."

Quinn held Marya, still unconscious, in her arms. Saą checked the child's heart and breathing. She called to another councilwoman, Pejeta, to examine the girl. Pejeta had brass-colored skin, expressive brows, and mischievous eyes. She had been the village's main healer for the last decade.

She put her hand on the child's forehead and said, "I believe she is healing a bruise to her head, but I need to examine her more closely. Can you bring her to the clinic? We can go now."

Quinn looked at Emerson who waved her on. "You go. We'll catch up to you later."

Quinn said to Pejeta, "Yes, that would be a relief—I know she is probably all right, but she hasn't woken up in a couple of days. I can't help but worry." They left together.

Plummer, the headless cyborg, exited the shuttle. Ana said, "He lost his head on the way from Beso Muerte. But I have plans to make him another."

India said, "What *is* it?"

On cue, Rat One and Two appeared next to Plummer's treads.

India stepped back, trying to suppress her horror. She said, "I think, maybe, these *machines* should stay with your shuttle. Our people aren't ready to see this yet."

Saą said, "Come, Kim and I will show you around."

Emerson said, "Plummer, can you and your rats create a shelter for us with Sandra and Anoush? Paxon, can you stay also and help? I don't want to overwhelm these folks with a huge crowd of outsiders." The refugees from the island weren't happy about staying, but no one voiced an argument.

"I will send an engineering crew up here to help. I know someone who won't find your appearance too discomfiting," Saą said.

"Emerson Lloyde," said India, "would you allow me to show you the village?"

"I'd like that," he said.

• •

As Saą and Kim showed Ana and Elli through the stalls in the market quadrant, Elli asked, "Why do you call this place The Land of the Crows?"

Kim said, "When we first settled here, this valley was home to thousands of crows. Something about the sheltered space at the top of a mountain made it a perfect home for them. As we grew, many of the crows found a different home, but we kept the name."

Quinn commented, "It's a mouthful."

Elli said, "So, Crow City, right."

Kim replied, "We do not consider our home to be a city, but you may call this place whatever you like."

Elli said, "Crow City."

• •

The stalls were filled with goods: food, pottery, cloth, shoes, sundries, clay pots, metal pans, eggs…

Ana said, "Chicken eggs? I have never tasted a real chicken egg. I thought they went extinct with the virus."

Saą answered, "We have been raising hybrid fowl for the last few decades. We crossed grouse with other wild birds to try and produce a viable chicken substitute, but altering the genetics takes time. I'm not fond of their eggs, but I never tasted a chicken egg."

Ana said, "I've had dehydrated eggs. Bletch."

There were stalls with birds and various other sorts of small animals in cages. Another had all sizes of hand-woven baskets. None of the items were salvaged; everything was meticulously handmade and assembled with a great respect for craft. Each item was unique with a keen eye for aesthetics and functionality. The artisans of Crow City, as Elli called it, were exceptional.

"I love your clothing," Ana said. "Is there a shop where I can trade for a pair of those pants? And I need a cap like this one." She pointed at the skin cap that hung from Saą's hip.

Saą said, "It is custom in *Crow City*, as you call it, Elli, for all citizens to make their own clothing. I made my first cap when I was Marya's age. My adopted mother made my vests and leggings until I became proficient. My first smock was so bad Mama wouldn't let me go out in public with it. She actually threw it in the fireplace!"

"Will you teach me?" Ana asked.

"It would be an honor, but I caution you—I have been sewing my own garments for several decades. Be patient with yourself and take your time. There is no substitute for practice." Saą untied her cap and gave it to Ana. She nodded, looking over the seams.

Saą said, "Do your hands a favor and get a thimble from Jan. He is a talented silversmith."

◆ ◆

Saą and Kim brought Elli, Ana, and LC to an open-air café and ordered for them. The proprietor, a woman with a shaved head and a dark blue pattern tattooed above her ear, who Ana assumed was also the cook and the baker, brought them ceramic mugs of steaming kiras and a platter of small sweet cakes made of some sort of sprouted grain.

Little Chandler ate three of the cakes before Ana saw what he was doing. The tattooed baker brought a damp cloth. She spoke with the traces of a brogue, "I have two babes myself. You can never have too many spare nappies. Do you think the little one would like some warm milk?"

Ana said, "I'm sure he would, but what sort of milk do you have?"

"We have tried to raise several types of ruminants. But sheep are best for milk, meat, and wool. They are small and hearty. I got my starter flock of three ewes and a ram from a nomad shepherd a decade back. We have over 100 now. They pasture in the hills to the east. My twins take turns watching them. We bring them into the village at shearing time."

Ana replied, "I've never seen a live sheep."

"Ahh, they'll be lambing come the cold weather. I'll introduce you to Cali. She's the current shepherd. You can go along with her when she checks on the flock in the fall."

◆ ◆

Ana was buzzed from her drink. She and the children rested on the comfortable bench as the sun crossed into the afternoon. Afterward, Kim and Saą brought them to Pejeta's house.

They'd put Marya in a cot and posted a nurse who would watch the child round the clock. Pejeta said she expected her to wake up soon. The lump on her neck had shrunk; the chamomile and willow bark poultice seemed to be having a positive effect.

◆ ◆

The crew got to know the village and its customs. India brought Emerson to the council chamber, a large, round, wooden structure with a dome-like roof. Even though the council wasn't in session, a small fire burned in a stone basin at the center of the hall. Seats were arranged in the round in concentric circles. Emerson sat while India walked around the room explaining the concepts of dynamic governance and restorative justice.

She was a natural orator, and the room was acoustically balanced so she could be heard anywhere speaking at a conversational volume. Emerson was enthralled. She said, "We are charged with creating a new, better world. A world where we avoid the mistakes of the old world. Our philosophy is to treat society as we treat family. And, of course, avoid falling for the lie that coin can be substituted for any value. The old world's punitive justice system does not work in a small family-based society. The old systems assumed the way to govern was to eliminate deviants. We see that as inherently evil. It was a system that used authority over the people to rule rather than helping people to take responsibility for themselves. No one is expendable in our family; therefore, every person deserves all the support our society can give."

"What about capital crimes, like murder and rape?"

"We prefer to speak in concrete terms and avoid hypotheticals. Murder and sexual assault do not happen that often here. When the circumstance aligns to produce such unfortunate events, the council takes everything into consideration before passing judgement. Regardless of the crime, we do not hurt or execute humans. We believe that a healthy individual punishes themselves enough when they make a mistake—with support, most people can forgive themselves and be forgiven. In the rare cases that someone cannot be rehabilitated and retuned to a life of contribution, we make sure they are as comfortable as possible, kept in a place where they can do no harm to anyone. But the focus is always on helping, not hurting."

"Are you sure of the safety of your people with murderers and rapists on the loose?"

"We lock them up, Emerson. We are not idiots. But we do not seek to punish as a way to modify behaviors. We believe that people become misled and confused or tricked. The job of justice is to interrupt undesirable behavior and teach better and more effective ways to deal with trauma and pain. Of course, sometimes there is no cure. We understand that you cannot fix people like machines. It is one reason that we eschew electronic tech. It is too easy to mistake it for something that is alive."

She sat down next to him and looked at his face closely. "You know, Emerson. It's not my job to be sure of anything. The council doesn't predict the future. Besides, security is a fool's errand. You know that."

Emerson said, "I'd like to watch a council meeting if I could."

"I'll do you one better; you can have a seat on the council at the next meeting. Four standing members are required to be present, but we can have as many as six. There is plenty of space for you."

India brought Emerson to Pejeta's house. Quinn, Ana, and Elli were already there.

◆ ◆ ◆

TERMINUS EXODUS

Not knowing when Lord Quinn's army would arrive, Eggert requested Laith send lookouts to a spot outside of The City wall. A sat-phone was too delicate to send, and there were no long-distance communications devices anymore, so they devised a signal. If a platoon was seen leaving the city, a two-meter-high pile of dry wood would be lit. Considering that the Enforcers would be traveling in shuttles, the fire would only give them a few hours' warning.

Eggert was an experienced strategist. He knew that they would need weapons and supplies. He and Emerson had traveled in The Black Mariah to retrieve stealth paint and plasma weapons from a bunker north of Outpost 212. Eggert and Emerson had only just scratched the surface of what was stored in that bunker. They had only opened three of the storage lockers' overhead doors. The hallway was at least 100 meters long with doors lining either side.

Eggert and Rosco left after dark to retrieve what they could.

Once they were airborne, Eggert said, "If the bunker were closer, I'd wager that the whole of Terminus could hide there. But Little Wing can only transport a handful, and our population is still in the thousands—that would take days."

They landed in a field of scrub grass, stunted trees, and brambles.

Eggert had the coordinates. He said, "Don't know how long the GPS network can be trusted. But without it, we'd be completely hosed. The shuttles largely fly on automatic. Oh, I can pilot her manually, but navigation would take on several new layers. We'd need to make compasses and sextants. The original mariners could steer by the stars and the moon." He sucked his teeth and added, "I think Emerson shut the GPS off on The Black Mariah. He and Ana created a magnetic field-based navigation system. Claimed it was more reliable."

The steel plates covering the staircase down into the bunker were completely grown over. Eggert had the location, but there was no sign of the door. He took a freight pole from the rear hold and walked around in circles banging the end on the ground. The sound changed from a thump to a muffled metallic echo when he located the coverings. They scraped away the soil and weeds. Eggert released the Interface-based lock with his implant and the computer on Little Wing. They lifted the heavy rusted plate and threw it back. Sunlight revealed the spiral stair descending into darkness. It smelled musty and wet. They lit a couple halogen torches and made their way down.

Eggert remembered lugging the rifles and fifteen-liter buckets of paint up last time and threw down a winch line tied to a net. He tapped the side of his head and said, "Getting old teaches you to work smarter."

At the bottom, they collected several crates of rifles and used the Interface-enabled line to bring them up. Rosco rode along in order to load them into the shuttle; then he traveled down for the next load. They found a bank of batteries that powered overhead lights and spent several hours searching and removing crates containing antibiotics, surgical kits, and canned and dehydrated foods. Most of the storerooms were empty. But there was one which was more of an office than a locker. Inside, Rosco and Eggert found treasure.

There were cases of short-range communication devices, laser tools, and a 3D printer complete with various resins, military-grade portable computers and tablets, and a book of old maps.

Eggert studied one of the maps and said, "I'll be damned, Rosco, my man. This bunker is part of a network of storage lockers, and guess what? There are a lot of them. One is less than a kilometer from Terminus."

Rosco looked at the book over Eggert's shoulder. He said, "Looks like there are living quarters there. A mess hall, bunk rooms, common areas. Thousands of people could live there for an extended period."

"And it's huge. They must have planned to come down here after the apocalypse."

"I guess they didn't make it, huh?"

"Their loss is our gain."

◆ ◆

Eggert and Rosco returned to Terminus with a full cargo hold and distributed weapons and medicines. Laith sent the lookouts on foot. She didn't want to chance flying anywhere near The City. After a short meeting, they decided that the healthiest citizens would migrate to the bunker first, scope it out, and report back. Eggert and Margaret went with them. Eggert located the door near a collapsed wooden barn on an overgrown farmstead. He didn't know the farmer, Eziah Carter, who had lived there decades ago. Emerson hadn't told him about the biannual pilgrimage he and his grandfather had made to Carter's for grain with a nano-carbon-fiber cart. They'd gotten their original buckwheat seed from the man. If Chandler or the old farmer knew about the bunker, they never mentioned it.

The plate steel doors were the same, but the lock was a standard tumbler-and-key device. Eggert melted it off, and they opened the doors. The advance crew took communicators and torches, but they found the generator and lights soon after opening the first overhead doors. Eggert left them to explore. He and Margaret went back to Terminus. After cleaning up the bunk rooms and the kitchens, which were equipped with 10,000-gallon propane reserves to power the stoves and generators, the advance crew would signal Eggert to bring the next wave.

They continued that way for the next few days. Luckily, Lord Quinn hadn't called out the army. Yet.

◆ ◆

In an attempt to mislead Quinn's Enforcers, Rosco and Eggert made it look like the citizens went further south. They created the illusion by cutting down a number of trees and roughing up the ground using plasma guns.

Eggert said, "That should slow them down."

Emerson called on the satphone, but the connection was poor, and there was no time to explain what they'd found or relay their plan. He sent them the coordinates to Crow City and warned that they should set camp next to The Black Mariah and not venture into the village until the council could meet with them.

Eggert, Pam, Grendel, and Margaret left the abandoned shell of their settlement at Terminus and set a course for Outpost 212.

Grendel said, "Why chance it? Shouldn't we just go west and get away from this madman?"

"Not enough fuel," Rosco said. "They purposely keep the shuttle range low with small fuel tanks in these standard shuttles. I outfitted The Black Mariah for extended range. She's much bigger, too, and can carry reserves. We are going to need a way to make concentrated hydrogen pellets, or we will never cross the Inland Sea."

◆ ◆ ◆

OUTPOST 212

Eggert was intimately familiar with most of the 300 outposts to The City. They were all pretty much the same: staging places for patrolling the area inside a 200-mile radius from the center of The City. As an Enforcer trainer and recruiter, he'd made the rounds looking for candidates and doing certifications. Every outpost was the same. They all consisted of an Enforcer station which was a block building with landing pads on the roof surrounded by a shantytown built out of the garbage the station made.

The town that grew up around the station was a vast sea of muddy paths when it was wet and a sweltering dust bin in heat. Most of the buildings were simple one-room shacks with plastic or tin roofs—except the Fly Saloon, which was built before the collapse. It was originally an ornate building, constructed as a boarding house in the late nineteenth century. Unlike most of the hastily slapped-together structures in the town, if you could call it a town, the folk-Victorian-style house had a basement with an actual stone foundation, plaster-and-lath walls, double-hung glass windows, and a slate roof. Several windows had stained glass along the top. The front porch sagged from termite damage, and the paint on its clapboard siding had flaked away to weathered grey long ago. But it was still more of a building than any besides the station, which squatted like a granite grave marker across the muddy street from it.

Since the last time Eggert had been there, the circular turret on the third floor had caved in on itself. The Fly Saloon was off limits to Enforcers, but that never stopped any of them from frequenting it. For Eggert, the problem was his face. Every Enforcer knew him; he was a legend. Most believed he'd died a hero in the siege at Blue Hole.

He landed Little Wing two kilometers out in the woods. Margaret, Rosco, and Grendel walked in, and Pam opted out. She was too weak. They each carried a pack full of antibiot injectors and a plasma rifle slung over their shoulders. Eggert stayed in the shuttle and played Gin Rummy with the doctor. She beat him mercilessly, calling Rummy on the board whenever he focused on monitoring the outdoor cameras, which was almost as often as he sucked his teeth.

The plan was to find and acquire a hydrogen pellet condenser. They brought valuable anti-inflammatory and MRSA drugs. There were several buckets of stealth paint back at the shuttle. Rosco was sure he could get what they needed.

Eggert had said, "Be vigilant. Lord Quinn has eyes everywhere. If you are asking about a hydrogen condenser, it is because you have a shuttle. Emerson and I have the only non-Enforcer shuttles."

Rosco said, "I get it. I'll keep it subtle."

As they were walking, Grendel said, "You don't do subtle, darlin'." Margaret laughed.

◆ ◆

Outpost 212 was a place where you could get anything if you asked the right person the right question. Asking the wrong person could get you killed. Its location near the edge of the Inland Sea helped connect it to trading groups in the north and, on very rare occasions, from the western side of the sea. Rosco knew he'd find what he was looking for at the saloon, but he wanted to see what sort of tech gear might be available in the shops first.

Grendel and Margaret went to look for fabrics and tools. Nearly everything they owned was destroyed at Blue Hole. Metal pots and glass jars were a luxury. They planned to meet at the west end of town in a couple hours and went off separately. The season had been relatively dry this year, so the paths between stalls were only a little muddy. At its worst, Eggert had told them, the sucking goo would take your boots.

Rosco watched a one-eyed man make polished steel parts on a Bridgeport lathe; an ancient Honda generator puttered behind his hovel. Rosco walked on. Another stall had several wooden cages of varying sizes lining the walls, some stacked two or three high. A short, heavy man stood to greet Rosco when he entered the stall. He was missing most of his teeth; his cheeks and nose were blotchy and red from broken blood vessels.

"Helloo, helloo, stranger, whot kin I do ya for, eh? I got sum fine specimens heya, fine fine fine."

Before Rosco could speak, the proprietor opened a chest-level cage and lifted out a small furry animal. Rosco couldn't tell what it was. The short man thrust the ball of fluff into Rosco's arms and said, "We breed the wild ones with our do-mes-tisticated female."

Rosco held the thing under its front legs and brought it up to his face. He said, "It's a dog? Aren't all the dogs gone? A boy dog, at that."

"Ah, thas the story they tell ya. But I'm here to prove the truth is a little harder to parse out, if you catch m'meaning." He winked. Rosco could only understand half of what he said, but he caught the gist. The guy whistled when he spoke. It distracted Rosco.

He said, "What sort of *wild one* was his mama bred with?"

"Not sure, some sorta canid, I guess. The babies survived, thas all I know."

The animal was certainly cute. Rosco couldn't tell if he was more dog or a fox. He was mostly grey with tan highlights on his face and paws. His nose was black, and his eyes were an odd dark blue. His tail was furry with a white tip and about a third as long as his body. He licked Rosco's nose with a pink tongue. Rosco laughed, and the shop owner went for the close.

He said, "You look like you could use a friend."

"How big do you think he'll get?" Rosco asked.

"No tellin'. Sometimes they stay small. But sometimes they grow. It's a gamble."

Rosco handed the furball back to the short man. He said, "I don't want no truck with live baggage. But if I found that I needed a dog or fox or whatever, what's this fella worth to you?"

"Whadda you got?"

Rosco brought a MRSA antibiot syringe out of his pack and said, "Would this be enough?"

Short Man handed the animal back to Rosco and inspected the syringe. He said, "Pretty out of date, but what isn't?" He smelled it, bit the cylindrical tube, and said, "Yeah. Thas fair." He slapped his right hand on top of his left fist and said, "Sold!"

"Hey, no. Wait a minute, I can't…"

"A deal's a deal."

Grendel and Margaret entered the shop and began fussing over the animal. Grendel said, "My leg ain't what it used to be. I had to stop."

The shop owner said, "Looks like you made the right decision, eh?"

Grendel asked, "What is he? Are we going to keep him?"

Margaret saw Rosco's face and began laughing.

Rosco shook the short man's hand and said, "Sold." After a few more minutes of petting the little thing, it fell asleep, and Grendel slipped him into her jacket pocket.

Rosco said, "You know anyone who can get me a hydrogen pellet concentrator?"

Short man looked at the floor. He mumbled, "We're closed now. Go talk to Miss Magg. She's the one. Now get going. Go on. Git!"

He pushed them out and unfurled an oilskin over the door.

Grendel said, "That was rude."

Rosco said, "No ruder than you hijacking me over this puppy or kit or whatever the hell it is. Shit! Eggert is going to freak." They walked toward the main street. He continued, "I knew I was already doomed. I was trying to get out of there before he sold *you* something else."

The sloped front porch of the Fly Saloon was filled with women of every possible size and color. Most were completely naked; two sat in a wicker love seat with their large breasts hanging over the wood rail.

As she passed in the street, Grendel said, "Better watch out for splinters, honey."

They had to push through the crowd at the double swinging doors. Margaret said, "Just like one of those bars in the old Westerns." She and Eggert had spent many afternoons watching archived television and movies when he believed he was locked up in Blue Hole.

Inside, the opium smoke hung around at eye level. The bass from the music throbbed insistently in time with the banging of beds on the floor above. The place smelled of mildew and piss. Fully clothed men walked purposely with naked women on their arms. Many of the men wore Enforcer uniforms.

A tall, gaunt, bald man in an ill-fitting suit stood in the center of the room. He greeted them with a deep, sonorous voice as they approached, "Welcome, pilgrims." He pointed. "The bar is that way. Place *all* of your orders there." He grinned, exposing one gleaming, gold incisor.

"I need to see Miss Magg." Rosco shouted to be heard.

"Go to the bar. I send her to you."

There were several empty stools. The bartender, dressed like a black-jack dealer from an old Western—including the waistcoat, string bolo tie, and green visor cap—appeared and set up three glasses, filling each with a thick, iridescent green fluid. He said, "It's on the house."

"What is it?" Grendel asked.

"Firefly juice. Drink it. It won't hurt you."

Rosco knew that when a bartender told you something would not hurt you, the chances were that it would. But he didn't want to arouse suspicion. He thanked the man and threw back his drink. Grendel and Margaret did the same.

It was warm and sweet. After he'd swallowed it, he realized it was actually burning his throat. He began to sweat. "What the hell was that?" His voice was squeaky and strained.

When he looked up, the room was no longer dark. Everything was clean and bright. Everyone was beautiful. He heard flute music. He looked at Grendel and was overcome with the urge to dance. It was amazing. His skin tingled.

A moment later, the room dimmed down to the same flat darkness. The sweet flute music evaporated, replaced by the low murmur of patrons and the squeaking of beds upstairs. The same redundant bass, off somewhere, everywhere, growled and bumped.

A girl arrived, dressed in the tattered remnants of a white wedding gown, the train dragging on the dirty threadbare rug behind her. It was stained and yellow. She stood in front of Rosco, her head only coming up to his waist, an unlit cigarillo clamped between her yellow teeth. She said, "Are you going to pick me up or what?" Her face was a nest of wrinkles. Rosco realized she was Magg and placed her on a stool.

"You big, manly men love to feel up an old lady, don't you?"

Grendel smiled. Rosco did not.

"I'm Magg. What do you want?"

The bartender set two more glasses in front of her and filled them all again.

Rosco pointed at the empty and said, "Who's that for?"

"The Domovoy," Magg said. "We must give the Domovoy his due, or he would be offended. Are you stupid or what?"

"What are we toasting?"

"The Domovoy, sheesh."

Everyone in the saloon thundered, "TO THE DOMOVOY!" and broke into a boisterous cheer, stamping their feet on the worn rug in unison.

When his head cleared, Rosco asked, "Where can I get a hydrogen pellet condenser?"

She squinted at his face. "You're not Emerson Lloyde. But I bet you came from Blue Hole. Uh-huh, I knew you people would be back. Lard Quinn is lookin' for you. He's lost what few marbles he had. Nope," She slipped off the chair and turned. "I'm not dancing with that bullshit. Get the fuck out of my bar, or I'll call the Enforcers." Rosco and crew sat stunned for a moment. She pointed and yelled, "Go! Now!"

◆ ◆

The sun was setting; they were out on the street. Rosco said, "Well that was a failure…" At that moment the one-eyed man from the Bridgeport lathe tapped him on the shoulder.

He said, "Splinter's the name. Magg says you have a need?"

On the way back to his stall, he said, "She needed to divert attention. Lord Quinn's people are everywhere."

He ducked under the oilskin curtain and led them past the lathe into a second room. The generator was off, and the cozy room was lit with oil lamps. A woman came in through another door dressed in a leather apron and britches, wearing knee-high leather boots. She was shirtless, and the leather bib of her apron barely covered her breasts. She didn't appear to care. Her arms were scarred with several red welts. But her face was angelic, auburn hair pulled back into a double ponytail.

"This is my mate, Mira. Hella smithy. Strong as a bull, too. Let's sit round the fire and have a nip. You can tell me what you're needing, and I can rest my aching back."

Mira said, "Rudy, you complain too much." His real name was Rudolpho.

"Yeah, yeah, maybe so, but I gotta tell ya, don't get old, friends. It ain't no fuckin' picnic." Mira gave an open jar of hooch to Margaret, as she was the eldest. She took a sip and passed it to Rosco and so on in the traditions of the rural folk. Grendel gave it back to Mira with a slight nod of her head. They had only consumed a small amount, but already, she was seeing double.

They made a deal to trade a pellet condenser for two buckets of stealth paint. Splinter fabricated the unit himself. It was untraceable. They arranged to meet in the forest at midnight. After thanking Mira for her hospitality, they walked back to Little Wing.

◆ ◆ ◆

MOTHER

runt woke from a feverish sleep. The last thing he remembered was crazy. He must have dreamed it. He was lying in his own filth. Dying, too weak to stand. A pack of wolves had him cornered. Then, just before they ate him, a giant, orange house cat appeared and chased them away. He never saw Mule before; she'd avoided him at the camp. He was *certain* it couldn't have been real.

Totally bonkers.

The light in the room was dim, but he could see. Before he even moved, he knew he was clean; his ankle and his head were bandaged. He was wearing a nightgown made of soft fabric, and he was covered by a light blue quilt. He lifted the covers; the sheets and shirt he wore were white. He had not seen fabric so clean since he was a little boy.

Something rustled outside the door to his room. He tried to sit up, but the pain in his solar plexus held him like a strap. The effort was surprisingly exhausting. He'd almost fallen back to sleep when the door opened. A barefoot woman in a tanned-skin vest and leggings entered the room. Though she dressed in a similar style, this woman was much older than Saą. Her long, grey hair was wrapped into a thousand delicate braids and twisted into a bundle that reached to the small of her back. Brunt was suddenly surprised to recognize that he was inside a house. The outer walls were thick and plastered, leaving deep shelves at the rounded windows. The forest outside shaded most of the sun, tinting the light emerald like it was shining through stained glass.

The woman sat on a three-legged stool near the bed and looked into his face. Her eyes were bottomless back pools. The wrinkles around them fanned out like the deltas of ancient rivers to her temples. Her skin was the color of the sienna-brown mud of her people's home, a home that hadn't existed for millennia.

Brunt couldn't look for long. He had to close his eyes and thought, *I must be asleep. I'm still dreaming.* That was the only answer for it. When he opened them again, he was sitting in a comfortable chair in a round room. The walls were the color of unbleached linen. A small fire glowed in a brazier in the center, and smoke twisted up through a hole in the ceiling. He could see stars through the opening.

The night was a bottomless blue-black that saturated the walls and rugs around him. He could feel the cold of the light though his eyes, melting down his face and over his shoulders. He was vaguely aware that he was seeing and feeling thoughts, but the idea evaporated when the woman spoke.

She sat in the chair next to him and cleared her throat. In a gravelly voice, she said, "Call me Mother. I am Mother to all."

He began to speak, but she cut him off. "I know who you are. And I know what you've done. It's not my task to judge you, Barry."

"No one calls me Barry."

"Your mother and father did. It is the name they gave you. More important, I'd say, than that derogatory nickname some deprived, oversized boys used to manipulate you, eh?"

Brunt opened his mouth but realized he had nothing to say and shut it again. The situation was out of his control. *Besides, this is just a dream, right?* he thought.

"Wrong, Barry. This is not a dream, and before you ask, no, you are not dead. We are in the Memories. It is a place all epochs share. You might say that it is where we are all from. Or maybe where we are all going. You are here with me because I found you near death on the side of a mountain, and I took mercy on you in the same way I would rescue a fledgling who'd fallen from his nest. I brought your battered body to one of our cottages and nursed you back to life. But I am aware that you are not a harmless bird, Barry."

"How long?" Brunt croaked.

"Weeks."

"But…" He realized again that he had nothing to say and went silent.

She continued, "You will be well enough to walk soon. For now, rest, Barry. Everything is right."

◆ ◆ ◆

CROW CITY

After Emerson arrived at Pejeta's house, he received a notification through his Interface. Eggert had made the necessary acquisitions and preparations. He predicted they would arrive in a day or so. Even though Little Wing could cover the distance in a few hours, Rosco and Eggert wanted to inspect other bunkers that were marked on the map.

Now that the refugees of Blue Hole were safely hidden, Eggert's responsibilities were concluded. He was free to explore. Margaret told him, "You should retire. You have done enough."

As India was leaving, Emerson said, "I have friends who are coming into this region. They will be here in a couple days. We will let you know so the rest of the council can meet them."

She said, "You forget. You are on the council too, now. I honor you rpast experience, yes, but I really want your outside point of view, Emerson."

"Right, but just the same, I wish to show the proper respect."

"Yes, thank you. We believe that if you want trust, you must give it. I trust you, Emerson. Until you show me that I shouldn't." She winked. "Good night."

Saą introduced Emerson to Pejeta as the eldest healer in the village. Elli watched her closely, and Pejeta noticed. She told the young woman, "I am always looking for helpers, Elli, in case you want to learn."

Elli nodded and looked down. She had come a long way from the girl Emerson rescued six years before, but her scars ran deep. He made a mental note to mention her history to Pejeta.

Są invited everyone to sit with her at the village meal that evening. She said, "There will be dancing. We celebrate the spring planting and the coming of the Worm Moon, which will be full and pregnant tonight." She invited everyone, but Quinn saw that she was talking specifically to Emerson. She hadn't noticed when they were still at the oceanside camp, but there was a definite attraction between those two. A feeling passed over her—a twinge. Not of jealousy but sadness. She wasn't sure why. Maybe she grieved the community and connection she'd felt when they lived together in the beginning. She felt that they were growing apart. But maybe they were simply growing. She wasn't sure that she was ready for that big of a change.

On the way to the central square, Quinn walked with Emerson. "You and Są seem close." She elbowed him in the side.

"She seems to like me."

"Everyone likes you Emerson. You are a good man. I'm talking about Są, tiger."

"Does that bother you?"

"I'm not like that. You know me, Emmer. I want you to be happy. Are you happy?"

"She's nice."

"Emerson, she's hot as a poker. In a rustic, earthy way."

"Do *you* like her?"

"Sure, she's intelligent and observant. And she has a sense of humor. What's not to like?"

"I want to invite her to join us."

"I guess. I'm a little preoccupied at the moment. Marya worries me. When can we set up the scanners? I want to believe the healers, but it's impossible not to worry."

Emerson said, "I'll get with Plummer, and we can set up the power supply we need for the MRI." They walked in silence a while.

Emerson said, "I got a message from Rosco. They found a map and an inventory book. There is a whole network of those bunkers where we got the plasma guns. It's astounding what's stored there. Someone thought they were going to live out the aftermath of a nuclear holocaust. Eggert wants to check a few out between Terminus and here."

Quinn was silent. Emerson said, "I thought you'd be more excited. Grendel and Margaret are with them."

She nodded.

He added, "I'm worried about Marya, too. We haven't had a minute to talk."

The commons were a shaded grassy area on a slight rise in the middle of the village. A sheltered outdoor kitchen was off to one side next to a large stack of split wood and a series of open grills. The firepit dominated the center, surrounded by wooden benches and small tables. They filled their plates at the serving table and found seats near the others.

When they were situated and Emerson had filled his mouth with the first forkful of bright microgreen salad, Quinn said, "Yeah, when I think about it, yes. I like Saą. She's kinda like the older sister I never had."

The meal was incredible. Ana brought a basket back to the shuttle for the others. Little Chandler had fallen asleep in her arms, and she wanted to put him down. "I'm wiped," she said. "We're just going to go to bed."

Quinn, Saą, Elli, and Emerson stayed until the moon was directly overhead and the drum circle had begun. At first, Emerson joined in on a large communal drum. He moved to handheld percussion, a gourd shaker, and later a couple of wooden blocks. Saą grabbed him and pulled him into the dance; Quinn followed. Elli was never comfortable in large groups, especially when it required her to move her body. She stood around and watched for a while and wandered off alone.

Quinn, Saą, and Emerson were mimicking each other's fluid movements pressed between hundreds of other bodies. Though the night was cool, they were sheened in sweat. Saą removed her vest. Emerson lost his shirt. No one wore shoes.

Before long, everyone was naked, and the dancing had become flamboyant and exaggerated. Groups had formed, slick limbs and torsos tangled in a rhythmic homage to the power of spring and rebirth. Soon couples began pairing off and retreating to more secluded areas. Quinn, Saą, and Emerson dressed and walked back to The Black Mariah. The moon cast an icy glow on the land and trees.

Saą bid them goodnight at Kim's. She said, "I'm still excited to sleep in my own space. That will wear off soon, and I'll be infected by my wandering spirit again. Good eve."

◆ ◆

When they returned to The Black Mariah, Plummer and the island refugees showed Quinn and Emerson a series of wooden lean-tos. Each included a warming stove and light. They were sealed and insulated.

Emerson said, "Perfect," though he was preoccupied and wasn't really commenting on the job. He would realize later that it was an incredible accomplishment to have created an entire camp in one day, but that evening, he was thinking about other things entirely.

There was a firepit surrounded by stones with a small but hot fire burning. Quinn said goodnight and left. Her lights were out soon.

Plummer said, "The engineers from the village were helpful, but they didn't stay long. I think my form may have disturbed them a bit…"

Emerson sipped from a metal flask. He offered it to Plummer who said, "Not tonight." Though Emerson wasn't sure where he would put it.

Plummer stirred the fire with a metal rod and tossed a black block of fuel on it. "They gave us a few kilos of compressed charcoal. It burns slow and hot. They say they make it in clay furnaces with a bellows as big as a man. I would like to see this mechanism."

"I hope they'll allow you into the village soon," Emerson replied.

After a moment, Plummer said, "I detected a signal I think you should know about."

"Signal?"

"A satellite phone made a call nearby. Maybe a kilometer away."

Emerson found it curious, but the thought left his mind when Saą arrived a moment later. She sat on one of the stumps Plummer and the engineers had arranged around the fire. Emerson offered her the flask which she took and emptied in a single drink.

She licked her lips and said, "Thanks. It's not kiras, but it will do the job. What do you call it?"

"Hooch. It's distilled corn mash. Used to be aged in oak casks to round off the bite; that turns it brown. This stuff is white lightning. Nearly 80 percent alcohol," he said. "I guess that wandering spirit came to visit."

"The spirit definitely moved me. Actually, I'm just not sleepy."

The wind picked up; Saą shivered. Emerson put his arm around her shoulder, bringing his face near to her cheek. She turned to him, their noses almost touching. He looked into her eyes; they were dark brown, flecked with gold. He felt her breath filling and leaving her lungs. He wanted to kiss her.

She said, "You have beautiful eyes."

"Oh, yeah. Thanks."

Quinn arrived and sat next to him on his other side. She said, "Somehow after all that dancing, I'm not very sleepy." She leaned her head on his shoulder.

Mule appeared behind them and pushed her large furry head between Emerson and Saą.

Saą looked into the fire and said, "What's good for the heart is good for the soul." She looked over at Emerson and Quinn and smiled.

♦ ♦ ♦

THE WORM MOON

The weather took a turn towards summer after the Worm Moon celebration. The day following the feast was clear and calm. Emerson and Są discovered their mutual love of elk jerky. They broke their fast while hiking the eastern ridge.

Są said, "What's it like, having an implant, controlling a machine with your mind?"

Emerson thought about it for a minute, The forest was still waking up—the dew hadn't dried. He stopped to inspect a wolf spider web in a sunbeam. He said, "It's amazing which animals thrived and which died. We've discovered species that we thought were extinct. We've found animals that never existed before."

Są raised an eyebrow. "Are you going to answer my question, Emerson?"

"I haven't figured out how to begin. It is a problem to explain something to someone who has no personal reference to understand the answer. So, when I am stumped, I sometimes let the question work itself out in the background. I guess having an implant helped me to develop that habit. When I began to rely on the Interface for most of my daily activities, I got used to letting processes run in the background. It's like splitting yourself in two or three and setting these other selves up with tasks. When the routine is complete, I get a notification, an alarm."

"That's very detached and analytical. I want to know what it feels like."

"There is only one way to do that. Try it."

"But it is against my family's belief system to have anything electronic implanted into my body."

"Ana is working on a temporary Interface connector. You'll stick it to the skin below your ear; it wouldn't need to be implanted. We were making it for the children so they could meet their great-grandfather, Chandler. He died several years ago. He only lives now inside a simulation cube. But we don't implant kids under six."

Saą didn't reply for a long moment. She said, "You entice me, Emerson Lloyde. Now I must know more about your mysterious grandfather who can only live inside a cube."

From the ridge where they stood, the Inland Sea was a thin shimmering line on the east horizon. As the day began to warm, Emerson took a drink from Saą's water skin, and Mule bumped his arm with her head. He wet the front of his tunic. And in mock anger, Saą chased her though the high grass playing hide-and-seek, peek-a-boo, or some new hybrid game created on the spot by an oversized cat and a catlike woman, two products of the forest and the wild.

Pejeta had just arrived with Marya when they returned just before noon. Quinn took her daughter and hugged her. The girl squirmed to be let down and ran off to find Little Chandler. Quinn said, "Did you find out anything?"

The physician said, "The swelling went down. She woke up." Quinn was relieved, but not reassured. Pejeta turned to Saą and said, "What do the Memories say?"

Saą said, "Mother was uncharacteristically reserved. She usually has plenty to say about anything I do or touch." She smiled, but it faded quickly.

Pejeta nodded. "I am sure it was just a bruise. She will be healing from it for several weeks."

Quinn frowned and said to Emerson, "We should still set up the scanner."

Emerson said, "I'm glad she's awake. We'll keep a close eye on her."

◆ ◆

The Black Mariah had a generator built into the ship's mechanical shop. It ran off the secondary reactors which meant it could generate power without firing up the noisy mains. Plummer and Emerson tested the output and determined that the electricity needed to be "cleaned up some" as Plummer called it.

"I mean, it wasn't shielded. The power supply for the MRI needs to be isolated and free of harmonic frequency distortion. These units draw a huge amount of power, twenty-five kilowatts when scanning. I created a filter circuit. It should be fine now."

After several tests, they scanned Marya. Plummer explained that the chamber would be noisy and that she shouldn't be scared; they'd be right outside. Pejeta came up to the North Quarter to watch the diagnostic. She'd never seen anything like an MRI, and her curiosity overcame her distaste for electronic tech. She stood a good distance away.

Marya was unfazed. She lay as still as a statue as the table fed her into the machine. Plummer monitored the output. "Just a little swelling, she should be fine."

Quinn said, "Good," and walked away. She still didn't seem satisfied.

◆

Saą asked Ana, "Emerson is on the council this afternoon. Would you like to join?"

Ana said, "I can't. I've got LC. He'll be disruptive."

"Nonsense," Saą said. "Mothers and fathers are encouraged to bring children to official village functions. That is the way we develop a dedication to justice. Besides, kids are safe here. Everyone watches out for everyone else."

"I'll take him for you if he gets fussy," Emerson offered.

Plummer rolled up. He had a new head made from a cracked plastic bucket. He said, "Ms. Saą, would it be possible to appear in front of your council to plead my case?"

Saą replied, "Honorifics are unnecessary here. What case is it you wish to plead?"

"The case for my value as a living being."

She looked him up and down. "I will see what I can do. It is India's decision."

He said, "Before I arrived here, I believed my life was a waste. But I see now how I can help in ways no one else can."

Rats One and Two stood up next to Plummer's treads. Their sudden appearance startled Pejeta. She jumped back and let out a little squeak.

Saą said, "It might be best if your assistants stayed with the shuttle."

"I see your point."

"I need to get back to the clinic," Pejeta said. "Is Elli around? She expressed an interest in helping out."

Quinn and Elli returned with both children, and Elli greeted Pejeta.

Quinn said, "I hear there is a learning house in the village."

Saą nodded. "Yes, it's on the way to the gardens. I'll show you."

As they were preparing to leave, Paxon appeared. "Excuse me, Anoush, Sandra, and I have decided to set out on our own. I used to have friends in the north, and now that the weather has broken, we are going to go."

Saą said, "Be sure that you are provisioned. The mountains north of here are treacherous. I recommend going into the flat lands to the west and then making your way north. But be warned. There are those who would take what you have and kill you without a thought, even if you have nothing. Do you have weapons? Can you defend yourselves?"

Paxon's face answered the question.

Saą continued, "Come into the village. I will be your guide. We can go before the council and discuss what would be best for everyone."

◆ ◆

Emerson and Ana went directly to the council chamber. Saą brought Anoush, Sandra, and Paxon to the public entrance. She waited with them. As the people waited for the hall to open, the line of petitioners grew. Council Day was a social event, and the line was more of a circle. Young and old stood or squatted, some smoking clay pipes and others sipping from waterskins, though most were filled with something more potent than water, and the conversations soon became excited and boisterous.

The man standing next to Saą introduced himself. "Hello. M'name's Coner. I've seen you before. Who are your friends?" Turning to Anoush, he continued, "I'm sure I've ne'r seen any a you." He was a thin man with small, piercing eyes and a high forehead. His hair was thick and brown, but his mustache, goatee, and curly sideburns were sparse and tinged with red. His face broke into a warm smile, and he said, "Welcome to The Land Ruled by Crows."

Saą said, "They just arrived. This is Anoush, Sandra, and Paxon." He shook hands with each in turn.

Coner said, "Requesting admission, eh?"

Saą turned to Paxon. "It might be best if you explain."

Paxon said, "We're not sure, yet. Maybe thinking we might fit in better up north where we have, ah, acquaintances."

After a moment of silence, Anoush moved close to Coner and put her hand on his arm. She said, "What brings you to the council today?"

He side-eyed her and said, "I'm here representing my quarter of the village. See, me and my people were driven out of our homes when our valley was flooded. Many died, and them that were left were invited here. We are refugees in The Land Ruled by Crows. And because we are new and lived through a terrible tragedy, the council says we need to keep our camp separate from the rest of the village in the southwest corner of the valley.

"Everything would be fine as frog hair if everything stayed the same, which you know it never does. I am here on behalf of the Southwest to seek permission for more integration between our people. There are young men and women wishing to have children, but our group is too small a gene pool for that. We have heard the stories, and we believe in the science."

Anoush said, "Maybe we'd feel more welcome with you." She touched his arm.

Coner said, "That may be."

The hall began admitting people. The mass of talking humans quickly assembled itself into an orderly line. Everyone knew the order they had arrived in; there was no argument. They signed into a ledger to be sure each had their chance to speak. There was no time limit for a council meeting—it lasted as long as it took for everyone to be heard. After signing in, they sat together in the petitioners' section.

India opened the meeting with a welcome and introduced the current council members including Emerson. She referred to him as a visiting council member with no other explanation. Ana sat next to him with LC in her lap; she was not introduced.

India said, "You should know by now that our newest visitors come from a highly technological society. They are implanted and operate computer-controlled machines using the Interface. They are here by my leave. Additionally, they brought four refugees. One of them is a cybernetically enhanced human. I brought him here to introduce him. His name is Plummer."

Plummer rolled out on the platform from around the corner. Several people gasped. A few laughed. He stopped and turned to the audience when he got to the middle of the stage. He said, "I lost my head on the flight out of Beso Muerte. That is why I am wearing this ridiculous bucket."

Ana cringed. Several pockets of people laughed. Emerson felt as though the room was loosening up. He realized he was tense and tried to relax.

Plummer went on, "I was born a human from a human mother and father. I became a cyborg after The Death destroyed what little of Earth we hadn't already destroyed ourselves. I wish to walk, er, um, roll among you, and I hope you will let me." There was a smattering of laughs, and a few people clapped.

He continued, "Even though I am dependent upon electronic tech, as you call it, I can still contribute to your community. I have tremendous data stores containing most of the engineering specifications from inventions up through the first decade of the twenty-first century. I am very strong. I am an experienced surgeon. And maybe most importantly, I am, at my core, still very human."

Plummer turned and rolled back to the corner and disappeared.

India continued with business before he was gone, naming petitioners and listening. After the initial statements were made, the other council members asked questions or made points. Unless the issue required outside input, like an absent person's perspective in a disagreement, India would make the final decision during the session, usually in ten minutes or less.

Each council member had an opportunity to add an opinion or move the discussion forward; each person knew the rules, the order, and the rhythm. Some people were more used to the process than others and came more prepared. In all cases, the session moved quickly with little friction. If there was a paramount objection, the discussion would focus on it until it was resolved. In Plummer's case, no decision was made.

India said, "Our next petitioner is Coner of the Southwest Quarter."

Coner stood and put his request in concise terms, as was the custom. He said, "I am the voice of the Southwest today, India. We have prospered within our borders and under the rules we'd agreed to when we were invited to The Land. But our people are straining the gene pool. Therefore, we request to intermingle, please."

India said, "How long have your people lived with us, Coner?"

"Near forty moons, I'd say."

"That was my memory. Yes. I see your dilemma. I think we can continue to coexist. But we will have to talk about the terms of this new agreement. Does anyone on the council have a question or concern?"

The discussion went to one or two of the members praising the relations with the Southwest people over the nearly four years of living together but apart. Saą told Emerson later that the biggest problem with the Southwest settlement was the unresolved trauma they carried.

"These are people who less than five years ago lost their families, homes, and possessions to a flood. Before that they had been a refugee camp," Saą said. "They have a lot of healing to do. If we let them in to intermingle with the population, we will have families who pass that trauma to their children and down the line. Though it is wrong to prevent people from mating as they choose, it is more of a wrong to poison the well from which our future children drink. We must take all things into consideration before normalizing our relations. The violence in the Southwest Quarter threatens to spill over into the village more every day." No one was talking about it, but violence in the Quarter was common knowledge.

"We will have open conversations about the process and hear from all sides before making an informed decision, but everyone will have to make agreements for those they represent, and that is always a weak link. It will look like a way to control people if that is what they want to believe. Which is why the Southwesterners are restricted."

Emerson asked, "What happens if your borders are breached by violence?"

"Violence will win what violence uses. We have no army, Emerson. We do not fight; we talk."

◆ ◆

Coming out of the council hall later that afternoon, Anoush, Paxon, and Sandra caught up with Coner. Saą stood nearby, as was her responsibility as a guide.

Sandra said, "We want to come to your Quarter; that's allowed, right?

There might be someone who knows my family there. And we are outside blood. We are willing to contribute."

Saą said from across the way, "They are not implanted. As long as they are your guests, you will be responsible for their behavior."

Coner said, "I know how t'werks, Saą, and sure, Sandra, you can come to the Southwest. I wouldn't care if you were a cyborg like that metal guy." He nodded at Plummer who gave him a small wave of one hand. "We have no problem with technology. We're just too poor to have any." He belly-laughed and spat on the ground.

◆ ◆

The council member who sat nearest to Emerson spent most of the day flirting with Ana. He was about her age, blond, and fit. He was also confident and observant. Leaving the hall, he picked up a paper that had slipped out of Ana's pocket and gave it back to her. Emerson knew it was a pretense to introduce himself, though India had already told everyone his name was Amrsal, lead planter and designer of the food forest.

He was taller than Ana with a strong chin and blue eyes; every hair was in its place. He worked outdoors year-round in the food forest which gave him a permanent tan, but also dried out his skin. Ana was attracted to his large forearms. Even through his linen shirt, she could see the defi-nition of the muscles on his back and shoulders.

Ana feigned disinterest. "Yes, I know your name. I listened to India when she introduced you. Unlike you spending all day making faces at me."

He said, "But she didn't introduce you."

"I'm Anastacia Moon."

"Well, Anastacia Moon, would you like to come with me to see the gardens and the food forest?"

"If you call me Ana."

Emerson watched the interchange. He took LC, who'd been riding Ana's hip, and said, "Marya and I are going to get some sweet cakes. I bet

LC would like to come." He side-eyed Ana, and she smiled and nodded. They walked away, discussing the finer points of butterfly wings.

Amrsal asked, "Is that a yes?"

Ana said, "Do you pester every stranger like this?"

"No. Sadly, most strangers are afraid and boring. Not like you. You're beautiful and mysterious." He expected her to blush. She did not.

"You must lead a pretty boring life if you think I am mysterious."

"Next to yours, my life *is* boring, but I'm satisfied with my companions—the plants and trees."

"I don't know who you think I am, but I *would* like to see the gardens and forest."

He said, "Let me show you then, this way." Emerson gave her a little wave.

◆ ◆ ◆

GSW

Elli spent the day at the clinic helping sign in patients, take temperatures, and record vitals. She knew the drill and was quick and efficient. Around one in the afternoon when everyone was sleepy from the noon meal and things had gotten pretty quiet, the emergency bell startled her out of a half sleep.

The bell signaled that a person or group was injured and being brought to the clinic. There were several bell stations beginning at the farthest points of Crow City. Each rang a specific note which let the bell ringers in the chain know where the alarm was raised and where the injured person was on the way to the clinic. A runner would soon arrive to tell Pejeta the nature of the accident and the number of people that she should expect.

The bells came from the Southwest Quarter. The runner, a barefoot, thirteen-year-old girl from that neighborhood, stripped down to a loincloth, burst in the front door a moment later.

She was winded, but she signaled three fingers. When she caught her breath, she said, "Gunshot wounds. Lotsa blood."

Elli was instantly alert and awake. The experiences following the siege of Blue Hole came back to her like a habit. She took control.

She called out, "Pejeta do you have blood? Can you do transfusions?"

The healer shook her head.

"DO YOU HAVE A SURGICAL SUITE?"

Pejeta said quietly, "We never get gunshot wounds. When people are shot, they die."

Elli used her Interface to make a voice connection with Emerson. If The Black Mariah were any more than five kilometers away, it would not have worked, but Emerson answered. Elli said out loud, "We have three gunshot wounds coming in here; there's no blood, no surgery. We need them to go to The Black Mariah. Open the triage hold. But we gotta hurry."

Emerson said, "I heard the bell."

The runner said, "I can try and divert them, but they are carrying the wounded on a cart. I would have to find them."

Emerson could hear the room in the background and said, "There's no time for that. If we are going to save these people's lives, we need to bring The Black to them. I can autopilot her. Plummer will make ready. I'll meet you at the clinic. The Black will land in the back. Make sure the area's clear. We don't have enough fuel to put the reactor on silent. It's going to be loud."

Elli looked at Pejeta and said, "If we are going to have a chance, our shuttle must come here right now!"

The healer nodded once. They cleared the area. Five minutes later, the reactor whine rattled the window glass and flushed birds from their nests. Emerson was there when the hatch opened. The carts with the wounded were brought around the cargo hold, and the three bodies put inside and doors closed. A crowd of people grew around the shuttle. Many laid their hands on the flat black skin but jumped away at the low pulsing vibration. The door opened for Elli and Pejeta, they entered, and the hatch slid shut.

There was no conversation. India stood with Saą outside the shuttle, the door outlined in pulsing blue. She looked into the younger woman's eyes and said, "Is this how it was in your dream, Saą?"

Saą said, "No. It was worse. Much worse." She followed Elli inside.

♦ ♦

"Will you take this stupid bucket off my shoulders, please, Elli?" Plummer was already wrapped in light blue gown fabric. A surgical glove was stretched over one hand; the other had a single scalpel finger extended. He looked at Pejeta and said, "I autoclaved my whole arm to be sure." He immediately cauterized the woman's open vessels. She woke up screaming. Plummer pinched a nerve in her neck, and she collapsed back onto the table.

Pejeta yelled, "This is a doctor? This abomination?" She backed against the bulkhead. Emerson gently pushed her down onto a fold-out seat and strapped the harness across her torso.

He said, quietly, "You wanted to come on board. But I am in charge here. If you want to stay, you need to observe without speaking, okay?"

She nodded, her eyes wide.

Elli and Plummer assessed the condition of the other two victims. One was shot in the chest, the other in the stomach. The gut shot was bleeding profusely, but the bullet went all the way through. They applied crisis bandages and administered a sedative to reduce the effects of shock. Both men remained unconscious. Emerson brought three bags of O-negative blood from a cooler in the medical bay.

The woman had suffered a massive shot to the left thigh which mutilated the artery and shattered much of the bone. The leg could not be saved. During the amputation, Plummer called to Rat Two for assistance. They set up transfusions and drip IVs for all three.

◆ ◆ ◆

THROUGH THE FRONT DOOR

A tall man appeared at the clinic. He stood off to the side, assessing the chaos as the victims were carried into the shuttle. No one seemed to notice the stranger in strange clothes.

He was a head taller than most, and he would have been striking for that reason alone. But there was more there than his freakish height. A glow seemed to radiate from his skin. A calm intelligence about him drew out others' loyalty after only a few words.

He wove though the frantic activity like he was stepping between raindrops. His confidence preceded him like a wave, gently clearing any obstacle. And unbelievable as it was, Terrence Brock was a surgeon. He went directly to the blue hatch outline on The Black Mariah and tapped the glass. Emerson opened the door. Brock went directly to the victims and took control.

"Get me a blood pressure on this man and give me a gunshot pack, stat!" He plunged his hands into the UV sterilizer.

Emerson recognized Enforcer high-level medical procedures. The man barking orders before him was obviously a trained surgeon, possibly a pilot, and most definitely implanted. He raised his voice and said, "Who are you? What are you doing on my ship?"

Saą helped him don gown and gloves.

Brock inspected the man's wound. The bullet had punctured his lung, which had collapsed. He said, "I can tell you, or I can save these men's lives. You need more than one doctor to deal with this many wounded." He paused and looked in Emerson's eyes. "Which is it?"

Brock reminded him of Eggert; Emerson smiled.

Elli was next to him in a second, pointing her plasma rifle at Brock's chest.

"What do I do, boss?" She was talking to Emerson, but she didn't take her eyes off of Brock.

"Help him, Elli. I can watch him. Let him work."

All three victims lived, though the third, the woman, lost her leg. Terrence Brock was considered a hero. Plummer was acknowledged by the medical people, Pejeta included, her suspicions notwithstanding, but no one outside of them, not even the patient, knew he was the surgeon who saved her life.

When they were done and the patients were recovering in The Black Mariah, Emerson confronted Brock.

Brock said, "I wouldn't trust me either, Emerson Lloyde."

Elli raised her rifle again, but Emerson pushed the barrel down and said, "I'm listening."

"I was an Enforcer, like you. But Lord Quinn has gone off the rails. I couldn't be a part of that train of fools any longer. I set out to find a better way. I've been searching for you, Emerson. You're a legend."

Elli said, "Bullshit, Brock. I don't trust a thing you say."

"We'll let the council decide if you are welcome here," Emerson said. "For now, stay with The Black Mariah and monitor the patients. I have scanned and blocked your implant in case you decide to take The Black Mariah for a spin or fancy using a plasma weapon. The citizens do not use electronic tech, and mistrust people who do. We are their guests."

He said, "Am I a guest or a prisoner?"

"You are a guest unless you show me you should be imprisoned."

◆ ◆

Emerson heard from the runner that the fight was over one of the strange new women. But the girl didn't know a name.

She said, "I only heard about it; I didn't see nobody get shot." She was grinning as though she wished she had.

Emerson didn't want to walk into the Southwest Quarter alone. The place was dangerous. This shooting reinforced his apprehension. Ana wasn't responding to communicator messages, and Quinn was back at camp with the children. He had a strong suspicion that Anoush was the strange woman who caused the fight, and he felt responsible for bringing her even if she did want to leave. So, against his better judgment, Emerson went alone to talk to Sandra, Anoush, and Paxon. He didn't think it would be hard to find them.

Just as he had made up his mind to go alone, Elli came out of the shuttle. She said, "I finished cleaning up. That Brock guy gives me the creeps. Do you want me to keep an eye on him while you're gone?"

"No, Plummer can watch him. You can come with me if you want. I'm going to visit Anoush."

She said, "I couldn't tell." She laughed and snorted.

Emerson said, "Am I that obvious?"

"No, but she is."

Pejeta returned to the clinic. The patients were stable, and she wasn't needed. Earlier that morning, Quinn confided to Saą that she had the worst and most debilitating cramps she had ever experienced. She added, "And I'm no stranger to painful periods."

Saą left the clinic, and instead of going to her bedroom at Kim's, she went to the North Quarter camp to look in on Quinn. As she walked, she realized she'd begun thinking of the northern Quarter as home.

◆ ◆ ◆

STARFLOWER

Amrsal and Ana went to the vegetable greenhouses first. They passed a number of farm workers, pleasant men and women who moved with purpose. He picked her a ripe tomato, a fruit she had never seen except the ones that came out of fifty-year-old cans. He gave her strawberries and a Meyer lemon which she tried to eat with the skin on until he showed her how to peel it.

She said, "We had hydroponics at Blue Hole, but the soil in the east has been so depleted and abused, we found it was easier to just add nutrients."

Amrsal explained, "Our plan is long-term regeneration. Most of the land in the mountains has never been cultivated. But that has not stopped us from reclaiming toxic lands too. We just don't grow food there yet. For example, we grow vats of beneficial bacteria that we then mix into the soil."

"Like compost?"

"More like nutrition. It helps the microbes in the soil. In return, they happily help with our harvests. In the later part of the twentieth century, they pumped crops with fertilizers. It made everything grow like crazy, but after decades without giving back to the dirt, and the overuse of herbicides and fungicides, the soil eventually died."

A crew of citizens were pulling plastic over a new set of spruce ribs. Ana and Amrsal watched them for a moment. His hand brushed hers.

She said, "These are pretty neat greenhouses. I thought you made everything from scratch; this looks like plastic to me."

"We avoid salvage as much as possible. But when it comes to food production and housing, plastic and glass are easy to find and hard to make. The ribs of our greenhouse are bent spruce, which we coppice. That way one tree can produce many cuttings. We stretch plastic sheets over the ribs and end walls to make microclimates."

They toured large rooms containing row crops in spirals: corn, buckwheat, and sorghum. Amrsal waved to an occasional farm worker, but they were more alone as they went deeper into the forest. Ana was silent. Amrsal kept feeding her amazing treats, like kiwis, ground cherries, sunchokes, and snow peas.

"In the summer we grow without the houses. But we have perfected it year-round, as a backup. Nature is resilient, but nature also creates multiple paths to success. Before the collapse, people believed that they could make huge amounts of food by growing one thing very, very well. But The Mother teaches us that success depends upon redundancies. When there was a break in the pre-collapse supply chain, the whole system crumbled. Too many shocks and the system failed completely. We listen to The Mother. She says, watch the trees and the animals who depend upon them. They will teach you how the forest cares for the people."

He picked a flower and peeled back the petals to reveal a single droplet of bright purple nectar. He held it out to her lips and said, "Taste."

She did without hesitation. "Oh, what is that?"

He touched his tongue to the nectar from another blossom.

Ana looked up at the sky through the tree canopy. It felt as though she was shot through a tube. In a second, she was looking out over the top of the forest. She looked down, expecting that Amrsal was still on the ground. He was standing next to her. They had not moved.

"Whoa." She lost her balance for a moment.

"We call it Starflower. It is a powerful mind-opening serum. The effects vary, but can last up to twelve hours." He put his hands lightly on her shoulders and peered into her eyes. Instantly, the world shrank down to a pinpoint of light. A second later, Ana was inside a warm pool. Amrsal's voice was coming from everywhere around her, but nowhere specific. He said, "You are in me, and I am in you. Pretty cool, eh?"

She blinked, and he was standing close, his nose nearly touching hers. They kissed quickly.

He said, "Come, I want to show you something else."

Walking was an experience. When Ana concentrated on anything, her vision expanded like looking backward through a sight glass. Anything she focused on filled her field of vision. She was disoriented and had to hang on to Amrsal's arm to keep from tripping over her own feet. She closed her eyes.

He said, "We're here. It's a hot spring. I thought you might really like a bath."

Ana hadn't been in a hot spring since before Blue Hole was obliterated. The entire village used to frequent the public baths; it was the reason for the village's name. They had their clothes off in seconds. Ana said, "This is hotter than the Blue Hole baths."

"There are a lot of minerals in this water. It makes you float like a cork." He dove the ten meters to the bottom, which was clearly visible in the turquoise water, and allowed himself to float back up. When he breached the surface, his body, all the way to his waist, shot out of the water and splashed Ana's face. They laughed and played in the water for an hour before their skin began to wrinkle. They found a smooth shelf to sit on and lay back against the moss growing around the edge so their legs and hips were in the water and their torsos were on the bank.

Amrsal rolled over and kissed Ana full on the mouth, pinning her upper body to the shore. They slid down into the steamy water again, hugging and caressing each other, bobbing under, kissing, nibbling each other. Amrsal's hand found Ana's breast. She hugged him close to her, sliding her hands under his buttocks, lifting his body up. The water made them buoyant enough to float vertically without having to tread water.

Their mouths locked together. He pressed his hand to her soft middle, and she opened to him. They made love luxuriously in the warm water.

The light of the forest lowered a few notches, and the wind reversed, blowing down the mountainside as the air cooled. Ana said, "I need to get back to my son." She jumped out of the water and dressed. As they walked back toward the village, Ana's Interface came into range. She got a string of notifications. They'd been isolated all afternoon. She read about the shooting. Emerson had been trying to find her; Quinn was with the kids. The last text was in caps:

COME TO MY LOCATION IN THE SOUTHWEST QUARTER ASAP.

It was ten minutes old.

She didn't want to break the mood with Amrsal by mentioning her Interface connection. Instead, she told him she had a premonition about Little Chandler. "It's nothing critical. Kids his age get hysterical when they suddenly miss their mommies." Amrsal kissed her in support. Ana felt a twinge of guilt. She couldn't keep her tech connections secret. Eventually, he would have to accept who she was. She chose to ignore her confliction.

◆ ◆ ◆

THE HARDWARE STORE AT THE END OF THE WORLD

merson and Elli had entered the Southwest Quarter a half hour earlier. The Quarter didn't look any different from the rest of the village. The boundary was a simple gate of branches lashed together. They stopped at a lean-to street café to ask about the strangers. Emerson felt it was only polite to have a drink. Elli wore her Colt on her hip and carried her rifle which brought stares and low murmurs that she guessed were about her.

Emerson ordered mead; Elli nodded.

When the dark-haired woman brought their drinks. Emerson asked if she knew about the shootings. The woman side-eyed him and walked away quickly. He said to Elli, "Touched a nerve."

Before they had finished their first sips, two men armed with revolvers arrived at their table. The one with a felt hat spoke, "Coner says come see him."

Elli grumbled, "Can I finish my drink first?"

The bald one said, "Coner says now."

Elli finished hers in one gulp and stood. Felt Hat said, "You gotta give up your guns."

Elli said, "The fuck I do."

Emerson didn't move; he sipped his drink. He said, "That's an Interface-controlled plasma weapon. Elli Moon can remove a pimple from your face with it, or she could remove your face. I suggest you let her keep it." He finished his drink.

They didn't argue. Felt Hat said, "Follow me."

Coner was a few doors down in a storefront named Hardware and Sundries. The walls were covered with tools, and there were hundreds of little drawers in the wall behind the counter. Each one was labeled with a number. He sat on a wooden chair in front of an unlit cast-iron Franklin stove. Emerson looked around the room. Obviously, the people in the Southwest Quarter had no reservation about salvaging and even trading for what they needed.

Coner said, "This part of Crow City was an old mining town. Most of it rotted away before the collapse, but this building was built the old way. Yeah, the rest of the village comes here to get stuff, too. They arn't as pure as they wantchu t'think." He stood up and greeted Emerson with a hug and a mighty clap on his back. He turned to Elli and raised an eyebrow as he said, "Who have we here?"

Elli stood a little taller and gripped her rifle. Emerson said, "This is my adopted daughter, Elli Moon." She frowned when he said it but didn't object.

Coner reached his hand to shake, and Elli took it reluctantly but looked at the floor. A younger, thinner man came in from the back room and said, "Such a lovely name, Elli. Is it short for Eloise?" He was seventeen or eighteen, gangly and thin. He wore the remains of a New York Yankees baseball cap, but it was mostly rags. He was missing more than one tooth.

"No," she said, but offered no more.

The young man said, "Shy, I s'ppose. Girls around here never want to talk." He put his hand on her arm in what Emerson supposed he thought was an affectionate gesture.

Emerson shook his head and murmured, "Oh, oh."

Elli reacted by putting him on the floor with the barrel of the plasma gun against his neck and the ready gauge in the yellow and beeping. It happened in an instant.

"Hey, Hey, cunt." The man on the floor held up his hands. His face was red with anger or embarrassment; Emerson wasn't sure. "You can't do that to me."

Coner said, "Seems she already has, Toms."

He blustered, face getting redder. "But, but—*she's* a cunt. She can't do that to me. I'm a *man*."

Coner said, "I think you are looking at this the wrong way, *boy*. You are on the floor, and *she's* got a gun to your neck. You aren't the one making demands."

Emerson said, "Elli, you can let him up."

Elli shut her gun down, put it aside, and helped him stand up.

He dusted off his pants and said, "You should…"

Coner slapped him on the back of the head. "*You should* know when to shut up, Toms."

"But Coner, she dresses like a whore. She looks like a whore. Why can't I treat her like a whore?"

Emerson stopped Elli with a look. But he smiled. She did not.

Coner said, "Listen to me. This is the reason why we are goin' extinct over here in the Southwest Quarter. If we don't learn to treat everybody with respect, we are going to languish and die. Now shut yer damn mouth. Yer foot is already halfway down yer throat. Yer got-damned brother is lying cold on a slab somewhere already because of that stupid mouth a' yers."

Elli said, "He's not dead. We saved him. And another man, and the woman, too."

Toms said, "Not dead, eh? That's a miracle, that's what it is."

"No," Elli continued, "it's good doctoring, done by me, the cunt," she spat on Toms's shoe, "and my friends the cybernetic rat and his master." She shook her head. She had to look up at the *boy*. She guessed he had at least ten centimeters on her.

She continued, "I was prostituted out from the time I was eight. It was the only life I knew until the Enforcers killed everyone and everything around me. As long as you men use women like tools, treat us, your fellow human beings, as if we are worth less than coin or land or power, eat us whole only to vomit us up again for no better reason than because you can." She had to take a breath. "As long as we are not equal people to you, you will battle against yourselves by willfully hurting us."

She turned as though she was done but spun around again and continued, "You will never be able to repay the debt of life you owe to the woman that bore you. So, you act as though she is your enemy when she is the only one who has ever truly loved you. Until you can see what you do to us, you will have forgotten the face of your mother." She spat on the wooden floor, wiped her eye with the back of her hand, and strode out of the building.

After a silent moment, Emerson said, "I need to see Sandra, Paxon, and Anoush. Can you take me to them?"

"Sure," Coner said. "Here we are." He spread his hands and grinned.

Toms recovered his voice and said, "They are below us, sir. You are standing on a trapdoor."

Coner and Toms cleared away the chairs and a thread-worn rug to reveal a door with iron hinges set into the floor. It took Coner and Toms to lift the thing. Emerson helped push it over to a stop block. A wooden staircase descended into the cellar lit by torches below. Coner went first. He said, "Follow me."

At the bottom was a long, low, arched, brick-ceilinged room with barred jail cells set into the rock along one side.

Coner said, "India didn't tell you about this place, did she? I wouldn't think so. She's a big believer in nonviolence, but when someone needs to be restrained, she always calls on us. This is the prison for the whole village, Emerson. Not just the Southwest Quarter."

They passed dozens of cells. The occupants sat in the shadows, silently.

Their faces were obscured. The cell containing Paxon and company was noticeably different: light, open, comfortable even. Anoush saw them first and stood up from the table where they were playing cards.

"Emerson, get me out of here. I've done nothing."

Emerson looked at Coner who shrugged and said, "There are always two sides. At least."

"Okay," Emerson said, "what's next? Is there a magistrate or something?"

Coner said, "We don't need no judge. I witnessed it; I'll be the judge." He opened the cell. Everyone met inside. It didn't seem like a prison. The room was decorated like a living room in a middle-class household circa 1975. Orange plastic chairs, an avocado-green shag rug, a standing lamp in the corner that looked like a series of planets suspended between floor and ceiling by slender pipes. Nameless jazz seeped out of somewhere.

Emerson said, "Electricity?"

"This place has a backup genny. We run it for a few hours a day to keep the freezers cold. You have good timing. It's due to shut off in a half hour."

Everyone found a chair. Emerson said, "Sandra, tell us what happened."

Sandra looked around at Paxon and Anoush. She took a breath and said, almost in a whisper, "I wish could, Emerson, but all I remember is all of us," she waved at Anoush and Paxon, "were in this bar, and I had just finished introducing myself when firecrackers began going off. Someone pulled me down behind a counter, and more fireworks went off. I stayed there, not moving until it was quiet. Someone else grabbed me and put me down here."

Emerson said, "Did either of you see what happened?"

Anoush looked at Paxon. Both began speaking at once and stopped. Paxon said, "I went to the bathroom. It was all over when I came back."

Anoush said, "I saw, but I don't understand what I saw. While I was waiting on Paxon, two guys came in. A woman yelled something that sounded like, 'You shitty weasel.' I thought we were going to see a class-A catfight. But she started shootin'. The two boys was backed in the corner;

they tried to shoot their way out. That was too much for me. I couldn't watch no more. Then this one," she poked Coner, "grabs me and puts me in this cushy cell. You should see the bathroom; I don't know how they found it, let alone brought it here."

Coner said, "I didn't put you here because I thought you were guilty of a crime. I put you here to protect you. The woman Anoush described is Teranel. She's Tams's mate. As near as I can figure, she shot Tams, who, by the way, is Toms's brother, because he was threatening to replace her with *fresh blood*, as he called it. That means one of you women.

"You have to understand the threat in that. If Tams actually cut her off, she would have no choice but to work the rest of her life in a brothel. The other guy was just an unlucky sod who got caught in the crossfire. He fired his hip cannon out of reflex and took Teranel's leg off with a single shot. Tams shot him in the chest for his trouble.

"Whatever the reason, and it is unfortunate that many of our people are highly traumatized and cannot control their demons, you three can't stay here any longer. The safest thing would be to leave with an armed guard. I can't guarantee your safety."

Emerson said, "I have a better idea."

◆ ◆

The whine of a shuttle reactor rose up around them. Even though they were in a cellar beneath the ground, the vibration rattled the walls and brought dust down on their heads. Little Wing touched down in the middle of the street in front of the hardware store.

Emerson had received a silent notification from Rosco that they were ten minutes outside of Crow City. He texted them back the coordinates to the street outside the Hardware and Sundries store.

Emerson and crew burst out of the front door just as the hatch opened and Eggert descended the stairs. Margaret was next to him helping him to stay balanced. He had time to suck his teeth once before saying, "Emerson!"

They hugged fiercely. Almost falling to the dirt street. Emerson said, "But we can't stay here. Our camp is on the ridge in the north. The Black Mariah is serving as a hospital in the village. Can we hitch a ride?"

As they turned to the hatch, Ana rounded the corner with Amrsal. She said, "My Goddess! These are my old friends."

Amrsal stopped, eying her suspiciously. He said, "Are you going to get in that thing?"

Ana said, "Yes, it's safe."

Amrsal grunted and walked away toward the gate to the main village.

Ana called after him, but he didn't turn. People began to gather around Little Wing. Coner said, "You better go now before anythin' else happens."

Emerson, Elli, and the island three boarded Little Wing. Before the hatch closed, Emerson nodded to Coner and said, "Thanks for keeping them safe."

There was no time to embrace. Eggert and Margaret were in the cockpit; Ana kissed Grendel on the cheek and strapped in. The little puppy barked, startling everyone. Eggert laughed and sucked his teeth.

Emerson said, "Where did you find that?"

"Outpost 212, where else?" Rosco handed the furball across Grendel to Ana.

She said, "Has it got a name?"

"I've just been calling it dogfox. I don't know."

"That's a terrible name. He looks more like a fox than a dog."

Eggert said, "When my son was young, we read him a book about a little boy and a dog called *Budrow Has a Ball*. Let's call him Budrow."

Ana said, "I didn't know you had a son."

"He's gone now. It was a different life."

The reactor whined. The crowd outside covered their ears. Just as the volume and pitch became unbearable, Little Wing lifted fifty meters straight up and hovered for a moment before shooting off to the north in a streak.

Once they were in the air, Emerson said, "Paxon, you, Anoush, and Sandra are going to have to work this out with the council."

Paxon replied, "We have already decided to head north. These people are crazier than the old farts on the island!"

♦ ♦ ♦ ♦

END OF PART TWO

INTERFACE

PART THREE

GIFT HORSE

Most people who met with Brock were taken in by his glamour. The weird part was that people knew it was a glamour; they just didn't care. It felt good to be around Brock; his past seldom came up. When it did, he always had a story ready to put any doubts to rest.

Terrence Brock was an open book. You could ask about anything, and he would answer without pretense. He did none of those avoidance techniques that the people in the village recognized. To all eyes he was the person he claimed to be, sincere and honest.

Except to Elli.

"Fuck that guy," she said. "He's hiding something."

Emerson brought The Black Mariah back up to camp as soon as the patients were out of intensive care. Brock came with them, and they cooked a meal together. Ana asked the tall man if he had a wife or a girlfriend. It was the one time he didn't want to answer.

After a long pause, Brock said, "Yes, I did have a family. But I don't like to talk about it." That was all he'd say. He had no end of opinions regarding The City and the Lords. He knew all about Elli Rattlesnake Quinn and Emerson.

"Lord Quinn has lost his mind." He looked sheepishly at Quinn and added, "No offense to your daddy."

Quinn spat on the dirt. "I should have killed that bastard when I had the chance."

Brock said, "Tell us how you really feel."

Ana laughed and said, "Well, we're safe now, so let's not poke the bear."

Brock described the heavy-handed Interface oppression Lord Quinn had implemented. He said, "The Enforcers are mostly thought police now. If you don't hold ol' High Lord Quinn up as the divine ruler, you might get mind-locked. Sometimes it's temporary. Other times, like in the case of his last Secretary of the Enforcers, Sarah Morton, it's permanent. She's been a drooling veg ever since she told him he was insane."

Elli was her normal sullen self. She acted as though the conversation was too boring for her to waste time on. At one point, though, she asked, "How did *you* escape, Brock?"

"Superior prowess and cunning." He smiled widely, and everyone laughed. "Really, I was on a medical census mission outside the wall and I just walked away. Boom. Gone. Never going back."

Ana said, "Medical census?"

"A group of Enforcer physicians would go just outside the wall to count and minister to the Dregs. We found that if allowed to fester, diseases we have eradicated find their way back into the general Middle population if we don't take care of the ones that live there. It's a service we provide."

Elli laughed. Then, she said, "How did you avoid the Interface mind control?"

"I'm a trained surgeon; I can program an implant. I could have even removed it without detection."

"You didn't say how."

He stopped smiling and looked at her seriously. "I locked my implant before I left but not before I was outside the wall so they couldn't nab me and drag me back in. Satisfied?"

"No, but that's fine." Elli left the table.

Quinn said, "Elli has trust issues."

Emerson wasn't sure of Brock either, but he kept his suspicions quiet.

At the meal, everyone was talking. Coner sent pitchers of Southwest Quarter mead, and Saą brought a few bottles of kiras. Conversation was lively. The food was great, and no one was watching the kids.

Suddenly, Quinn yelled, "Marya is choking!"

Brock was closest to the child and performed a chest compression from behind. The strawberry shot out of her mouth and across the table; Marya burst into tears. After Quinn calmed her down, she said, "I'm so glad you were here. You have to teach us that technique."

He said, "That's what I'm here for. I took an oath to save lives."

After that, mistrusting Terrence Brock was frowned on. And as his reputation grew, even Emerson's suspicion waned. Elli, however, never trusted him and even followed him around for a few weeks. He always knew she was there and talked to her when no one else was around just to piss her off.

On the last day before she quit trying to sneak around behind him, she told him, "I don't know what it is yet, but there's something wrong with you, Brock. I'll find it. You'll see."

♦ ♦ ♦

THE MEMORIES

Children in Crow City grew up parented by the village. They were usually with their mother until they ventured into independence. Some youth chose to live together in small communal houses. Most fathers lived with their children too, though men often had more than one family. Parents maintained tight relationships with their children and each other. The pressures of survival after a near-human extinction event like The Death required all resources, including reproductive capability, to be shared. In most cases, citizens of the village were more concerned about genetic traits than they were about sex or appearance. This led to open sexual habits in the main village. Obviously, folks in the Southwest Quarter were less relaxed. Since there was an agreed-on reason, no one complained about it. And there was no social pressure and very little jealousy.

Over the years, it became an ingrained custom. If a couple decided to stay dedicated to each other in a closed union, it was their choice. Most adults chose to have many sexual partners. All citizens considered it their responsibility to raise the entire village together, and village health was openly discussed and communally addressed. There were no sexually transmitted diseases in Crow City. The lack of shame and guilt regarding sex made them easy to eradicate.

Brock did not cultivate intimate relations with the citizens of the village or any of the members of Emerson's team. He was sociable and seemed to enjoy company as much as the people enjoyed him. But he never touched anyone aside from an exam, a cordial handshake, or a chaste hug. Of course, Elli thought this was the key to his mystery. She made up scenarios in her mind about him: he was a spy from across the ocean, or he was working for Lord Quinn and would attack the village at night.

Emerson listened to her, but she knew he didn't take her seriously. She was used to it and continued looking for evidence to back up her suspicious itch.

◆ ◆

Saą was born with the gift of The Memories, meaning she could contact The Mother and acquire knowledge that she had no other way of knowing. The Mother was a spiritual guide who took the form of Saą's birth mother—at least for Saą. She was actually a consciousness, like a goddess, who rose from the soil. The Memories were a crystal matrix woven into the nodules and feelers of the living mycelial network. They were the mind of the planet. For Saą, Mother was the voice of The Memories.

Most people were unaware of the network, much less possessed the ability to communicate with it. Even so, the society of Crow City based its moral compass on the teachings that came from The Mother. But Saą had noticed more children were being born with the knowledge and ability. She petitioned the council to set up a school for these children to learn more about the awareness they possessed and to help them learn to use their connection. She suspected that Marya was able. She exhibited no sign of it until the summer solstice, a few weeks shy of her sixth birthday, which may have offered some clue. The council had been considering it for months.

◆ ◆

Brunt grew stronger. The Mother fed him bone broth and rare venison. She inoculated a bloodskin—a bear's bladder containing enzymes which, when activated by fermentation, produced an elixir of unparalleled effectiveness. The contents of a bloodskin activated the body's cells to put all their energy toward healing. The elixir turned most of Brunt's life force to rebuilding his damaged cells. It required a lot of sleep, like eighteen hours a day. For the first few weeks, that was all he did.

But he was not idle. During sleep, The Mother brought Brunt, who she called Barry, to her round room and tutored him in techniques to call and listen to The Memories. By the time his body was healed, he had advanced enough for her to call him a novice. Most of his desires from the past and, in fact, most of his memories had melted away by that time. The motivation that replaced them was singular. He yearned to know more of The Memories; he had fallen in love with The Mother. When he was not with her, she was all he thought of.

The Mother fed him, washed him, sewed his clothes, and nursed him. She also spent time with him, either silently walking in the small, fenced garden outside her cottage or talking about his past and future. Brunt no longer thought of himself as Brunt. He was twenty-five kilos lighter and clean-shaven; his curly, light brown hair had grown to shoulder length. He didn't look like the same man. She gave him a linen tunic and drawstring pants.

He told her about his youth in Beso Muerte. After his father died, a gang of boys became his only family. Together they tried to avoid the slavers. He never had enough to eat, scratching out survival from the leftovers in the crumbling city. He became a bodyguard because of his formidable height and weight: 180 centimeters and fourteen stone. It made him look much older; few people would chance him in a fight. Of course, Brunt didn't fight. Which was how he was captured and brought to live on the island.

But that man was dead. The wolves had eaten him on the side of the trail so many weeks ago. Barry emerged from the cottage in late spring with a light heart and a clear purpose: to gather the children who could hear the call of The Memories and lead them to The Mother.

On the day that She found him, wretched and beaten by the side of the path, She also collected the plasma rifle but kept it hidden until he was ready to leave. They had a leisurely morning, and after tea and groats, she gave him the gun.

"I can't use it, you know. It's an Interface weapon," Barry said as he looked at the dull metal surface of the weapon.

Mother said, "All things exist within the laws of The Memories, Barry. I think you will find all tools sympathetic to the requests of The Mother. You will have it for a reason, though you may never know what it is."

Mother took Barry into the Memories.

Instead of the round room with a hole in the ceiling, they were standing in a field of tall grass. Barry had never seen the prairie; the endless space was disorienting. He put his arms out and nearly fell. When he regained his balance, Mother said, "You can always call me here, son. I will always come. No matter where you are or what is happening. Call me."

They embraced as mother and son, and when She released him and he looked in her eyes, he found himself looking into a stream. He was in the same forest She'd found him. A light rain fell. He tightened the strap on his day sack, slung the plasma gun over his shoulder, and continued up the path toward Crow City.

◆ ◆ ◆

A DAY IN THE LIFE

The council took a collection for the three island refugees and had a feast as a send-off. The citizens of Crow City mobilized at any reason for a celebration, which always included food, drumming, and dancing. The reason was irrelevant.

The early summer weather meant that most days were warm, with long afternoons best spent in the shade with a cool, alcoholic drink. But when the sun went down, the temperature cooled quickly. The summer foliage at that altitude was sparse, but it released its humidity beginning at dusk, creating a low-lying mist that hung close to the ground around the ankles of the people gathering in commons. Torches were lit. The drummers tuned up while children chased fireflies in the gathering dusk.

Crow City knew how to throw a party.

Polly Burdock, born and raised in The Land Ruled by Crows, was the head chef in charge of celebrations. She'd been doing it faithfully for twenty years. There were always plenty of people around to help, but Polly ran the show. It was a full-time job. Polly was a big woman, and she loved to eat—but she loved to feed people even more. Her head was shaved, and she wore a gold hoop in her right earlobe. She'd tell say, "Hair and fire are a bad mix. Better to have none than to get it burned off!" It was unusual to see Polly without the oil-stained leather apron that covered her from neck to knee. She kept a glass bottle of kiras in the front pocket. The bottle was kept filled by one of her omnipresent helpers.

On such short notice as this, there was no guarantee that they could have a large animal to roast. All large animals in Crow City were wild-caught. But there were domestic fowl aplenty. Polly set up a station behind the woodshed, and five local kids took care of the processing. She estimated they would need 100. Caren Cara and her daughters brought the birds. Polly sent a runner to the food forest with a list for Amrsal. He needed most of the day to collect everything.

Polly always had two or three kids hanging around ready to run an errand or a message. Some wore linen slings that helped them carry more. One girl had a folding cart she found and repaired. The children raced each other to see who was the fastest.

The drummers didn't need any organization. They set up in the early afternoon with a barrel of kiras and a basket of bread. More players trickled in as the afternoon wore on. By sunset, the circle would include twenty of the village's oldest, surrounded by children, newcomers, and other curious citizens. Everyone attended. There were reed baskets of every sort of percussion instrument ever found, alongside homemade versions like tin cans filled with rice or dried peas and old plastic bleach bottles filled with acorns.

Children ran free in Crow City. Everyone looked out for everyone else. Everyone knew the children belonged to the future instead of the present and that the world they were living in was theirs. The village was small enough that everyone knew whose children belonged with who even if they didn't know everyone's names. The kids formed their own groups and played games in the darkness: hide and go seek, jail tag, kick the can. Games older than memory where the rules were reinvented by each generation.

The kiras flowed. Residents carried their mugs tied to their belts. Some drinking vessels were more ornate than others. Carved wood, clay, metal, or horn, they were crafted out of anything a person could find to drink from. The people of Crow City were proud of their celebratory nature. They toasted it frequently and with gusto.

The three island refugees danced and sang with the rest of the revelers. They ate and drank too much, along with most of the people in the village. Just before he went to bed, Emerson told them to stay in touch, but he was pretty sure they wouldn't. The next morning, they were gone, and life in Crow City went on.

◆◆

Emerson's camp didn't much look like a camp by midsummer, but even so, the infrastructure they'd built was largely invisible. The entire village was calling it the North Quarter by then, and it looked much the same as the rest of the village. The buildings were smaller and the roads wider, but the architectural style of Crow City had taken on a uniformity that it had not had prior. Plummer's construction ability and historical understanding of structural engineering created an unwritten code which sped new construction.

The buildings were faced with wood when they were finished, but the initial structures were made of loam cement. A mixture made on site that contained 80 percent aerated earth, wood ash, and lime mixed with water and formed into walls and bricks. It was the foundation of all new structures. In older buildings, wood was the primary material. The lime was stored in the cavernous Ag barns. The resulting cement was light and water repellent, and it cured in two hours. They mixed batches in salvaged barrels: put the ingredients in, roll it around for a few minutes, and pour it out.

Emerson's close family included Quinn and Marya, Saą, Ana and Little Chandler, Plummer and his rats, Eggert and Maggie, and Grendel and Rosco. Their houses were arranged in a wide semicircle around a common area, much like the beach camp, with a heavy wooden table and a frame suspended over it from four thick posts. The frame was handy for hanging things like lights, flowers, sun screens, and rain tarps. When the weather was nice, they congregated outdoors around the table for meals, meetings, and sometimes to work or read alone.

The firepit was further away from the buildings and the table but still central. This design was common in Crow City. The main differences between the North Quarter and other areas, aside from two flying machines parked a few hundred meters from the houses, were the plumbing, electric, heating, and sewage systems.

Also, most of the tools they used were Interface-controlled. All of the locks, monitoring cameras, and appliances were Interface-only. The houses in the North Quarter looked like any other; the differences were well disguised. Each one of Emerson's crew had a preference for different types of heating. He used the compressed charcoal that the rest of Crow City used for indoor cooking. But the cooking stoves in the North Quarter ran on biogas which they made from food scraps in large, heavy rubber bags, which were pressurized by balloons filled with water attached to the top. As the food scraps and other waste decomposed in the main chamber, methane filled the flexible plastic bag, but as it filled, the weight of the water kept the chamber under the needed two kilograms per square centimeters of pressure.

Gas was piped into each house to be used how the occupant saw fit. Eggert heated with it. So did Ana and Rosco; they were used to houses with modern amenities.

Meanwhile, Plummer had engineered a passive solar design. His operating parameters were broader than most humans. He was comfortable as long as his nutritional fluid didn't freeze. All of his organic functions were inside the temperature-controlled pod at his center.

The North Quarter had its own vegetable beds. Emerson and Plummer constructed a hoop house from some spruce ribs that Ana got from Amrsal and sheet plastic that they found in a grower's supply warehouse in the valley. He made it mainly to extend the growing season for his small field of corn.

Long ago, the council had ruled that corn could not be grown or consumed as food for humans. The dead culture had become addicted to corn, and the plant had become the vector for many of the poisons and pesticides responsible for the degradation of health that preceded the end. By the time of the collapse, something like 90 percent of all food was based on or completely created from corn. The people of Crow City had a justified bias against the plant.

Emerson made the case, before the council, that he had no intention of eating the corn. He had never tasted corn and didn't even find the smell of it appealing. When asked what he was growing it for, he replied, "We want to drink it. Sour mash whiskey, councilwoman. We want to make hooch." The request was unanimously approved. The Crow City council was an exuberant supporter of all things alcoholic.

When he started it, the weather was too cold even for the growing season Emerson hoped to extend into, but he planted his dwindling supply of Jimmy Red corn and set up an auto irrigation system. The rest of the North Quarter camp was using Ana's pH and H_2O monitors. Emerson attached one to his soil. He would have to wait to see how well the plants survived.

The grey water systems from the houses' gravity fed the irrigation systems. They were accustomed to composting toilets, but Emerson and Plummer designed an underground humanure composting system that created fertilizer and deposited it in a hopper near the gardens. It used a solar-powered mechanism that mimicked peristalsis, taking the inputs through the stages of compost in a slow corkscrew-type conveyer.

Emerson's grandpa, Chandler, had designed and fabricated several types of materials during his life. But his finest creation was his modified photovoltaic matrix; Chandler perfected a paint-on solar cell. Not only was it powerful on a single coat, but successive applications could be layered and switched molecularly to operate in parallel or in series. The North Quarter was powered with personal arrays that tracked the sun. They made enough current to power reduction space heaters, but nobody had or needed one. The inside of their homes was coated with another Chandler innovation: a super-insulating paint-on coating, based on the principals found in sheep's wool. The paint was a spreadable medium for billions of microscopic tubes. The properties of this were cumulative as well—the more that was painted on, the higher the R factor. It was difficult to fabricate, so Emerson was stingy with it. Besides, one coat was enough for this zone, even at the higher altitudes in the mountains.

The people of Crow City had no problem with mechanical tech, as long as it was controlled by human hands. And salvaged items were structurally necessary for the community to have clean water and adequate sewer. They were carefully hidden, but the civil engineers used copper pipes as well as steel reinforcing rods. Even if the community did not have milling machines or other precision metal working tools, they knew where those tools were and made regular pilgrimages to nearby cities to make and or find parts. They developed strict rules regarding imports. And as with any rules, there was commensurate resistance in the form of a lively black market centered, of course, in the Southwest Quarter.

◆ ◆

Barry arrived at the border gate at the edge of the North Quarter and stopped. He sensed that someone would come to him. He didn't have long to wait. Ana arrived and asked him what he wanted. He had stashed the plasma gun off the trail in a hollow tree because he didn't know how to explain it without lying, and he'd learned from Mother that lying made it harder to contact The Memories. She taught him that the heart and mind must be clear to make a good connection, and keeping track of lies clouded the judgement. "Too much stupid crap to remember," Mother had instructed. Barry never lied unless Mother told him to.

He said, "You don't recognize me. Do you, Ana?"

She looked into his eye. "Nope. Can't say that I do. Wait here. I've called Emerson. He'll be here in a minute."

Emerson arrived with Saą, who said. "Hello, Brunt."

Ana and Emerson recognized him then. Barry smiled broadly. He said, "Not anymore. I was rescued from death, and I've decided I want to be Barry again as my father named me. Barry is who I am. I come with a message for everyone from The Mother." He opened his arms in a gesture of inclusion. "I need to speak to India Tarn."

Saą raised her eyebrows. She wanted to hear more. Emerson was guarded. Ana said, "One of us needs to stay with you while you are inside our boundaries."

They walked back to the communal table where Quinn and the children were eating a fruit salad of berries and melon. Elli had already gone to the clinic.

When Barry approached the table, Marya said, "Hello, Barry. I wondered when you'd get here."

Everyone was shocked, except Barry. He said, "I've just arrived!"

"Marya, what are you talking about?" asked Quinn.

The child looked confused. She said, "What, Mama?"

Quinn said, "You just called this man by name and said you wondered when he'd arrive. Do you remember him?"

Marya said, "That's Barry." She looked at her mom, emotionless.

Quinn said, "Never mind. You and LC finish your breakfast. We are going to visit the school this morning." LC had made a tower out of scrap wooden blocks. It toppled over, and one fell into Marya's breakfast. The kids laughed.

Barry said, "The little one can see The Mother?"

"You are being weird, Barry," Ana said. "I don't like it."

Emerson put his hand on her shoulder, but he said nothing.

Saą said, "I see The Mother. How do you know The Memories? I was trained from birth."

Barry replied, "It is true. I am not the man I was. Mother rescued me and brought me to her cottage in the forest. She taught me about The Memories and told me to come to you."

Saą said, "There are no cottages near here."

◆ ◆

Emerson brought Barry to India. She listened to him speak for a moment and agreed that he should have freedom within the village. Emerson was surprised, but he had learned that recognizing The Mother was a peak spiritual experience to the people in Crow City. Not everyone could see or talk to her, but everyone aspired to a greater connection. India heard truth in Barry's story. Emerson remembered that Brunt stole food and a plasma rifle even though he couldn't fire it. To him, Barry had simply cleaned himself up and adopted the language of believers; Emerson had seen it before. But he cloaked his mistrust and kept an eye on the man.

◆ ◆

Emerson asked India about the façade the leaders of Crow City created about not salvaging from the past.

India listened patiently and said, "We are trying to avoid the mistakes of the past, to give humans a chance at coexisting with the planet they are born of. We make no secret of what we are doing. The citizens of The Land see and understand all of our measures, even when they seem to encroach on personal freedoms. Life here is not so concerned with absolutes, Emerson."

He guessed that was reasonable. They avoided the sort of tech they believed was ultimately harmful but embraced tech that supported life and perpetuated their philosophy. It was a noble goal: don't repeat the prior civilization's mistakes. But, he thought, it led to making some pretty dubious distinctions about what being helpful or making a mistake even meant. Emerson kept his thoughts to himself.

◆ ◆

Ana spent most days working on code in the cockpit of The Black Mariah. Plummer, and his new retractable head, spent time building new rooms and finishing buildings. Ana called on him to discuss ideas. She was completely stumped by the problems with her temporary Interface connection. She had built an eight-centimeter-wide, paper-thin disk of programable nano fibers and burned circuitry similar to the implant into it. But all of her tests failed. So, she began again, thinking that something was amiss in the nano structures, or possibly with the base machine operating system. She had no trouble cloning the implant inside one of The Black Mariah's virtual machines. Those tests all came back within specifications. She knew she needed expert help, and there wasn't anyone with more experience except Chandler Estes, but he only lived inside his Interface cube simulation. Emerson controlled access which he never loaned anyone. C. Plummer was close, so she enlisted him.

Plummer read over all the code and logs in thirty seconds. He said, "It looks right. But it doesn't work?"

"I ran a simulation, and it failed. I don't get it. Maybe we need a human subject to try it on."

They asked Saą.

She said, "What do I have to do?"

Ana explained, "Just stick this to your neck below your ear."

"Uh-huh. Now what?"

Ana opened a simulation, but she was working with the Interface. It looked to Saą like she was staring into space. Saą was excited and wanted direction. She asked, "What now?"

Plummer said, "Ana is testing to see if you have made a proper connection. When she is sure you do, she will ask you to perform a series of tests."

"Yeah! That's more like it," Ana said. "Okay, Są, close your eyes. Do you see the red square in the upper right corner of your field of vision?"

"Yes. Yes, it's bright red. I don't think I've ever seen such a vibrant glowing red; it hurts…"

"I'll lower the intensity. How's that?"

"Better. Yes, I see a red square."

"Okay. Make it blue."

"How?"

"Think blue."

"Blue," she said, as if commanding it. "Right. Nope. Still a red square."

"Try this. Red is hot. Blue is cold. When I touch your hand, my finger will be so cold it will burn."

"Ow! Oh! It turned blue."

"Good. Having an Interface connection makes your brain more open to suggestion. Now try to turn it back…"

"It's red. Now it's green, blue again, purple—wow, this is amazing. I can move… Oh wow. I can move it and make it bigger and…"

Ana and Plummer could monitor the visuals that Są was seeing. Plummer sent Ana a private message that said, "Don't let her do too much. She'll get a hangover."

Ana texted back, LOL, and shut down the sim. She said, "That's enough for the first time."

Disappointed, Są said, "But we can do it again, right?"

"She's hooked," Plummer said.

◆ ◆

Ana continued to see Amrsal on a regular basis. She stayed away from any conversation that might come back to her use of the Interface. He'd made it clear that he would prefer that she remove the implant. Ana didn't react when he said it. She forced her face to not betray her and said she'd consider it. He hadn't brought it up since.

He liked to bring her to the warm springs, and as much as she liked having sex with him, she was growing tired of his predictable routine. When she suggested they go somewhere else or do something else, he'd become quiet and introspective, asking if there was something wrong with him wanting her to be more present.

Ana saw through his manipulative behavior, but she was unsure of how far she should push him. So, she played along, answering his questions truthfully but avoiding the real subject which she was sure would make him cross. He had already walked away from her in the middle of a conversation in public.

Ana was close to Emerson, but she couldn't talk to him about Amrsal. He'd get jealous, even though he thought he was above such base emotions. She avoided sticking it in his face.

Elli and Ana were lovers off and on. Elli had no intimate relations with anyone but Ana, but she wasn't possessive. They were both able to allow the other to live their independent lives and still spend occasional nights together. Amrsal knew about Ana and Elli. That didn't seem to bother him. Ana knew he had an intimate relation with a boyfriend from school when he was young. But it ended in conflict.

Elli didn't like Amrsal. She thought his infantile behavior disqualified him. His handsome-boy persona made her want to poke fun at him. But Ana didn't need advice; she needed to talk. No convenient time presented itself.

At the hot springs, after they made love, Ana said, "Amrsal, we need to talk."

But he was distracted and didn't hear her. He said, "I love you, Anastacia Moon. I want us to be exclusive and have many babies together."

Ana was surprised and struggled to keep her face under control. She liked Amrsal, but hearing him say *exclusive* and *many babies* was too much of a stretch for her, and a laugh escaped her throat. It sounded like a bark.

She knew it was a mistake and immediately said, "I'm sorry, Amrsal. Really, I'm not laughing at you. I just…" But he was striding naked into the forest.

Ana called after him, "I'm really sorry."

He didn't turn. She called louder, "Hey, you forgot your clothes."

He kept going. After a half hour, she got dressed and walked home alone.

◆ ◆

When Quinn and LC were on the way to the school building, which was just one high-ceilinged room with several tables, a few cases of books, and shelves of supplies, Little Chandler noticed a box turtle in the grass next to the path and picked it up. By the time Quinn realized he was holding it, she had no idea how long he had it.

She stopped in the road and stooped down to his level. "Hey, LC, where'd you get that cool turtle?"

He held it out for her to see. "Turtle."

Quinn said, "I see. But I bet the turtle has a family. Why don't we put him back where you found him?"

Chandler stood up straighter and said, "No."

Quinn was raised by caregivers who never said no to her. She didn't believe in disciplining children to modify behavior, but LC could be belligerent at times, and she didn't know how to react. Rather than force the issue, she said okay and continued walking.

When they arrived, another mother found a wooden box, and the children gave the turtle grass and a dish of water. For most of the morning, they watched the turtle or looked for books about turtles. Quinn stood back and observed, looking for ways to be helpful. She felt isolated from the other parents who were there with their children. The woman who found the box brought her a cup of chamomile tea. She was wearing a plain, sleeveless, ankle-length dress.

She said, "I put a little honey in, I hope that's okay. My name is Sury. That's my daughter, Sanka." She pointed to a teen dressed in the traditional skin leggings and vest.

"Thanks," Quinn said. They walked along the bookshelf, sipping their tea. Quinn ran her finger along the spines. There were only a few books. "Is this the only library in the village?"

Sury said, "I'm afraid so. I hear there are still libraries in the ruins of the bigger towns, but they are far away, and no one has made the journey for books in a long time."

Quinn said, "I know your views on electronic tech, but we have nearly every book ever written in our data stores on the shuttle. For example, I looked up the sort of turtle Little Chandler found and…"

"You can look up books from here?"

"Yes, and if there were a screen here, I could cast what I find to it so everyone could see. She's a northwestern pond turtle. The locals used to call them red sliders."

Sury was surprised. "That's amazing. We need more books. That's certain."

◆ ◆

At the end of the day, Quinn called Emerson's children to gather up their things and get ready to walk back. Little Chandler brought the turtle.

Marya met a girl her age and had spent the day with her. She was breathlessly describing everything they did. Quinn asked LC if he'd named his turtle.

LC said, "He's not my turtle. Besides, he's already got a name."

After a while, when he didn't continue, she asked, "What's his name?"

"I can't pronounce it. It's in turtle talk." He squatted in the dirt at the side of the road and put the turtle down. "Go on home now. Thanks for coming to school."

After they walked for a bit and Marya exhausted her narration, Little Chandler said, "He wanted to come with me. For the other children, I promised I'd bring him back."

◆◆

Emerson and Ana were entertained by the turtle episode. Quinn tried to get across how weird it felt, but LC's parents didn't let Quinn's concerns pierce their pride.

Instead, Quinn changed the subject and said, "Emerson, we need to find a way to give Crow City a real library."

"We have every book, movie, and show ever recorded in our data storage. What do they need a library for? Books are difficult to preserve. Without climate controls on humidity and temperature, paper deteriorates. But our data cubes are radium powered and will last indefinitely as long as they are recharged in the sun once every few months."

"You know the citizens of Crow City will never go for it."

"Maybe not, but transporting books here without a building to preserve them in would be like dumping them in a big pile and lighting them on fire."

"Maybe we should build a library."

Plummer added, "From what I've seen, we'd have more luck getting them to accept a climate-controlled building than a database."

Saą said, "Plummer is right, but people change. We should be patient. Keep our eyes and ears open for the way. Mother will provide solutions for everyone's needs."

◆◆

That night, Saą came to Emerson's cottage. They sat at a wooden worktable. She said, "I want you to implant me. I need to experience the Interface."

Emerson said, "It's risky for you. Your people may reject you if you embrace this technology."

She stared at the ceiling for a long minute. Finally, she said, "Mother asks me to do it. She says the people need it."

He held her hand and said, "I know this is a crisis for you."

"Mother knows what she is asking."

◆ ◆

Quinn brought a supply of implants when she left The City. They were the modified non-surgical type that could be administered with a pressure syringe. Saą sat on the edge of Quinn's sleeping platform.

Quinn said, "This will sting for a moment, but it contains a topical anesthetic so, as it threads into your nervous system, it will feel like streams of cold. You may feel a little sore for a day or so."

"It would be best for you to immerse yourself in Interface simulations while you are acclimating to the implant," Emerson said. "There are a series of tutorials you can try, and later tonight, I'll introduce you to my grandfather."

Emerson invited Plummer to come along that evening. And because Ana had finished testing the temporary Interface disks, Quinn brought Marya. The sim ran inside The Black Mariah. The shuttle was one of the few places where Emerson could lock out the rest of the world.

They sat in the main cabin seats because they were the most comfortable. Emerson turned the lights down to a soft emerald color. He initiated the cube and placed it on the seat next to him. Saą had spent a few hours studying the basic introduction to the Interface tutorial. It was part of the Enforcer orientation program. She was not prepared for the totally immersive experience of the Chandler Cube.

When it powered up, each of the participants felt the familiar vibration in the center of their brains. Saą was looking at the latched cabinet doors lining the bulkhead. Her vision doubled and split into red, green, and yellow outlines. She blinked, and the scene changed completely. She was sitting in a leather sling-back chair in front of a huge stone fireplace. The fire was mostly glowing coals. A moist pocket inside a log snapped, spitting an ember onto the wood plank floor. The floor was pitted by hundreds of burns.

For a second, she was looking at the bulkhead again. The light flickered, and she was back in the cube again. She felt pressure in her ears for a moment, a feeling she recognized from diving into deep water as a girl. She looked to her left.

An old man with shaggy grey hair and piercing ice-blue eyes grinned at her from a similar chair. Emerson stood; he and the old man hugged. "Grandpa, I want you meet your great-granddaughter, Marya."

Chandler bent to the girl's level and said, "Good to meet you, sweetheart. I am your daddy's grandpa, but you can call me Chandler."

Marya shook his hand firmly and said, "My half-brother's name is Chandler, but we call him LC. I guess you're big Chandler, huh?"

"Can I give you a hug?" Chandler asked.

She hugged him tightly around the neck and said, "You smell good."

Emerson said, "And this is our friend, Saą. She's one of the people you told me about when I was a kid. I know you said they were all gone, but Saą found us and brought us to her village, Crow City."

Chandler said, "Glad to make your acquaintance, dear. My grandpa used to tell stories about people who lived off the land. It was an inspiration to my mom and dad and uncles. We learned how to live independent of society. That preparation and knowledge served us pretty well after the collapse. But tell me, Saą, what about your people? Where are you from?"

Saą said, "They say there were once tribes of people who populated this continent before the colonizers came, murdered them, and stole their homes. I am descended from the handful of those people who survived The

Death. They already lived outside the Interface-controlled part of society. The collapse changed little for them day to day. But there were only a few. And we needed greater numbers in order to survive, let alone thrive. Since my family was killed, I have only The Memories to tell the stories. My people came from the Arapaho, but none of my direct relatives survived.

"The founders of The Land Ruled by Crows were nomads who traveled from group to group gathering families together. There is strength in numbers, and at least we could watch each other's backs. We have built a village of about 5,000. New pilgrims come every day."

Chandler said, "You'll have to tell me more about your Memories sometime, dear."

Plummer stepped forward and stumbled. He extended a hand and said, "Glad to meet you, Chandler Estes. I have heard a lot about you outside the sim. I am mostly machine, you see. I haven't had this form since before the collapse and The Death. I remember things that most men have forgotten. I have to say, being in this simulation is the closest I've felt to my humanity in fifty years. It seems strange to say, but you and I are close to the same age."

Chandler touched Plummer's hand and then gestured for them to go. "Yes, yes, we should talk, but right now, I need to spend some time with my great-granddaughter."

Everyone sat silent for a moment. Chandler said, "You can go. I want to talk to the girl."

Emerson looked at Quinn. Chandler added, "Oh, you can stay, Elli Rattlesnake. Everyone else, out. Vamoose!"

When they had gone, Chandler said, "So tell me, little one, what's your favorite color, eh?"

◆ ◆

Plummer worked out the details with Emerson to use the cube in his absence. He and Chandler planned to go over weather history that Plummer had stored to see if together they could develop better models for prediction. Chandler didn't have access to history following The Death, and Plummer didn't have access to the modeling platforms that Chandler had salvaged.

Plummer could visit with Chandler while his cybernetic body was doing other things, like recharging or carrying boxes, a job that people in Crow City were always asking him to do. During the first meeting, Chandler asked Plummer if he preferred being a cyborg to being human.

"There's a question." Plummer paused. "I never had a choice, so I never gave it much thought. But now that you mention it, I would much rather be a flesh human."

"Well, Charles, in this simulation, you can be anything you want."

"Novel thought."

"You're a programmer; you can figure it out."

Next meeting, Plummer appeared as his human self with one of his cybernetic arms. His voice still sounded artificial to him, but it was a pleasure to have a functioning body again, even if it was a technical illusion. He looked in the mirror at his thirty-year-old self. It was the last time he remembered seeing his face. He had black hair and grew a dark beard, which, even shaved daily, always had a five-o'clock shadow at two. His eyes were brown and his skin more olive than pink due to his mother's northern Italian heritage. He turned his head to get a better look at his left ear, the ear that Joey Lindstrom bit off while he was a cadet in military high school.

He never got the chance to repay Joey, who was killed when a tractor rolled on him cutting grass. Charles realized he didn't have to keep his image true. He was the only living soul that knew anything about Joey. While he was thinking about it, the bit-off part of his ear rematerialized. Plummer said, "Huh," and sat down to work.

They took a break after five hours of number crunching. It was becoming clear that there were few patterns they could tease out of the emerging climate data.

Chandler shook his shaggy head. "They really fucked it up, didn't they?"

Plummer said, "It started to get bad in the late 2010s: strange variations in temperature, shifting jet streams, ocean currents moving, ice melting, sea levels rising. But after that, the *real* mega-storms began. The coastlines became unrecognizable which disrupted shipping to such a degree that people in first world countries were going hungry. But the climate change was only getting started."

Chandler said, "I was just a little kid, but I remember. Storms that filled up the subways in New York City, hurricanes in Southern California."

Plummer continued, "After all my cohorts died, when I was studying cybernetics and Interface programming, the hurricane season began, except we seldom had hurricanes in that part of the continent. And as if that wasn't bad enough, most of the people had died, and there was no infrastructure anymore. Nobody to repair what broke. Nobody to bury the dead. After a while, everything was broken, and most everyone was dead. That's when the tornados began. Sometimes two or three at a time. I'm no expert, and I didn't have access to measuring equipment, but I'd guess that the ones that ripped through Beso Muerte were at the top of the Fujitsu scale. I'd call them F6s if there was such a thing.

"Those storms changed the landscape. They made new rivers where deserts had been. They created a huge lake in the middle of the continent, tying the waterways of the northeast with the ocean in the gulf. And still, the storms got worse. Drastic changes in the water weight at the edges of the continental shelves created slippage between plates. The earth's crust snapped back like a rubber band, except this band was made of rock and spanned hundreds of kilometers.

"By the time Emerson came to live with you, probably about

twenty-five years ago, most of the drastic shifts had settled, but anomalous inversions still caused bizarre, unpredictable weather. You can see why the maps are so useless. No one could have predicted the kinds of changes the coastlines and lowlands experienced. The climatologists imagined some of it, but the full power of the planet's climate system is more than anyone could imagine. We, as a species, are lucky to have survived." He thought about what he'd said for a moment and added, "If we survive. Some days I have my doubts."

Chandler asked about Plummer's surgical capabilities.

"I guess I'm as good as any surgical robot," he replied. "I amputated a leg a few weeks back. And I made Rat One and Rat Two."

Chandler said, "Say what? You can do amputations? Did the guy live?"

"Woman, and yes. I am making her a prosthetic. I don't want to tell the council about it."

"That seems fucked up."

"It is their culture; I didn't ask if I could save her life. And neither did Brock. He works at the clinic now. He's a City-trained doctor, and they let him use anything he can to repair damaged citizens."

"Brock, eh? How did he get here?"

"Terrence Brock appeared the day of the shooting. He's been here since. Told us he got fed up with Boston Quinn's strong-arm tactics. He's a hell of a surgeon."

"I think I knew his father, Lord Eustice Brock. He was my wife Ciara's enemy. Hard to believe his only living child is here by chance."

Plummer said, "His story seems pretty tight. People like him."

"I'd keep an eye on the silver. The Brocks always had a loose concept of ownership, if you catch my drift."

"I enjoy your archaic language, Chandler, and I can usually figure it out. But *the silver*?" Plummer asked.

"It was an old saying. If you had a servant who wasn't trustworthy, you might have to count your silver knives and forks."

"Ah, right, when knives and forks were really valuable."

"No, you idiot. Because *silver* was valuable."

"I'm not an idiot, Chandler."

"I know. I'm sorry. When this sim was made, I was an impatient old man. Sometimes I lose myself in the character."

"So do I, sir. So do I."

◆ ◆ ◆

THE NEWCOMERS

Pamela P fit right in with Elli and Pejeta at the clinic. She was vocal about their lack of pharmaceuticals and test equipment and just about everything else they didn't have. It was just Pam's general cantankerousness bleeding through, and both Elli and Pejeta understood and ignored it. Something about being the only people left in the world made everyone more tolerant of eccentricities.

They didn't know Pam was in the late stages of breast cancer, and she wasn't going to tell them. *It wouldn't make any difference anyway*, she thought. The last thing she wanted was to navigate everyone's sympathy and pity. *Christ, that would be harder than dying.*

Consequently, Pam lived at the clinic. She was used to sleeping where she worked. Her Blue Hole office had a small cot and a closet with some clothes in it. She had a house, but she never went there. There was always too much to do. When medicines they salvaged ran out, she made her own salves, decoctions, and remedies. Willow bark for pain and valerian for a sedative, plantain to sooth bites and bread mold for penicillin. She sent a note to Emerson to send Eggert for a restocking. There was a bunker they located a few hours away. The late rains came early and stayed for weeks, turning every path to mud and halting construction on the library.

The clinic had an increase in water-related injuries and diseases like foot fungus. It was running them all ragged, not to mention that the roof leaked and drainage water ran through the center of the building. At least the charcoal was stored up high so the room was warm, even if it was often annoyingly dark. Elli mentioned more than once that she could bring a battery-powered light from The Black Mariah that would light up the room like day if they wanted. But Pejeta waved her off like it was too much trouble.

Pam had a different approach. She told Elli to bring the light, and she set it up and turned it on. Pejeta looked at her and opened her mouth.

Pam said, "We need two more of these, Elli. I can't help if I can't see."

This ruffled Pejeta's feathers, but she needed all the help she could get.

◆ ◆

Eggert and Margaret had discovered the peace and beauty of working with the trees. They named the foxdog Budrow, who was looking more like a fox every day. The pup was growing long and lanky and had attached himself to Maggie and Eric. Eggert couldn't go anywhere without him.

Once the weather turned wet, they stayed inside. Eggert had developed a cough; cold and damp made it worse. They spent their time reading and playing with Budrow. Margaret helped at the communal kitchen and brought meals from the main table. On one of the rare days that the rain only threatened to burst through the squatting, grey sky, Eggert and Margaret took Budrow for a walk.

The village had grown to nearly 6,000, but most people knew Emerson's crew, as they were called. Eggert and his mate walked slowly through the market stalls and were greeted by name. Children and adults both stopped to pet Budrow, who would flip over on his back, exposing his belly. He could bark like a dog but laughed like a fox when he was excited. And it didn't take much for him to get wound up. He would run ahead of them and run back, traversing at least three times the distance the old couple walked.

They met Barry. He seemed to know everyone's name. Because of his professed ability to communicate with Mother, he was regarded by most in the central village as a holy man. When he spoke, people stopped and listened. Barry was overwhelmed with Budrow's exuberance. He sat on the plank-covered road and let the little animal run circles around him. Both Budrow and Barry laughed uncontrollably.

Eggert was introduced to Barry by Emerson, who warned him to watch out for the man. He said, "The citizens of Crow City accept Barry because he says the right words. They give him their trust because of who he says he is. But I am watching actions, and so far, I haven't seen any reason to trust Barry."

Eggert didn't want to get overfriendly with him; religion hurt his brain. He had heard from Elli that Barry was one of the refugees from the island and that, originally, he was weak and shifty but ducked out as soon as he heard about the quake. Elli didn't trust anyone, but mistrusted Barry more than usual.

Still, his playfulness with Budrow was infectious. Margaret began a tug-of-war with a branch, and Barry had a chance to stand up. He watched the two for a while, then said, "Margaret has a pure heart. The Mother can see her."

Eggert tried to ignore him. Barry continued, "I expect that she can see and hear Mother as well. It is a rare ability of which she should be aware."

Barry's speaking seemed wooden and unnatural, but he caught Margaret's attention. She gave Budrow a jerky treat from her pocket and asked, "What should I be aware of?"

Eggert sucked his teeth.

Barry said, "You have the gift."

"Why, thank you, Barry. That's nice of you to say. Do you want to walk with us? We're going to have a cup of tea and should get back to the North Quarter before the rain starts up again."

"Thank you," he said. Eggert sniffed and walked on ahead. "But Mother says it will not rain until tonight."

Margaret side-eyed him. They walked a few meters. He added, "Mother is never wrong, you know."

◆◆

The communal table, a massive oak block big enough for forty people, was nearly empty. They sipped their tea from mismatched ceramic coated tin mugs. Eggert sat on the end petting Budrow, pretending not to listen, picking burrs and twigs from the animal's fine hair.

Barry said, "The Mother sent me here to Crow City to lead all of her children. Marya and you clearly have the gift. I'm not sure yet about Little Chandler; he's young."

"How did you say you found Mother?" Margaret asked.

He grinned and set his cup down, leaning into the role of storyteller. He cracked his knuckles by bending his fingers backward, a habit that Eggert found as offensive as fingernails on a chalkboard. Barry's father tried to break him of it by hitting him with an old flyswatter, which created a degree of trauma in Barry as a boy. But since his rebirth, as he called it, he reveled in little rituals like that. Especially the ones that would have annoyed his father.

"I was near death. Mule saved me from a pack of wild wolves. I had dislocated my shoulder, sprained my ankle, and been ravaged by poison ants; I was covered with welts and sick with a fever, poisoned from some bad berries. I gave up."

"And?"

"I woke up in her cottage. She cared for me, fed me, and washed me. I slept most of the time, so she taught me in dreams. She showed me how to contact The Memories and ask questions. Here, let me show you."

They stood. Eggert's muscles twitched, but he resisted intervening. Barry hadn't done anything yet, even if Eggert felt the threat level rise. Barry knelt on a patch of dry earth.

He said, "Here, now you do the same." She knelt.

"Place your palms on the ground."

Margaret copied his actions, putting her hands flat on the earth. She felt a tingle and said, "Oh, am I supposed to feel something?"

Barry said, "Close your eyes and look up into the inside of your forehead, right above your brow. Tell me what you see?"

"It's black. I don't see anything."

"Keep looking."

A couple of people had stopped and were watching. A local woman, wearing a thigh-length linen dress over the traditional leggings, hiked up her skirt and knelt next to Margaret. She put her hands on the ground. Soon, several people had joined them, and a crowd had formed. Barry pretended not to notice. Eggert began to sweat; he fidgeted. The overwhelming urge to grab Margaret by the arm and drag her away nearly overtook him. Budrow began to growl, low in his throat.

Barry said, "Do you see anything yet? Maybe just a dot of light?"

Some of the others murmured. Margaret said, "I think so. Is it supposed to be, like, orange?"

"It can be anything you want, Margaret. When you see it, go through it."

Margaret didn't know exactly what Barry was asking her to do. Her Interface training was limited to oven adjustments. She had never gotten any advanced certifications that would have trained her in the focused use of her imagination. Still, she reasoned that if she tried to conjure the feeling of going into the pinpoint, something might happen.

And as she approached it, an iris of light opened like a soft lens. It was an entryway. She had to duck. The top of her head brushed the lintel which proved to be soft and spongy like moist rubber. When she passed through, all sounds from the outside world were sucked away in a vacuum. She stood in a round room. The walls were a soft blond color like weak tea. A small fire glowed blue in a brazier at the center of the room. Looking up, she saw the midnight sky, sprayed with a billion stars, revolving though the cosmos. She became dizzy and sat heavily on a pile of pillows.

"Hello, Margaret."

She heard the voice and looked around for its source.

"I'm glad you could make it." A wrinkled woman with burnt umber skin materialized before her. Her image looked to be arriving out of a fog, yet She was standing still, dressed in a natural linen dress embroidered with red and black symbols. Her hands were spotted and her fingers long with knobby joints, but her nails were short and clean with neatly trimmed cuticles.

Margaret was captured by her eyes. They were blue, and then green, and then brown. She felt her balance slip suddenly and tensed.

Mother's voice was close. "Relax, dearest." She fell into a dark pool.

When Margaret opened her eyes, Barry was staring into them. They were both on their hands and knees, surrounded by several others in the same position. Eggert stood next to her, his hand hovering above her shoulder.

Margaret asked, "Was that The Mother?"

Barry grinned. He said, "You know in your heart, Margaret."

◆ ◆

Later that evening, after the rain began again, Margaret tried to reconnect. She goaded Eggert into trying with her, but he claimed he felt and saw nothing. When they finished, she said, "I want us to remove our implants, Eric. How do we do that?"

"You know I can't, baby. I need to be able to fly Little Wing and help when Emerson needs me. But Plummer can remove yours, if you want. I'm sure. If that's what you really want." He knew removal was a tricky process in the well-equipped medical center at Enforcer headquarters in The City. But he didn't mention it. Plummer was a wizard, and Emerson trusted him. Eggert would too. Besides, Eggert loved Margaret and would have promised her anything.

◆ ◆

Rosco and Grendel sat in on the council. There was some objection, but the critics were persuaded to wait and see by India Tarn. Rosco had more experience with governing processes than many of the permanent council members. He had led the team that developed dynamic governance rules in Blue Hole. Although they didn't call it restorative justice, the system he created rested on the foundation of human value rather than order or commerce. He was a firm believer in the philosophy that no person should ever be sacrificed, and he'd dedicated his life to the practice of forming individual representative channels to facilitate direct governance. If they listened to him, they would have recognized a kindred spirit, but many believed the North Quarter people to be a threat. With the addition of yet another flying machine, they believed that threat was growing.

Of course, the people in Crow City had developed their own form of government, and Rosco would not challenge another group's sovereignty. It made him a unique volunteer because he could make decisions from a truly dispassionate attitude. But the people of Crow City didn't accept him. He was challenged at every turn. Grendel sat next to him, nodding, which made his opinions more meaningful for the women. But he got little traction.

Rosco was surprised to learn that there were more women than men in Crow City. Unlike the controlled genetic and reproductive habits of the "Middles" in The City, the population of the village was communally responsible for maintaining functional population levels. Being a group of intelligent people with a high degree of group consciousness, it was acceptable for women and men to have as many sexual partners as they desired. Couples and groups of people of all sexualities still formed lasting bonds and many became exclusive over time. But the acts of procreation in Crow City were much more open and unattached than the cultures of the past.

As a result, women, as the creators of life, were valued as individual members of society, and their opinions and attitudes were highly respected simply by nature of their being fully engaged humans. And yet, as Grendel brought up, "The citizens know that at the core, we are all people and that we are stronger together."

"Yeah," Rosco said, "and we are dead apart."

But Rosco and Grendel could see their opinions on the council weren't making a lot of difference. It was disheartening, even if that wasn't the reason they were doing it. In conversation with Emerson and Quinn, Rosco admitted, "I don't think we are going to fit in here. For me, the Interface is like another limb. I can't imagine living in a society where it was deliberately cut off."

Quinn said, "I have to agree. While the people of Crow City are creating a world where they try to avoid the mistakes of our recent ancestors, I can't agree with the lines they have drawn. There are no books here. Marya won't grow up in a world without books. I won't allow it."

"We can't stay in our Quarter," Emerson said. "There must be another way. Even with Interface technology, a group as small as ours can't survive alone."

Ana said, "Chandler did it."

Eggert replied, "Not alone he didn't. I helped Ciara and Chandler. Most of the homeplace was brought there by my shuttle."

"We have a shuttle. Two, actually."

"Yes," Eggert said, "but Chandler had a community of independent homesteads to draw upon, even if they were far away from each other. We are exposed and vulnerable."

Quinn said, "I'm uncomfortable here. But frankly, I was uncomfortable on the beach. It was beautiful, but I miss my apartments!"

Marya called from the other room. Quinn went to help her. When she left, they could feel the weight. Everybody was thinking the same thing. Everybody but Plummer, but he would go along with them as long as he was part of the family. They were eager to find a home. And somewhere else was calling; they just didn't know where.

◆ ◆

Elli and Grendel had been close, but they hadn't seen each other for more than six years. Elli had been nearly aphasic when she arrived at Blue Hole. Grendel could read the girl's damage as clear as she could see the triangle tattoo on Elli's hip—and she knew what it meant.

She and Rosco had a house of their own in the North Quarter. The Black Mariah was cloaked nearby. Once the rains ended, the humidity became overwhelming, never going below 90 percent. The locals called it "full of moist." When there were no official duties, it was too hot to do anything but sit in the shade and drink. Eggert and Rosco made whiskey, which was nearly pure alcohol, and they spent many afternoons soapy-eyed.

Grendel found Elli sitting topless in a puddle on the shady side of her house. The cement there was covered with moss which was always damp, making the temperature at least fifteen degrees cooler. She'd been sipping Rosco's hooch all afternoon. It was nearly four, and Elli Moon was zozzled.

Grendel said, "You look comfortable."

Elli held up her cup up. "I'm drunk and dirty, don't you know."

Grendel said, "Yeah, I hear you. I have a surprise. Can you walk?"

"Does a goose shit in the woods?"

Grendel looked at her, laughed, and helped her stand.

She slurred, "Are there geese anymore? Hey, where're we goin'?"

"Just hold my arm."

They walked out into the blinding sun. Steam rose off Elli's shoulders. After a few hundred meters, the trail turned downhill into the cooler forest.

Elli said, "Hooboy. That's a little better. At least I can see."

Grendel had to hold Elli's hand to keep her from sliding down the rocky embankment. As they went, Elli heard the waterfall.

"Oh, damn, Grendel. Water!" She began to run, hopping on one bare foot to pull off her shorts. Grendel walked. Her leg had not healed completely after the bombing in Blue Hole. She had to take it a little slower than her twenty-six-year-old companion. Elli's body was all muscle.

She rounded the corner and heard the splash as Elli cannonballed into the water. The hazy sun shone through the waterfall's mist and created tiny rainbows that wavered in the air and disappeared.

Elli surfaced with a hoot. "Ah, Grendel, you are my savior. Come, swim with me. The water is *fine!*" She let out a laugh and dove. It was refreshing to hear Elli's laugh.

Grendel didn't need coaxing. She was stripped down and in the water before Elli surfaced.

They bobbed and dove, swimming under the pounding waterfall. After they were cooled off, they explored the rock depressions behind the falls and collected tiny yellow flowers from the moist outcroppings. Clumps of grass and moss were perpetually wet by the falls.

The two women lay out to sun-dry on a huge slab of purple-grey shale. Elli drew spiraling designs on the smooth surface with her wet finger. Elli watched a crow cross the sky, high in the canopy. She said, "It seems like I haven't rested in a lifetime."

They rolled over on their bellies to dry their backs. Elli said, "I find men gross. I thought it was just because Michel forced me, and I just needed time to recover, you know? But I'm much more attracted to women."

Grendel sat but didn't speak. She noted the differences between their bodies: hers, sagging and scarred, skin loose but comfortable, like a worn caftan. And Elli's taut as a bowstring, not an ounce of fat on her with tiny breasts and wide shoulders. Her cheekbones were angled and red hair cut short. Grendel noticed the fine fuzz on her upper lip. When Elli stopped speaking, Grendel leaned over and kissed her.

Elli smiled. "I love you, too, Grendel."

Grendel's face was still close. She said, "I'm proud of you, girl. You are finally comfortable in your own skin. I remember you when you were more Mew Mew than Elli. Scared and silent and quick to fight."

They hugged.

Grendel went on, "You love whoever you want, girl. You can be attracted to women or men or nobody! It's your body for as long as you live in it. Do what you wish with it."

They hugged again. Grendel lay down on the warm rock with Elli on top of her, pressing her slight frame into Grendel's more voluptuous one. Elli cried into Grendel's neck, and Grendel kissed the tears away. They stayed there like that, as the sun sank and the breeze reversed up the mountain. Birdsong echoed through the valley as their bodies fused into one another.

◆ ◆ ◆

ELLI MOON

When Elli first moved to Blue Hole, she filled her days with a game she made up following different people around the village. The rules of her game were simple. Follow all day without being seen or caught.

After Blue Hole was decimated, Elli took on fighting, hunting, and guarding responsibilities. While they were trying to survive the first six years on the beach, she hardly had enough time to sleep, let alone fill idle time.

Six months after arriving at Crow City, Elli was bored and looking for drama. The village was calm. When people weren't getting hurt or sick, they ate and drank. Being uncomfortable with people, Elli drank alone. She began tailing people again for sport.

Since the days at Blue Hole, Elli had gotten an implant and become a proficient markswoman with various traditional and modern firearms. Her standard was the plasma rifle, but she loved her vintage .45-caliber Colt Buntline Special. The damn thing had a forty-cemtimeter barrel and kicked back so severely that she had to learn to fire with loose shoulders. She and Quinn crafted a leather holster for it that tied the barrel securely to her thigh. Elli had deadly aim with anything she touched. But with the Colt, she never missed. She said it was because there was no electrical interference. Ana called bullshit. Elli stood by her theory, and the proof was in her record. Since the first day, when she missed her first shot, she learned how heavy the weapon was and how to hold it. She never missed again.

Crow City was fairly safe for its regular citizens. Even so, the forest could be dangerous and weather in the village was unpredictable. Most wore some kind of weapon, though crossbows and knives were more common in the main village. Gunpowder had to be formulated, and the only gunsmith in the village lived in the Southwest Quarter. Pretty much, everyone was on their own. There were no police. The Crow City council didn't believe in behavior coercion. People were left to defend themselves or each other. Elli was never without her Colt.

She chose Brock as her subject. *My prey*, she thought. Partly because he posed a challenge and partly because she didn't like him. She learned from Chandler that the Brock family was an enemy to his in-laws, the Cokes. He never talked about it, and no one in Emerson's camp brought it up. It frustrated her, but she kept her thoughts private.

Elli followed him on a day when she didn't work. He went from the clinic to a café, to a knife shop, and home. He was almost as boring as the rest of Crow City. The next time she followed him, he visited a boarded-up house near the border of the Southwest Quarter. He stayed for an hour and went to the community table for dinner afterward, hung around listening to the drum circle for a while, and went home.

Brock visited the house once every two weeks. After a couple of months, she decided to see what was inside. At first, she tried looking in windows, but they were blocked inside and out. She went around back and hid, but no one came out, and no one went in. After coming back a few times, she decided that Brock visited at a prearranged time. The next time he went, she used Emerson's Interface scope to look into the momentarily open doorway.

She was shocked to see Brock shake Paxon's hand. They closed and locked the door; she checked it. Brock emerged an hour later. This time it was Anoush who let him out. She was naked. They embraced before he strode away. Elli went directly to Emerson and told him what she'd seen.

Emerson smiled. He said, "Yeah, they didn't leave. But they couldn't stay either. They couldn't contribute, and there is really nowhere to go, so Paxon set up a brothel. It only caters to outsiders. Apparently, the regular citizens of Crow City don't use prostitution. The business only caters to the displaced and the traumatized. The council knows about it."

Elli said, "What about Brock?"

"I guess he has a right to intimacy, too, even if he needs to make it transactional."

"I still don't trust him."

"I learned my lesson with your suspicions, Elli Moon. I say follow him all you like. I don't trust him either, but he has saved a number of lives since he arrived. It will be hard to convince anyone that he is dangerous."

"Well, the technology on The Black Mariah saved lives, and nobody wants that."

Elli continued tailing Brock. He was so predictable she almost quit. Besides going to the clinic, the café, and the brothel, he usually went home after getting his rocks off. But one time he surprised her. It was getting dark; she supposed that he didn't think anyone would notice. He left the village and went to the pine forest in the east.

She kept far back. It was unclear how good of a tracker he was, but it was obvious that Terrence Brock was highly trained. She trailed him until the moon rose. He removed a box from the trunk of a hollow tree. She used the scope on infrared. He unfolded an item in the box; she realized it was a phone. She used her Interface as an amplifier and listened in on the call but could only hear his side. It took a moment for her to connect, and by the time she could hear him, he said, "I love you," and closed the phone.

As he was returning, she stepped out of the brush with her hand on the hilt of the Colt. She said, "Give me a good reason not to shoot you dead right here?"

Brock was surprised but not shocked. He said, "My wife, Thilda. I can only speak to her at designated times. She's in prison, you see, and…" Tears welled in his eyes.

Elli said, "I'm touched, but that's not a reason."

"I guess I haven't got one, then. I left The City because I couldn't live that way anymore. But Thilda was jailed after I escaped. My brother smuggled a phone to a guard, and we make contact once a month. But she's sick now, and I don't know how long we can keep this up..."

Elli said, "It wouldn't be any of my business if I believed anything you say. But I don't. So why don't we go on back and tell Emerson all about it?"

She walked behind him, back to the village. She texted silently to Emerson:

```
I caught Terrence Brock with a satphone. We
           are coming to talk to you.
```

As they walked out of the woods, he said, "I'm the victim in all this. My wife is being held hostage. What would you do?"

Elli said, "I wouldn't do what you are doing."

As they stepped into the sun, Brock spun around behind Elli and pinched a nerve in her neck. She collapsed, and he ran back into the woods. By the time she woke, he was gone.

◆ ◆

Emerson and Quinn listened to her story. "It's possible that he was a spy for Lord Quinn."

"High *Lord* Quinn," Quinn added.

"Right. So, we need to be extra vigilant."

Elli was rubbing her neck. "Next time I'll shoot the bastard. Fuck!"

◆ ◆ ◆

THE FALL

Emerson came into The Black Mariah. Ana was working on a code problem, lost in thought. She looked like she was sleeping in the pilot's seat. Emerson sent her a nudge. She opened her eyes.

"Hey." He leaned over and kissed her cheek. Emerson and Ana didn't have an ongoing intimate relationship. They had been lovers long ago in Blue Hole. He was Little Chandler's father. They were partners in helping the community and raising LC, and Ana occasionally came to Emerson's bed.

"Hey," she said and held up the temporary implant disk. "I tested it, and it works. I want to bring Little Chandler to meet his great-granddad. You game?"

"Yeah, yeah, sure. Anytime, Ana. But I was really wondering, do you have the code for The Fall Simulation?"

Ana smiled. "You want to 'Fall' with someone, Emerson?" She raised her eyebrows seductively.

He blushed. He didn't know why. He and Ana had no secrets. But she could still embarrass him that way.

"I love to tease you, Emerson. You look like a little boy with his pants down. You're so *cute!*"

Emerson nearly turned away. "Thanks, Anastacia Moon. I love you too." He kissed the air.

"Who's the lucky girl? Oh, no. Let me guess. It's not Quinn, is it? No." She made an exaggerated face as though she was hard at thought. "It's Saą! You want to Fall with Saą." She grinned widely. Emerson didn't respond. "She is beautiful, in an earthy sort of way. No, unfortunately, The Fall was lost with Blue Hole. I have some of the working files, though. I can put something together. Give me an hour. I'll copy it on to a cube for you."

Once she began the process, she said, "That will be a second. Hey, wait. Does Saą need my temporary?"

"Saą has an implant. She's met Chandler."

"You really like her, huh? Even brought her to meet your grandpa. How's Quinn feel about that?"

"Oh, you know Quinn. She's an adult."

"I do know Quinn. I'll bet she is far from alright with this. Does she know what The Fall is? The version I have begins at the cliff." Ana stood up and began pacing. "I can't believe you aren't considering her in all this." She looked in Emerson's eyes. His cheek twitched.

She said, "You're not hiding from her, are you?"

"No. I don't know. There's nothing to hide."

"Yeah. And she feels the same?"

"Sure, I guess. How do I know what she feels?"

"Listen to yourself. Emerson, sometimes you can be an ass. You know she's not alright with you falling with a new woman. She might not want to, but she loves you, man. You need to talk to her before you do this. The Fall will change everything."

He put the cube in his pocket. They hugged. She whispered in his ear, "I'd Fall with you again anytime, cowboy."

He blushed but hugged her tighter so she wouldn't have the satisfaction of seeing. As he left, she called after him, "Maybe you should Fall with Quinn *and* Saą. Hey, maybe I can come too."

◆ ◆

Emerson said, "Quinn, remember that time you brought me to the Red Palace?"

She was brushing Marya's hair. "How could I forget? That's the day you met Boston, the son of a bitch."

Marya said, "Bitch!"

Quinn said, "That's right, honey. A female dog is called a bitch."

"So, your daddy is a dog?"

"Yup."

"But I like dogs. At least I like Budrow. But he's the only dog I know."

"It's just a saying, dear."

Emerson held up the silver Interface cube. He said, "I have something like it. It's called The Fall. Ana and I did it back in Blue Hole. I want to share it with you. With you and Saą."

"Is this a virtual sex thing, Emerson? 'Cause I've been a little busy lately, and I don't have time to play a game with you."

"Come with me. You'll love it. I want to experience it with you. No virtual sex."

"And Saą."

"Well, you said you liked her."

She rolled her eyes at him. "Alright, Tiger. Tell me when."

"How about tonight?"

◆ ◆

Saą was eager to do the simulation. Ana agreed to watch the kids. The three sat together in recliner seats in the main cabin of The Black Mariah. Emerson initiated the sim and entered. The gravity was different; the light was intense and had a golden tint.

He called, "Quinn, Saą? Hello? Are you here somewhere?"

The two women appeared at his shoulder.

Quinn said, "This is different."

"It's hyper-real."

Quinn said, "What do you mean by hyper-real?"

He opened a pocketknife and said, "Show me your wrist." He held her hand, palm down. "What do you think I mean?" He pulled the blade slowly across the flesh on the back of her wrist. She sucked in her breath. The skin peeled back and showed an intricate maze of patterns, like brightly colored revolving gears. Looking closer, she recognized the flow of energy moving up and down her arm. She flexed her fingers and watched the muscles and vessels move and pulse, sending out little bursts of light like miniature fireworks.

Saą said, "I like this place. It feels dreamy."

He winked at Quinn and said, "The fun is just the beginning."

When she looked back at her wrist, the skin knitted itself back together until it was just a thin scar, which faded as she watched. Quinn spent her youth inside simulations and games like the Red Palace. But nothing ever felt like this. This was real. It was nearly impossible to hold on to the thought that it was a simulation, and the feeling was so delicious that thinking about anything seemed like an unwanted distraction.

Saą brought Quinn's chin up and kissed her firmly. Her body felt as though it were filling with life, making her stronger and fuller. Saą looked the way Quinn felt: flushed skin, muscles rippling; the light reflecting off her hair in little swirling rainbows. Both women felt as though the atoms of their bodies were swirling around each other in a whirlpool of sensations.

Emerson pulled Quinn and Saą by the hand through the open French-style double doors and onto the thick grass leading to the sea. They held hands, walking barefoot across the dew-damp lawn. The surf pounded in the distance. Sea salt and iodine washed over them. They came to a smooth pathway at the end of the grass.

Emerson said, "When Ana brought me here, she didn't give me a clue. She tricked me into jumping to try and save her life. I can't do that to you, even if it means ruining the experience. I want you to hold hands with me and jump."

Though it looked from the house that the ocean began at the end of the lawn, in reality, the shore was at the bottom of a 100-meter cliff. There was a crumbly-looking edge about a meter wide between the walkway and the drop.

"This is your choice."

Quinn looked into Saą's eyes. She said, "This is real, even if I know it is a simulation."

Saą said, "Everything is real, Quinn. If it weren't, it could not be."

They stepped toward the edge and held hands. Quinn froze when she looked down.

Emerson said, "You don't have to."

Quinn said, "Yeah. Maybe next time, huh? I liked the other part, though. Yeah, thanks for that. But this, ah, no thanks…"

The earth beneath their feet gave way, and they fell.

Quinn's hair swirled around her head like a flame as they plummeted toward the rocks. She screamed, but no sound penetrated the wind. She looked down and went into shock, frozen, staring.

Emerson held his panic down. He knew that he was in a sim, but the body sensation was overwhelming. He glanced at Saą. She watched the horizon. Her face was relaxed. A toothy grin stretched it. She was not terrified; she was in ecstasy.

Emerson fought the fear. He was holding Quinn's hand, but she was limp, in shock. It threatened to overwhelm him. They fell toward the rocks. When he looked down, the ground sped towards him so fast that he had to look away, out over the ocean. The sun was setting, and in that moment, the red orb dipped just below the horizon, streaking the wisps of cloud with lavender and purple. For a millisecond he forgot that they were plummeting to their death. When he looked back at the ground, the rocks were right before his eyes.

The world went black and soundless. Slowly, a blue light grew around him. He heard his heart and felt his breath. It was slow and steady. He remembered the moment before hitting the rocks, and the terror shocked him, causing a fast, deep inhale. *Did that really happen?* he thought.

The room was lighter now; he was lying on a pile of pillows. He looked at his hands and wiggled his fingers. *It seems like my body*, he thought, suddenly stuck with the oddity of the thought. Why wouldn't he trust that he was in his own body? He suddenly wished he had a mirror and half expected one to appear in his hand.

Quinn moaned from the pile of pillows next to him. She stretched and yawned. They both sat up. Emerson remembered what had just happened. Emotions flooded him, and he began to cry. Quinn was more reserved, but she had tears in her eyes as well.

She said, "Did we just die together?"

She sat next to him and hugged him around the shoulders. He said, "Yes, I think we did, love."

He looked around the room. They were not in The Black Mariah. The walls were soft ivory and round. A fire crackled in a ring of round stones at the center, and, looking up, stars rotated around the twist of smoke drifting into the blue-black night.

Saą sat on a single pillow on the other side of the fire. She said, "Welcome to Mother's house."

Quinn said, "Is this part of the sim?"

A woman materialized next to Saą. They were was dressed in similar tanned-skin leggings and vests. She had long, grey, dreaded hair. Her eyes were black pools and her face a river delta of deep creases.

She smiled, showing a full set of perfect white teeth, and said, "Nope. Not a sim, Elli Rattlesnake Quinn."

Emerson said, "What did you think of The Fall, Saą?"

She said, "I want to do it again."

◆ ◆ ◆

MOTHER

"Hello, Emerson Lloyde. Chandler told me you'd come."

Emerson said, "You knew Chandler?"

"I know everyone, boy. I'm The Mother."

Quinn said, "What does that mean? Where are we?"

She picked a stick out of the fire and used the flame to light a clay pipe. She blew out a cloud of white smoke.

Inside the smoke, Marya was sleeping, Little Chandler was hugging her. Quinn began to cry.

Mother said, "It's okay, child. Everything is okay. As for where? We are nowhere. I am the place you came from. Did you think that because you stopped thinking of me, I had forgotten you?"

Emerson said, "Why are we here?"

"Because you can see, Emerson. You all can. You can see, and you can do. That is a rare combination, son."

Quinn regained her composure. "What do you want from us?"

Mother laughed. "I don't want anything, dear. But I am here for you, if you need me. I will never lie to you or be untrue. You only need to ask."

Quinn looked at Emerson and said, "This is a dream, or some part of that sim, right?"

He shrugged. "I've never seen this room before."

Sąą said, "It takes time to understand. Our minds have been trained for centuries to ignore the truth. You can't rush it."

When Quinn opened her eyes, she was in The Black Mariah, in a reclining seat, looking at the pulsing blue lights in the ceiling.

Emerson said, "That was different."

Quinn sat up and looked around. She said, "Where's Sąą?"

"I don't know."

"Was that real or a sim?"

"I think we'll have to wait and see, Quinn."

◆ ◆

Sąą remained with Mother after Quinn and Emerson returned to The Black Mariah. As she stood to leave, Mother put her hand on the younger woman's shoulder and looked into her eyes. Mother's eyes contained the depth of the universe. Sąą didn't hear Mother's words as much as feel them vibrate through her heart.

"The future is simply a set of causes and effects flowing forward from this moment. It is as changeable as the mind, which is to say that some people are more flexible than others.

"Stay close to Emerson, daughter, and direct the stream's course. But take my warning seriously. Interface technology requires more responsibility than the people can manage. You must understand this. The natural boundary to such powerful technologies was breached by the greed of men before it was disrupted by the collapse.

"Emerson needs to realize that the Interface must be protected at all costs. Hidden away and possibly destroyed. He will face this decision alone. You must be there to give him strength."

◆ ◆

That night, Emerson went to bed alone. When he woke up to pee after midnight, Quinn was sleeping beside him. When he returned, they made love.

As he was drifting back to sleep, she said, "I love you, Emerson."

◆ ◆ ◆

ATTACK

The next morning, just before dawn, Marya woke Quinn by holding her cheeks between her small palms and speaking close to her face. Emerson was gone.

The child whispered loudly, "I can go to the round room and talk to Mother too. That's why I had to sleep. Not 'cause I hit my head. So, you don't have to worry about that anymore."

Before Quinn could even focus on her daughter's face, the peace of the morning was shattered.

The roar of the gunships was deafening. The first low pass over the village toppled several incomplete buildings. The vibration shook the ground. There were six, small, armored shuttles outfitted with two forward rotary guns each that fired 100 antique M16 Vulcan missiles per second. They were old, but they were effective. Each rocket was twenty centimeters long with an exploding tip. They looked like miniature Flash Gordon rocket ships. The show of force was overwhelming. Hundreds of men, women, and children were brutally dismembered in ten minutes.

When the shuttles landed, the speaker systems on board announced, "THIS VILLAGE BELONGS TO HIGH LORD QUINN. RESISTANCE WILL NOT BE TOLERATED."

A hatch opened in the top of one shuttle, and an Enforcer in full battle gear used a plasma rifle to cut twenty people in half. Terrified citizens scattered. The other shuttles opened their doors, and rows of Enforcers emerged in lockstep.

The man with the plasma gun used his Interface to amplify his voice: "BRING ME EMERSON LOYDE AND ELLI RATTLESNAKE QUINN, OR I WILL LEVEL THIS ENTIRE SETTLEMENT."

◆◆

Emerson, Ana, and Elli made their way into the central square. They crossed several trenches of devastation where the rocket fire had torn the earth into troughs strewn with body parts and blood.

Emerson and Ana carried plasma rifles. Elli had the strange nuclear cannon she'd acquired at Outpost 212 in addition to the plasma gun slung across her shoulder and her long-barrel Colt strapped in its holster. Five of the six shuttles were parked in a row near the open area where drum circles and dances took place. A large fire burned in the central pit, and Enforcers sat or leaned on the wooden benches, drinking hooch, laughing, and smoking.

As Emerson crept behind them, he overheard one say, "They didn't mention that these people have no weapons. What a bloodbath."

Another said, "Shut up, idiot. It's bad enough The Authority can hear everything you think without you making it easy to mind-lock us both!"

Emerson texted Ana:

```
Stay here. Elli and I will take cover across
the square. On my signal, we take them out.
```

Ana said,

```
Kill them all? And what about the other
                gunship?
```

Emerson said,

```
            On my signal.
```

Ana couldn't reply.

Elli had only fired the cannon once. There was really nothing to it, just a bulky cylindrical case with a stubby barrel sticking out of one end and a handle with a trigger on the other. The gun came alive when Elli lifted it. She held it cradled in her arms, pointed at one of the gunships, and waited for Emerson's signal.

Emerson texted,

```
        Three, two, one.
```

Elli pulled the trigger. A red light lit on the top near the sight, and a whine rose from inside, shooting up the scale to a nearly deafening pitch before a ball of silver matter shot out of the barrel with a FUMP, hitting one shuttle. Static-like veins of electricity covered it accompanied by a sizzling sound. The ship vanished. A few sparks remained, snapping in the air, whizzing around like flies.

Ana and Emerson stepped up to the group of shocked Enforcers. She had switched on an Interface blocker which effectively cut contact between every man in the area.

Emerson shouted, "Drop your weapons! Get down on the ground! These are plasma rifles. One move and I will liquify your bones."

Elli turned her attention to the next ship, and the next, until they were all vaporized. Enforcers scattered. When she removed the vape from the captain's hand with the Colt, every Enforcer dropped to their bellies. Ana collected weapons. Citizens slowly emerged from buildings and behind walls. Elli and Ana tied the disarmed soldiers' wrists. They were marched off to prison in the Southwest Quarter.

Emerson spoke to the captain. Her name tag, Nelson, was sewn to the left breast pocket of her uniform. He said, "You are obviously finished. Tell me where the sixth shuttle is."

"What are you going to do?" Nelson asked. "Kill us?"

"The council will put you on trial. These people don't believe in killing, though after this, I wouldn't be surprised if they let the families of the dead tear you apart with their fingernails. Now tell me."

"I have no reason to talk to you."

Emerson said, "I have no reason to let you live." He brought the barrel of his rifle up, not quite pointing at her, but showing that it was there. The power gauge beeped. The meter showed red. "So? I don't have time to chat."

Plummer called on a voice channel. His gain was turned up too high, and it fed back in a screeching whine. He mumbled something about Marya.

Emerson said, "Turn down your volume. I can't hear you over the feedback. Where's Quinn? What the hell happened?"

"They took Marya!" Plummer replied. "Repeat, the Enforcer gunship has kidnapped Marya."

Emerson pushed the captain on her way and said, "We need to get back to camp."

Ana said, "Where the hell is Elli?"

They locked the Enforcers in the Southwest jail, and Emerson called Eggert, "Pick me up at the hardware store. I need to get back to camp, STAT!"

◆ ◆

Quinn had been overpowered; she wasn't hurt, but she was livid. "They only took Marya. We have to go, Emerson. We have to get her back. I know who took her. I'll kill the fucking son of a bitch this time." She broke down in tears thinking of Marya saying, *Your daddy's a dog?*

Emerson said, "The attack killed a lot of citizens. I am going to go look for Saą and see if we can help with the wounded. We'll go as soon as the village stabilizes."

"Fuck no, Emerson. What the hell is the matter with you? We need to go now!"

He resisted putting his hand on her arm and said, "We can't take The Black. She has the only triage. It's going to take some preparation to outfit Little Wing. We're not wasting time, babe. We'll leave as soon as it is possible."

Elli had dressed in her hunting gear; she looked like a wiry red-haired ninja with her black bandanna wrapped around her forehead. She went with Emerson and Plummer to the triage at the clinic. Pejeta and her helpers were run ragged. Brock showed up and went to work. Elli cornered him and said, "After this you are going to jail." The tall man nodded but said nothing.

Elli and Pejeta sewed wounds and set bones. Brock did amputations. Plummer did vascular reconstructions. They worked nonstop for twenty hours.

Coner lost his left arm. Toms and Tams had been caught in a building collapse and were feared dead. The recovery crews found Pamela P's body. She died shielding a child who survived without a scratch. They never found any trace of India Tarn. Brock worked on Anoush's wounds; he listed her as dead.

By the dawn of the next day, Emerson had arranged with Eggert to leave The Black Mariah in his care while it was being used as a hospital. He and Quinn would fly Little Wing back to The City to rescue Marya.

When he landed the smaller craft at the North Quarter, Saą was waiting, outfitted for travel with her sling and day sack.

Emerson said, "We are going to The City."

She said, "I know. I'm going with you."

◆ ◆ ◆ ◆

END OF PART THREE

INTERFACE

PART FOUR

THE RESERVOIR

After the attack, Rosco and Grendel helped organize the members of the council who were left. The level of fear and mistrust was nearly too much to work around, but Rosco knew how they felt. He also knew they needed help, even if they were in too much shock to realize that Emerson's crew were their allies.

Saą explained that she was helping a woman give birth when the gunships arrived. The new baby could see Mother in the room. It was powerful and miraculous.

Saą said, "There are massive changes coming. We are witnessing the birth of a new consciousness." Emerson was sure she was right, but he wasn't sure how positive the changes would turn out to be. He didn't have time to ponder it then.

Emerson asked Ana to create a special mass group simulation. It was a huge job, and he would need it before they left for The City. She worked on it with Plummer all night. Ana requested that Emerson open up access to the Chandler Cube for her, which he eventually did. The cube was specially protected, but, even so, Emerson was hesitant to let it out of his possession. He realized Ana and Plummer would need all the help available, so he reluctantly acquiesced. Plummer was able to clone it into his own neural circuitry, though he didn't tell Ana or Emerson. They completed the final test on the sim an hour before Emerson, Saą, and Quinn left.

◆ ◆

Once they were in the air, Saą retreated to her cabin. She could see the bond Emerson and Quinn had. Their years together allowed them to work from a single mind. The urgent need to act required them to focus. Saą could see and understand what they were doing. She would be a distraction, so she made herself invisible.

When Quinn learned that Pam was dead, she locked herself in her cabin and wouldn't come out until Emerson told her they were leaving. Getting into her harness, she said, "That man does not deserve to live." She didn't say another word until they reached the opposite side of the Inland Sea and found a place to land the shuttle outside of the security zone two days later. They planned to rest there and work out the remainder of their plan. They were still several miles from the edge of The City.

And once there, they would still have to figure out a way across the body of water that Emerson's parents died on when he was a toddler, leaving him alone on a sinking boat. Quinn said, "I have a plan, but you aren't going to like it."

The reservoir was a huge lake protected on two sides by cliffs and by The City's west wall on the third. The majority of it stretched out toward the Inland Sea. It provided fresh water for the entire population. There was a maze of maintenance tunnels under Founder's Quarter in the northern part of The City. When The City was carved out of the rock of the hillside, the builders used the tunnels for access. The entrance opened out to a small jetty extending into the water and was sealed by iron bars. Quinn intended to enter The City at this point, but they would have to cross the water to get there.

Quinn explained that the water's surface was patrolled by drones monitored by a team of operators. Unbeknownst to Quinn, the positions were not being filled as regularly as they should of late. Partly because the department was terminally disorganized. But High Lord Quinn's control measures made the population noticeably preoccupied. They required more supervision, and the increased stress took up a huge part of everyone's attention.

The citizenry's impairment didn't always exhibit itself as slowness or a difficulty in performing tasks; sometimes it displayed itself in emotional crisis. Other times, it made the host physically sick. With jobs like security and policing, the pressure disrupted continuity and made the protection it was supposed to provide porous. Consequently, essential operations like the drone-monitoring processes had unexpected gaps. On top of the problems with the general population, the Enforcers' internal regimentation was deteriorating for the same reasons.

Quinn knew nothing of this. For her entire life, The City was run by experts, people who put their heart and soul into their jobs. When she was a kid, the general citizenry of The City believed that all hands were required for survival and that everyone was guaranteed a place in the whole. Most of the Middles that she'd known truly believed they were supporting each other communally, even though the Lords and their families lounged in actual towers above them, living opulent lives off their sweat and labor.

Quinn's plan was to find a boat and cross the reservoir to where the old engineering tunnels opened onto the water. There was a ruined marina on the western shore. They would certainly be able to find a suitable boat. After that, it would be easy to get to Lord Quinn's apartments without being noticed. Once they had him, he would lead them to Marya. The two hitches in the plan were the security drones and a boat.

Saą arrived with a cup of tea.

He said, "You know, Quinn, I have an aversion to water as it is. And this water is the seed of my fear. So, the idea of sitting out in the open in some ancient boat seems a little too much like a reoccurring nightmare to me. Besides that, we would need a way to propel it." He paused to catch his breath. When Emerson got going, he sometimes forgot to breathe.

"But as we discovered by accident on the Inland Sea, Interface Industries corporate shuttles float. I bet we can use the main fuel tanks as ballast and make Little Wing sink and surface on command."

Quinn said, "I'm no engineer, but didn't we nearly flip over? I remember something about poor Mule hitting the ceiling. Won't we need some sort of stabilizers?"

Saą said, "Fins. If you watch fish, you learn how they swim."

Emerson's eyes seemed to turn inward. They were open, but he wasn't seeing through them. It was same look that stole over Chandler when he was gripped with an idea for a new machine or program.

"Fins!" he said to no one.

He opened a design space in Little Wing's Interface computer and made a few drawings. He showed Quinn and Saą and said, "If I repurpose the side shutter servos as motors, I can make a dorsal for the top, and two pectorals for the sides. Hopefully, that will be enough to keep us upright. We'll run the shuttle on Eggert's auxiliary tank and use the main tanks for ballast."

It took a couple of days to outfit Little Wing. Emerson mashed his fingers more than once. Near 6 p.m. on the second day, a light rain started. By sunset, all three were soaked. They tested the fins and the ballast pumps after dark; Saą held a halogen torch. The wind had picked up. As Emerson closed the hatch, a branch the size of a man slammed into the hull and broke into pieces. He closed the door just in time to avoid a shower of hail. The rattling on the outside of the hull was deafening, like they were being buried by stones.

While they dried their clothes on the back of the main cabin seats, Emerson cooked a pot of groats in the microwave. The noise of the hail receded. Saą and Quinn toweled their hair dry. All three wore white maintenance jumpsuits.

Quinn said, "These are pretty stylish." She spun around like a model and shook her ass. "Maybe we should wear them when we break in."

Saą looked at her, expressionless. She said, "I can't stand this material against my skin. No, thank you. I'd rather go naked." She took the coveralls off and folded them neatly.

Emerson said, "Wow. I didn't see that storm coming. But we'll be safe inside. I suggest we get some sleep and start early tomorrow." There was murmured agreement. They shut down the lights and went to retreated to their respective cabins.

Emerson woke suddenly. Sitting up, he smacked his head on the low cabinet over his bunk. The siren blared. He opened a monitoring screen, but all the sensors were blank. It seemed like a problem with the batteries. Saą and Quinn met him in the cockpit. Emerson shut off the alarm and tried to run a diagnostic. The power shut down. The cabin went dim.

He said, "The emergency lighting and ventilation will last for ten minutes." There wasn't enough auxiliary power to even try starting the reactors.

Saą said, "What then?"

"Then we'd better get the doors open, or we will suffocate in the dark."

◆ ◆

Emerson plugged a temporary power supply into an Interface jack near the main hatch and tried to open the door. It opened a few centimeters and jammed, chattering for a moment before the auto sensor sealed it shut. Emerson used the power supply to activate the exterior cameras. Each one showed featureless static.

"What does this mean, Emerson?" Saą said.

Quinn answered, "He's working on it. He'll tell us when he knows. But my guess is that we're iced in."

Emerson said, "Mmm." His eyes were unfocused, looking inward.

Quinn added, "And if I'm correct, we can't start the reactors, which is the only way to charge the batteries. They are probably plugged with ice."

Saą said, "So we need to go out and clear them, correct?"

"Except that the doors are frozen shut, so we have to wait."

Emerson came out of his daze. The top and side hatches opened a few centimeters each. Cool, fresh air sifted in. He lit a halogen lamp and set it on a seat in the center of the cabin.

"Now we wait." He sat and put his boots up on the back of the seat in front of him. "As soon as the sun comes up, the ice will melt, and we can charge the batteries."

They didn't have long to wait. Except, when the ice began to melt, the shuttle slipped, throwing everyone against the wall, which had temporarily become the floor. The shifts didn't stop there. Before they could get strapped in, the shuttle tilted again. This time, it slid off a loose mud embankment and fell, nose first, into a fresh sinkhole. Everyone was thrown to the front of the ship. Little Wing became wedged in between the rocks, and water poured in through two open hatches.

Emerson manually shut the hatches. "Get strapped in. This ride's not over…"

They felt like they were going over a chute in a barrel. Quinn had to grab hold of Saą's arm to help her get a seat. The craft hit several large, hard objects, rattling the fuselage and battering anything not tied down. The halogen lantern went out after the second hit.

Little Wing streamed down a mud waterslide in the dark. They shot along a newly formed canal of frothing brown water. The large objects they rammed into were mostly uprooted trees and forest-floor debris churned up in the landslide. One loud impact came from a chunk of limestone bedrock which ripped a six-meter-long gash in Little Wing's underbelly.

The slide ended abruptly, depositing the shuttle on the broad floodplain at the edge of a tall grass marsh. Miraculously, everyone seemed okay. It was dark inside the shuttle. After a moment, Emerson unstrapped and tried the hatch. No response.

Emerson had to use a flat bar to manually open it. The craft was level, more or less, rolled partly on its side, away from the hatch. He climbed out and jumped down. Saą and Quinn followed. Emerson inspected the gash.

The sky was a swirl of pink and grey with the cerulean blue of morning peeking through the thinning clouds. The breeze was light and dry.

Saą said, "It will be cool here in the night. Even though tonight will be clear. I'm going to go search for wood."

"I'll go with you, Saą." Quinn threw her a plasma rifle. "We have no idea where we are."

Saą said, "I have some idea. But the gun is a good idea. We are going to need to eat, too."

◆ ◆ ◆

MEANWHILE IN CROW CITY

The temporary council, including Rosco and Grendel, passed judgment on Brock—he was subdued with an herbal extract and put into prison in the Southwest Quarter until they decided his permanent fate. Many people wanted him dead.

At his hearing he said, "Lord Quinn forced me to betray you by torturing my sweet, sweet Thilda. Do what you want to me, but please make a place in your hearts for her if Emerson is successful in bringing her here."

And of course, the peaceful, tolerant, people of Crow City screamed for blood. "It's the way of trauma," Saą would later say. "It gets passed around like a hot potato, reenergized by shame and rebounded by guilt." Barry stood on a table in the public meeting space and tried to tell them Mother's way of forgiveness, and many stopped and listened. But after a few days, when the initial shock wore off, after people buried their dead, a huge fire was lit in the square to signify rebirth, and a feast was prepared to celebrate the lost people's lives.

Food preparation for the ceremony took days. Margaret and Eggert worked alongside Polly and her helpers. Elli hunted with Mule and brought back more than her share of game. The hunters found several elk and processed them. The farmers brought the best summer vegetables, nuts, and roots. The milkers separated cream from milk, and the children made butter.

When the drumming began after sunset, twelve days following the massacre, it came in sparse and uncoordinated from several separate pockets. By the time the Full Buck Moon rose that night, 100 drummers played in unison, creating intricate side rhythms that combined and syncopated with the deep core.

And the people danced. They call it dancing with abandon, but the people of Crow City were dancing to abandon. More and more citizens joined until it seemed the whole village was undulating together. They danced to exhaustion, until they collapsed. Until their grief became exuberance. Until the trauma began to find a way out of their bones.

The tables overflowed with every food imaginable, from roasts to stews, plain steamed greens to complex soups, and every kind of nut, fruit, berry, and melon they grew. The celebration went on for days. The food and drink never ran out, and the drumming never ceased. During all that time, the survivors stood one by one and remembered the dead. Everyone told stories about their lost brothers and sisters, daughters and sons, mothers and fathers. The loss touched everyone. Everyone participated and was accepted. Except the men in prison. Terrence Brock was lucky there were bars keeping the citizens out.

It would not happen overnight. It would take years, and maybe the people of Crow City would never be completely healed, but the weight would be borne. As long as they drummed, and danced, and remembered.

♦ ♦ ♦

OUTPOST 212 REVISITED

While Emerson walked around the shuttle, which looked a little like a beached white whale, grumbling about the damage, Quinn and Saą went into the forest to search for firewood and game. The marsh began where the woods ended at the beginning of a steep incline. Mudslides had given way to several spontaneous rivers, cutting ravines of churned-up earth and stone like veins in the hillside. Little Wing rested a thousand meters from one such tributary, though by then the flood had dried to a trickle.

Quinn waved to Emerson as she and Saą stepped into the line of trees. He was distracted and didn't see. She thought to send a text, but her Interface was offline. As long as the computers on Little Wing were down, she would remain disconnected.

Saą felt the loss as well, but for her it was a different sensation. For the first time since she was implanted, she was able to feel the subtle connection to The Memories without having to focus. The Interface didn't block her connection to Mother, but it competed with it. Now that the implant was dormant, she could see and feel just how much interference it caused.

Quinn switched on a portable power supply, and both women were immediately connected to one another and the plasma rifles. Quinn said, "We can stay in contact as long as we are no farther than 100 meters."

They were climbing through the trees on a narrow trail. Conversation quieted. Saą said, "I enjoyed the increased awareness I felt when my implant was off."

Quinn took a moment to respond. She leaned against a fir tree to catch her breath and said, "You can turn your implant off any time you like, but the gun won't work if you do."

"This is not a hunting weapon. It is a defense tool. I can hunt more efficiently when I am connected to the earth."

"True," Quinn said. She began climbing again. "Just be sure you can turn it on when you need it. Even you can't run from a grizzly."

They decided to collect wood on the way back. Near the crest of the hill, Saą indicated a depression in the ground near a large rhododendron. They made a nest and waited.

Saą texted Quinn:

I saw signs of a burrow. I believe there is a rabbit den nearby.

The wind picked up after an hour or so. Saą sniffed and said, "I smell a predator."

"Rabbits are not predators."

"I know."

A sudden rustling on the opposite side of the brush startled them. Saą stood to see, and a large, orange-and-white striped tabby cat strolled around the corner with a large hare in her mouth. She was easily the size of an adult coywolf, at least twenty kilos. She dropped the rabbit, which twitched once and lay still.

"She looks just like Mule," Quinn said.

"She's smaller and missing the tip of her ear."

The large cat rubbed against Saą, nearly knocking her over. Quinn put her hand into the animal's thick neck fur. She began to purr—the normal fifty-five hertz rumble of a house cat, but louder.

Quinn said, "I don't think I've ever heard Mule purr. At least she was never that loud."

The cat froze suddenly and stared off into the woods. She leapt away and disappeared into the brush. Saą said, "We have a hunting partner."

◆ ◆

Back at the shuttle, the wind had picked up. Emerson went back inside to inventory his repair supplies. He knew he didn't have what he needed. But first he needed to put Little Wing back online.

The auxiliary reactor was functional. The conduits that controlled the mains were shredded. He began a list. Once the core batteries were recharged, he was able to test the reactor and run some diagnostics. But without repairing the cables and conduit, Little Wing could not fly.

He noted that the servos for his homemade fins had been torn away in the mudslide. The outer shell of the shuttle was ripped up, but it would self-heal if he could cover the holes up with temporary patches. The problem was he didn't have any. Once the computers were back online, he could communicate with Saą and Quinn.

He plotted their position using what was left of the GPS system. The Black Mariah had a navigation system based on the earth's magnetic core which was more reliable. From what he could figure, they were only eighty kilometers from Outpost 212. While that was good news in regard to getting the parts they needed, it was bad news as well. The Enforcers patrolled this close in. If they could not disguise the shuttle, they might be found and captured.

Quinn and Saą returned with the rabbit and a pallet of dried branches. Soon the animal was roasting on a quickly made spit. Meanwhile, they cut and collected pine boughs and used them to cover Little Wing.

Emerson said, "As an Enforcer, when I patrolled the outskirts of The City, we never cared about individual fires and camps. There are many independent people roaming these forests. As long as the shuttle is disguised, we won't draw attention."

As it was, nobody flew near them the entire time they were there.

Emerson explained that they should be able to get the parts they needed from Outpost 212.

They set out in the morning.

The outpost was west of where the shuttle rested. They followed the forest, along the edge of the marsh. Each had a plasma gun and a day sack. Quinn wore Max's wool stretch hat and Emerson his double-breasted peacoat. Saą had a buffalo-skin jacket with the fleece turned inside out. Instead of her leggings, she wore elk-skin pants.

Just before noon, Saą felt a presence. She said, "Someone is following us."

Emerson and Quinn turned around just as a large orange-and-white striped cat stepped out of the forest. A moment later, another cat of similar size, with black-and-white markings, emerged to walk beside the first cat. They were both huge with ice-blue eyes.

The cats sat before Quinn, Saą, and Emerson like they were petitioning the king. Emerson extended his hand palm down, and the orange cat put her head under it.

Saą said, "This is the same cat that brought us the rabbit."

Emerson said, "This is one of Mule's kits. I recognize the missing ear tip. She lost it to a sibling in a vicious mock-battle when she was a kitten the size of a normal housecat."

"Do you recognize this other one?" Quinn said.

"Never seen a black-and-white one before."

The cats followed them at a distance; sometimes Quinn saw them. Other times, they disappeared for hours. Near dark the first day, the orange cat, which Saą had named Nimue,[1] returned with a brown bird of

---

1   Pronounced Nim-Wah

some sort. Ten minutes later, the black-and-white cat showed up with a couple of squirrels.

Emerson said, "I guess it's time to set up camp."

◆ ◆

The following day, just before the shantytown surrounding Outpost 212 came into view, Nimue and her consort, whom Quinn was calling Romeo, vanished. A few minutes later, the humans were walking down the muddy main path. It would be a stretch to call it a street. The Fly Saloon was abandoned. It squatted at the opposite end of town, across from the tomb-like block bunker of the actual outpost. A shuttle occasionally landed or took off. The paths were empty except for the occasional pedestrian, stumbling along the wood plank sidewalk, trying to avoid the mud.

Emerson said, "Something ain't right."

Quinn set her gun to yellow. "No shit."

As they walked toward the saloon, a figure in the shadows caught Emerson's attention with a hand motion.

When Emerson turned to him, he whispered, "Git da fug offa the street before the fuggin Enforcers shoot off yer dick, ya idjit!"

A short, black crossbow arrow appeared in the wood post near Quinn's head.

"Down!" Emerson yelled.

A volley of similar arrows peppered the stall behind them. The voice from the shadows said, "Dissa way."

They scrambled between shacks and emerged in an alley. The shadow man turned and extended a hand. "You're Emerson Lloyde. Remember me? I'm Splinter! Cummon."

They followed him through a maze of narrow alleys and around tarp-covered boxes. As they walked, Emerson said, "Sure, I remember you. You helped Elli and me the last time I was here."

Splinter pulled open an oilskin door flap and ushered them inside. He lit a lamp with a carbon-embedded wick, and the room was illuminated with sun-bright light.

Splinter's mate, Mira, brought in a flask and passed it to Saą. She bowed her head and said, "I can see The Mother on you, girl," and handed her the hooch.

Emerson said, "This is Saą." She nodded in reply. "And this is Quinn." Mira said, "Pleased."

Saą took a ceremonial sip and held the vessel up to the Goddess for a moment, honoring the deities that Mira and Splinter worshiped.

Emerson had a sip, as did Quinn. He told them about Crow City and Lord Quinn's attack and the kidnapping.

Splinter explained, "After Eggert visited, an Enforcer platoon raided the Fly and shut it down. The Enforcers patrol day and night. There's a sundown curfew. They arrest people. We never hear from them again."

Emerson explained the parts he needed. Splinter had several. He could fabricate the rest except the temporary healing patches for the rips in the fuselage. "We gonna have to git them from an Enforcer. And that's beyond my talents at the moment."

"What happened to Magg? She used to know how to get anything."

Mira said, "They say she was abducted. That Lord Quinn had her brought to The City. But I heard that she got away. That she went into hiding and is rallying an army to take back the saloon."

"Poppycock." Splinter spat. "That's a load of bullshit, and you know it."

"I don't know, Splinter. The stories keep hope alive."

Emerson added, "If we can't get the patches, we are stuck."

Quinn said, "There might be a way. Do you think you can find the parts in the outpost building?"

"I used to work there. I know that building inside and out."

Saą said, "I might be able to get you in there, but you have to know where you are going and get out quickly."

Emerson said, "What are you suggesting?"

"I have a plan."

◆ ◆

"No fucking way. That's too risky."

"You have a better idea?"

"Than to walk in there with you projecting some sort of glamour over me so these highly trained Enforcers will simply look the other way? You have to be kidding me."

Saą said, "Mira, may I project a glamour on you to show Emerson how it works?"

"Sure," Mira said, "but I gotta warn ya, you cain't hypnotize me. Nobody in mah family is susceptible."

Saą said, "Thanks." She closed her eyes and hummed a middle-range note. After a moment, she raised the pitch. A second later, she raised it again and stopped.

She said, "Mira, this is Emerson. He is a senior Enforcer officer. He wants to ask you some questions."

Mira dropped to her knees with her head bowed. The color drained from Splinter's face. Saą touched Mira's forehead and said, "It's okay." Mira was shaking and sweating.

"Whot just happened?" Splinter asked.

Saą said, "I just proved my point."

◆ ◆

Quinn stayed behind at Splinter and Mira's stall. Saą and Emerson went to the outpost building. At the main doors, she closed her eyes and created the illusion.

"Okay, Emerson. Go get it."

He was apprehensive.

"Go. Go on! These glamours don't last forever."

Emerson entered the building through the double glass doors. He saw his reflection as he entered. A high-ranking Enforcer office he was not, but each person he met froze at attention until he released them with a salute. He texted Są and Quinn:

`I guess it's working...`

The parts department was on the third floor. Emerson arrived at the desk and told the clerk what he was looking for. The clerk, Enforcer Private Munday, looked up the number via Interface and cast the listing to Emerson.

But because Emerson's Interface was logged into his own server, he was not able to receive data from the Enforcer network. He pretended that he could see the listing and nodded.

The clerk said, "There's seven in stock, sir."

He would need at least twenty to make the repair; he would have to make do. The clerk gave him the patches and asked him to sign off, which was also an Interface process that he could not access.

While he was trying to figure out what to do, the pilot of a surveillance shuttle landed and arrived at the desk. He looked at Emerson and did a double take.

"Hey," he said, "you're Emerson Lloyde."

Emerson froze for a moment, looking side to side. The scene would have been comical if they weren't about to imprison him. Another pilot entered the building from the roof. Emerson looked past him to the landing pad outside the glass doors.

A whooping alarm sounded, deafening everyone.

Emerson ran out to the landing pad before the glass doors could swing shut. A shuttle waited, refueling at the end of the platform. He sprinted toward it. A group of Enforcers appeared behind him and took aim with their crossbows.

Emerson stopped, looking for a way to escape. The officer that recognized him called out, "You're trapped, Lloyde. Give it up."

Emerson put his hands up. An Enforcer walked toward him while others kept their weapons trained on him. Just as the Enforcer reached him and began to tie his wrists, he heard Quinn shout, "Emerson, duck!"

Her plasma pulse sliced their crossbows in half; parts clattered to the floor. Quinn grabbed his arm and pulled him to the refueling shuttle. Their Interface implants registered automatically to the ship's network, allowing Emerson complete control. The hatch sealed, and the reactor screamed as they shot off the roof. The fuel line hose tore off and flapped behind them as the shuttle disappeared. Luckily, there were no other shuttles to pursue them, but they had definitely given up the element of surprise.

Once in the air, she said, "Saą did a glamour on me so I appeared as my father. Everyone looked at the floor when they saw me. I was able to walk right in."

Twenty minutes later, they met Splinter, Mira, and Saą at the edge of the forest.

There were hugs all around. Mira said, "If you ever need anything, just ask." They were back at Little Wing before midnight.

Emerson was able to salvage what they needed from the stolen shuttle, and the spare parts contained enough healing patches to save some in reserve. They salvaged the right front landing arm to replace the damaged one and locked the Interface computers so even if their parts shuttle was found, it would be bricked. They stripped anything usable from the supply lockers and covered the ship in brush. Emerson marked the geolocation before they left. The shuttle would be there for them if they needed it.

It took a few days to fix Little Wing and rebuild and test the fins.

◆

Before dawn the following day, Emerson flew Little Wing in silent mode to the edge of the reservoir and hovered.

Quinn said, "The drones fly a few meters above the surface in a grid formation; you can never be sure where they will be. But their weapons are short-range, and no one drone has much ammunition. So, we should be able to dive beneath the surface before they see us."

Emerson opened the ballast tanks, tested the stabilizer fins, and said, "Here we go." He tipped Little Wing's nose to the water and dropped. The shuttle slipped into the dark liquid with only a small ripple. Thirty seconds later, a security drone zipped by.

"I am guessing everything is okay," Saą said. She looked unsure. It was a new look for her.

Quinn said, "We'll know if anything goes wrong. The shuttle notifies all passengers of an impending catastrophe."

"That makes me feel so much better."

Emerson said, "All systems appear to be operating within spec. It's hard to tell. Little Wing was not built to go in the water, and she hasn't been subjected to more than rain in her entire history. Your guess is as good as mine."

"I estimate we are halfway across," said Quinn. "Here's where I believe the tunnel entrance is." She made a mark on the display map.

"You don't know where it is?" Emerson asked.

Quinn said, "I'll find it."

"We don't have an unlimited supply of oxygen, Quinn."

"I can find it. Don't worry."

"Have you ever been to this place?"

Quinn walked away. Saą said, "You didn't have to do that."

"What?"

"You love her. You should trust her."

Emerson called back, "Probably about two more hours of air here, that's all I'm sayin'."

Saą shook her head.

◆ ◆

The security monitoring crew from that morning was shorthanded, as usual. The lead officer, Calib Stern, called out sick with a herniated disk. He'd twisted his back helping his pod-sister move into his house. His pod-mate, Sylvia, quit working and spent most of her waking hours playing Mashup, a new simulator that allowed its participants to combine the bodies of more than one extinct animal and interact with them in a virtual world. There were few rules—if you crossed the wrong player, you would be ejected. Ejected players didn't return. Only the most powerful could eject people, but it kept everyone else in line.

Sylvia was trying to get that sort of power, but she didn't have the intellect for it. Eventually, players like her suffered breakdowns and couldn't get clearance to play *any* games. It made Sylvia's stress levels peak. She was no longer present in the day-to-day tasks of running the pod. She stopped washing and was only surviving by drinking plain mushroom nutrients—the raw materials for replicator food. In the past, The Authority would have stepped in and modified her behavior, but citizens were left mostly to their own these days. As long as they didn't interfere with the lords or their plans.

Calib hoped his sister would be able to help out, but he didn't have the time to get anyone to help him move her, and he tried to do too much. He was in bed for a week. His team was one person short anyway; now they were down by two. Four people could not effectively patrol the reservoir, which should have been a big assist for Emerson and his crew.

But the four cadets that were in the terminal room that day were really only first-years, and they were bored. Without supervision, they were normally prone to screw things up. Today, the boredom bordered on deadly.

Calib asked his superior officer to look in on them once or twice a day, but Crane was sporting an epic hangover. It would be miraculous if he performed any of his own duties, let alone help Calib. He said, "Yeah, yeah," and disconnected.

The "cadets" were on their own.

Martin Greer, Ted Asa, Beverly Matts, and Phill Laurie never saw any action. The security monitoring terminal room was where Enforcers went to languish and die. They had all been sent there because of similar behavioral problems: a lack of foresight and executive function. Why they were all assigned to Calib Stern was a mystery, but there was an overall cognitive decline in The City, so there it was.

Matts saw it first. She said, "Holy shit, guys, look at this." They crowded around her external display which was divided into six blocks. Each was a video feed from the point of view of a drone, essentially the same hue, color, and texture, rushing by at the bottom of each block. Each box was nearly the same.

"What the fuck, Matts?" Greer smacked her on the back of the head.

"No wait, look. There." She pointed at the screen.

In the segment at the bottom of one box was a large white fish. Its tail and fins wavered slightly in the current as it sped just a few meters beneath the surface.

Laurie said, "Well. Fuck me running."

Asa said, "Shoot it."

Matts offered no resistance. There was no debate. She picked up the targeting set on her Interface and shot three of the drone's missiles into the back of the huge white fish.

◆ ◆

The projectiles went through the outer hull and into Little Wing's rear cabin and made dents but were not strong enough to penetrate the floor. The cabin began filling with water. Emerson got the notification and went back to check. He called Quinn, and together, they applied quick patches to the holes. Within a few days, the ship's skin would heal. By the time they returned, Eggert wouldn't even be able to find marks. Emerson accelerated. To the monitoring station, it looked as if the big white fish vanished. Emerson vacuumed up the water and checked the patches.

Back in the cockpit, he explained what happened. As he slowed, the shuttle began to drift. He said, "They must have damaged the right pectoral. We are going to have to fix it before we get near the shore."

They surfaced and opened the top hatch. Emerson climbed up, but he nearly lost his balance and fell to his hand and knees. He got a quick look at the fin but heard an approaching drone, scrambled back through the hatch, and submerged.

"I will need both of you to look out. I should be able to fix the fin quickly, but we have to dive if a drone shows up."

Saą stood at the bow and Quinn at the stern using an Interface scope. Emerson hooked a tether from his belt to a ring on Little Wing's fuselage using carabiner clips. He slid down the hull to the pectoral fin and used an epoxy pack to re-glue the servo, allowing the line to hold his weight while he worked. He used his Interface connection to do a quick test.

Saą said, "Drone."

Emerson was satisfied that the fin was repaired and began climbing back up. At the top, Saą was down inside, and Quinn was waiting by the hatch. Emerson's carabiner jammed.

He said, "Be ready to dive."

Quinn said, "What the fuck, Emerson?"

They could hear the drone buzzing.

"Get inside now!"

She gave him a lingering look but jumped down into the ship. The hatch snapped shut. Emerson accelerated and dove at the same time. His body was pulled to the end of the tether where he bounced off Little Wing's skin and dangled, spinning and semiconscious, in the wake of the speeding shuttle.

The Interface was designed to overcome the rigors of quantum acceleration which was several orders of magnitude greater than the fastest Little Wing could ever go. Even though Emerson was nearly unconscious, he was still in control. He sent Quinn and Saą a message to monitor the surface for drones.

The terror of being pulled down into the dark water with no control paralyzed Emerson's body. His mind retreated into a room of memories in order to survive. He found himself sitting at a luncheonette counter he'd seen in a book on art deco style once. It was Woolworth's in the mid-twentieth century. His mother, Deborah Soo, and father, Mark Lloyde, sat on either side of him. His mother took a sip of coffee and left a red lipstick print on the rim of the thick white china cup.

His father emptied a paper packet of Domino Sugar into his black coffee and stirred it with a chrome spoon. The tinkling of the metal on porcelain was loud and distracting. The scene was surreal and at the same time as natural as a spring day.

Mark said, "We didn't mean for you to watch us die out there."

Deborah Soo put her hand on Emerson's wrist. His shirt was wet. She said, "We made a terrible mistake, and you paid the most for it, son. We love you, always. We were trying to give you a better life."

Emerson wanted to hold her trembling hand and tell her that he was alright. Chandler raised him, and he knew they loved him. But tears choked him. He opened his mouth but couldn't speak.

An instant later, Quinn gave the all-clear, and they surfaced.

Saą pulled his limp body up onto the ship and lowered him down the hatch. Just before it closed, Quinn saw where they were, less than 100 meters from the shoreline with the wall of The City glittering golden in the sunset above it.

Emerson submerged the shuttle to keep them hidden. Then he turned to his side and vomited a lungful of water on to the floor. Saą and Quinn rubbed his body and turned the cabin heat up to thirty-three degrees.

Quinn said, "I guess you have bested your fear of water, considering that this is the reservoir that started it all."

Emerson replied, "I saw my mom and dad. They said they were sorry." He began to tear up again, sneezed, and spat up a puddle of water. Quinn and Saą laughed. Quinn offered some jerky and a cup of water. He said, "Yeah, but all the same, I think I've had enough water for today."

They waited until dark to begin exploring the shoreline. Quinn said that the drones used infrared at night, which increased their visual range, but their missiles were twice as inaccurate in the dark. They located the tunnels before hearing another one. Quinn used her plasma gun to slice open the metal bars. They closed the hatch, and Emerson used his Interface to submerge Little Wing. They rewelded the opening, and Saą agreed to wait and stand lookout. She could contact Emerson and Quinn via Interface as soon as he plugged in and registered them in the local system. Quinn and Emerson disappeared into the dark tunnel.

◆ ◆

Emerson and Quinn used red headlamps to see, and Quinn called up the underground maps. They were a gift from her best friend, Max Hamp. He researched old sayings and found construction maps in the archives. Max was killed saving them in Blue Hole. Six years later, Quinn still wore his stretch hat. When she thought of him, her heart constricted, and her eyes leaked. Max was in love with her, though she never thought of him that way. But since he was killed, she realized that she loved him too—and her heart ached.

She pointed and said, "There. The corridor splits up ahead. We'll take the passage to the left. It goes up a steep set of stairs carved into the rock."

Emerson followed her. She moved with single-minded determination. He hardly recognized her. She seemed so focused.

"We need to plug into a terminal port so you can shut down the Interface security and lock everyone's implant. Once Boston is isolated, we can enter his apartments, and no one will be notified."

Emerson went over the plan in his mind. He said, "We will need to disarm him as soon as we enter the room."

"I don't know what sort of weapons he'll have. Or if there is a bodyguard."

"Or anyone else."

◆ ◆

There *was* a bodyguard, but he was asleep in a chair outside the outer doors of High Lord Quinn's rooms. He was close enough to enter when summoned, but the doors and walls were sound-tight. If Boston didn't call him through his Interface, he would never wake up.

There was also someone in Lord Quinn's bed. Sally Mink had become his concubine. He had semi-mind-locked her to make her compliant but not so strictly that she was non-functional. He had no idea what she really thought or felt because her implant and Interface programming suppressed that part of her personality. She was just as Boston wanted her—a warm, willing, flesh-and-blood doll.

The doorway in from the tunnels was hidden next to a massive oak wardrobe that Boston had salvaged from a palace in Northern England. It reminded him of *The Chronicles of Narnia*. He aspired to be as regal and powerful as the White Witch, but of course, he never finished the first book. Boston Quinn was unconcerned with the fate of the children in the story—to him they were of little importance.

He was trying to penetrate Sally. She was lying on the bed underneath him, moaning. He liked her to moan. And grunt. Sally was a good grunter. And she knew how to orgasm when he did, too. She was just the perfect little sex toy. Boston liked her the best, though he could have anybody in The City. They all acted exactly the same. He had them programmed that way.

But his overweight body wasn't cooperating. He tried rubbing against Sally but got no stiffer. He commanded her to suck on it. Sally never objected. She was so much better than any of his wives had been—though he had liked Lucia. He couldn't remember at that moment what had happened to her. He supposed that was the whiskey. High Lord Quinn liked his whiskey. That night, he'd had at least a quart. It made him feel disconnected from that black hole he felt whenever he was alone. Though, lately, the alcohol wasn't working.

Sally wasn't helping. He pulled his flaccid member out of her grip and went to the bathroom. "I have to pee. Clean yourself up."

She wiped her face on a towel by the bed and applied a refresher to her bright red lipstick, looking in the mirror. The thought that she was pretty crossed her mind. For a moment, the real Sally Mink saw her bloated, puffy, overly made-up face and nearly spat up. But it passed in a second, and she thought, *Wow, I really am a pretty girl.*

◆ ◆

Emerson plugged into the Interface socket he found recessed into the tunnel wall next to the secret door to Lord Quinn's rooms. Once he completed the authentication series, he used the security override routine that Ana created and entered administrative mode. He would be detected and blocked if he didn't shut down security fast enough. It had already sensed his presence and notification alarms were poised to go off. He uploaded the simulation and the routines that would scrub the programs when they ended.

He created a group rule to allow him to open implants selectively and then included all. He initiated the change. It would take sixty seconds for the permissions to replicate through the network. Emerson set a countdown. They would enter the room the second the system locked.

◆ ◆

Emerson's count was off by four. The locks snapped off the moment High Lord Quinn exited his bathroom. Sally heard the toilet flush and the door open. One second, she was randy as a cat in heat. The next second, she saw Boston Quinn for what he was and what he had done to her. She could remember every episode in crystal clarity. The hatred and disgust she felt overwhelmed her. She lunged for the silver letter opener on his desk.

Boston had terrible gas. The bathroom break did nothing to relieve him. As he exited the toilet, he was going to tell Sally to fuck off. He was drunk and exhausted. When he looked up, she was diving at him with a knife. He put up his beefy arm to shield his face, and she stabbed him. The point of the letter opener poked through the opposite side of his arm, stopping a few centimeters from his nose. He screamed.

Quinn and Emerson burst into the room. Sally, still naked, backed into the corner. The letter opener stuck out of Boston's arm. He gurgled an unintelligible sound and collapsed in a heap.

Emerson wrapped a sheet around the trembling woman and sat her down in the desk chair. He looked into her unseeing eyes; she was obviously in shock.

He said, "Sally? Sally Mink?" Emerson and Sally had been close years ago.

She didn't look at him but said, "Yes," devoid of emotion.

Elli Rattlesnake said, "Well, that was easy. Next, we have to wake him up and find out where Marya is."

Sally seemed catatonic, but she said, "Your daughter is with Doctor Sailor. She's safe and knows you are here."

Quinn said, "But how do you know that?"

Sally slumped to the floor unconscious; her legs splayed. Emerson asked Quinn, "Do you know where this Sailor person is?"

"Yes, but what about my father?"

"It would be easy to kill him now. That's what you want to do, isn't it?"

"Yes. I do." She ramped her gun up to half power and pointed it at Lord Quinn, cowering and bleeding on the slate floor. "Get up, Father."

He said, "I'm bleeding. This thing is dirty. I need a doctor."

"You won't need a doctor for much longer, Father. Your wounds will be mortal."

"Elli. Daughter. I only did what I had to, to bring you home. You must believe me. We need you here in The City. Don't you want to come home? Everything can go back to the way it was…"

"Fuck you, Father. You killed my mother in front of me. Did you forget? You ordered a strike on thousands of innocent people, twice. You murdered two of my best friends and kidnapped my daughter. It could never be the way it was. That was an illusion, just like all this is. No, Father, you are going to die. Your time is up."

Doctor Sailor opened the door to High Lord Quinn's bedroom, and Marya ran in.

"Daddy! Mama! I knew you'd come. Mother told me. Where's Saą? Isn't she with you?"

Emerson used his connection to take control of High Lord Boston Quinn's Interface, essentially restraining him with a mental handcuff. He took the gun from Quinn.

She ran to her daughter and scooped her up. Doctor Sailor bandaged High Lord Quinn's arm and revived Sally Mink. The woman wiped the red lipstick on High Lord Quinn's pillow and wrapped herself in his silk dressing robe. Doctor Sailor turned to Emerson and Quinn and said, "The City is in chaos. I suggest you leave quickly. Some factions are still loyal to High Lord Quinn, and they will arrive soon."

Quinn said, "Come with us."

"No, I'm too old for that. But this one should be punished for his crimes." Doctor Sailor poked High Lord Quinn's meaty shoulder. "Now go! I'll be fine."

The secret passage closed just as the Enforcers splintered the front door. Doctor Sailor, a life-long betel nut addict, spat a stream of orange juice on the floor and said, "They're not here, idiots. They were gone when I got here. Go! Go find them!"

When they ran out, she laughed and laughed.

◆ ◆ ◆

LADY BROCK

On the way through the tunnels back at The City, Emerson said, "We need to rescue Brock's wife." Quinn held Sally's arm. She was waking up, but the suppression systems Lord Quinn had implemented were slowly wearing off, and she was still in a fog.

Quinn replied, "You have a fucking strange sense of loyalty, Emerson Lloyde. That man was responsible for hundreds of deaths and the kidnapping of your own daughter. Why do you give a shit?"

"It's not for him, Quinn. It's for her. She's innocent in all this. Plus, it was never him. It's High Lord Quinn who is responsible."

When they reached the bars at the mouth of the tunnel, Quinn sarcastically introduced her father to Saą as the late High *fucking* Lord Quinn. The Interface-drugged man stumbled along in a trance. Emerson still held Marya, who acted like she was on a grand adventure rather than traumatized by a violent abduction. Quinn asked her if she was really okay, and Marya said, "Of course, Mama. Mother told me everything would be okay, and I trust her. Don't you? She's always right."

Quinn wanted to object that *she* hadn't even known it was going to be alright, so how could The Mother, but she was too glad to have Marya back and didn't want to fight. Saą helped Sally Mink wrap herself up. The woman was trying to regain her dignity; she needed all the support she could get. They settled in on the sand floor at the tunnel's entrance.

Emerson said, "We need to find her."

Sąq replied, "Mother can tell you where she is."

Emerson looked at Quinn, who shrugged. He said, "Marya, can you ask The Mother where we can find Thilda Brock?"

Marya didn't hesitate. She said, "Lady Brock is in Mom's apartments. And Mother says that Tanya would very much like to see you." Tanya had been Elli Rattlesnake's maid since they were both teenagers.

Emerson said, "Quinn, do you know how to get there?"

Quinn grinned and pulled Max's hat down tighter. "We grew up in these tunnels, Emerson. I could find it in the dark."

Marya said, "Mother said something else."

They turned to her.

"She said you could have asked yourself, and next time you should."

◆ ◆

Emerson initiated the simulation that Ana, Plummer, and Chandler wrote. It created a huge virtual meeting room and linked the computer on board Little Wing with The City's Interface network. It made the shuttle vulnerable, but in five minutes, all connections would be automatically severed. As soon as the simulation began, every resident of The City with an Implant was instantly brought to this room. The chances of being hacked were low—there wasn't anybody left to do it.

The simulation Ana created hijacked the Interface connections for everyone on the server—even those implants which were locked. It was only temporary. The network's internal security would eliminate the app after five minutes. When everybody arrived, Emerson and Quinn were already standing at the front on a raised platform, waiting for the crowd to quiet.

He said, "I am Emerson Lloyde, and this is Lady Elli Rattlesnake Quinn." Quinn cringed but kept the smile on her face. "We have freed you. It is your choice to stay or go. We are taking Boston Quinn away to trial. He is responsible for countless deaths. If you wish to join us in a settlement across the Inland Sea, I have embedded the coordinates in this simulation. You can stay or leave. It is your free choice. Goodbye."

The disorientation of being suddenly cast back into a damp tunnel only lasted a second.

Sally Mink said, "Take me home. I need to go home."

Quinn said, "I'll drop you off on the way. Come on." To the others she said, "I should only be a moment." She grabbed Sally's hand and sprinted into the dark.

◆◆

The secret door to Quinn's apartments came out in her bedroom closet. It was a large walk-in with mirrors on each wall. The door was one of the mirrors. Quinn peeked around the corner to see if it was clear. Tanya was entering with some clothes. When she saw Quinn, she dropped them and ran to hug her.

"I can't believe you're here."

"I can't stay. Where is Thilda Brock?"

"In the sitting room."

Lady Brock was sunken into one of Quinn's overstuffed recliners. She was reading a Stephen King novel. The dust jacket was missing. Her long auburn hair was tied into a messy braid that draped over her shoulder. Her fingers were unusually long with cleanly trimmed, unpainted nails.

Quinn said, "I always liked *Cujo*. I have a soft spot for bad dogs."

Thilda put the book in her lap and slipped the reading glasses off her nose. She said, "Elli Rattlesnake Quinn. I just saw you in a simulation. I was wondering if that was true. So, you mean to tell me you have deposed your daddy? Bravo! You've done the rest of us a favor. I suppose you want a title now." She winked and smiled, raising a mischievous eyebrow. The smile didn't reach her steel-grey eyes. She took a sip of bourbon from a Waterford crystal.

Quinn said, "Enjoying my things, I see."

"Well, one must make the best of the situation, I always say. So, is it true that I am free?"

"We blocked all the restraints and locked down all the implants, not just for the Elites, for everybody. You are free, but so is everyone else."

"Small minds are easily controlled."

"I'm leaving. You can come. Your husband is waiting."

"My husband is a greedy ass. I never want to see him again."

Quinn said, "He's in prison in Crow City, said you were kidnapped and he was blackmailed into kidnapping my daughter in return for your freedom."

"Unmitigated bullshit. I had an affair with Lord Fat-man so I could be close when his brain finally melted down the rest of the way. It was *our* plan, Terrence and mine. But he got greedy or jealous or stupid—I don't know, maybe all three. He confronted your daddy who threw him out, told Terrence he'd consider allowing him back if he brought the *High Lord* your daughter. That was his plan all along. I told him not to go. He never heard a word I said, the bastard."

She drained her glass, and Tanya refilled it. She said, "I'm not going anywhere. I have a shot at being a queen here. I'm taking it."

Quinn hugged Tanya. "Do you want to stay here or come with me? I'll warn you—it's rough."

Tanya cried, "I missed you so much. But I can't leave. This is my life."

Quinn hugged her and left the way she'd come.

Emerson had the gate open and Little Wing idling in the shallows when Quinn returned. The craft was airborne and headed west over the reservoir ten minutes later. The drones had all fallen in the water.

Quinn brushed out Marya's hair; they watched the birds diving for fish on the forward monitor.

She said, "A part of me wishes we could stay."

◆ ◆ ◆

HOOCH

Emerson passed the responsibility for his cornfield over to Rosco and Eggert while he was rescuing his daughter. He also showed them the still, which neither knew he had set up before he left.

Rosco said, "You've been holding out on us, brother. We've been using that makeshift thing that Eggert stuck together out of a pot and some old pipes."

Emerson grinned and said, "We didn't have the corn. I planted the last of it in the hoop house."

"I could have gotten you all the corn you wanted back in Blue Hole."

"Yeah, but in Blue Hole there was no shortage of hooch." He added, "The corn should mature before the first frost."

Emerson was prepared either way. He'd installed biogas heaters to keep the temperatures up. He also showed Rosco a set of corn kernel extractors he'd fabricated which were essentially steel blades curled into a circle the diameter of a corn cob and attached to a block. Once the corn was dried and husked, it could be forced through the extractor, leaving a basket of kernels and a bucket of cobs. Corn cobs were a great insulator and all-around core building material.

Margaret and Ana organized a family husking party and corn roast. Mule provided the game: four large rabbits. Elli burned husks which scented the air; she claimed the smoke was cleansing. Little Chandler fed them into flames. The next day, Rosco and Eggert mixed up a big pot of sour mash. They used a modified grinder to crack the corn and mixed it with water, and several cups of honey. Then they put the pot in the corner of Emerson's bedroom and let it ferment.

Margaret asked if it didn't need yeast. Eggert said, "Yeast is everywhere, floating around in the air. Like sourdough, our yeast will be different from yeasts anywhere else."

Rosco said, "So our hooch will be unique. If it's any good. It would be best if we could store it in oak barrels for a few months, but then it would bourbon! Ha."

The mash bubbled and stank in a corner. No one was living there, and no one complained.

A few days later, Pejeta called a meeting with Plummer and Eggert. Rat One brought her a mug of tea. Eggert showed up late. She said, "We are low on supplies. I need you to fly The Black Mariah to the bunker."

Eggert sucked his teeth and said, "Hey, Rat, can you get me a cup of tea or, even better, a flask of hooch?"

Rat One scurried off. Eggert said, "Seems you've gotten used to some of our technology."

Pejeta said, "I surrendered when Rat One and Two stopped the bleeding on a six-year-old boy with a chunk of iron embedded in his leg."

Rat Two said, "Timothy and I became good friends. He makes his mama bring him to visit." But Pejeta couldn't hear him, so Eggert translated.

Eggert said, "When should we go? I promised Quinn that I would find a library to bring back here. I'm ready when you are."

◆ ◆

The bunker was two hours south of Crow City. Plummer, Elli, and Eggert used the belly cameras and their Interface connections to scan the landscape below. They cruised as slow as they could without losing lift at 1,500 meters.

Eggert said, "We are looking for a medium-sized city with little or no activity. We can call up a map when we find a suitable candidate and check for a library."

The first town was a ruin and seemed populated solely by aggressive grey woodchuck-like creatures. The animals were engaged in repetitive skirmishes where two would scramble around, fur flying for a few moments, and then walk on. There were hundreds of similar fights going on simultaneously.

Elli said, "I don't want to have anything to do with them. They look nasty."

The animals scrambled around the piles of rubble, frantic and agitated.

Eggert added, "They look diseased."

The Black Mariah veered off the direct course to the bunker in order to pass another town. The buildings looked mostly intact, and the streets were deserted.

"You never know who might be hiding in the shadows. We can't let our guard down." Eggert sucked his teeth.

The sign on the outskirts said the town was called Groveland. Elli located the library. They landed in the middle of Main Street. The downtown area was mostly in the woods; the library was a brick building with a metal roof. Its windows were intact, and the roof, though covered with pine needles and fallen timber, seemed solid.

The door was locked, but Elli plugged an Interface power supply into the key socket. The mechanism clicked and swung open. Inside was dry and dusty. It didn't look as though anyone had been in there in half a century. They spent the rest of the day loading books out onto the street. Plummer could carry more weight than would fit though the hatch. So, they staged all the library shelves on the road next to the shuttle's rear bay doors.

Around four in the afternoon, Elli and Eggert sat on a picnic bench outside the museum chewing jerky. She'd brought apples, and they each enjoyed one—core, seeds, and all. Plummer recharged in the street next to the shelves.

No one noticed the stooped, grey-haired man dressed in a threadbare park ranger parka and a pair of patched chinos. He limped up Main toward the shuttle. The name patch on the jacket was torn off years ago. He reached Plummer and nearly exploded with vitriol.

"Who THE *HELL* are you? *WHAT* THE HELL ARE YOU? And *why* in the name of the baby Jesus are you puttin' the got-damned library out in the middle of Main?" He was missing most of his teeth. Plummer could smell him, which was an accomplishment since his olfactory sensors could only detect toxins and fluorocarbons.

Elli and Eggert walked over. She was just finishing the last bite of her apple. Eggert sucked his teeth and said, "Pee-yew, old man. Don't you bathe?"

"Water's in short supply these days."

Elli said, "There's a lake not more than a mile north of here."

"I can't walk no mile. I'm lucky I could make it all the way of here from my house. Hell, I gotta rest going out m'front door t'piss." He used his thumb to point over his shoulder. After an awkward pause, he added, "You get used to it—dying, I mean."

"There's a shower in the shuttle," Eggert said. "You're welcome to it."

"That's mighty kind, but I'd need help to even get up in there."

Plummer retracted his solar collector. "I will help you. My name is C. Plummer. I am a cybernetically enhanced human. And these are my assistants, Rat One and Rat Two."

The old guy peered at the rats, standing side by side on their hind legs. He said, "Don't look like any rats I ever seen."

Rat Two said, "We're cybernetic rats. Plummer built Rat One, and she helped build me."

The grizzled guy grinned a toothless grin. "They're kinda cute, ain't they?"

Plummer realized that the old man couldn't hear the rats, so he repeated Rat Two's statement. He asked, "What's your name?"

The old guy looked confused for a moment and said, "Ah, nearly forgot! Been a while since I had so much English spoke at me at one time. Randorn, Silas Randorn at your service." He tipped his head forward in a little bowing motion, but he got a crick in his neck and shouted, "Oh shit!"

Elli said, "I hate that. You need some deep tissue work. But not until you wash."

Eggert said, "We live in a settlement up in the mountains. We are moving your library there for our children. You can come back with us if you want. Does anyone else live here?"

"I'm the last. Our kids left as soon as they could. My wife died a decade ago. I've been alone since."

Eggert said, "We need to stow these books. You and Plummer and the rats go on in and get cleaned up. If there is anything you want to bring, we can go get it when we're loaded."

He nodded; Plummer carried him inside. Elli and Eggert stacked books from floor to ceiling in the hold and then used freight bars to wedge them in. By sunset, they were ready to roll. Eggert found Randorn, sitting on a bench next to a collapsed bus stop, untangling his stringy hair. When he saw Elli, he said, "I haven't had a comb in twenty years!" He had yanked out a clump of matted hair but was gleefully pulling out more with the comb.

"Here, let me help you with that," Elli offered. "I comb out LC's hair all the time, but it just turns back into a rat's nest." She turned to Rat One and said, "No offense."

Eggert snared a couple of rabbits and built a fire. He'd prepped them on a spit over the hot coals and passed a flask of hooch to Randorn.

After swallowing a mouthful, the old guy yelled, "WOOT! DAMN SON! That's rocket fuel." He passed it to Elli. When she finished her swig, Randorn was snoring with his chin to his chest. Eggert covered him with a thermal sheet and put a pillow behind his head.

◆◆

The old codger was up before the sun the following day with a filled backpack and a blackened coffee percolator nestled into the embers. When Elli stretched, he said excitedly, "I broke out the good stuff!" and poured a tin cup full of the steaming black liquid. "There was a McDonald's warehouse in Sonora. We salvaged all the coffee, sugar, and creamers before the tornada came through there and ripped the place to little pieces. Then them rabid gophers moved in, and, well, that was years ago, and I ain't been there since. But I still got some coffee!"

Elli wasn't used to caffeine. She was jittery and animated all morning while they broke camp. By the time they were in the air, she was snoring in the copilot's chair. Randorn was like a little kid. He talked nonstop. He told stories about raising a family and living in the town alone. "There used to be others here, but it got too hard to be so isolated. Everybody moved away. I was the only one left." He looked out the view screen in awe. "I always dreamed I could fly."

They reached the bunker before noon.

◆ ◆ ◆

WELCOME BACK

ggert landed in a field of dead avocado trees. He used a cargo pole to bang on the weedy, brush-covered ground, seeking the hollow. When he struck metal, he knew he'd found the door.

No one had been in this bunker since the collapse over fifty years ago. The lock was a standard key-operated, mechanical one. He melted it off with a plasma gun set at two. Plummer lifted the steel plate door and let it fall back on the ground. It sounded like striking a gong. They stood around, peering down the dark hole. Randorn startled Eggert. He said, "I can't see a got-damned thing."

Eggert sucked his teeth and resisted telling him to go back in the shuttle. He smelled considerably better, but he was somehow twice as annoying.

Elli said, "Plummer, shine a light down there."

The cyborg switched on a magnified beam of light and widened the aperture until the entire stairwell was illuminated. Elli squinted in the glare. "Tone it down some, man."

Eggert said, "I'm going to use the winch on The Black Mariah to lower a cable. Elli knows what we're looking for, so she needs to go. Plummer can watch the ship."

"What about me?" Randorn asked.

"I need strength, Silas. You sit this one out."

The codger strode away muttering to himself. Eggert went back to planning. "Plummer, you keep an eye on things." He tipped his head in Randorn's direction.

After Eggert and Elli had descended the well, Plummer went in search of the old man. The shuttle winch was controlled by Eggert. It didn't need his attention. After poking around in the brush, he called out.

Randorn called back, "Over here, by the stream."

Plummer made his way over the rocky terrain, his treads crunching on the gravel, ripping up the grasses next to the trail. Randorn was standing on the edge of a wide stream. It was shallow, but more than 100 meters across. He said, "I just love the water."

Plummer was about to tell him to come back when a huge mountain lion rushed out of the trees near the bank, grabbed the old guy around his middle, and dragged his limp body into the brush.

Plummer raised his weapon, but the Kill Switch interlock prevented him from firing without an okay which would never come. Randorn realized what was happening and began screaming. Plummer turned on his treads. He couldn't stop the cat. He was powerless. The man's screams intensified, louder and more frantic. It seemed they went on too long. When they stopped abruptly, Plummer rolled back up the embankment to the bunker.

◆ ◆

Eggert and Elli wore LED headlamps. He called up the map on his Interface. "Med supplies are in locker 543," he said.

"This room has lockers one through twenty. We got a ways to go." She carried her plasma rifle cradled in her arms and turned her head from left to right, sweeping the light across the dusty hallway lined with rolltop doors, scanning for movement and calling out numbers.

Elli spun around to a scurrying behind her, pinning the rat in her headlamp beam. The animal was large and blue-black. She had an involuntary shiver. They walked on. At the room labeled 兵工廠, Elli looked at Eggert, who shrugged.

She ran the image through the translator on The Black Mariah.

"Arsenal," she said.

He shook his head and said, "Not this trip, but you and I can come back later."

They walked for several minutes. Eggert opened rolltop door number 27 for lockers 228 to 248. Inside were twenty, two-by-eight-by-five-meter steel boxes. Number 243 contained cardboard boxes stacked from bottom to top stenciled with other Chinese characters.

"What does it say?" Eggert sucked his teeth.

Elli said, "You know, you have an Interface connection too." She sent an image of each label.

"Now why didn't I think of that?" He grinned.

They took boxes containing anesthetics, antibiotics, anticoagulants, fungicides, bactericides, and a host of other drugs. Elli also grabbed a case of sterile bandages. They had been using steamed cotton cloths. She said, "In an emergency, a ready supply of gauze can sometimes mean the difference between life and death."

After the supplies were stowed and they were preparing to leave, Eggert said, "Plummer, where's Randorn?"

Plummer rolled up. "Dead, I think."

"What? How did that happen? What do you mean, you think?"

"It was a puma or a cougar. I get them mixed up, but I don't think he could survive. I didn't check. It was huge."

Elli arrived and was drinking water from her skin. "What?"

Plummer said, "Randorn wandered off down by the stream, and a mountain lion grabbed him."

Eggert was shocked. He yelled, "Why in Christ's name didn't you stop it? You could stop a freaking freight train."

"FSX7: the Kill Switch."

"Pardon?"

Elli explained, "When they authorized the soldiers in Plummer's unit, the World Government forced Interface Industries to hard program FSX7 into them. He can't hurt a living being without expressed approval from a trusted source. The source is gone."

"I'm sincerely sorry, but I couldn't do anything."

Eggert said, "We'll see about that. I'll talk to Ana. There should be a way to transfer the trusted authority."

"Yes, I hope so," Plummer sighed. "Just because you cannot see my emotions does not mean I don't grieve for my actions and inactions, Eric. But you cannot alter my core programs without killing me. That was the way I was designed."

◆ ◆

As Emerson, Quinn, Saą, and their captive Boston Quinn flew in Little Wing over the Inland Sea, the neural sedative that Emerson had given to Boston began to wear off. It essentially put him in a coma for a twelve-hour cycle. Quinn stood over him with her rifle, the glowing power gauge wavering orange-red, between two and three. Emerson came back from the cockpit and said, "I was wondering where you went."

She said, "I could put a pinhole through his heart. He wouldn't even feel it." She put the barrel to her father's chest. "He looks pitiful, weak." His head was cocked to one side, tongue out, drool dried on his cheek and shoulder. "I should put him out of his misery."

Emerson put his hand on the gun and said, "You'll regret it."

She switched the rifle off and walked away. "You're right, Emerson. That would be too kind. The son of a bitch should suffer."

The sunset left a blazing line of violet and orange along the western horizon. The smooth surface of the Inland Sea was broken by the occasional cluster of rusted and broken windmills poking up from the water like stalks of metal grass.

At the end of each twelve-hour cycle, Emerson allowed Boston an hour to eat and pee before putting him back into the coma. The transition was painful and disorienting. Lord Quinn was in poor health anyway, which exaggerated the effects. He retched with cold sweats for the first ten minutes, curled into the fetal position on the main cabin deck.

Saą fed him a protein drink and allowed him time in the toilet. When it was time to put him back under, he put up his hand up and said, "You have every reason to hate me. But you must listen. Armies are coming from the north. We must prepare. We must defend ourselves."

Emerson strapped him into a shuttle seat and said, "You should be happy your daughter can't hear you. I've had to stop her from killing you three times already."

When Emerson returned to the cockpit, Saą said, "I have a child, Emerson. She lives with her mother."

Emerson said, "Her mother?"

"Yes, she lives far away. Across the sea. I have been feeling her pull. I fear that something is wrong."

Emerson said, "Can we contact her?"

"That's part of the problem. The child and I are mother and daughter. We should be able to hear one another through The Memories. But since midsummer, she has not replied to my concerns. I am frightened. When I ask, Mother only looks at me expressionless."

Emerson hugged her. "I'll talk to everyone; we'll figure something out."

◆ ◆

Back in Crow City, Eggert, Elli, and Plummer arrived back as the sun set. They landed near the clinic and unloaded the medical supplies. Pejeta put them away. The next morning at dawn, the word had already circulated that Eggert and Elli returned with a shuttle full of books. The main square was filled with people cleaning up from breakfast when The Black Mariah landed near the fire pit. Plummer reassembled the shelving,

Eggert, Margaret, Ana, and Elli put books out, and, as was the custom, everyone took what interested them. It was cause for a celebration, but what wasn't? The people of Crow City celebrated whenever they could, even though this time there were clots of citizens who stood on the periphery and shouted slurs and insults.

Margaret said to Ana, "They blame us for the massacre. And I'm afraid they are right."

The large reference and early childhood reading sections were put aside for the learning building. The event felt like a circus with kids running around playing games and groups of people gathered together talking about their favorite stories.

There were still so many books left by the end of the morning that Plummer decided he needed to build Crow City a library. He went to the council for permission to build it in the center of town. They put him at the end of the day's business and claimed the time ran out. He came back the next day, and the next and the next.

Finally, on the morning of the third day, he interrupted the meeting. "Madam Speaker, please allow me the floor for one minute." The room went silent. "I volunteer to build a climate-controlled building to house the books Eric Eggert and Elli Moon salvaged and brought here. I only need the ground on which to build. Crow City need not give me anything else. It is a gift from Elli Rattlesnake Quinn and Emerson Lloyde."

There were random shouts from the chamber of "Abomination!" Someone shouted, "We don't want your dirty gifts." There were random calls to get out and leave them in peace.

The speaker motioned for quiet. She said, "If the council has no paramount objection, I say we allow the library to be constructed on the ruined indoor market space at the East Quarter."

There was muttering, but no one objected.

"Decided. C. Plummer, from the North Quarter, will donate the labor and materials to construct a climate-controlled library. Next order on the docket?"

◆ ◆

It was midnight when Emerson landed Little Wing outside Hardware and Sundries in the Southwest Quarter. Coner came out to meet them, his right shirt sleeve hanging empty at his side. He removed his hat with the other and brushed the hair out of his eyes with the brim.

Grinning broadly, he said, "Got something in there for me?"

Boston Quinn, dressed in a white maintenance jumpsuit and dizzy from the transition to wakefulness he'd experienced moments ago, stepped through the hatch and vomited the residue of his last protein drink on Coner's shoes. He stood in front of his jailor trying to focus his eyes and wiped his mouth while two boys tied his hands behind his back. Emerson assumed these were Coner's replacements since Toms and Tams had been killed. Boston burped, and Coner skipped back to avoid more possible spewage.

Quinn and Saą stood on either side of the unsteady prisoner. The two boys walked him into the building. Coner said, "We'll put him next to Brock. They'll have a lot to talk about."

Emerson said, "Has the council come to any decision about him?"

Coner said, "No. And if you're asking me, they won't. You can't restore justice from war crimes. There's no way to undo that kind of damage."

◆ ◆ ◆

TURN TURN TURN

Things didn't return to normal in Crow City, not that relations with Emerson's camp and the citizens were ever normal. Life evolved. Eggert and Margaret went on donating time to the cooks and farmers. Plummer broke ground on his library, though making a climate control system without central electricity was more challenging than he originally anticipated. People side-eyed members of the North Quarter. Emerson's crew did their best to ignore the taunts and jeers.

Near the autumnal equinox, Paxon and Sandra returned to camp and announced they were pregnant. The council granted them citizenship. They moved from the Southwest to the North Quarter so Sandra could be closer to the medical systems on The Black Mariah. She got regular exams from Elli and Saą. She had never even known anyone who was pregnant before, and it both excited and frightened her. Like many women post-collapse, she'd believed she was barren.

Emerson gave the MRI and CAT scanners to Pejeta, which put her up against the village's bias and the council's avoidance of electronic tech. Emerson attended council meetings where he made impassioned pleas to make an exception for responsible use. The members were still new and unsure of their standing. So, they thanked him each time and took no action.

Emerson was beginning to understand why Chandler hated politics so vehemently. The old man would say, "A politician is a person who would cut off their left hand to make a deal for gloves."

But it wasn't just the council's inaction on progress; they also seemed unable to move forward on the subject of Boston Quinn and Terrence Brock. It had been weeks without any discussion. Coner said, "What'd I tell ya?"

Ana and Amrsal moved into a house in the central village, but after they slept there one night, councilman Daris Clute served them an eviction. Apparently, Ana was no longer considered a suitable mate for a citizen. Amrsal was humiliated. He muttered something about how he'd told her and stormed away. Ana was crushed. She never saw him again. And though she didn't talk about it, it was clear to Elli and Emerson that she was grieving his abrupt exit. Saą offered to do a releasing ritual with her, but she declined and concentrated on her programming projects.

Emerson and Elli went to the council to complain and were denied access. The guard muttered something about official business, but he wouldn't look at Emerson. Elli nearly lost her temper which made the guards nervous. She got that look in her eye that just begged for someone to try and stop her.

Emerson pulled her away from the door before she caused an incident. Later that evening, Emerson and crew had a meeting around their fire pit. Everyone sat on logs or benches, wrapped in quilts or winter weather gear. Nights in the mountains were cold. The temperatures had hit zero the last two nights. Emerson had broken out his grandfather's Enforcer peacoat. It was more insulation than he needed, but the coat always made him feel more secure and closer to Chandler.

He said, "You all feel it. We are not welcome here anymore."

Saą looked at the ground. Emerson put his arm around her. He said, "Saą, you can't be responsible for the way the people are responding. If it weren't for us, there wouldn't have been a massacre. Even though we saved lives. Even though we've given a library full of books and a clinic with advanced medical diagnostic equipment, we will always be seen as the reason all those people died."

Saą said, "I understand it, but it feels bad. I know causes and effects brought death to Crow City, and that we're not responsible for Brock or Lord Quinn's actions. But I think it would be best for everyone if we moved on. We should give them the space to heal."

No one spoke. They'd all felt the same thing. Eggert said, "I'm done, Emerson, too tired to run anymore. I have friends here. They don't mind that I use tech. And hell, I wouldn't care if they did."

Saą said, "It grieves me that more of the people cannot accept you and see you the way Mother does. I think that some do, but they are less vocal than the frightened ones. Fear has a way of plugging our ears and our mouths. But I am committed to my new family, here with you. And I will go where you go."

Marya, who was making figures out of thread and straw, said, "Are we going to cross the ocean?"

Emerson and Saą looked at each other. Quinn said, "What?"

Saą said, "I have a daughter who's living on the other side of the ocean."

"Marya, do you know something I don't?" asked Emerson.

When she didn't answer, he continued, "We won't be going anywhere until the spring. I hear the snow can get pretty deep up here."

Plummer said, "I know these people are afraid of us, but they also need us. I am afraid that we have attracted attention from other far-away groups who will come and take what they have built. I want to stay and create a militia. Give the people of Crow City a chance to defend themselves."

Eggert sucked his teeth and said, "I'm all the way in with that, Plummer."

Elli said, "We can check out the arsenal!"

Eggert nodded.

Grendel said, "I hear you, Emerson. We don't feel welcome here either."

"They locked us out of the council," Rosco added. "I'm thinking of going back to Terminus or maybe even The City, now that everyone's implants are locked."

Paxon sat with his arm around Sandra. Ana thought they were a cute couple. He said, "We've been granted citizenship and could live anywhere, but Sandra has decided that the North Quarter is the safest place for us to be, even if we are insiders now." She leaned over and kissed him. "Besides, I don't know the first thing about babies. We need all the help we can get."

Barry said, "Mother says I must go with you. I don't know why. I like it here. They accept me. But Mother says I should stay with you and the children."

Elli said, "Who said you were invited, fat boy?"

Barry didn't retaliate; he looked at the ground. Marya said, "Barry's not fat anymore, Mew Mew."

Elli squinted at the little girl who squinted back at her in a mock staring contest. Elli suddenly lunged forward and tickled Marya's ribs ferociously. The girl squealed and ran away giggling with Elli in pursuit.

When they woke the next morning, it had already snowed a foot. It continued to snow all week.

◆ ◆

When Budrow went out by himself, he wandered. Everyone knew him and greeted him by name. He had the notable position of being the only dog in the entire village. Mule would have gotten the same sort of welcome, but she preferred solitude where Budrow craved attention. He also liked to eat. He discovered that humans derived a mysterious thrill from feeding animals, especially when those animals demonstrated exuberant appreciation. The people of Crow City fed Budrow whenever he asked. No amount of warning from Eggert made a difference. They would nod while he explained that Budrow had a good deal of wild DNA and his metabolism wasn't geared for the high-fat diet they were giving him.

And then they'd go right back to feeding him, saying, "I can't resist those eyes. He's so *cute*!"

Budrow *was* cute. He possessed all the traits of a red fox in his face, ears, and tail. And though his leg coloring was foxlike, his paws and chest were all dog—a medium-sized breed with stubby legs, like a corgi. He had the heart of a puppy and the cunning of a trickster. He made the rounds almost every day—and Budrow was getting fat.

When Ana turned twenty-six, she realized her body was changing, painting the final strokes of maturity on her hips and butt. She began to fear that her sedentary habits were catching up to her. Lying in a lounge chair most of the day, only getting up to eat and care for LC, was not enough exercise, even though Little Chandler never sat still. So as soon as she could stamp down the snow enough to create a clear trail in the woods, she began running around the settlement every morning.

She'd heard Eggert say to Budrow, "Bud, you are going to end up looking like a coffee table if you don't quit the sweets!" He sucked his teeth.

Ana said, "I can take him with me on my runs if you want," which was how Budrow met his future mate, the melanistic fox.

At first, Budrow was excited to be out in the crisp early morning air with Ana. He would never venture into the forest by himself. As smart as he was, Budrow was a coward. Something about his mixed-up genes short-circuited courage and loyalty in his dog/fox brain. Running with Ana shielded him enough from reality for him to believe he was safe. Until he fell off the trail.

He was sniffing after some scent, something foreign and intensely attractive. When he looked up, he was on the edge of the hillside. The drop-off was steep. The snow crust gave way under his paws, and he tumbled down the embankment, rolling and flipping all the way to the bottom. He was lucky he wasn't stopped by a tree. When Ana realized he was not behind her, she doubled back but didn't see his tracks and went too far. Following his tracks back up the trail, she saw the disturbance in the snow. She called his name.

Budrow's ears were plugged with snow. He shook his head to try and clear them, but they were packed tight. All he could hear was the sound of his own breathing, his heart, and the blood pulsing past his ears. He couldn't hear Ana.

He looked around, trying to get his bearings, but the snow in his ears made his head feel swollen and heavy. His sense of direction wasn't working. That was when he saw the fox. She was sitting calmly next to a Douglas fir. Budrow shook his head. The snow had begun to melt, but his ears were still plugged.

The fox stepped toward him. He looked around for support, shook his head again, and barked. It sounded to him like he was underwater. The fox didn't flinch. She was interested in him as well.

Ana heard the bark and called to him. Her voice echoed off the adjacent hillside. Crows launched out of a nearby alder. She called again. Nothing. "Well, shit, Budrow. I guess I need to go down there," she said to the crystalline air. She dug her boot into the snow and carefully stepped off the trail, holding the trees for support and making her way down, digging her heels in and testing that it would hold her weight for each step.

Budrow shook his head a final time, freeing the snow and clearing his hearing. He listened for Ana. She was too far up to see, but he heard her coming down. He crossed the space to the fox. She stood her ground, and he circled her. She favored her right hind leg. It looked mangled. She smelled him; he smelled her. His ears pulled back from his head as he crouched down into the snow and postured to her: *wanna play?*

She might have, but Ana snapped a branch and came into sight. The fox bolted into the brush. Budrow sat looking in the direction she went.

Ana arrived. "Hey, Bud. Where'd you go?" She inspected her footprints and said, "You had a visitor."

They continued their morning runs until spring. Budrow looked for the melanistic fox every day at the spot where he fell off the trail, but she didn't show herself.

◆ ◆

Quinn avoided visiting her father. She was angry. *If I went,* she thought, *I'd just end up screaming at him.* Thinking about him spiked her blood pressure. Emerson reminded her that they would be leaving soon.

He said, "I don't know when we'll be back. He's your father, good or bad. You need closure."

Quinn frowned and said, "You mean as disgusting and evil as he is, he's still my blood so I should want to see him? Fuck, Emerson! He throws me into a rage."

"That's what I mean. You can't carry that around with you. It's not healthy. You need to go talk to him. Clear the air. Close the book."

Quinn walked to the Southwest Quarter jail slowly, by herself. She was rehearsing what she'd say: "Father, I hate you, and I never want to see you again. I'm leaving, goodbye." That one left her feeling madder than before. She tried again. "Father, you have killed everything I ever loved. I hope you rot in this cell." Better. But not quite right. "Father, if I had a gun right now, I'd shoot little pieces of your body off and watch you scream and bleed to death."

Well, maybe she'd tone that down some. She did have her gun.

She met Coner sitting in his place by the Franklin stove in Southwest Quarter Hardware and Sundries. Since the attack, they'd rigged a counterweight on the heavy trap door. He was able to open and close it with one hand. Before they descended the staircase, Coner said, "Might be a better idea to leave yer gun up here, yes?"

The hallway was dimly lit. She passed several empty cells. It was dark in Brock's cell. She heard someone snoring softly. Boston was in the cell adjacent. He was sitting in a reading chair, but he didn't have a book. They'd traded his white maintenance jumpsuit for a pair of baggy Dickies and an oversized Carhart work shirt. He stared out through the bars at something on the other side of the hall.

Quinn said, "Father?"

He was skinny. It surprised her to recognize that his clothes weren't just baggy; he'd shrunk. His hair was growing out, fuzzy white patches on the sides and back. He'd grown a beard, but it was sparse, straggly, and grey.

"Father?"

He seemed to wake up then, looked at her, and smiled. He said, "Lucia. Why did you lock me in here, baby? Whatever I did, I'll make it up to you. Open the door and let me out. I'll get a bottle of Dom, and we'll drink out of the bottle in the bath."

Quinn was revolted. "I'm Elli, Father. You murdered Lucia, remember?"

But Boston couldn't hear her. He cried, "C'mon, baby baby. Let Daddy out of here. Whatever I did, I'm sorry. I'm *so* sorry, baby."

Quinn looked at the dregs of a man who used to call himself High Lord. His cracked lips were pulled away from his teeth, exposing receding gums. Several teeth were loose. His bloodshot eyes bulged.

He croaked, "*Please!*"

She turned and left the hallway without looking back.

◆ ◆

On the morning of the first day of spring, a messenger from the council arrived. Emerson called a meeting. When everyone was in the main room of his house, he relayed the message, "I have just been informed that we are no longer welcome here in Crow City. With the exception of Sandra and Paxon and, strangely, Plummer and his rats."

Plummer said, "The council made an exception at Pejeta's request."

"Where will we go?" Quinn asked

Emerson said, "I'll go talk to Filine. Since she was nominated speaker, we've been discussing options."

"So you knew about this," Ana said.

"Well, let's say I had my suspicions. Filine is reasonable. She and Saą grew up together."

Eggert said, "Me and Maggie have to stay, and this speaker friend of yours better understand that." He sucked his teeth but began to cough and winded himself before he could stop. Margaret helped him recover and fed him some warm tea.

She said, "Eric is sick, friends. He can hardly walk to town, let alone move to some new place. He needs to fly Little Wing to help Plummer finish the library. Even Cyber-man can't pick up some of those girders. But we can't leave."

Emerson said, "We shouldn't try to make decisions without all the facts."

LC said, "I'm hungry, Da."

Emerson said, "You're always hungry, buddy. How about some oatmeal with nuts and raisins?"

Quinn asked Marya if she wanted oatmeal. Marya said, "I had a weird dream, Mama. I dreamt that I was with Mother, but you were there too."

Quinn put a pot of water on the biogas burner. She said, "What was weird about it, baby?"

"I mean, you and The Mother were, like, one person. And you told me that the other people would call to us from the new place. Do you know what that means?"

Quinn looked at Ana. She said, "No, I don't. Did anything else happen?"

Marya curled her hair around her finger and asked, "What's a shortwave?"

Plummer said, "A wave that's not tall." He laughed his braying donkey-on-helium laugh, which was funny in itself. LC began to laugh too.

Ana didn't. She said, "Shortwave is a high frequency analog radio band. It goes from three to thirty megahertz. It's archaic. Nobody uses it. I don't think. Why?"

"That's who Mother said would call. She said there's a place."

Quinn said, "Who would call, baby?" She stopped what she was doing, obviously not following her daughter's reasoning.

Marya made her annoyed face. "SHORTWAVE! Mama, aren't you listening?"

Ana said, "Plummer, can you receive transmissions in the shortwave range?"

He said, snidely, "Do I look like a radio to you?" Which sent LC into another fit of giggles. When the boy calmed, Plummer said, "No, but an RF transceiver back-end connected through the Interface could."

Ana was already thinking about the architecture. "After breakfast, let's work that out." She served LC and Marya bowls of warm cereal.

Emerson said, "I'm going to see Filine. I'll be back." He put on his coat and boots and left, slamming the door.

◆ ◆

Elli went to the clinic after doing a quick fetal heart check and blood pressure on Sandra. Elli used a forehead-mounted stethoscope rather than an Interface-contact microphone; it gave her a better feel for the mom's connection to the baby. She wondered about how much the Interface technology interfered with communication between people, especially in medicine. She said, "Everything looks and sounds great, Sandra."

Ana and Plummer went to The Black Mariah. Quinn practiced the stitches Są taught her with Marya. The girl was already better than she was at her age. LC was digging canals to float woodchip boats on. The snow had mostly melted, though there was still enough around for him to craft roads and landscapes. He had created a game where the boats were merchants moving goods up and down a river. He got the idea from a first reader book Quinn found called *Life on the Nile*.

The melanistic fox hid around the corner of a water barrel watching Little Chandler prattle and speak for each of his twig people. She knew which house Budrow slept in and went around the back, climbing into the sixteen-centimeter-deep depression surrounding the window. She stood on her good hind leg and let the other atrophied limb dangle. Budrow was curled up at the foot of Eggert and Margaret's bed. Eric was under the quilt asleep, breathing slowly. The fox used her front claws to scratch the window glass. The sound was too high-pitched for Eggert to hear. But the scratch was like a dog whistle to Budrow. His ears stood up, and he tracked the sound across the room to the window. The fox licked the glass and jumped down.

Budrow pushed the bedroom door open and went outside through the flap that served as his private entrance. He tasted the air. LC was still playing in the mud. He went around the house the opposite way. The fox sat prettily and tilted her head when she saw him. They touched noses and ran into the woods together, crested the hill, and followed the trail down to the stream. She released a laugh that echoed off the far hillside.

LC stopped playing when he heard it. He'd never heard a fox, but he knew laughter. He smiled and listened for it again. After a moment, he went back to his game. By that time, Budrow and his girlfriend were at the water, hunting minnows in the clear shallows through the thin scrim of ice.

Mule crouched, silent and watchful, halfway up the hillside. She followed Budrow whenever he snuck out. Mule knew the forest. Budrow could sense mystery, but he didn't know danger. Mule stood guard.

◆ ◆

Emerson caught up with Filine on her way to the council hall. She paused to talk.

He said, "We got the eviction."

"It's out of my hands, Emerson. The rest of the council voted me down."

"You let Paxon and Sandra stay. And Pejeta wrangled an exception to allow Plummer and the rats. Can you make one for Eggert and Maggie? He needs to help Plummer finish the library, and frankly, I don't think his health will hold up much longer."

She shook her head. "I'll make a motion today, but there's no guarantee.

The council is worried that your influence is bad for the community. They cite the unrest as evidence. But I see more and more salvage incorporated into our way of life. For decades, we have been able to keep the technocratic impulse from gaining a toehold. We are losing control over it, and it scares them."

"And you? Are you frightened by technology?"

"That's an unfair generalization, Emerson. I believe it's inevitable that we, as a people, embrace the responsible use of electronic tech. It should be needs-based. But in a nonviolent community like ours, it is very difficult to regulate behavior. We've done better historically by keeping the evidence of tech to a minimum. You are a constant reminder. I know we are going to have to change. But I must agree with them. We should be cautious of *being* changed."

Emerson was disappointed, but he took a breath and said, "I hear you. We'll move on when the weather gets warmer. But I need to know I am not abandoning my people. Please push this if you can. Eggert has made Crow City his home, and he's dying. Don't make me drag him away."

◆ ◆

Ana and Plummer coded a basic shortwave receiver utilizing a universal radio module. Gain, frequency, and volume were all managed by Interface connection. She was running it in the sandbox, an isolated virtual machine on The Black Mariah.

Ana wasn't sure if she believed all this *Mother* talk, but she tried to keep an open mind. She had personally experienced enough miracles to know she hadn't seen everything. She would wait, and the truth would make itself apparent. Until then, anything was possible—and it was likely that if someone was broadcasting anywhere, it would be on shortwave.

She switched on the circuit. Silence. She increased the volume. Nothing. It was empty. She slowly panned the frequency range. The silence was occasionally punctuated by repetitive clicking sounds. Ana didn't think these were made by people and continued the sweep. When she reached the top end of the band, she stopped and coded a loop to creep through the frequency range from top to bottom and back automatically. She also set up a data recorder and a notification alarm if it encountered a transmission.

She'd learned from Plummer that when shortwave was in regular use, transmissions were sometimes sent in Morse code. He played a close approximation of the sound of electronic dots and dashes so she could hear it. Ana wrote a translation program and set the alarm trigger to recognize Morse code. If someone was sending, it would be forwarded to her, translated.

She just had to wait.

◆◆

Eggert, Plummer, and Elli used Little Wing to do a supply run to the bunker. It had snowed the night before, and the view of the forest from the sky was breathtaking. When the trees were bare, she could see the slope and curve of the hills. It looked like a woman's nude body, her back, shoulders, hips… She became aroused unexpectedly and shifted in her seat. "We are getting rifles and ammo, right? Not just supplies."

Plummer said, "We have to keep the weapons secret for now. The Crow City council would be unhappy if they knew."

Eggert said, "I'll feel better knowing that they will be able to defend themselves if anyone else comes for them." He cleared his throat, but it became a cough that went on for nearly a minute. When he finally stopped, he spat blood into his palm and then wiped it on his pants.

"You mean *when*," Plummer added.

They set down in the same area as before. The dead avocado grove looked ghostly in the mist. Snow blanketed the world, softening the sharp edges Elli knew were there. As they landed, she saw the wide, shallow stream where Silas Randorn had been eaten. Her Interface suggested the trivial fact that there were forty different English names for a mountain lion including puma, panther, and cougar.

After retrieving drugs and other supplies, they used Little Wing's winch to raise fifty crates of plasma rifles and five high-voltage solar field generators. Once they were stowed, Elli stood at the edge of the field, some twenty meters away from Little Wing, looking at the rows of distant hills beyond the river. Plummer and Eggert were already back on board. Deciding to go, she turned and came face to face with a huge mountain lion which froze ten meters in front of her. The animal's head was level with Elli. She'd surprised it. Another second and her bones would have joined Randorn's.

She raised her rifle and said, "I got no beef with you, mister lion. Everybody's gotta eat. I'd rather not kill you, but if you move toward me, you're dead."

The lion growled low in his throat. Elle sighted the center of its skull, between the eyes. The big cat's tail swished. After a moment, he turned his massive head toward the stream and slowly walked away, growling, leaving platter-sized prints in the snow.

Eggert was standing in the door of the shuttle. "I was a split second from killing that devil."

Elli said, "We came to an agreement."

◆ ◆ ◆

FOGHORN

Coner said yes before Eggert finished explaining his plan for training a secret standing army. Eggert and Plummer had come to him at the hardware store jail. Rat One and Two scurried through the aisles picking up items, sniffing them, and putting them down. One of Coner's new boys, Mitel, was doing a poor job of chasing after the modified rodents, putting items back in their proper places.

"We felt that your people down here in the Southwest Quarter might be better suited for the job," Eggert added.

"I can see that," Coner said. "I know just the woman to head up recruitment. She's missing her left leg from the thigh down, but Teranel is a hardass normally. She'll make a great drill sergeant."

"I have the rifles stored in Little Wing. See who signs up. We need twenty to start."

They shook hands.

◆ ◆

Ana said, "I don't know, Plummer. My shortwave receiver isn't picking anything up."

He reviewed the code.

"I have notification alarms set up, but all I am hearing is random clicks from all over the range."

Plummer didn't say anything. Sometimes it was difficult to know if he was offline. She tapped his shoulder. "Plummer? Hello?"

"I think I found your glitch," he said. "Your code translated megahertz into kilohertz. You've been listening to longwave. It should be right now." She listened a while, then set it to scan.

Ana said, "I've been thinking about how to become your trusted authority. If you can give me read permissions to your core processing, I might have more luck."

"Done. Anything else?"

"Rosco wrote a routine to bench test a satphone when we were living at Blue Hole. Long-distance communications are problematic, but as long as the satellites haven't crashed into the earth, we could still keep in touch. I modified the code and put it up on our Interface server. I think everyone should have it in their personal bag of tricks."

"Yeah, good." Plummer was preoccupied, distracted by something.

Ana said, "The code will run in the background with a notification if anyone calls. Each iteration creates a unique number and passes that to the contact list of every other iteration. That way we can always call one another."

Plummer said, "Right," and rolled away. Ana shook her head and went to the family meeting.

◆ ◆

Emerson took a sip of tea and said, "I got an agreement from the Crow City council to allow Eggert and Maggie to remain here when we go."

Elli said, "Yes!"

Quinn said, "Yeah, but we still don't have any idea where *to* go."

"We have a shortwave receiver program scanning the range," Ana said. "If we interpreted Marya's dream correctly, we should hear something soon."

Emerson said, "If we don't hear about something better, I've been thinking about going back to Chandler's homeplace and rebuilding the cabin." The others murmured about this idea.

"That was a hell of a tornado," Ana said.

"That never happens," Emerson added.

Quinn said, "It happened."

That silenced him. LC was getting restless and squirmed out of Ana's lap. Emerson said finally, "We have to go someplace. They want us out next week."

"Next week? How can we pack everything up in less than a week?" Quinn stood and paced, chewing the cuticle on her left hand.

Emerson said, "We can leave anything that's not essential. It's not like we're dumping it in the ocean. We can come back, just not to stay."

Quinn looked at him, shaking her head, and strode out of the house.

Ana said, "We'll figure out what's essential."

Saą walked to the door. "I'll go talk to Quinn."

Emerson said. "Has anyone seen Mule lately?"

"She's around."

"I don't want to lose track of her in the confusion of the next few days."

Eggert said, "She's been hanging around with Budrow. They've been exploring the woods."

Ana stood up. "Shit! Shit, shit, shit. I got a notification. There's a transmission! Somebody's out there." She called everyone into The Black Mariah and put the transmission on the speakers.

An electronic voice repeated, "46.0211 degrees north, 123.7653 degrees west."

Emerson said, "It's obviously a set of coordinates."

"But to where?" Quinn came in with Saą.

"Northwest of here."

Ana said, "But we don't know who it is."

"We don't even know when it was made or how long it's been repeating," Emerson added.

"I found it on the map. Look, there," Ana said. "It's near the ocean." She cast the display to everyone.

Elli said, "Oh, fuck that. I don't need any more quakes."

Saą replied, "Mother says the seismic activity is further out to sea that far north."

"And it's not on the ocean. It's in the mountains, see?" Ana used an arrow to point at the spot and scrolled out. "The historical map says it used to be called Oregon. A place called Clatsop, twenty-five miles from the ocean."

Emerson asked, "Can we transmit to it? Maybe someone is monitoring."

"I doubt anyone is listening. It's an automated recording. But I can try," Ana said.

"So that's it," Emerson said. "We are going to the Pacific Northwest."

Quinn said, "Whoa, wait a minute, Tiger. How do we know what we'll find? We have children. We need to think this through." She was getting aggravated.

Saą put her hand on her arm and said, "Breathe. We'll be okay."

Quinn pulled away and said, "Don't patronize me, Saą."

Saą was stung, but did not react. "You're right. You're apprehensive for a reason. I can respect that. Do you know why?"

"Besides what I said, no. I'm not ready to jump back into the fire. I'm worn out."

Budrow came into the room and sat in the middle of the floor, looking around. When he'd gotten everyone's attention, he turned back and nosed his flap door.

The melanistic fox popped her head through, looked left and right, jumped into the room, and sat next to Budrow with her tail curled around her atrophied hind leg.

Emerson said, "Hey, I cut a snare off that fox. The day we left the beach."

Quinn knelt by the pair and put her palm out toward the fox. Budrow licked her face. The fox sniffed at Quinn's hand and then nestled her chin into it.

Elli said, "That's amazing."

"We are all related. When there is balance, we can see it and naturally work together to each other's benefit," Saą said.

The fox made the rounds, coming to meet each person in Budrow's family. She went directly to LC and licked his nose; he giggled. She jumped into Marya's lap last and fell asleep.

Margaret said, "I think she's going to be a mama soon. Her nipples are swollen."

Elli said, "She's beautiful."

"Melanistic," Emerson said. "Rarer than rare. Even before the collapse."

Saą said, "Mother says that in the new world, the rarest will be the survivors."

"What does that mean?" asked Ana.

Emerson said, "I've been thinking about this. Mule is a strange anomaly. But not so strange that she couldn't mate. That suggests the rare ones are the ones who survived. The fox is another good example. If there is one thing Chandler impressed on me, it's that life is persistent and tenacious. It always finds a way. Just not always the way you'd think."

"Let's hope the kits survive," Ana said.

Elli said, "Damn. I hope these fox-things take after their mom in the looks department. I mean, I love you with all my heart, Budrow. But you are a mixed-up-looking boy." She took the sleeping fox from Marya and put it in her lap.

Budrow didn't understand a word that Elli said, but he knew love when he felt it. He wagged his tail so hard it made his rear wiggle.

LC pointed at him and said, "Wigglebutt!" Both he and Marya dissolved into giggles and ran from the room screaming.

◆◆

Later that evening, after the kids had gone to sleep, Quinn came to see Emerson.

He said, "What's up?"

"I want to go with Rosco and Grendel. I need to go home." When Emerson didn't speak, she went on, "Boston is gone. Everyone's Interface is locked. There's food and water and electricity. We can go back to some sort of normal."

Emerson said, "Wait. Are you asking me to go back to The City?"

"No, not really. Unless you want to. I mean me and Marya. I don't want our daughter growing up in the wilderness, Emerson. She needs kids her age and a stable life."

"How does Marya feel about leaving her dad?"

"I haven't told her yet; I'm just talking to you first."

Emerson said, "You have to do what you think is best. LC isn't going to be happy. But I won't ever stand in your way."

LC was much more than unhappy. When he realized what Ana was telling him, he screeched and ran away. Several hours later, Emerson found him crouched behind a water barrel. He sat down next to his son and gouged a new canal in the earth with a sharp stick. As he worked, he said, "It makes me sad, too, Chandler. I've been with Marya every day since she was born, but Mama Quinn needs to go with your Uncle Rosco and Aunt Grendel. They have important work to do at The City. And we'll see them again. I promise."

"But you said The City was a bad place." He was looking up into Emerson's face with such complete trust and openness, Emerson's heart nearly broke. LC reminded him of himself when his grandfather would tell stories about The City. He said, "Mama Quinn is going to make it a better place. It used to be her home."

Chandler didn't reply. After a while, Emerson ruffed his son's shaggy hair and stood. "I'll be in the house getting ready. You might want to spend as much time with your sister as possible. I'm just saying." He walked away.

◆ ◆

Barry lived in the North Quarter. He made a show of helping out when Emerson was around, but most of his time was spent at the Crow City market, drinking strong tea and preaching to a small group of citizens. Mother came to him in a dream and told him he had to go with Emerson, but he didn't want to. He liked being the center of attention, even if his congregation was five crippled men and a blind woman.

He decided to simply refuse. The citizens of Crow City welcomed him. He didn't need to obey her. Who was she after all? His memory of her rescue had faded. He doubted that it even happened. In the days before Emerson and crew left, the dreams became intense. Still, Barry believed that it was all in his head. And besides, they were only dreams; what could she do?

The night before leaving, Emerson came to Barry. He said, "Are you still coming with us? We are going at first light."

"I've reconsidered. The people of Crow City need my guidance. I will sacrifice my own desires and stay where I can be of the most use."

Emerson raised an eyebrow but said nothing.

That night, Barry closed his eyes to sleep and was immediately pinned against a wall with a blinding light in his eyes. He struggled to free himself, but invisible hands held him fast. They dug into his shoulders. He opened his mouth to complain and found no air in his lungs. His eyes bulged.

A voice spoke from behind the light. It was calm and quiet. It said, "You will go with Emerson, and you will stay with him at all times. I need this from you, Barry."

It was minutes before grey dawn when he opened his eyes. One word repeated in his mind over and over like an echo. Barry took his pack and walked to the hatch of The Black Mariah. Emerson was checking systems. Mule sat next to his leg, cleaning her paw.

Emerson said, "Changed your mind?"

Barry opened his mouth, and the word that was echoing in his mind came out. "Yes," he said. "Yes."

◆ ◆

Emerson landed The Black Mariah in the center of Founder's Square in The City, just 500 meters from the dead-end street where Boston Quinn killed Lucia Rattlesnake in front of her daughter, Elli.

A few of Quinn's friends, Amber Luce, and Max's younger brother, Mariel, came to meet her. Tanya helped with her duffle. She and Ana hugged. LC had tears in his eyes, and he shivered. Marya hugged Emerson around his neck for a long minute. She climbed down from his arms and stood leaning against his leg.

Quinn said, "Call me on the satphone. Tell me everything." She began to say more, but her voice cracked, and she stopped trying, hoping to get into her apartment before she began to cry, knowing she wouldn't be able to stop.

Elli stood near the hatch looking down at the slate pavers. Quinn opened her arms and said, "Come to me, girl." They embraced tightly.

Elli Moon cried into Quinn's neck, "I don't know who I am without you."

When they broke apart, Elli ran to the back of the shuttle and locked herself in her cabin where she cried herself to sleep. She was not aware that below her bunk, Budrow and his mate had made a den in her clothes bin. Three tiny kits suckled at their mama's teats.

Rosco and Grendel said their goodbyes. Quinn had acquired apartments for them a level below her.

Emerson hugged Quinn quickly and kissed her behind the ear. He couldn't look at her face. To Marya, he said, "I love you."

She said, "Me too, Daddy."

He turned and climbed back into the shuttle. The hatch closed, and ten minutes later, The Black Mariah lifted into the sky, slowly turned to the west, and shot into the distance ahead of a streak of blue light.

◆ ◆ ◆

END OF PART FOUR

INTERFACE

PART FIVE

ARE WE HOME YET?

Plummer held regular drill sessions. The Southwest Quarter men and women were surprisingly dedicated to protecting Crow City, especially considering their second-class status. Coner told the small group of eleven men and five women, "We have little hope of survival without being a part of the greater village. I'm not telling you to love 'em, but they are all the humanity we got. Our best chance of acceptance is to be there helping every time they turn around."

The militia they formed was not regimented. Eggert doubted that they would follow any orders in the face of battle, but what they lacked in training, they more than made up for in dedication. "What my Grand called gumption!" Eggert said and sucked his teeth. "I'd be proud to stand alongside these folks defending our home."

After a month of drills, Plummer explained the guns.

He said, "Hi, y'all."

The group was standing at some semblance of attention. At least they were all standing in a line. They stared blankly at Plummer. He pushed forward. "The weapons that you are going to be assigned are early twenty-first century plasma weapons. They are adjustable to a micro-degree. Only problem is they are Interface weapons."

When the platoon didn't react, Coner said, "Don't you get it? He's tellin' you you're gonna get implants. You got to be Interface users to shoot these guns."

Some grinned, and small talk sprang up. Teranel shut it down with a look.

She had large eyes and a wide face. Her rust-colored hair was shoulder length. There was always a licorice stick in the corner of her mouth.

To Plummer she said, "Speaking for the platoon, sir, we're over the moon with the thought. Y'see, most of us come from generations of poverty. No one in my family has ever had an implant, and even though the world has pretty much gone to shit, sir, having an implant is a thing of status."

They lined up, and Eggert implanted each one. Coner was at the end of the line. He said, "Got one more there, Eric, my friend? For security's sake, right?"

◆ ◆

Plummer registered each user as they were implanted and ran the initial diagnostic. It would take several weeks for the implant to fully connect to their neural networks, but the basic interface would be ready to test as soon as it was initialized.

Eggert said, "Now the fun begins. Each of you will need novice Interface training. I did this class at Enforcer school in The City for thirty years. Most of the exercises should be done as a group."

They all sat on the lawn and listened. He set up a remote screen on a stand outside Little Wing. Eggert cast his personal Interface display to it and said, "This is my basic desktop. You can see yours by looking up and behind your eyebrows. If it helps, close your eyes. You should see something like this, only yours will have your name, vital signs, heart rate, BP, blood oxygen, and any warnings there in the upper right. All of this is customizable, but for now, you will use the default setup. You can play with it on your own time. Don't worry. You can't break it. Either Plummer or I can do a reset if you get hopelessly tangled. Better to screw it up now than when you are in an emergency. The Interface is an amazing extension of your body and mind, but it can also be a deadly distraction if you do not control it."

He scrolled through each trainee's display up on the projection. He continued, "Your Interface mind is a muscle. Since you've never used it, the muscle is weak. These first exercises are meant to build strength and coordination. Next, we'll work on controlling simple machine functions. Then we'll move on to accessing databases and communications. Finally, we will practice controlling and firing the plasma rifles."

Eggert had taught this class for so long he was on automatic. His Enforcer students were never as attentive or quiet as this group. The Southwest Quarter militia learned quickly. Within two weeks, they were practicing cutting paper and glass with the guns set to three. Target practice showed his militia to be especially good shots.

"Well," Coner said, "we've had to hunt for our food most of the time since the collapse. We've only been here in Crow City for a few years. Before that, we roamed."

◆ ◆

Late one evening, after a day of drills, Plummer sat with Eggert as he sipped hooch in the growing dusk. "Ah, Plummer. It might seem weird after doing this sort of work for the Enforcers for so many years, but I'm prouder of this unit than any other I've trained!" He sucked his teeth. "Damn proud!" He took another deep drink, but it triggered a coughing fit. By the time it settled, he was too exhausted to stand. Margaret came out to help bring him inside.

Near the end of the third week, Eggert didn't come to training. Plummer was staying in the village, working on the library with every spare minute. The wielding on the steel frame was complete, and the outer shell was nearly done. He oversaw several local Crow City engineers who had volunteered, and the work on the interior was progressing steadily.

He went directly to the clinic when he couldn't raise Eggert.

Margaret was there. She said, "He fell. We think he broke his leg, but when Pejeta did a scan, she found the tumors. We consulted The Memories, Plummer. Eric has lung cancer. We don't know how long he's got, but he's too weak to work anymore."

Plummer said, "If I could hug, I would hug you, Margaret. But don't worry about anything. We got this. You take him home and make him comfortable."

Eggert was sedated but awake. Plummer said, "I'll carry you home, my friend."

Eggert sucked his teeth. "I'd appreciate it."

He picked the frail man up and held him like a child, slung across two of his four arms.

Pejeta was there. She and Margaret hugged. Plummer put one of his free erector-set claws on Margaret's shoulder, but it looked creepy and felt wrong. He removed it and rolled out of the building.

◆ ◆

It was dark in the cells except for a small candle they left burning in the hallway. Brock said, "Boston, are you awake?"

There was a moan in the darkness.

He continued, "If we can get out of here and into the woods, I have a satphone hidden in a hollow tree."

Boston said, "What good is a satphone if we have nobody to call? Besides, they keep me so drugged I can hardly see, let alone walk."

"Stop drinking the water. That's where the sedative is. I think I can get us out of here."

"And die of thirst?" He was silent for a minute. "Who would we call?"

"There are Enforcers who are loyal. I'm sure they are plenty pissed that Lloyde put you in prison. But we need to get out of here first."

"It's too fucking cold in here. I can't even feel my fingers most of the time."

"Stop whining, you fat asshole. I have someone in the village who can help us."

• •

Anoush was not killed. In the confusion, Brock only listed her as dead. He warned Paxon and Sandra about the attack; the two fled and were hiding in the forest when the gunships arrived. After the funerals and life in the village settled down, Anoush snuck back to the brothel and had been living there since. She had patrons in the Southwest Quarter who kept her presence a secret. She did favors for food and tradeable trinkets like gems and clothes.

Before the gunships came, Brock told her he might be imprisoned or killed. If he was still alive, she should hide until everyone had forgotten about her. Then she should help him escape, and they would return to The City together where he would be a senior Lord with real power.

Brock had no idea that Quinn, Rosco, or Grendel had returned to The City. He expected Anoush to visit soon. He planned to have Boston pass the scepter to him so his position would have some legitimacy. But if the Old Shit couldn't see or walk, he'd just as soon leave him to rot.

He needed Anoush. He was waiting patiently until then.

• •

The transit over the Inland Sea was quiet. Emerson reread *Sometimes a Great Notion*. Or at least he tried. He kept losing his place when his thoughts drifted off to Quinn. He hadn't thought about how attached they'd become. He told Saą, "We never talked about it. I just assumed she wanted to be with me. I wanted to be with her."

Saą said, "Relationships require work, Emerson. Spontaneity will only take you so far."

Ana and LC spent time playing Go Fish with Grandpa Chandler in the Sim. LC described in detail his Nile merchant game and how, when they got to their new home, he was going to make an even bigger river with pyramids!

Barry didn't like air travel. When he wasn't self-sedated on the secret stash of hooch he kept hidden in his bunk, he was in the head, purging from both ends.

Mule slept when they flew. Emerson made her a padded box, and she stayed in it. Memories of unexpected flights through the main cabin kept her still.

Elli tried to stay in her cabin, but after she'd been awake for a while, she got bored. Just as she was putting on her shoes to go see what everyone else was doing, she heard a squeak from under the bunk.

She came into the cockpit and said, "Budrow and his girlfriend came along with us, and she had her kits. They're in my cabin."

Everyone had to come and see. LC pleaded with Ana to let him tell Grandpa Chandler. But then he remembered that he couldn't tell Marya, and it made him sad, and he wanted to go to bed. Ana hugged him in her lap.

Emerson said, "It's going to take a while to adjust to Quinn's absence. I hope he'll be okay." Ana nodded, wondering if Emerson was going to be okay.

Saą cooed over the kits for a bit and went back to her seat in the cockpit. She watched the dark horizon at the edge of the water. The stars above were like chips of glass thrown on black velvet.

They landed on the western shore and set up camp. Emerson wanted to run diagnostic checks and do a surface inspection of the shuttle, and everyone needed a rest. The weather was hot and humid during the day, but the evenings were cool. They stayed for a few days.

It was cloudy and cold the next day. They stayed inside the shuttle watching the featureless grey shift shades through the view screens. Outside, the temperature was negative ten. Wild temperature fluctuations were normal near the Inland Sea. Sąą kept to her bunk. The weather cleared on the third day, and they continued on northwest.

◆ ◆

They approached a mountain. Its peak poked through a thick cloud cover, making it appear like a volcano in a whipped-cream sea. Emerson did a search for the name, but Ana beat him to it.

She said, "Wy'east. That's what the Northern Paiute people called it."

He brought The Black Mariah down to 4,000 meters under the clouds and opened up monitors from the bottom and front of the ship. The shuttle flew a wide circle around the mountain. It was so close you could see animal tracks. The north face was covered in snow.

"This is amazing," Elli said.

Barry came forward to see the source of the excitement and stood with his mouth open, watching the extinct volcano drift past. His beard had grown back, and since his diet had lately consisted mostly of sweet cakes and fatty meat, so had his prodigious belly. Chandler would say, "You can put lipstick on a pig, boy, but it's still a pig."

Ana noticed a group of people a half kilometer away. She pointed to them.

Emerson said, "They look like scouts. I don't want to stick around in case they've seen us." He took The Black up into the cloud cover.

"There were six," she said. "They were carrying longbows."

Emerson replied, "Yeah, maybe they are from the army in the north that Boston was warning us about."

"Too far away for that."

"Or he's just crazy." Emerson used the scope to see if the scouts were tracking them, but they had disappeared.

Ana said, "Like a fox. Speaking of which, I guess Budrow and the melanistic fox were compatible enough to breed."

Emerson sighed. "Cute little buggers."

Ana said, "In a dying world…"

Saą added, "Life finds a way."

Ana put her hand on Emerson's wrist. "It's hopeful, isn't it? With all this death, life still prevails."

After checking the vitals of The Black Mariah, Emerson said, "We're about 160 kilometers from the source of that transmission. It's getting late, and I'd like to arrive in the light. So, I'm going to find a place to set down, and we can make camp." He landed, and they set up a fire pit on a sandy patch next to a lake, still in the foothills, just northwest of the peak.

◆ ◆

Severn Milk was commander of the third division of the Roze City Scouts. He and each of his five companions carried small day sacks and a quiver of titanium-shank razor-tipped arrows. Their longbows were always in their hands. Trained as teens, he and his mates were the third of three teams patrolling the boundary: a circle around the city 100 kilometers in diameter.

Deeter gave the silent signal, and the platoon dropped into a crouch, heads bowed, bows planted in the earth before them. Severn used his peripheral vision to glance at the aircraft. He had never actually seen any aircraft, but he'd heard of them. The shuttle flew out of sight.

Soo pulled the hood tighter over her small cage of carrier pigeons and murmured shushes to calm their agitated cooing.

"*That* was not a bird," Severn signed to the others.

A moment later, Deeter signed back, "It's gone."

Nevera said, "What then, eh? Some kind of boat in the sky? Have you evea seen such a thing, Severn? You're not just looking for a way to spice up a night's duty, are ya?"

Severn didn't look at her; he was tasting the wind. He said, "I know you too well to let you get a rise outa me, Nevera." He stood and looked at the sky in the direction of the ship's disappearance. "There. It landed there."

Leebla said, "Not meanin' to question yer expertise, sir, but how's it you know?"

The six gathered around to listen. Severn was a master tracker. He was born with special powers of observation. Part of it he would have called a photographic memory if he'd known the term. As a scout he had very little contact with the world outside of his station. He lived and breathed the natural world. Severn Milk could read it like a map.

He said, "I know where the horizon begins. Even when the sun is setting, I can tell. The flying ship landed vertically, and it landed *before* the horizon. I'd say it is no more than fifteen kilometers—about four hours' hike in this part of the foothills. They'll be gone by tomorrow."

Vischek said, "What's the point of waiting? Let's go."

"You have an opinion, Soo?" said Severn.

She shook her head. Deeter said, "We might be walking into a trap. We don't know what weapons they have. But if they can fly…"

Vischek, always the impatient one, said, "I say we go now."

"And when have we ever done what you say?" Deeter asked.

"We'll go in the morning," Severn said. "No sense rushing into the storm. We'll inspect the landing site tomorrow. Soo, send a pigeon. Warn the Wall to look out for a flying ship. Everyone else, find shelter. The rain will get here in an hour."

◆ ◆

Emerson had just finished making a fire when the first drops splashed on the dirt next to him, kicking up little puffs of dust. It wasn't the first time he'd cooked in a rainstorm. Mule returned with a couple of rabbit-like animals. They were reddish brown and at least three times the size of normal rabbits.

When Ana saw them, she yelled, "ROUS!"

Elli looked at her sideways.

Emerson said, "No, not really. Just mutant rabbits."

Elli asked, "Is there a nuke site near here?"

Ana looked it up. "The Hanford waste site is 150 kilometers northeast."

Elli asked, "What's ROUS?"

Emerson said, "Rodents of unusual size. It's from an old movie called *The Princess Bride*. I showed it to Ana. You should see it."

"Do you think they might be radioactive?" Saą was basting the animals as they roasted over glowing coals. She ducked back into the open bay doors where the others were sheltering as dinner cooked. Rain drops hit the glowing embers, occasionally spitting and popping.

Emerson said, "Mutation comes from damaged or modified genes. But they would only be radioactive if they were living in the waste. At that far away, I doubt it. Radiation poisoning would kill it before it could get this far."

They thought silently in the growing dark. Emerson added, "But we don't know why they are so big. Nuclear mutation is just one guess."

After everyone had fallen asleep, Saą and Emerson watched the fire burn down. The rain had turned to a mist, and the air was humid but warm.

He leaned his head against her and said, "I feel like my heart is in two places. I hope Quinn and Marya are doing okay."

Saą said, "Quinn needs to get her head and heart clear. She will come back to you. I can see the silver cord between you two."

"I hope you're right." Mule stretched on the other side of the fire and rolled on her back with her massive paws in the air and fell back to sleep.

In the morning, after coffee, Emerson cleaned up. Chandler instructed him to never leave a trace, but he was not as observant as Saą. She spent that morning with LC and Ana in the shuttle. They left before the sun was above the hills and flew north with a plan to follow the river most of the way to the ocean.

◆ ◆

Severn Milk and his scouts arrived at the camp around nine. His platoon rested near the lake while he inspected the dirt where the shuttle had landed. He discovered compressed earth where the landing pads had been. And even though the fire was out and the ashes were scattered into the sand, the ground was still warm.

Rummaging around in the brush, he found their covered latrine and a place near a tree where the rabbit bones were buried. 100 meters along the bank, he found one of Mule's pawprints. His findings were coded and written by Soo onto a strip of Tyvek in her tiny precise calligraphy. She tied it to a pigeon's leg and sent it to the Wall at Roze. There was nothing left to do but continue on their scouting route. The matter was now out of his hands. It was the Defenders' responsibility.

◆ ◆

Emerson navigated The Black Mariah outside the boundary of Roze City even though he didn't know it was there. The river was wide and spectacular. They spent the remainder of the morning flying low on the northern side. When the tall buildings came into view, he increased altitude to 13,000 meters. The risk of antiaircraft guns went up drastically in urban centers. Even though the city that stretched out as far as he could see was crumbling in ruin, he wanted to avoid being seen.

The Defenders of the Wall guard saw that something passed high up, but they did not get a good look. Severn's first pigeon arrived twenty minutes later. Lican Troom read the Tyvek and snapped the bird's neck, tossing its carcass over the stone abutment that formed the northeastern parapet. He was the commander of the Wall. He would pretend the pigeon never arrived and send a platoon west to investigate.

He said out loud to himself, "No sense giving that scout Milk any credit." He laughed. The guard standing ten meters from him didn't dare even look in his direction.

He called for a messenger, "Assemble a stealth team. I want that flying craft found and brought to me!"

◆ ◆ ◆

HOUSES IN THE TREES

Barry said, "If I never fly again, it will be too soon."

Elli said, "Fine with me, fat boy. I don't like you stinking up the head."

He stuck his tongue out at her. She walked away.

The shuttle had landed in a wide area that looked like it could have accommodated hundreds. A blackened ring of stones marked where the firepit was, but it had been years since there was a fire in it. Several of the thick-trunked deciduous trees in the valley were connected by ramps. Above the suspended paths were houses, multilevel homes, built into the massive tree limbs.

Ana opened the sim with Grandpa Chandler so LC could stay safely in the shuttle while they went out to explore. The boy loved his great-grandfather and never complained about spending time with him. As she left, she heard the old man say, "So, boy, have you ever seen the documentary *The Pyramids of Egypt*? No? Oh, you're gonna love it!"

Outside, Saą said, "The trees gave their consent to build these homes. The people who created this lived in balance with them. It is truly a unique relationship."

Elli said, "But where are the people who built it?"

Ana said "And what is powering the shortwave transmitter, hm? This place doesn't look inhabited."

Saą replied, "There are a few people. They are afraid of us. And they do not live in the trees."

Emerson looked up at the sprawling structures and said, "This is so huge. I bet 2,000 people could live comfortably in these trees."

Elli climbed up and grabbed a staircase and pulled it down, clipping the stringers to an iron latch staked into the ground. "C'mon, let's explore!" She skipped up the stairs and disappeared down a lower pathway. Her voice echoed, "Hey, this place is cool."

The others climbed up. Barry looked pale. He was the last up the staircase. He said, "I don't like heights."

Ana said, "You can always stay by The Black Mariah."

"No," he said, "I can't. Mother made it clear. I must stay with Emerson. She gives me a headache if I try to ignore her."

On the second level, the ramps ran from tree to tree. Each tree was like a separate building with many upper floors and rooms. Ana said, "These are homes."

Each one had a common area with a cooking and heating stove. Water was piped in from a network in the upper canopy. Black and grey water sewage were piped out in two lines that ran down the main trunk and into the ground. Later, Emerson traced them to a rudimentary septic black water treatment basin and a subterranean growing cave. Light was piped in through reflective conduits with large glass prisms near the entrance. The rooms were so bright that he had to shield his eyes. There was evidence of fruit trees and vegetable beds in the high-ceilinged chambers. But nothing had grown there in years.

Another tree—a massive oak—housed several floors of what looked like merchant stalls and storage lockers, all open and empty. Another one appeared to be a school of some kind with chalkboards lining the walls. On the top floor of the largest tree was a locked room. A wraparound porch provided views of the forest above the canopy. Emerson could see the thin line of the ocean in the western distance.

He inspected the lock and texted Ana:

```
These people were Interface users. I found a
room with a neural lock. I am powering it up
                  now.
```

Ana and Elli found him a few minutes later. Barry stood on the deck with his back pressed against the wall farthest from the edge. The trees all swayed in the wind, and this high up, they swung from side to side in a wide arc.

Elli said, "Barry, you look fucking green, man. Don't you puke on the floor up here. I can't deal with any more of your stink."

Barry hiccuped with his hand covering his mouth and looked at her apologetically. She said, "I'm serious, man. Close your fucking trap."

Emerson unlocked the door. It swung open with a muffled click.

Inside they found a bank of computers and thick cable feeds from solar panels higher up in the trees. Emerson used his Interface to access the control panel and switched on the power. The processor lights blinked. Fans spun, and recessed ceiling lights slowly illuminated, glowing amber first and brightening to creamy yellow before snapping bright white.

Emerson received a request to open a channel with the local Interface processor, which he accepted. It instantly opened a session inside a simulation. Before surrendering completely, he registered Ana, Saą, and Elli's implants, and the three women joined him in the sim.

A thin woman with straight blonde hair appeared in the center of a simulation room, which looked like a mirror of the computer room they were actually sitting in, but the floor in the simulation was carpeted with a living grass rug, and moonlight shone through the opened windows.

She said, "Welcome to The Haven. My name is Kindra. The year is 2062. I assume that you are experiencing this in the future, and that I am most likely dead. I hope you are comfortable. I am your virtual guide. I can answer any questions about The Haven, and you are welcome to live here as long as you like." She had a strong chin and robin's-egg blue eyes. Emerson noticed a small scar on her forehead.

Elli said, "What happened to you? Where are your people?"

"Good question, Elli Moon. All in good time. For now, I want to instruct Emerson and Ana in the process of waking up the systems. Once you have water, sewage, heat, and shelter functioning again, I will tell you the entire history. I suggest we break out the wine and have a celebration. The Haven was created for you. It was designed to fulfill all human needs and prepare you for the journey. But we have plenty of time to get to that. Come, let me show you the initialization routines. Once you are moved in, we can meet again."

The systems were cold and stiff, but Emerson, Ana, and Elli were able to lubricate and initiate them. Before sundown, several tree houses were illuminated in the upper branches. Blue and yellow lanterns glowed from embedded niches in the trunks. The Haven, as Kindra called it, looked like a glimmering city of fairies. Everyone's heart felt weightless. The idea even crossed Emerson's mind to bring Quinn and Marya here. Like the storm clouds of the past year had finally lifted, warming them with the sun of a new hope. They would begin a community here and invite others to join them. The settlement would grow.

♦ ♦

Elli saw the girl hiding around a corner. She was dirty, dressed in torn clothes. Elli sat on the ground and took a piece of jerky out of her day pouch. After a moment, the girl was standing in front of her.

"Want some?" Elli asked. She tore off half. "Here." She held it out and popped the other half in her mouth.

The urchin grabbed the slice out of Elli's hand and stuffed it in her mouth, but she didn't run. Elli nodded and took out another piece and gave it to her. The girl held it while she chewed the first piece. Elli said, "If you need anything, come and find me, okay?"

She looked frightened for a moment and walked away.

◆ ◆

Everyone felt the sun of hope but Barry. Barry was constipated. Their new diet consisted almost entirely of uber-rabbit stew with local wild onions and tubers. It often included a prolific green leafy plant called licorice fern that carpeted the temperate rainforest floor. He'd been ill since they landed and didn't know exactly what he was reacting to since he had never eaten any of it before. So, he just suffered.

He was impacted so badly that he walked bent over, which made him look a little like a troll from a distance. Barry was much too big to be a troll, but an Orc, maybe, or some sort of goblin. He had been unable to go for so long that any hint of an impending bowel movement would send him straight to the latrine. He was often disappointed.

Barry followed Emerson, who was tracing a buried cable with a makeshift metal detector Ana had cobbled together. They still had not found the location of the shortwave transmitter. He was convinced it was not in the cluster of tree houses. Discovering a buried cable was the best clue he'd had in days. Barry was walking alongside Emerson asking questions, trying to act interested in the answers, when the urge suddenly struck him. They were on a narrow trail through high grass. Barry sprinted toward the woods where he squatted, leaning back against a tree. It was the most satisfying shit he'd taken in his entire life, and he rested there, panting.

Barry had a bad relationship with poison oak—the hairy vines of which covered the trunk of the tree he'd leaned against for support. A day later, he had a screaming red rash up and down his back, neck, and the backs of his arms.

Saą made a salve out of comfrey and plantain. It didn't help much and left his skin with a greenish tint, causing Elli to make frequent remarks about his goblin heritage. He tried to stay in and rest up, but on the second day, he woke with a migraine. It felt as though his eyeballs bulged out of their sockets in time with his heartbeat and made him so sick that he nearly puked. It seemed his head pain vanished the moment he met up with Emerson. Barry mumbled, "Mother isn't going to cut me any slack."

♦ ♦

They entered the sim again after the systems were up. Kindra welcomed everyone. LC nursed and fell asleep on Ana's lap. Saą sat next to Emerson. Elli squatted near the door in the corner. Since he had no implant, Barry couldn't hear or see Kindra and waited outside.

Kindra said, "The Haven was envisioned and constructed by Professor Albert and Doctor Anya Gillespie. She was an Interface engineer in the mid-2000s, and he was a genius inventor, a scholar of Traditional Ecological Knowledge.

"They anticipated the collapse and began creating the infrastructure for The Haven before the virus swept the earth, which unfortunately took both Doctor Gillespie and her husband. They were survived by their children, Dol and his sister Arn. It was the twins who salvaged the rest of the raw materials to build the city in the branches as you see it today. They recruited scientists, engineers, and farmers from all over the world to come to The Haven and complete their parents' dream." Emerson noticed her clenched jaw and the scar on her forehead.

"The Community grew and prospered for close to forty years when we were attacked by a hostile group from the east. Dol was killed along with many of the men. Most of the women and children were taken back to Roze City where they were made slaves. Arn and the remainder of The Haven citizens left in search of a new home. She created me to help others who hear the beacon.

"Be warned. The soldiers of Roze are brutal and angry. Whatever you possess they will believe it is theirs. They take with no care for the consequences to others. They live by the rights of force. We could not defend ourselves. We kept no defensive weapons and no trained army. I sincerely hope you can."

Emerson said, "Where did Arn go? How can we follow if we haven't a clue?"

Kindra said, "I am sorry, Emerson Lloyde. But I was recorded before Arn left. I have no way to know where she went after that. She had no intentions where I was concerned." The simulation rubbed the back of her neck and looked away. "But I will tell you the soldiers from Roze City probably know you are here already, and they will want your shuttle. Prepare to defend yourselves. The people in Roze City do not have Interface technology."

The sim ended.

Emerson was visibly stressed. He said, "I need to get some air and think about this. Saą, get everyone close to the shuttle. If what she says is true, and I have no reason to doubt it, we need to be ready to go. I have no intention of doing battle with LC present. I'm afraid we can't stay."

He walked into the forest, not following any sort of trail, just moving aimlessly, staring but not really seeing, trying to process the news.

When Barry realized Emerson had left, he stumbled down the steps. On the ground, he looked around for some trace of Emerson's direction.

Mother pushed his back and said, "That way!" He followed her direction into the forest.

A few minutes later, Emerson began to calm down. He took a breath and sighed. *Shit*, he thought. *Just when I began to think we're home.* He thought of Quinn and Marya. It felt like tearing the stitches out of a deep wound. He tried to look for the positive side but couldn't see one. *There will be time later to think about it*, he thought, *but now I need to act!* He took a deep breath and turned to walk back. Emerson nearly walked into a wall of dark brown fur.

The grizzly was nearly five meters tall and stank of rotting garbage.

The odor completely enveloped Emerson as the animal roared, spraying his face with spit and bits of her last meal.

Emerson froze. He didn't have a weapon. The bear roared again and began to move. At that moment, Barry arrived, out of breath, shirtless, and beet red. He screamed at the bear, grabbed a handful of rocks, and threw them, hitting her in the head.

She turned to him, shook her head, and stumbled. Barry held his breath. He couldn't possibly outrun a bear. She took a step and stumbled. A trickle of blood ran into her eye. She shook her head and roared again.

Barry screamed, "AAAAAAHHH! GET, GO! HAH!"

Saą, Ana, and Elli were running into the woods from the tree house. Elli pointed her rifle. The bear took a step toward Barry and swung her paw at him, carving four deep grooves in the side of his head and snapping his neck in one smooth movement. Barry's body crumpled into the underbrush. The bear turned back. Emerson heard a rattle behind him.

Saą bent down to check for a pulse, but Barry was dead. Even if the bear had not broken his neck, he could not have survived the wounds to his skull.

Elli fired a pulse at the animal's back. She'd set the power to five, not knowing how tough a grizzly's hide was. The beam hit the animal directly in her spine, but instead of making a hole, the massive bear exploded. The sheer force, including bits of her partly disintegrated anatomy, threw Emerson backward into a depression in the ground. He was unconscious when Saą reached him.

Mule arrived just following the blast. She moved next to Emerson, licking his face with her coarse tongue. The women picked up his body and carried him to the shuttle. Mule followed.

Just before they left the woods, Mule collapsed into the weeds. But no one noticed.

◆ ◆

Anoush arrived at the hardware store jail at three in the morning. The night guard was passed out drunk on the floor next to his chair. She went to Brock and kissed him hard through the bars. He squeezed her breast with one hand and groped her with the other. She broke the kiss and backed away.

"Here." She squeezed a fat waterskin through the bars. "I'll bring more tomorrow. Kendry Brown is passed out. He won't be a problem."

Boston croaked, "Give me that!"

"You'll get your turn, old man." Brock guzzled half of the skin and passed it through the bars into Boston's cell.

To Anoush, Brock said, "I need you to sneak out into the woods and make a satphone call for me. Can you do that?" She nodded. "Here's the number. I'll draw you a map. Don't let anyone see you. Remember, you're dead."

"And you'll make me your queen, right, Terry? You'll put a baby in me. She can be our heir, just like the stories," Anoush said.

Brock replied, "Yes, yes, baby. Just call this number and tell them it's time for part two. Come back and tell me what they say." He didn't bother to tell her that he, like most men from The City, was sterile.

Boston was still in the dark. He said, "More. More water, please."

Brock said, "Go now before anyone comes."

After she'd left, he said, "Man up, fat boy. Don't drink the water they give us. The sooner you are fully awake, the sooner we can break out of this poor excuse for a jail." But he was limiting the amount of clean water Boston was getting.

◆ ◆

They laid Emerson on the mess table in The Black Mariah. Saą put her hand on his head.

Elli checked his pulse at his wrist and then his neck. "It's so weak. He must be injured; he isn't just unconscious."

"You are right, Elli," Saą said. "Mother says look deeper."

In the urgency to bring Emerson in, they left the shuttle door open. Budrow, who hadn't been out that day, took the opportunity to pee against several trees. He followed the scent Emerson left. The smell of the exploded bear was strong, but there was another smell. He put his nose to the dirt and followed the microscopic particles aging and swirling together with the breath of the grass and moss and trees. His olfactory bulb was well-developed, giving him an extra edge, a gift from his ancestors on both the wolf and fox side. He easily sorted the different smells and uncovered the identity of the other: Mule.

He ran directly to her. She was lying on her side, her breathing shallow, unable to move or open her eyes. Budrow barked. The cat didn't move. He barked again and again. He set a rhythm. He sang a warning. His song cried for Mule, pleaded for help, shouted with urgency and anger that he could not be clearer. He barked so hard his heart broke. And they heard him.

Ana and Elli picked Mule's limp body up and brought her into the shuttle. They laid her on the floor. Saą checked her eye and the color of her gums. She listened to the breathing. Then she inspected the big cat's body, running her hands along Mule's paws and legs.

"Ah! Here." She parted the fur on Mule's hind flank. There were two puncture wounds. Both were angry, red, and inflamed. She prodded the flesh. Mule drew a shuddering breath, held it for a moment, and then deflated as her spirit left her body.

Ana said, "Oh my Goddess, is she gone?"

Saą shouted, "ANTIVENOM! GIVE EMERSON ANTIVENOM! IT WAS A SNAKE! A DEADLY SNAKE! HURRY!"

Elli used a pressure hypodermic to force antivenom into Emerson's neck. His body jerked, but his breathing remained depressed. They put him on an IV to keep him hydrated and strapped him to a bunk.

They turned him over and found several bites on his shoulder and neck.

Elli locked Budrow in her cabin. She said, "I'm grateful that you found her, but I want you to be safe. We might have to fly at any moment." She didn't think the little foxdog could understand her, but it made her feel better to get her thoughts lined up. Before she closed the door, she said, "Thank you." Though at that moment, she wasn't sure why.

Back in the main cabin, Ana said, "One thing is sure—Emerson wouldn't want us to remain in danger for him. I suggest we leave now and regroup."

Elli said, "We need to stay away from that mountain. Those scouts."

"I agree. Can you fly the shuttle?" Saą asked.

Ana replied, "I'm going to damn well try."

Elli used her plasma gun to dig a grave for Mule. She couldn't stand the idea of just leaving her body out for the vultures to pick clean. She, Saą, and Ana held a quick ceremony. She wanted to just leave Barry.

Saą said, "I believe that we owe Emerson's life to Barry. And even though he is no longer in that body, I want to honor him too. Can you dig another grave, please, Elli?"

They did not mark either burial site. The purpose, as far as they were concerned, was not for them or Mule or Barry. Saą nodded her head and said, "We care for these bodies as an honor to The Mother. For all things come and go from her. She helped Barry protect Emerson, and we give thanks."

Elli said, "That's all well and good, but he saved Emerson from a bear so I could knock him into a snake's nest."

Saą said, "You may blame yourself, but Mother saw the snake as clearly as she saw the bear. You played your part in saving Emerson, too."

Elli walked away. Ana said, "I won't feel better until Emerson wakes up."

"He's awake. I have spoken with him. As with Marya, his body simply needs time to heal. Emerson will sleep until that healing is complete," said Saą.

"But if he's in a coma, how can you talk to him?"

Saą said, "I believe you know the answer." She tapped the spot below her ear.

"Right! The Interface implant was designed to allow the control of complex machinery when the body is incapacitated during high-G acceleration. I guess this proves the idea that coma patients are aware but unable to use their body."

◆ ◆

Ana entered the Chandler Cube. He was tinkering with a small machine on the kitchen table. The kettle was whistling. He looked up and said, "That's not a good look on you, pretty lady. I'd ask you what's wrong, but I already know. So, you want to create a simulation room for Emerson, while he is healing."

Ana had tears in her eyes; she nodded. Chandler hugged her tight. She forgot that he was only a simulation and sank deeper into his warm flannel. He smelled like cedar and bay rum. She didn't even wonder where it came from or how he made it. She just faded away and cried into the worn fabric of his shirt.

When her breathing calmed, she pulled away. He gave her a cup of sassafras tea and bid her sit at the table. He said, "I have a suggestion. Why not port Emerson into this simulation? It would be easier than creating one from nothing, and if he were here with me, the wait would go much faster for him."

Ana thought about it for a moment. "How can I get consent from a man who is not awake?"

"Some part of him is, or Saą wouldn't be able to talk to him. Ask her to help. She's implanted."

Ana said, "Right." She stood up from the table and hugged him around the neck. "Thank you, Grandpa."

He said, "Anytime, love. And bring Little Chandler to me soon. I want to teach him to play chess. That boy has the mind of a master."

The sim ended, and Ana ran to find Saą. She had just finished the checklist for takeoff and was closing the hatch.

Ana said, "We can port Emerson into the Chandler Cube, but I need his consent. Can you talk to him?"

Saą said, "I don't see why not. He would be able to interact with us from inside, presumably, while his body heals."

A moment later, Emerson's disembodied voice spoke through the ship's speakers. "Hello, Ana, Saą, and Elli. It's the strangest thing. I don't seem to have any body anymore. Except The Black Mariah, I can *feel* her systems."

He began the charging sequence for the reactors. "Did you clear out all of our stuff? I don't want to leave any trace for the soldiers."

Ana said, "Wait, Emerson. Someone is banging on the hatch."

A view window opened to the other side of the door. A woman with matted grey hair dressed in torn jeans and a stained smock backed away from the glass and shouted. Her cries were ported through the speakers. "WHAR'S MY LITTLE GIRL? YOU CAIN'T TAKE M'LITTLE GIRL!"

Ana opened the door.

She pushed past Saą and Ana and began throwing open bin doors and closets.

"PIN!" she shouted. "Pinny, cummout now, girl. The raiders is cummin. We gotta go!"

Emerson ported his voice to the overhead speakers. He said, "We don't have your little girl. You should leave now."

Through the front view screen, they saw a band of three men carrying longbows appear at the edge of the clearing. When the men were 100 meters away, a fourth man emerged holding a small child by the wrist, her filthy feet and legs dangling off the ground. The other three had nocked arrows and were pointing them at The Black Mariah.

"Can they do anything to the shuttle?" Elli asked.

Emerson's disembodied voice said, "I doubt it."

The four advanced. The man with the child held her in front of his torso. All four wore matte-black breastplates and shin guards. The woman rummaging through the cabinets suddenly screamed, "PIN! THAS MY PIN!"

Saą grabbed her arm and said, "No, wait." But the frantic mother twisted free.

The man with the child yelled, "Surrender the flying machine or I kill the girl."

The ragged woman jumped through the open shuttle door and sprinted toward them. The archer on the far left put an arrow through her heart, killing her instantly. The girl squirmed and screamed. Her captor smacked her into silence.

Elli had followed the woman, and she was standing, legs apart for balance where she fell. She held her nuke cannon. As it began changing, she said, "Well, that was pretty stupid. What are you going to bargain with now? That woman was the only one who cared about the kid."

The man with the child said, "So you won't mind if I break its neck, right?" He shook her by the leg.

Ana fired her plasma rifle, and the top of his head disappeared. He crumpled to the ground. The girl ran to her mother. The other three archers turned toward Ana. Before they could draw their bows, she fired a stream of plasma that cut them in half. Their bodies fell in a pile. Elli's gun finished charging, and she fired at the pile of dead men. The gun made its normal FUMP sound. Veins of static electricity covered the bodies, and they disappeared, leaving a few snapping sparks and buzzing fireflies of electricity.

Saą went to the girl sobbing over the body of her dead mother. She said, "Is there anyone else? A brother or sister or father?"

The girl shook her head. The tears had cut clean rivulets in her filthy face.

Saą took her hand. "Come, you're with us now. We are your family."

Ana buried the girl's mother. Soon after, The Black Mariah lifted into the clouds and left that region of the continent. Ana took over flying to allow Emerson a chance to rest. She said, "We need to regroup and weigh our options."

Saą said, "I am sending you the coordinates for a house in the mountains southeast of here. We will be safe, and there are supplies I will need for Emerson."

Ana set a course and engaged the autopilot.

Everyone sat together in the main cabin. They were dazed. No one spoke. Ana said it would take about four hours to get there. "Everyone should try and rest until then."

They set a schedule to check on Emerson every twenty minutes, but Saą sat with him through the night.

Elli gave Pin a slice of jerky and brought her to the shower room where she removed the girl's rags and got into the shower with her. The recirculating water finally ran clean after three soapy washes and rinses. She tried to use an electric dryer on the girl's hair, but there was no way to untangle it. Elli shaved the child's head and disinfected the bites and scratches on her scalp. She cut her fingernails and toenails and brushed the dirt from her cuticles. It was as if the child had never seen water, though she sat, staring at the wall, while the shower ran.

Elli incinerated the dress the girl had been wearing. She had a worn cotton T-shirt of Ana's from her days in Blue Hole, back when there was a robust trade between The City and the small villages surrounding it. It was soft and worn and always made Elli feel better when she wore it. She put it over Pin's head; it looked more like a potato-sack dress than a shirt on the small child.

Elli said, "It'll have to do until we can ask LC for some of his." *It will have to do.* The phrase made her think of Eggert, though she wasn't sure she'd ever heard him say it. She wondered how he was. She thought about Quinn and Marya and decided to message her distant friends. It had been too long. Pin looked small in Ana's Foo Fighters shirt.

◆ ◆

Ana said, "I am getting a notification from Plummer. He's calling on my satphone." She ported the call to the shuttle's speakers. "Hello?"

Plummer's voice was phase shifted and obscured by waves of static. He said, "Hey, how's everything in the Pacific Northwest?"

"We were forced to flee." She told him about Emerson, Mule, and Barry.

"Damn."

"We haven't heard from Quinn."

"Me neither, but I have some bad news too. Eric Eggert died this morning. I know Emerson would want to know."

They chatted about Crow City and the library for a few minutes. He told them about Eggert's memorial and the choice of burial decisions.

"There will always be a tree there when you want to visit him."

Ana said, "I'll tell Emerson. Keep in contact. I'll let you know where we land."

◆ ◆

As per Eggert's wishes, his body had been buried with a fir tree sapling in his heart. Margaret stood by silently looking at a bald eagle circling high above them as they dug his grave and planted his tree. She wanted to remember him smiling, sucking his damn teeth, and nuzzling her neck.

Few citizens attended Eric Eggert's memorial. Margaret didn't want to receive mourners at all; she just wanted to sleep. Plummer conspired with Pejeta and Coner to find a reason to get her out of the house, but she wouldn't hear it. In the end, they went to her.

The people who missed Eggert the most needed to get together and remember. They showed up at her door with food. Once everyone was inside, Margaret accepted what was happening and put the kettle on. She said, "There are only a few of the people that Eric touched who are still around. We *should* sit and remember him; I think he would have liked that."

Teranel was among them. She offered her condolences and told Margaret that Eric changed her life. She said, "I don't know who else would have believed that a one-legged chick could lead a militia full of first time

Interface users. He gave me a chance, and it opened the doors to my new life. I wish I could thank him myself…" She started to cry. Margaret hugged her and rubbed her back.

Plummer said, "He was prouder of your platoon than anything he'd ever done."

They went around the room until the lamps were lit. And the stories flowed. By the time everyone said their goodnights, the sun was lightening the eastern horizon. Margaret realized she felt better. She said to Plummer, "I'm glad you came. I needed this. Thank you."

◆ ◆

Ana contemplated calling Rosco, but Elli came into the cockpit, and it slipped her mind.

Elli said, "Emerson gave his consent to enter the Chandler Cube. Są says we should all join him to talk about our next steps."

When Ana entered the sim, the room was different than before. Instead of Chandler's fireplace room in the homeplace, she found herself in a library with rows of empty shelves on several levels. Są and Chandler had done a redesign.

Są said, "We decided a strategy and research room was more important than Chandler's homeplace at this point."

The bookshelves had staircases at either end of the room, which was at least 100 meters long. The ceiling was vaulted and had large glass windows embedded every twenty meters or so. The sky outside the windows was black. Looking closer, Ana saw the stars, revolving around them.

Chandler said, "We'll be done in a moment."

"Right," Są said, "where were we?"

"Filling the shelves," said Chandler.

As Ana watched, the bookshelves began to fill. The effect was mesmerizing. Books of different sizes and colors popped into being. They appeared in the final order they would be in. To Ana it looked like books were randomly manifesting all over the room. She couldn't keep track and had to look away.

Chandler said, "We are making the entire digital library into physical books. Much easier to find your way through, I think. When it is done, all you have to do is call out your subject, and the library will illuminate the books relating to it. You can access it through your Interface when you are outside the simulation. And look at this." He led her to a large globe on a wooden stand. Chandler touched the surface, and it became a three-dimensional holographic representation of Earth, showing the topography in miniature. Chandler touched a spot, and a readout of data appeared in a thought balloon. He scrolled down the list to open submenus and links.

"The routine that creates it is interactively building depth by searching archives and memory. It becomes more detailed as it learns."

Ana said, "This is completely amazing. I love the sky."

Saą said, "Mother had a few suggestions." She winked.

LC sat hunched over a large chessboard with oversized pieces; the queen, an intricately carved jade figure, was at least eighteen centimeters high. Ana saw Emerson and went to him. He looked washed out, dressed in his customary long-sleeved tunic and canvas pants.

They embraced. She said, "You look tired. How are you feeling?"

Emerson pulled back and said, "Like I was almost eaten by a bear." Shocked, he suddenly realized that Mule was gone. He said, "Mule is dead, isn't she?"

Ana said, "She was bit by the snakes that bit you. Some sort of hybrid timber rattler. We took a biopsy, but it isn't helping us find an antidote."

"It's like there's a hole in my heart." He looked into her eyes as the tears spilled over. "She was my sister. I don't know how I'll live without her."

Ana hugged him tightly.

The globe continued to populate.

Saą said, "The Haven just appeared. You can see Crow City and The City."

Ana said, "You even have the beach camp on here."

"The Interface connects each user to the sim," said Chandler. "It knows and stores your memory as it knows everyone else's. Everything you have done and every place you have seen is part of the sim. And because we're translating the data to physical books, your history and knowledge is also written here."

Ana said, "I'd love to see the code."

"It probably wouldn't make much sense to you. You would need to decompile it, and I'm not sure that would even work. You're welcome to try. But I'm actually a part of the simulation which is written in Interface machine language. I program in numbers in hexadecimal, Ana. On that level, I have no need for words."

Elli said, "So you have access to everything if you want it."

Chandler said, "Only if Emerson grants me the permissions."

Emerson added, "There are rights I retain."

Saą interrupted, "The concept is the same as The Memories. An adept would have access to all the same knowledge."

"The question remains: where should we go?" asked Ana.

Emerson said, "While I am convalescing, we can search for where the citizens of The Haven went."

Elli said, "How do you expect us to do that? That Kindra simulation didn't give us a clue."

"I think the Kindra sim was made by an actual person. And that real person knew very well where they were going. She has scars. A completely artificial, digital person would not. Chandler and I think her memory *is* a part of that sim!"

Elli said, "That's no help. That sim is back in the treehouse."

"I cloned it. The Haven programmers weren't as good at protecting their work as Chandler," Emerson said.

Chandler harrumphed. "I invented the simulation process. Nobody is a good as me."

Elli said, "Ana will give you a run for it." Ana blushed; Chandler nodded.

Saą pointed to the 3D map. She said, "This is where The Cottage, as my family called it, is. The elevation is around 1,500 meters. Anyone else would have to hike in, and the trails are rugged. They require a good deal of rock climbing. We'll not be bothered."

Elli whined, "Why can't we just stay there? I am so tired of running."

Saą answered, "It should be clear that if we expect to survive, we need a community of other like-minded people. A group as small as ours cannot be resilient enough to stay independent for long—we are unsustainable. We would eventually die out or be absorbed into a stronger group that might not share our values. The Cottage is a small stone house that has grown over the years. It is surrounded by a homestead terraced into the hillside. My family, the brother- and sisterhood of The Memories, contribute to the house and grounds whenever they stay. It is a tapestry crafted over decades, made by many varied hands. It is a sacred place of rejuvenation and replenishment, and it is a place I share with many other people. People like me who are on pilgrimages to purify themselves so they can be clearer agents for The Mother. Therefore, we cannot stay longer than one season, but I don't expect to be there that long."

Ana asked, "When are we going to call up Kindra so we can get started unlocking her protections?"

Chandler said, "I've already broken all the Mickey Mouse protections they had on that sim."

Elli said, "Mickey Mouse? Is that some new form of security I've never heard of?"

Emerson laughed. His grandfather had shown him the history of animation beginning with Walt Disney's original flip drawings of Steamboat Willy. He said, "It's a euphemism. It means amateurish, weak, and ineffective."

Chandler said, "Yeah, so if you are done criticizing my word choices, would you like to talk to Arn? That's Kindra's real name."

He didn't wait for an answer. The woman they recognized as Kindra appeared in the empty chair next to Elli. Her image blinked off and on once before she stabilized.

"You got me. What can I tell you?" asked Arn.

Chandler said, "Tell them what you told me."

"What?" Arn said. "I don't know where we were going."

Chandler said, "After I unlocked the sim, I knew everything you knew at the time you recorded yourself. You told me where you were going. Tell them."

She sighed. "This feels coercive. Isn't it unethical somehow?"

Chandler blew an impatient sigh through his teeth. "You can take me to court if you can find one. But since you and I are fucking programs of dead people, I don't think ethics apply. I for one am against giving the rights of consciousness to electronic beings, sorry."

Arn frowned and said, "We don't know if I'm dead, you know. I was still pretty young when we left." She walked to the globe, and used her finger to spin it like it was a planet floating in the air. It slowly spun past the equator, and she stopped it with the same finger.

"There." She used both hands to enlarge the area. "Here is where we proposed to relocate. But we were walking, pulling carts, carrying children. There were 500 of us who had escaped the Roze City armies. We left in the spring. There's no way to know how many made it."

"When?" Emerson said. He sat. His coloring was thin, somehow watery.

Arn said, "Ten years, give or take."

"We could ask Plummer to fly down in Little Wing and check it out while Emerson is recuperating," offered Ana.

Emerson said, "He would need more fuel than Little Wing can carry to get there and back. Call him and bring him here. We can outfit Little Wing and give him extra fuel."

"And I can go with him." Elli beamed.

Ana got a notification that they were close to Saą's coordinates. She took manual control. Emerson said, "I think I need to rest."

LC said, "Check."

They all laughed including Arn, who added, "I like you people. I sure hope I'm still alive to meet you."

Emerson's image blinked out and then back. He looked sorrowfully at Saą and disappeared. Saą left the sim, returning a minute later. She frowned and said, "Emerson's heart rate is slowing. It's going to be best if he rests away from the simulation. I think it was draining him."

Chandler said, "Arn, how did you get the scar? It's how we knew you weren't artificial."

"My twin brother, Dol, hit me in the head with a stone when we were twelve. Gave me three stitches."

◆ ◆

While Plummer was performing the preflight checks before leaving to meet up with Emerson, Boston Quinn, Terrence Brock, and Anoush cornered him against the shuttle. Brock held a plasma gun. Lord Quinn's eyes rolled around in his gaunt skull, which, along with his wispy white hair sticking out in all directions, gave him a crazed look. Anoush had a purple bruise spreading up her neck that was growing more jaundiced by the second. She also gripped a fourteen-year-old boy around the neck, one of Coner's boys, Kane. The kid had wet himself; he stank.

Brock said, "You know where the bunker is. Take us there or I start carving pieces off this kid."

"Why would I let you do that?" He rolled a meter closer to the three.

"You can't stop me," Brock laughed. "I know all about the Kill Switch, FSX7. You aren't allowed to hurt me."

"I guess you got me then, boss. Okay, I surrender." The kid looked like he was going to pass out.

Brock said to Anoush, "Get in, strap down, and shut up." Plummer closed the hatch. Brock sat in the cockpit, the others in the main cabin.

Plummer said, "What's with Lord Quinn? He seems pretty out of it."

"They drugged him bad. I think there's still some kind of neural lock on him. He's been like this since they brought him back." The truth was that Brock continued to give Boston drugged water. He decided that the lord needed to be compliant when they landed in The City. Boston was his key to legitimately assuming the throne. There was no throne, but that was the way Brock wanted to think of it.

Anoush had found the satphone. She also stumbled on the plasma rifle that Barry had stashed. She brought them both to Brock, but the satellite network was down, and he threw the phone on the slate floor, smashing it in a rage. That was when he remembered Plummer and his supply runs. They would need guns to take over The City.

The flight to the bunker took close to two hours. When they arrived, Plummer set down on the river side of the avocado field. He opened the bunker doors. Brock said, "You need to get the guns."

Plummer hooked a winch cable to his torso and lowered himself into the shaft. After he brought up ten cases, he said, "Enough?"

Brock said, "Stow them and let's go."

"Just a minute. I need to recharge."

"Screw that, cyborg man, charge later."

"I have no choice in the matter. If I don't go, my programming will take over. It should only take a little while." He rolled off toward the river and opened his hood.

Twenty minutes later, the sun was setting. Brock called to Plummer. "Hey, Plummer, let's go."

Plummer didn't move. After a minute more, Brock walked over to where the cyborg was sunning himself and shouted, "Let's go, Tin Man!"

The mountain lion didn't make a sound. Brock never knew what broke his neck. The plasma rifle fell to the ground as the big cat dragged the giant man's dead body away toward the river.

Plummer imitated Brock's voice; he yelled, "Anoush, Quinn, get out here, now. Leave the kid. Hurry, Plummer is getting away!"

When the woman and Boston stumbled out of the hatch, Plummer sealed it, locking them outside. He picked up the gun and rolled toward them; they jumped out of his way. He opened the hatch and entered the cabin. Before closing the door, he turned, pointing, and said, "He went that way, down by the river." The hatch sealed with a thump.

Plummer did not look at the site as he lifted off. He set a course for Crow City and used his scalpel finger to cut the boy's bonds. He said, "Don't worry, son. They can't bother you anymore."

◆ ◆ ◆

THE COTTAGE

Not wanting to disturb the wildlife around the cottage, Ana switched the reactor to silent and set The Black Mariah down in a grassy field adjacent to the house. The light around the cottage was different in an indescribable way. Brighter? Golden? Ana couldn't put her finger on it. It was almost like they were landing on a different world.

And even before the craft set down, she felt a wave of relief wash her, like the pressures of the past several months drained away. She entered the protective bubble surrounding the house, and time, which had felt lately like a hungry animal snapping its sharp teeth centimeters from her, seemed to relax. She sighed and thought, *It feels so good!*

As they drifted toward the earth, Saą said, "The stone section of The Cottage was built by my grandfather and his mother. It started out as a lean-to and has grown into a stout homestead over the years. Several such houses are scattered throughout the thousands of hectares in these lands, high in the mountains, protected by the veil. My family used to roam with the seasons. When I was still a babe, my father settled the family near the ocean, and created the homestead where he, my brothers, and my mother lived.

"We were raided when I was ten, and the rest of my family was killed. I hid in a vinegar barrel for days. Kim's father found me and brought me to Crow City. When I was fourteen, on the date of my first moon blood, I was shown The Memories by my adopted mother, Kaianian.[2] When the wandering came over me, she took me on my first long walk and showed me a dozen or so of these cottages. Over the course of that year, Kaianian told me the old stories: about the creation of woman and the balance that the earth requires, which can only be held by a woman.

"She taught me Gaelic and the ways of the ancient druids, how to clean drinking water with a reed, and the languages of the animals of the wild. But most importantly, Kai taught me my history.

"She walked with me for many seasons before she left this world. I still see her as The Mother; the face of my actual mother is so long forgotten. I learned much later that Kaianian was my mother's sister. She'd been my blood all along.

"We share these cottages with other seekers in this region, the guiding rule being to leave more than you take. Over the decades, the buildings have grown, and the surrounding land has been cultivated into walled gardens and terraced pastures." She scanned the land for a moment and continued, "No one has been here in a while. The gardens and fruit trees are calling."

Elli and Saą laid Emerson in a wide bed in one of the bedrooms. Saą let the spring fill a bucket while she rested on a moss-covered outcropping. The trickle of icy water sang harmonies with a nearby robin. She said, "I have loved this place since I was a girl."

Ana, LC, and Pin chased after Budrow and explored the farm. The melanistic mom and her kits, who were looking more and more like pure red foxes, lazed in the shade of a rock wall and batted at flying insects. Elli hung around the kitchen watching Saą, not saying much as was her way. Saą set a hammered copper pot to boil on the alcohol stove. She said, "Once the house has awoken, the composting system will charge, and we can use the biogas heaters. Our backup is fuel-alcohol distilled from fallen fruit. We make a cider for drinking too. I'll bet there's a jug in the cold cellar."

---

2 Pronounced: kiyen-éan

She used a worn cloth and warm water to cleanse Emerson's skin, drying him with a cotton towel. "My aunt's favorite," she said and held it up to her nose, breathing in its scent. "Each item in this place was donated by one of the hundreds of visitors over thousands of stays. Many were made by my family before I was born. Everyone contributes in their personal way. In return, this sanctuary belongs to anyone who has the vision to find it. Gifts are donated in the spirit of love, which in turn permeates the buildings and the grounds."

Hours before the sunrise, Są woke to Pin screaming. Her eyes were squeezed shut, and her arms flailed. She'd knocked over the bed table. Są held the girl's shoulders and hugged her to her chest, whispering at her sweaty temple, cooing to the feverish child. Są rubbed her back, calming her.

Pin's breathing slowed as she fell back to sleep, turning twice, moaning and whimpering. Są pulled the quilt to the girl's chin and returned to her bed, but she was awake. There was no way sleep would find her now. The air on the mountain was too cool to walk around unclothed at night. Są searched the closet, found a bolt of dyed cloth, and wound it into a sari draped over one shoulder fixed with a large clasp-pin she'd found in a drawer. A voice in her mind (she wasn't sure at first if it was Mother or the Interface) said, "The Celtic brooch, more properly called the penannular brooch, and its closely related type, the pseudo-penannular brooch, are types of ornamental clothes fasteners, often rather large; penannular means formed as an incomplete ring…" She let the data pass over her like a breeze.

Są went into the pre-dawn mist to search for herbs. She found some blackberries for breakfast, which she could grind in a mortar and pestle and mix with honey to strain into Emerson's liquid diet. He needed ready nutrition to survive even if she had to feed him with a dropper. If she could keep him alive through the next few days, she hoped his body would stabilize and strengthen, speeding healing in his brain. She needed to search The Memories. She thought, *I am not a master healer.*

Mother's voice rose up in the back of her mind and said, "You are all he's got, daughter. With or without the title." It was clearly Mother and not a disembodied encyclopedia of archaic trivia.

She suddenly pictured a glass of *fresh milk* and smiled. Mother put ideas in her mind sometimes. She murmured silent thanks, unsure if she could find a lactating doe. The few hybrid goats in the valley were descended from abandoned farm animals, living in the caves and crags, eluding predators. She would call to them at sunset and leave the pasture gate open; the reward of tender grass might coax them. As an incentive, she scythed a bit of the tall fescue, releasing its scent.

At dawn, three does and a single kid were nibbling the new shoots. She closed the gate and hand-fed them with a bit of dried honey cake.

Emerson would also require a collagen-rich broth to build strength quickly enough to save his life, but for that she would have to hunt. Later that morning, she cooked a stock of boiled roots with a handful of dried wild oats from the cellar. It was delicious. Ana, Elli, Little Chandler, and Pin were grateful, though the little blue-eyed girl still hadn't spoken.

After she'd washed Emerson's bedclothes, while there were still hours of light left, Są went to hunt, but only saw squirrels and an owl, nothing that would suit her needs. Emerson needed dense protein: meat one mouth from a green plant. Sacrificing a goat would be foolish; her people had spent decades developing relationships with the wild herds. They had a mutually beneficial agreement. And these strange hybrid goats that occupied the valley were freakishly smart and had generational memories.

She would need to take one of the stunted elk that had replaced the whitetail since the collapse. A small buckling would do. It would provide Emerson the life he needed, and she could leave a tanned hide as her contribution to the house. There would also be jerky and meat enough for weeks. Winter was months away—but when it arrived, the weather would snow them in. After it turned cold, they would either have to be stocked up or be elsewhere. This would be her first step.

◆ ◆ ◆

THE BLOODSKIN

The next day, Saą organized a group house cleaning and inventory. Elli found a wheel of cheese and a sealed container of einkorn grain. Saą ground it into a flour and baked a rough bread. They also found a pound of dried currants which she mixed with oats and honey and baked. "We could live on this trail mix for months if we had to," she said. The goats were in the paddock, and she milked. But even after getting a half-liter into Emerson, his skin was still grey and clammy.

Saą said, "Emerson's treatment requires aggressive steps. I must hunt."

"I'll get my rifle and go with you," Elli said.

"I must do this alone, Elli Moon. It's okay. Mother will help."

Elli didn't handle disappointment well. She strode away without replying.

Saą sat cross-legged on the ground in the courtyard and put her palms to the packed red earth. Mother appeared to her, and the woods around them transformed into the high-ceilinged round room. They embraced, touching their fingers to the center of their foreheads, an ancient greeting symbolizing the imaginative quality of the meeting.

Mother said, "He is fading, daughter. What will you do?"

"The venom damaged too much. The milk isn't helping. But broth might."

Mother nodded and said, "Charge the bloodskin."

Saą said, "Yes. Help me to find a herd; I worry about leaving Emerson unattended for long." The scene changed around them, the walls growing brighter. Like ink dropped into a dish of rain, color and light transformed until they stood together outside of the cottage. Moonflowers twined the porch posts as Saą watched.

Mother pointed up the hillside and said, "Find the three on the ridge. But give them until dusk to say their goodbyes. They do not know what is coming, even as they sense the transition."

Saą thanked her with a slight nod. They embraced, and she opened her eyes, still sitting on the packed earth; only a moment had passed. Ana watched at the window, though Saą didn't see her. Just before sunset, Saą left to hunt.

After winding her way up the mountainside, weaving through the trees and avoiding the path, Mother whispered, "Ana is following."

Saą paused with her eyes closed, sensing the surrounding environment. She absorbed the activity of the high forest, the birdsong and breeze, synchronizing herself to the rhythm of life surrounding her. Warm air drifted uphill from the valley; dust lazed in the slanting beams; the shafts looked like solid columns of light. A cardinal called from above and behind her. She put her hand to her heart.

When the sun dropped behind the west range, Ana's presence stood out in relief to the sudden shadow. A moment later, she snapped a twig. Saą stopped, tasting the cooler air as it reversed, now flowing downhill carrying the herd's scent. Up the slope, she saw the backs of three elk grazing together just over the crest. A pair of straight, slender antlers marked the buckling.

Ana rustled some leaves. The herd tensed, but Saą calmed them with her song, humming at first, murmuring the ancient words of culling: "Deònaich dhomh do bhàs, damh mòr, gu bheil mi a 'fuireach dòcha." *Grant me your death, Great Stag, that I may live.*

The young bull raised his head, nose pointed toward her. Saą stepped into the open; the buckling's companions turned away. He stood still, breathing in short puffs, his heart pounding in her chest. She crept toward him, and he toward her.

Saą looked down at the ground, bowing to his symbolic power. The elk stepped on a branch, snapping it in a loud report. A flock of sparrows launched, and the stag's herd-mates scattered. Saą and the stag met. His unfocused gaze looked through her, beyond her. She offered her opened palms; he bowed his head. His antlers nearly touched her shoulders, as though she were being knighted.

Saą said, "My thanks, young wapiti. To The Mother with you," and she broke his neck with a swift twist.

Surprised, Ana slipped and rolled a short way down the hill, her body striking the base of a redwood, and tumbling over. Mother said, "She needed to see you hunt."

When Ana opened her eyes, Saą was looking down at her. The stag was draped across her shoulders; she towered over Ana like The Great Huntress. Saą helped Ana stand. They did not speak. Ana had twisted her ankle, and it took until nightfall to limp back to The Cottage leaning on a twisted branch.

When they got to the courtyard, Ana said, "I have never seen anything like that, and I've done some hunting. The quarry always runs. I would run. Why did that animal surrender to you? What sort of power did you have over it? Did I hear you singing?"

"Power? What do you mean?"

"A trick. Did you fool it somehow?"

"Of course not. It is natural for our relatives to make sacrifices for our benefit. I would never think of taking another being's life without their consent."

"But how do you talk to a wild animal? You make no sense. And I saw you before the hunt. It looked like some sort of prayer. I was taught to depend on what I can see and touch, what's real. It's ignorant to make up fantasy beings and then pretend to speak to them."

"Mother is always with me. I did not *make her up*, as you say. I see her as you see me. She sends me The Memories. They are part of the earth and every living thing on it including all of the people who have ever lived. There is nothing fantastic about consulting them. I quiet my mind and concentrate. It was difficult to learn, yes. Mother says humans are easily distracted, so she helps focus my attention to make contact. She appears to me in Kaianian's form because she is imprinted upon my heart. I use my imagination, but I assure you, I learn things I did not know and I find things I did not hide. The Memories are always correct, always true." She paused a moment, laying the elk on the outdoor butcher's block table. She began sharpening a large carbon steel knife with a shinbone handle. The stone was set into the table. She spat on it and used both hands to slide the rainbow-patterned edge against it.

After a few minutes, she said, "Chandler Estes only exists in the cube. You can only see, hear, or touch him because of a connection in your mind—it is the only 'place' he actually exists. And yet, you do not consider it an ignorant fantasy to speak to him, do you?"

◆ ◆

By next morning, a bone broth was simmering, and the rest of the elk was butchered and hanging in the cold cellar. Saą fed Emerson warm stock and sat him in the sun while she stretched jerky and brined the haunches and shoulders. She told Ana, "I might fire up the smokehouse, make some sausages."

Ana said, "When I was little, Grendel's aunt used to call them lil' ol' bags-o-mystery."

Ana was trying to stay off her ankle. She hobbled around leaning on her crooked makeshift crutch and following Saą while she worked.

Saą said, "I charged the bloodskin. It's a hide-covered bear bladder. Every cottage keeps one to aid in healing. Farm work is dangerous. I have been alone in the woods for over four years and never got a serious injury, but the bloodskin is a required tool at the homestead. My adopted mom made this one when she was a girl. It's inoculated with an ancient yeast cultivated in gut bacteria and is very potent.

"Kaianian taught me that we humans are made up of much more than our own bodies. We are a coordination of many relatives, both inside and outside, functioning as one. This morning I filled the skin with the buckling's blood. A bloodskin ferments its contents into a concentrated beverage; the process works with any liquid whether it's a tea made from roots or the serum from a reptile's brain. The resultant elixir possesses powerful healing powers. I'm hoping it will help Emerson. This is my last option."

The following morning, when the bloodskin elixir was ready, Saą drank some of the fermented beverage. She gave a thimbleful to Ana and said, "It's a general elixir. Try it."

The thick serum was spicy and sweet and left her feeling giddy. Ana's color rose up her neck from her breastbone when she drank it. Saą fed a dropperful to Emerson every few hours. It didn't seem to have an effect.

She tried to look hopeful, but Elli moped. Ana, LC, and Pin took a long walk. Ana could hardly tell her ankle had been hurt; the bloodskin had healed her. It gave her hope.

Four days after the bloodskin regimen began, Saą said, "I'm afraid this isn't working. He may have been too far gone before we administered the antivenom, and we are going to run out of elixir soon."

Ana said, "I've never thought about a life without Emerson."

"I don't believe it," Elli said. "He'll be fine. Just the other day we were playing chess in the Chandler Cube."

Saą said, "We might need to consider the possibility that he won't wake up, Elli. We can't force his body to stay alive much longer."

Elli marched to the door, turned, and shouted, "You've just given up!" She slammed it shut behind her. A stuffed doll fell off the shelf set into the plastered wall.

Ana said, "C'mon, kids. Let's go see what Budrow's up to." She and the children went outside.

Sąą was left alone in the bedroom with Emerson. She noticed that his face might have more color, but *no*, she thought, *I am only projecting my hope*. His breathing remained shallow.

Mother's form didn't materialize all at once. For a moment, Sąą could clearly see the finch perched on a branch outside the bedroom window through her. A sudden cramp knotted her belly, and she said, "Oh."

Mother's gauzy image crystalized into solidity. She said, "You ask for help, daughter. You know that nothing in this world is free. You must always give something in return."

Sąą rubbed her tender stomach. She felt a slight tug on her center again, gentler this time, a mere aftershock of the initial spasm. Mother put her hand on Sąą's shoulder. She put hers over it. Though the skin was loose and soft, Sąą could feel the strength within it, the strength of an ancient oak.

Sąą said, "Already the cord between us is strained. It will soon break. I have done everything I know how. What more need I offer?"

Mother raised her eyebrows and smiled broadly. Her teeth were perfect and bright in her sepia complexion. She said, "For his life, dear? I'd say your life might cover it."

"Yes. Take my life for his."

"Wait a second, daughter. I already have your life. Besides, that would be too easy. No, Sąą, you must give your life to *him*."

"What does that mean?"

"You must want to stay with him and watch over him, like a lover."

"But Emerson loves Quinn. They belong to each other. I can't come between them."

"Yes. And there's the rub, eh? Yet, that is the price of his life."

"I love Emerson, yes, but this…"

Mother squatted next to Sąą and looked into her eyes. Mother's eyes were like peering into the night sky. Saą felt like she was floating in the vacuum of space for a moment.

Mother said, "You will be his advisor. Destined to be always by his side, for the rest of his life. And you cannot explain it. Tell him to come and see me if he wants to know more."

She vanished, but the warmth of her body lingered next to Saą's side. She stood and sighed. When Saą looked at Emerson, his eyes were open.

He smiled and said, "Did you miss me?"

◆ ◆ ◆

KAIANIAN

Back in Crow City, Plummer dropped the boy off at the clinic where he picked up Rat One and Two.

Pejeta said, "We are going to miss you, Plummer. I already miss the rats."

He'd repaired Brock's satphone and given it to Pejeta. She almost wouldn't let him show her how to open a connection and make a call.

He said, "My number is programmed in. I can't guarantee that the satellite system will last, but as long as it does, you can call if you need me, and I will come."

Pejeta said, "This is where I hug you, but I don't know how."

"I understand." He held out his mechanical hand. "A shake will have to be enough."

Before taking off for The Cottage, Plummer had one more errand. He landed Little Wing in the vacant lot across from the Nova Café in the Southwest Quarter. Teranel was behind the bar. He rolled up.

She said, "Plummer, you don't drink, do you?"

He put a brass-clasped, polished wooden box on the bar and slid it toward her. It was a meter and a half long, thirty centimeters high, and deep with a hinged top.

She put down the towel she was wiping glasses with and said, "What is this?" She was grinning.

Plummer said, "Open it."

Other patrons gathered around. Everyone in the Southwest Quarter knew Plummer, and a few guessed what the cyborg brought in the box.

When she flipped the lid open, Teranel sucked in her breath. She said, "No!" and lifted the mechanical leg out of its case. It was constructed in the same style as Plummer's erector-set arms.

Plummer said, "It's best if these types of cybernetic enhancements are grafted directly to your skeleton. When I did your amputation—"

She interrupted him, "You? You saved my life?" The tears spilled over. She picked the limb up and held it in her arms.

Plummer went on, oblivious to her emotions. "I fused a titanium connector to your femur. You probably didn't even notice it. The prosthesis plugs into it."

"Don't my nerves have to be connected somehow?"

"It's an Interface limb, Teranel. Try it on."

She sat and snapped the leg to her stump and moved the ankle joint back and forth. "That was easy. Damn."

She stood on the limb tentatively at first and said, "It feels just like a leg—I can feel the floor. Hey, everybody! I got toes!" She held the metal leg up high and flexed each of her mechanical toes one after the other. After a moment, she ran to Plummer and hugged him, pressing her cheek against his metal chest.

He raised both sets of arms away from his body and said, "I'm not good at this, I'm afraid."

Teranel was crying. She said through her sobs, "I love you, Plummer. You've saved my life twice."

He said, "Eric wanted you to know how proud he was of you. He believed the militia was one of the most important accomplishments of his life."

She didn't let go of him or speak for a solid minute.

◆ ◆

After fifty years of solitude, Plummer's interactions with non-cyborgs were still exhilarating and fresh. He should have been happy, but he was not. The heart he didn't have ached. Seeing Teranel so overwhelmed, he felt the urge to cry himself, even if it was for other reasons than her joy. Plummer grieved for his own humanness, and he knew there was nothing he could do to stop it. As much as he tried to use his superhuman strength to master it, grief consistently overpowered him.

He mulled over it while Little Wing's autopilot took him to The Cottage. During his half-century alone, he had given up the part of himself that craved human contact. He was only alive as a result of his extraordinary will to survive. But he owed that life to his ingenious adaptation of the technology he was left with. And now there was little but that technology left. Only the smallest most vital part of his original self remained.

It was true; he had developed reciprocal relationships with people despite the fact that all of his humanness was hidden inside a metal casing. When he thought of his friends—Emerson, Saą, Quinn, Ana, and Elli—he felt warmth where his chest and face should have been. He loved these people. He loved Eggert, and the fact that his friend was dead added to his dull but constant pain.

He yearned to cry it out, but the anatomical release of weeping had no cybernetic corollary. He didn't have eyes, and therefore he couldn't make tears. The feeling would just build if he let it; he knew that from experience. The pain would build and build and become unbearable, but still it would not end. In the past, he would shut it down rather than hurt himself further.

And even that, his ability to change emotions and control the path of his thinking, depressed him. These practices set him far apart from other humans and only isolated him further. Conflicted and restless, he decided that talking to Chandler would help and entered the simulation.

Chandler said, "Hello, Charles. Come here. Give me a hug."

No matter how many times Plummer entered the Chandler Cube, he was always shocked by having a body. He remembered from somewhere that in an Interface simulation, your avatar was created by your residual self-image, which was a science fiction term if he'd ever heard one. He supposed that a strong mind could imagine any form it wanted. He was satisfied having his original back.

The hug felt real. His hands and face felt real. He wondered why he didn't come back more often.

Chandler said, "Because you'd want to stay. And because this sim wasn't made for you and I wouldn't allow it."

Chandler lit his pipe and offered it to Plummer, who declined. "Don't start believing in your own genius, Charlie. I let you copy this sim. Live in the moment, I say. Take the break. But you can't stay in the dream." He exhaled a cloud of smoke and said, "And you don't have to worry about disease in here, Charlie. There's no cancer in the Interface."

Plummer did cry then. He wet Chandler's flannel and actually had to blow his nose, which was another treat he'd forgotten about.

Chandler said, "If you really want an experience, go to the outhouse and take a good dump."

When they both finished laughing, Plummer said, "Since you know my thoughts, you know that Emerson is in a coma from a snakebite. Eric Eggert died, and Mule is gone too. I'm having a hard time seeing the reason. We're all going to die."

"Maybe not you, son."

"I'm working on that. But honestly, we all die. And after a long enough time, nothing remains. I fall in love with people who will be gone in the blink of my eye. It seems like pain for pain's sake. What the hell is the point?"

Chandler said, "It's a weird world of dualities. You can't have pleasure without pain. There would be no urgency in life if there were no death. No, not everything is black and white, but what would sadness mean without joy?"

They sat and watched the fire together until Plummer got the notification that Little Wing was only a half hour from The Cottage.

They hugged again. Chandler said, "But what do I know, son? I'm just an old man frozen in a simulation. Ask Saą when you see her. She's got more of an idea of what's behind the curtain than I do."

◆ ◆

Emerson was weak, but his body felt intact. He had feeling in all of his fingers and toes, and his equilibrium was back. But his muscles had atrophied while he slept. It would take time and exercise to rebuild his strength.

Saą told everyone, and they had a happy reunion in the bedroom. Emerson sat up and sipped broth. Ana and Elli laughed at Emerson's stale jokes, and the kids played with marbles in the corner.

After about an hour, Saą told everyone to clear out and give Emerson a chance to rest. When they'd all gone, she sat next to him under the quilt.

She said, "I thought we were going to lose you there."

Emerson said, "I had a weird dream just before I woke up and saw you, looking at me like an angel."

"Can you remember it?"

"It was weird. All I have is this image of everyone around me, you and Quinn and Ana, and I could see these thick silver cables that tied me to each of you. Coming out of my belly button and running like a tube to yours. We are all connected."

"That sounds like a good dream." She had two fingers over the bottom of his wrist, taking his pulse.

"Yeah, I guess. But then I was going away and we were all still connected. It hurt, Saą. I mean, I was in agony. And then I opened my eyes, and you were there."

"You are with us now. But we still have to build your strength back."

◆ ◆

Plummer landed just after sundown and parked Little Wing next to The Black Mariah, which dwarfed it. He went directly to Emerson. Saą sat in a wooden chair reading a worn paperback copy of *The English Patient.* Emerson drowsed, but he opened his eyes when he heard Plummer's treads.

Plummer said, "So, you just woke up, eh?" He stood near the bed.

Saą said, "Just in time to see you."

He told them about Brock and Lord Quinn. They reminisced about Mule and Budrow, and LC brought a kit in each hand to show him. The mama fox followed him intently, but kept her distance.

Saą told the story of the past several weeks. Plummer met with Kindra/Arn in the Chandler Cube and determined the probable location of The Haven community. As soon as he could fabricate an extra capacity fuel tank for Little Wing, he'd leave in search of their possible new home.

Saą mentioned to Emerson that her daughter and Nahal, the child's mother, were living in a mountain enclave in what used to be Florence, Italy. That if other options failed, they could try going there.

"And going to see her would put my heart to rest." She bowed low before him.

Emerson said, "You don't need to bow to me, Saą. We're family."

"Yes, Emerson. But I want to clearly define our relationship. I will take on the responsibility of being your advisor, in all things. I vow to remain by your side and to remain unaffected and neutral. It seems as our family grows, you will be responsible for more and more lives. Four eyes and two brains are always better than one."

Emerson said, "You make me sound like a king or something. I'm no king, Saą."

"Trust me, Emerson. I can see many possible futures, but in all of them, you are a king. Whether you want it or not."

◆ ◆ ◆

QUINN

Back at The Cottage, a few days later, Emerson said, "I miss Mule."

Są said, "We were too late to save her, but she saved you."

"It doesn't make me miss her any less. It's like I went to sleep, and my friends died. I didn't get to thank her or say goodbye." He had tears in his eyes.

Są put her arms around him. She said, "You can meet with her anytime you like. You only need to enter The Memories. Mule is with Mother."

"I wish I had your faith, Są."

She kissed his forehead. "I know what I know, Emerson. I don't need faith. Think about what I said. You can be with her."

◆ ◆

The weather was changing; everyone felt it. Są said, "I have been waiting for this day since the days began to shorten. I call it the turning day. It's the first day you can really feel the fall. The light feels different, and the air smells drier. It's only an early warning, you know; the time of changing leaves is still far off."

LC said, "Telling the animals to get ready! Right?"

"Right, and that day is today."

"Turning day, I like the sound of that," Emerson said. They were having a breakfast of berries and tea with honey on the patio. The sun had heated the slates, and though there was a little wind, they were warm and comfortable.

Plummer left the day before, after getting The Haven people's coordinates. He estimated the trip would take him two days before he'd be in the region. He was going to send word then. They sent him off with an expanded fuel tank full of hydrogen pellets.

He said, "I can fly three times the distance on that much." Emerson was satisfied.

At the last minute, Elli decided to stay. She didn't give a reason, just simply said, "I'm staying here, Plummer. Have a good trip."

Ana thought she'd cracked the authorization code problem for Plummer's Kill Switch, but she was still working out the fine tuning between the call and response. If it wasn't perfect, it wouldn't work. So, she needed more time to experiment with it. Plummer was going to be far outside their sphere of protection. It seemed absurd. He was twice as capable and stronger than any of them. Still, she worried about him and made time to tell him so.

She came to him as he entered the hatch and put her hand on his shoulder. "Plummer, be careful, okay? It scares me that you can't defend yourself."

"I appreciate your concern, Anastacia Moon. In the Chandler sim I would certainly kiss your hand for such a noble impulse. But I assure you, I can defend myself. Just not proactively. FSX7 also prevents me from committing suicide, remember?"

She took his claw in her hand.

He continued, "But I will take your love with me, and I'll return. Don't lose any sleep over *The Tin Man*." He released the synthetic hyena laugh and rolled inside as it faded away.

◆ ◆

LC woke Ana. "Mama?" It was still dark; the room was a faint outline in grey.

Ana said, "Here, baby. Did you have a bad dream?" Little Chandler climbed into Ana's bed and nuzzled into her side, turning so his small spine was pressed against her. She hugged him. "Tell me."

"I dreamed of Marya."

"It was a good dream then."

"It was Marya, but she was different, older. She scared me."

"Why were you scared, baby?"

"Her eyes, they were glowing. And lights were streaming all around her like fireflies. I called her name, but she didn't hear me. It was creepy."

Ana hugged him tighter and whispered, "It was only a dream, baby."

LC was already asleep.

◆ ◆

They were having a late breakfast outside on the slate patio. The wisteria leaves covering the bentwood arbor above them cast dappled shadows. Emerson received a notification that someone was calling his satphone channel. When he answered, the line was static.

He said to Ana, who was finishing the last of her tea, "I think we lost a satellite. Or the phone is getting glitchy. Can you trace that notification? It might have been from Plummer."

A few minutes later, Ana returned from the shuttle and said, "The call was from Rosco, Emerson. I tried pinging him back, but you're probably right. A satellite in the array is probably smoked. He might have sent a text after the call failed. If it comes back online, you'll get that message."

Emerson nodded. "I'm going to send Rosco a text asking that he call me again. The degrading system passes SMS messages more reliably." *I wonder why Rosco didn't do that first*, he thought. Emerson's nerves were raw. Then he thought, *Maybe it wasn't important. Maybe he was just calling to say hello*, which made him feel a little better. But "chatting" was out of character for Rosco. He wouldn't call unless there was a reason. Emerson began pacing. He sent the text, but it failed. He wasn't surprised. They would have to wait. His imagination filled in the unknown with terrible possibilities.

Twenty minutes that felt like two hours later, Emerson received a text from Rosco:

UNDER ATTACK SEND HELP.

◆ ◆

Elli said, "Under attack? The City? Lord Fathead must have really let things slip. The Enforcers have aircraft with guns!"

Saą said, "Mother suggests that they are the attackers from the north that Lord Quinn warned about."

Ana said, "I tried him back just now. No good. The array must be damaged."

Emerson said, "I'm going." He tried to stand but sat back down heavily.

Elli said, "Like you are strong enough to go anywhere, eh? Are you going to bring Ana and the children into a war zone too?"

Emerson looked like a scolded dog. Elli went on, "I'm going, and Emerson, I doubt I can stop you, so stay out of my way."

He murmured, "Yes, sir!" She ignored him.

Saą said, "I must stay with Emerson. He just came out of a coma; he needs care to heal." And then to Emerson, "Just remember, you haven't got your strength back. Strain yourself now and you could do permanent damage..."

Elli said, "I'm going to get ready; we leave in an hour." She left the room.

"Elli is like a war chief," Emerson said.

Saą said, "And I am your steward."

◆◆

Just before leaving, Emerson tried Plummer again. But the system was still offline. Ana created a test routine to send a notification when it came back up. They all entered the cube to consult with Chandler.

Once there, Elli said, "You guys are always talking. I'm going to go take a rest in Chandler's bed and watch some TV."

As she walked away, Chandler said, "Have you seen *The Last of Us*? It's pretty funny considering the way things turned out."

Emerson did not know that Plummer cloned the Chandler Cube. And since they were totally separate simulations, Emerson's Chandler had no way of knowing anything about Plummer's. However, somehow, Emerson's Chandler had an inkling. He could sense it, but he didn't say anything specifically.

Instead, he asked Ana, "Have you made any headway with replacing the trusted authority for Plummer's Kill Switch?"

Emerson said, "That's random."

"Not really, Chandler and I have been working on the solution." To Chandler she said, "When he was here last week, I tried some diagnostics, but his core system kept locking me out. That program is a persistent bugger. From what I can tell, it's tied to his life support. If we tamper with it too much, it might kill him."

Chandler said, "Think about it this way. Figure out how they are verifying the trusted authority and imitate it."

"But if I can't inspect the code, how can I figure out anything?"

Emerson added, "What about interrupting it at the machine level?"

"We'd need to take him offline—like a general anesthetic. That makes me nervous. You know his processors are degrading, right? If we shut him down, we might not be able to revive him."

"Oh, I fixed his degradation problem."

Emerson said, "When was that?"

Chandler didn't answer.

They were silent for a moment following that revelation.

After a while, Ana said, "Too bad Plummer is hundreds of kilometers away."

The array came online and sent Ana and Emerson a notification. She said, "Hey, the sat system is up!" They stood. Ana said, "Later, Grandpa," and closed the sim. She opened a channel and tried to call Quinn. The system rang, but she did not answer. She tried Rosco next.

After six rings and a screech of static, Rosco answered, "Ana! The City is burning. They took Quinn."

Ana shouted, "What?" She was answered with more static.

Elli came closer.

Rosco said something garbled.

"We're losing the satellite," Ana said.

Emerson said, "Hold on, Rosco." The line went blank. "We can push The Black Mariah into overdrive and make some time."

Elli said, "Strap in!"

◆ ◆

The top speed of a normal Interface Industries Executive shuttle was 700 KPH. But before Emerson acquired The Black Mariah, Eggert had modified her. She was larger to begin with, built so the chairman could run the company from the sky if there was ever a chemical or nuclear attack. Eggert expanded her range and installed weapons, expanded cargo holds, and added cabins for a crew of seven and two staterooms for VIPs. It already had a kitchen and stocked medical facility. Eggert added a triage pullout, X-ray capability, and several winches. Plus, he modified the tie-downs. The top speed of The Black Mariah had never been reached, though Eggert bragged that he took her to 900 KPH. But in order to push her any faster, they had to ride in the pressurized cockpit and have safety life support interlocks engaged with their helmets. It took a little preparation.

When Elli engaged the turbo, they were pressed into the seats for eight seconds until the gravity compensator caught up. When the forces equalized, Saą said, "Oh my Goddess."

Elli said, "Gave me an orgasm."

"It throws your insides around a little. I wouldn't doubt it," said Emerson. "First time I accelerated like that I nearly threw up."

"Oh, I like my sensation better."

They arrived twenty miles west of the reservoir at five o'clock. The sun was nearly set. The shuttle hovered at 1,000 meters near the eastern shore, scanning the area. But even in the twilight, it was obvious that something was desperately wrong. Black smoke billowed from several locations in the direction of Founder's Quarter beyond the wall, and the shores of the reservoir were littered with broken drones. A gouge in the earth, 100 meters wide, snaked away over the horizon to the northwest, the obvious direction the attackers had taken in their retreat. It reminded Elli of the path the tornado's devastation left after the homeplace was obliterated.

Emerson said, "It won't be a problem getting in unnoticed."

"I don't think anyone is looking anymore," commented Elli.

Saą said, "It doesn't look like anyone is here."

They flew slowly over the water. At the far shore, Elli set The Black Mariah down on the narrow beach. She reopened the iron bars with a plasma burst and cloaked the shuttle. Saą carried only her sinew sling. Elli brought her Colt, the nuclear cannon, and her plasma rifle. Emerson used a cargo stick as a walking staff and limped after them.

When they got to Lord Quinn's apartments, the door was blown off its hinges, and the passageways were charred black from fire. A burned skeleton smoldered in one corner. Elli took the lead; Emerson and Saą followed.

The hallway and stairs were also charred. The front doors of the building were gone. The courtyard was deserted except for the bodies of a few Enforcers who looked to have died running away. Emerson pointed across the square to the row of townhouses carved into the rock face. They looked untouched. "That's where Quinn's apartments are."

When they got to Quinn's building, Emerson pointed out the hidden door. At the top of the stairs, he turned and disappeared through a stone wall.

He poked his face back through and said, "It's an illusion. Come on."

Elli walked through. "You were in the dungeon. Max brought me and Ana here, but it's still fucking disorienting."

He put his hand on a matte-black panel in the smooth clay wall. A door traced itself and opened. He entered; the others followed.

A woman's automated voice from inside the apartment said, "Good to see you again, Emerson Lloyde and Elli Moon."

Elli said, "How is there electricity here? It's off everywhere else."

"Backup solar panels on the south walls," Emerson said. He was already in the apartment.

He called, "Quinn! Marya!"

Inside her bedroom they found Tanya, drowsy against a wall. She had a cut on her forehead, and her arm was wrapped with a bloody bandage. Blood had soaked into her tunic. She held Max's stretch hat. Quinn would never go anywhere without it.

Emerson said, "Where's Quinn? What happened?"

Saą brought her a glass of water. After a sip, Tanya burst into tears. "I don't know, Emerson. They came at night; it happened so fast."

Emerson hugged her and carried her to a chair. He said, "Okay, it's going to be okay. Tell me from the beginning."

"Fire. They used a fire weapon. It burned everyone in the Lord's quarters alive in seconds." They both looked at the hat. She pushed it into Emerson's hands.

Emerson said, "Did they have guns? Airships? How many were there?"

"It was all on fire when I woke up. Quinn was already outside. They took most of the people. Put them in containers and pulled them away with huge, armored tractors. And there were hundreds of soldiers, Emerson. All dressed the same in black armor. I've never seen anything like it."

Rosco and Grendel entered the apartment. When Elli saw them, they hugged.

Grendel said, "Come with me, Tanya. They didn't get to the birth corps or the hospital. You need to see Doctor Sailor."

Rosco clapped Emerson on the shoulder and said, "From the north. They came from The Iron Belt, the band of dead lands just south of the Lake Country. We avoid it because of the toxicity from hundreds of years of chemical and steel manufacturing. It's an industrial wasteland surrounded by a desert. They have oil. Millions of kiloliters. And industrial electricity supplied by five nuclear power plants. We'd heard that they'd successfully shut them down after the collapse, but these people may have learned how to keep them from melting down.

"They've welded together gargantuan earth-moving machines, protected by thick plates of sheet iron and rebar. They surprised the Enforcers, wiped out the shuttle corps, and incinerated the armory.

"They had inside information and took out the monitoring systems and the power grid first. Then they razed the lord's housing and offices of The Authority. They killed anyone who opposed them and herded hundreds into shipping containers outfitted with bulldozer treads. They just drove through the wall like it wasn't there. It took less than ten hours."

Saą said, "This is just so evil and violent."

"Slaves!" Elli said. "They made them slaves."

Rosco said, "You are both right. They are an industrial society built on the trash they've salvaged from a dead civilization. They have power, but running tech requires skills few have. Human labor is cheaper and easier to control."

Elli said, "Easy to replace, too. If you have females, you can just breed more." She spat on the floor.

Emerson said, "That kind of power is never satisfied. Its appetite just grows. You can be sure they will be back. And if they could have taken the shuttles, I am sure they would have."

"You don't think they have the Interface?" asked Saą.

Emerson said, "No. But if they get it…"

"And access to the plasma weapons…" Rosco said.

Emerson sat down heavily with his head in his hands. "I should never have let her go. I knew something like this was going to happen. My god."

Saą sat next to him and hugged him around the shoulders. "We'll find them, Emerson."

He looked her in the face and said, "I can't live without her, Saą. Quinn *or* Marya. I'm just lost without them."

"Let's go after them," Elli said.

No one disagreed, but conversation evaporated. Grendel returned. They looked at one another for a long minute. Finally, Emerson said, "Well, like Chandler used to say, small talk is for people who don't have anything better to say. Are we ready?" Saą put her hand on his shoulder.

END OF BOOK TWO: CROW CITY

◆ ◆ ◆ ◆ ◆

EPILOGUE

MOTHER

Barry woke up to a bird singing a repetitive song. It was familiar. He listened with his eyes closed, but he couldn't quite follow the pattern. It was just beyond his understanding. He opened his eyes and took in the round room, looking up at the fire hole and the swirling stars to be sure. He sighed. Barry knew where he was. Mother squatted near the fire stirring the coals. He sat up. She didn't seem to take notice.

Barry looked across the room. There were two men sitting shoulder to shoulder on the other side of the fire. He recognized the unusually tall one as Brock. The other stared into space. Both men looked unhappy. Mule yawned and stretched to his left. He scratched behind her ear. Eggert sat next to him on his right. He'd been feeling apprehensive, but seeing Eggert there relaxed him.

Eggert sucked his teeth.

Barry said, "Ha, for a second there I thought I was dead. But seeing you here, Eric, showed me that's just silly."

Eggert looked at him sideways. Barry wasn't wearing a shirt; his skin was still blotchy and red.

Eggert sniffed and said, "Oh, you're dead, alrighty, Barry. You're as dead as they come."

Mother said, "I never hurt you, Barry."

He said, "But the headaches and the dreams…"

"It was the tumor, Barry. You were dying. But you made the honorable choice, son, and that made all the difference."

Mule began to purr and pushed her head under Barry's hand.

Mother smiled. She said, "You did good, Barry."

Barry smiled.

◆ ◆ ◆ ◆ ◆

SNEAK PEEK OF BOOK 3
INTERFACE: THE ALICE SIMULATION

High Lord Quinn's modification of the Middles' behavior through their Interface connections had unwelcome effects. At least they were unwelcome for the Middles. Lord Quinn got what he wanted. He'd stopped caring a long time ago what it cost in blood. The people who lived in The City were compliant and calm and yet able to carry out their duties, mostly, without all the problems that went along with personal rights and freedoms, without the pressures those pesky notions put on the lords' lifestyles.

The Interface was a neural implant that gave the ability to run machines and experience virtual states of consciousness, all within the mind. It was developed before the collapse to enable pilots to function during the intense pressures of quantum acceleration, though no one was concerned with interstellar travel any longer. The Interface was the most comprehensive technological advance ever imagined, granting the individual nearly omnipotent powers. It was also the most powerful mind control device ever created; he who controlled the Interface servers controlled the implanted.

The people had no recourse. They could feel something was off, but in most cases they couldn't even identify the problem. Being so taxed, the Middles developed an underlying lethargy. Nothing seemed to have changed, at least nothing that they could remember. But everyone could feel it.

The Interface was an invincible weapon in the wrong hands. Lord Quinn's hands were about as wrong as you could imagine. He was an autocrat, in cognitive decline, with control over a whole city of compliant robot people.

And while Lord Quinn's neurons atrophied from a lifelong diet of preserved, toxic foods, The City deteriorated from the inside. It's ironic when you consider that the lords were among the few citizens of The City who had access to fresh, clean foods. High Lord Quinn had lost the tenuous grip he'd had on reality sometime in the six years since his daughter and granddaughter escaped with Emerson Loyde. He'd turned his attention away from leading The City and instead concentrated on assuring his legacy. Boston Quinn had much more power over the people in The City than he had over his own faculties.

But this is a story about the Middles in The City. One Middle in particular, named Ahlise. She grew up in Talor's pod. A Middle could use her pod name as a surname if she needed it. Normally, it didn't matter because everyone was implanted at six years old and could be identified by registration number at any time. She still liked to think of Talor as her mother, and she hung onto the name as a way to keep her pod mother alive.

Ahlise Talor repaired food replicators. Middles got all their nutrition from a specially developed fungus delivered through the replicators, which were a sort of advanced 3D printers. The taste and smell of the "food" was delivered though the Interface. There were many problems associated with the system. One was that the flavor profiles had become corrupted over the past fifty years. But since no one remembered what the foods actually tasted like, the problem went unattended and largely unnoticed.

Ahlise felt this was wrong. She was proud of her work. It was hard for her to eat replicator food. She was always questioning, which led to everything tasting wrong. Unlike most Middles, she had a reference point.

Her pod, like many others, grew flowers in window boxes and large pots. Mama Talor loved the dirt and spent hours with Ahlise and her sisters, planting, transplanting, and pruning her roses and flowering vines. Mama Talor, like her mother, saved seeds. She told stories about the times before the collapse and how she would dry and store them. Mama Talor was born before the collapse. Some of her seeds came from her birth mother, kept in tiny waxed paper envelopes and sealed in an airtight tin box.

Most of them were flowers. But when Ahlise was young, one germinated into a smelly stalk that only sprouted a few tiny yellow flowers. She wouldn't allow Mama Talor to pull it out for a weed; she claimed it deserved a chance to live. The tiny flowers became green balls which ripened into cherry tomatoes. Ahlise had seen pictures. They tried to save the seeds, but none of them germinated. Ahlise had tasted a real tomato. The memory was indelible.

And so, when it came to correcting the flavor profiles, she stood up for the quality she knew she could achieve. Her superiors ordered her to leave them alone. No one else was concerned. Ahlise felt the resistance her implant fed her. But Mama Talor taught her children to believe in themselves, and Ahlise used her will to push through the resistance.

An Interface server detected Ahlise's fight reflex and automatically countered it, as per the lord's mandates. The result was a blank spot in her memories. Even though she couldn't articulate why she shouldn't be concerned with the taste profiles, the fact that she couldn't even think about them threw Ahlise into depression. Well, first it made her angry. Livid would be more precise. But when she fully realized that her thoughts could never be her own, she gave in to the futility.

Her depressed state should have alerted a human monitor that Ahlise needed help, as it did before the new mandates. But now, mental health issues were referred to an online help server that was repurposed from the year 2035. The outdated program suggested nonmedical solutions be tried first. It said she should play board games with people, take long walks, and try meditation. The choices were ridiculous.

Ahlise attended a few sessions with an AI therapist, but the programing was so out of date for her culture and situation in 2090, it all seemed like a poor attempt at satire. After the second session, Ahlise briefly considered suicide, which the Interface servers responded to as a threat to life. Again, had it happened before the mandates, humans would have been notified. But because resources were budgeted tightly, Ahlise wasn't even contacted, and the suspensions were implemented instantly. They had the same effect as if she were injected with a general anesthetic.

Ahlise was cast into a flat, black void. She couldn't see or feel anything. Just a numb mind in endless space.

When she regained normal consciousness, she had received a secure message from an unknown source. She followed the link in the message which brought her to a server where she was plunged into a detailed simulation. The scene looked like Wes Anderson designed it, not that Ahlise had ever seen one of his films. A serene instrumental rendition of the late twentieth-century hit, "Somewhere My Love," oozed from somewhere overhead. She was in the waiting room of an upscale lawyer's office from early 2000, sitting in a light brown, seventies-style, pleather chair. The surface of the coffee table before her was scattered with glossy glamor magazines. A copy of *People* rested face up in her lap.

The light was somehow clearer in the simulation. She felt lighter, like gravity was no longer holding her body down so firmly. She thought out loud, "Why am I here?"

The answer came in her own voice. "Because you can be free here. You can do whatever you want."

The thought was intoxicating. Ahlise laughed out loud. She stood and looked around. The canned music continued in the background. She didn't know the tune. She yelled, "IF I'M FREE, THEN LET ME GO!" And ran to the door, expecting someone or something to smack her hand away from the knob. When it didn't, she stepped onto the sidewalk.

The late afternoon sun blinded her. She stumbled out into the heat. At the corner, the traffic light changed, and a stream of actual automobiles seemed to erupt. She had never experienced real traffic before. The dirt, heat, and noise of the crowded macadam streets pummeled her. The smell of open storm sewers assaulted her. Across the way, on the hillside, she saw the Hollywood sign, its letters propped against the scrubby Los Angeles brush. Ahlise had never seen it before. Bodies crowded the sidewalk. The sun was too hot. An unidentifiable pressure built inside her skull. She felt like there was grit in her joints, sand in her eyes; an oily layer of grime covered everything.

The signal changed, and the throng carried Ahlise across the street. She couldn't resist. On the opposite side, she collapsed onto a bench in a covered bus stop. It was shady and cool; the relief nearly brought tears. The signal changed. She closed her eyes, hoping the dizziness would pass. Nothing made sense. The crosswalk whistle signaled the light change several times. Ahlise lost count.

She opened her eyes to a light-brown-skinned woman dressed in a blue blazer and a white silk blouse who leaned toward her ear and whispered, "You can't sleep here. The cops will lock you in the drunk tank." She had a pink carnation in the buttonhole of her jacket. It was a flower Ahlise had only seen in pictures. It emitted a strong sweet smell.

She sat up and wiped the drool from her cheek. "I'm not drunk, am I? *Where* am I? What is this place?"

The blazer woman said, "You're in a simulation, Ahlise. The year is 2024. This is Los Angeles. Pretty cool, eh?"

"How? Where? I don't understand. Are we still in The City? I've never experienced a simulation that was this real before."

Indeed, the sim was becoming more intense every second, as though the closer Ahlise looked, the more detail she could see. Sims were usually simple cognitive façades. Everyone knew it was an illusion, and they just ignored the frayed edges. Close inspections quickly became pixelated. Not this one. In this sim, the complexity compounded. Every moment, there was more. More noise, more heat, more light, more people... It became oppressive. Ahlise nearly vomited.

The woman in the blazer extended her hand in the early twenty-first-century gesture of peace and said, "Nice to meet you, Ahlise. I'm Aver, your Spirit Guide." Ahlise held Aver's fingers in her limp hand.

She said, "I'm still confused."

"I'm your *Spirit Guide*, like your personal technical support agent. Only you can see or hear me, and no one else will see you speaking or interacting with me. I am simply not there to everyone else in the game."

"Game?"

"You know, Ahlise, you are smarter than that." Aver shook her head in an exaggerated gesture. "We would have never invited you in if you were just any run-of-the-mill Middle. Wake up, lady! Game? Yes! Of course this is a game. Otherwise, The Authority would shut us down. But while you are a patient, there are servers you can live in which The Authority can't see. This is one of them."

"Patient?"

When Aver didn't answer, Ahlise continued, "Is there an object to this *game*?"

Aver moved close to Ahlise's cheek and brushed it with her lips. She whispered, "To stay alive, Ahlise. The same object as any game. Except, when you die in this sim, you never come back." Aver kissed the corner of her mouth, and her lips actually burned. Ahlise put her hand to her cheek, but it was only wet.

She said, "What about my job? I have to go to work."

"That's part of the beauty, dear. This is therapy. You are in our care. You work here in this world now. What kind of work would you like to do?"

She didn't want to think about her actual life. Being in the sim was so much easier. She couldn't remember much about it anyway, something about repairing machines. Her memories were like looking at a picture through steam; the image was blurry and indistinct. It actually hurt to try.

She said, "Can I be Alice? Just plain old A-L-I-C-E? Sometimes I think Mama Talor named me Ahlise as a punishment."

"You can be anyone and anything you like, Alice. You want to be a boy?"

Ahlise's physiology morphed where she stood. Her breasts flattened, and hair appeared on her cheeks and chin. She put her hand in her pants and gasped.

"No. Definitely not."

Her body resumed its original form.

Aver said, "What would you like to do?"

"I'm starving," Alice said. "Can we eat?"

They walked to a hot dog cart. Alice ordered a foot-long with kraut. The flavors were intense, clean, real. She got ketchup on her shirt and said, "It tastes like a real tomato. How did you ever get the profiles right?"

Aver touched the stain, and it disappeared. Alice said, "How could this be? Replicators can't produce flavors this bold. If we have this technology, why don't we employ it?" She had a twinge when she said replicators, but it didn't derail her. A moment later, she wondered why it would.

Aver said, "Because, Alice, this simulation was not written for you. It is an elite construction; we cloned it. It's running on a rogue server. The City Interface network can't find us because of a cycled address routine."

"But why? What's in it for you? And how do you keep The Authority out of my Interface connection when I am here?"

"We are sanctioned by The Authority as a therapy. That's all they know. We lock them out of your implant while you are under our care."

The sun began to set, and streetlights came on. Alice said, "Where do I sleep? Do I need to leave?"

Aver replied, "Follow me. No, you don't leave the game, Alice. Ever. If you leave, you can never come back, remember?"

They walked on a sidewalk for a few blocks, but as the day turned to dusk, the landscape changed drastically. Instead of a downtown street with high-rise buildings and lanes of noisy traffic, they were in a quiet, green, neighborhood. Alice said, "Are those birds? I have only ever heard recordings of songbirds."

"This simulation is a representation of the southwestern coast of the United States in the year 2024. Everything from the air pollution to the wildlife is accurate down to the microbial level. We run the sim on a quantum processor. No one uses this technology anymore."

Small bungalows and high stone walls flanked either side of the street. Alice marveled at the tall palms and overgrown yucca plants near the side-walk. Aver turned up the driveway to a cottage about 100 meters from the road. The lights were on; buttery yellow glowed through gauzy curtains.

A brown Border Collie burst through the front door screen and bounded across the lawn. Alice had never seen a real dog before. The animal wagged its tail and licked her hands. She knew her name. "Rosey. Rosey, is that you?" Memories of childhood flooded her brain. Rosey as a puppy playing fetch with a tree branch in a large, grassy park and Alice stroking the dog's head.

Alice looked at Aver and said, "I remember things. Things that didn't happen."

"That's the sim, Alice. You have a life here. You should forget about your old one."

After a moment, Aver said, "I'll go now. Spend the evening with your mate. You might want to talk about what you want to do, eh?" She tipped her head in Alice's direction and grinned. "Well, goodnight, Alice. Sleep well."

Alice thought, *Mate?*

◆ ◆

Aver vanished. Alice was left kneeling on the lawn with her arms around her dog. Rosey licked her face, and the sprinklers came on. She squealed and ran toward the front door, arriving just as the screen opened and a thin, blond man stepped out. She nearly ran into him. Rosey wiggled in the door around them. He embraced her, and she reflexively put her arms around him.

The information about Peter May flooded her mind. She suddenly knew everything about him. They had been together for a year. He was an advertising agent in a downtown LA firm. They owned the bungalow. It was close to downtown. Amazingly, Alice knew what all of it meant. She could find his office from memory. She even remembered where they met, at an art opening in Beverly Hills.

Alice began to cry.

"What, baby? What's wrong?" Peter asked.

Alice said, "I'm just so happy, Peter." She shivered. She was happy, but she was also unnerved. She wanted it to be real. It seemed real. But she knew it wasn't. She couldn't ignore the feeling that it was distracting her from something else.

He said, "Let's get inside, get you out of those wet clothes."

As he closed the door, she said, "What's that delicious smell?"

◆

They had a bottle of Tuscan wine with dinner. Alice had never tasted anything like the Trambusti Brunello di Montalcino. The roast was perfect with a crisp fat cap on top and the center rare. Peter served it with new potatoes and fresh asparagus with a light Hollandaise. Alice marveled at the intense flavors. She wanted to lick her plate. Everything was vibrant and delicious. She and Peter sat on the back screened porch and drank the rest of the bottle. The sounds of downtown were a distant background hum.

Peter said, "What would you like to do tomorrow, dear?"

She didn't plan it, but thinking about Aver had the same effect as freezing a reel, except the whole world suddenly paused. Aver appeared.

"What's up?" She was oddly chipper, dressed in a pair of pink flannel pajamas with tiny elephants in repetition printed on the fabric. It felt incongruent for her to be in the scene with Peter. Peter didn't notice. He was stiff as a statue, frozen in mid-sentence.

"Oh, nothing, I just thought about you. Sorry."

Aver said, "You don't need to apologize to me, Alice. I'm a simulation. And yes, you can call me by simply thinking of me. Anytime, anywhere. I am your guide, remember. All you have to do is…" She vanished, and the world took on its normal cadence. Peter finished his sentence, but Alice didn't hear him. Aver's voice echoed and faded, "…call me." Her voice trailed off as she sang the old Petula Clark song, "Don't be afraid, you can call me…"

Peter said, "Alice? Hello?"

"I'm just tired. It's been a long day and the wine… I'm a little spaced out."

"Oh, babe, I hear you. Go on and start a bath. I'll clean up and be there soon."

Alice had never seen a modern bathroom. Water was scarce in The City. Flush toilets were a thing of the past. Sitting in a bathtub filled up to her neck was beyond luxurious. The water pressure was high, and the sunken tub filled in minutes. Resting in the steaming water, Alice tried to wonder about her actual body. *Where is it? Who's caring for me?*

But it was no use. She couldn't pay attention to that reality when the world she was experiencing was as powerful and arresting as this one. It seemed she floated in the tub for hours. The water didn't get cold. Of course, Alice wasn't expecting it. When Peter came in, he dried her with a plush bath sheet. It was like being kissed by a thousand butterflies. She was too exhausted to resist him seeing her naked. More and more, it felt like they'd known each other for years. He slipped a cotton nightgown over her head and led her to bed, where she sank into the feather mattress and drifted into a dreamless, rejuvenating sleep.

◆

"What do you want to do?" The words swam in her consciousness as she surfaced from sleep. Peter's words, Aver's words, she couldn't tell. What *did* she want to do? If nothing else mattered, if age and sex and power meant nothing, what did *Alice* want? She had never asked herself that question. It was always *what can Alice do for them?* And it was never *what can Alice do for Alice?*

She sat up. The room was filled with golden light. Peter came in. Alice said, "I want to paint!"

"What, like paint the walls?"

"No, Peter, I want to paint with oils, on canvas. I have always wanted to be an artist."

"And so, you shall be."

◆ ◆

There was a spare bedroom next to theirs and an office downstairs. When Alice suggested making the bedroom her studio, Peter said, "That's for the baby, right?"

She could feel the wave of emotion coming, but she didn't want to break down in front of Peter. He was so earnest and sincere; she couldn't bear explaining it to him. Instead, she conjured Aver and stopped the sim, even freezing the blue jay who had just launched off the birdfeeder outside the window.

Alice broke down when Aver appeared. They hugged, and she sobbed into her guide's shoulder, leaving a damp spot. She said, "Babies? I can have babies here?"

Aver held her by both shoulders, an arm's length away. "This is your life. This is where you live. You can do *whatever* you want here."

Alice recovered her composure and nodded, wiping her tears. When Aver was gone, she said to Peter, "Oh right. The baby."

381

◆

They set up her studio in the downstairs office. It turned out to be the better choice. The light wasn't blocked by the side yard trees. Once her easels and pallets were set, brushes in jars, and a few white smocks were hanging near the door, she locked herself in and stared at the blank canvas. It was intimidating, but of all the memories that Alice had lost, she remembered Mama Talor telling her to believe in herself, that she could do anything she put her mind to. She squeezed out a fine pile of ultramarine blue onto her pallet. It was creamy and rich. She wanted to feel it on her tongue, to press her lips into it. Alice dipped her brush in turpentine and used a thinned bit of burnt sienna to begin sketching.

She worked for ten hours without a break and wouldn't even let Peter in. He offered to push sandwiches under the door, but she told him to go away. As the last glimpse of sun flashed off the copper wind chimes hanging from the eave of the back screened porch, Alice opened the door. Peter handed her a ham sandwich as he passed her on the way to the canvas.

Alice ate the whole thing without stopping. She followed Peter and stood by him, chewing. He said, "This is amazing. How did you learn to paint like this?"

The canvas was covered with thick, pallet-knife-shaped swirls of shiny, rich color. It was a picture of the bungalow painted in Van Gogh style. The indigo night sky spiraled around white and yellow stars over the little house with glowing buttery windows and a wavering, deep green lawn. Rosey slept curled nose to tail on the front porch.

She finished the last bite, swallowed, and said, "I didn't. I've never painted anything before."

Peter looked at her with awe and shook his head. "You're a savant."

Alice thought of the sim and Aver, but quickly changed her mind, not wanting to interrupt the moment.

He said, "Can you paint any other style?"

"I don't know. Maybe I'll try to do a Vermeer tomorrow. But for right now, all I want is to fall into bed. I'm spent."

"How do you know so much about art?" He was walking her up the carpeted stairs to their bedroom.

"I had books when I was a kid. I read them over and over. I memorized the ones I liked: *Starry Night* and *Girl with a Pearl Earring*." A memory bubbled up; she was in a huge marble room with high ceilings. Large oil paintings lined the walls. She said, "My dad took us to the Chicago Museum of Art when the traveling Van Gogh show came through." She knew this was an implanted memory. Alice grew up in The City. She had different pod-fathers throughout her youth, but she'd never been to Chicago. She didn't even know what it was.

Alice was asleep before her head hit the pillow, and she slept till the afternoon the next day.

◆ ◆

Alice and Peter lived together for several years. She became pregnant with their first daughter, Marne, nine months after she arrived and their second daughter, Mellissa, eighteen months later. When she wasn't tending her children, Alice painted. She favored Van Gogh and Vermeer, but she could copy any style as long as she'd seen enough examples. Peter brought her thick coffee-table art books filled with color plates.

Her children were beautiful and well behaved. She had a storybook life, illustrated in masterfully executed oils in the styles of several master Impressionists. Peter was a talented cook, which was fine with Alice, though she made delicious meals in her own right. She'd tell her daughters, "Anyone can learn to cook if they can read." And the produce and meats available at the local market were always fresh and in good supply. Alice had little time to reflect on how perfect her life was. She seemed to have boundless energy, and years passed quickly.

Peter always agreed with her. Days were smooth and routine. They enjoyed hanging out with friends from the block. The girls grew up strong and healthy. She almost forgot Aver, though the guide did make occasional appearances to check in on her. In Alice's estimation, she'd been living in the bungalow with her new family for close to ten years. Peter was getting grey at the temples. Most evenings, they sat together on the couch and watched Netflix shows. Alice nearly forgot about her other life.

The confusion and frustration that caused Alice's breakdown faded. This was her life now, and it seemed to Alice that it would go on forever. That's always a bad sign. She knew she was in a simulation, but she ignored it. Thinking about herself as Ahlise in The City was painful; she avoided it. But there were hints that not everything was as perfect as she wished. Alice noticed that she wasn't aging. When she asked Aver about it, the guide said, "It's a sim, Alice. Anything is possible in a sim."

"But what about the real me?" The thought turned her guts to water. She nearly ran to the toilet.

Aver said, "It's better if you don't think about her."

Aver's response didn't satisfy Alice, but she didn't want to experience that terror again. Avoiding it didn't help her fears. If anything, over time, it became a hungry animal waiting in the shadows. She couldn't think about her body back in The City—why would she want to? And still, there was a lingering question: *What is happening to me while I am living out a different life? Am I alright?*

She soon found out.

◆ ◆ ◆

Emerson Lloyde and Elli Rattlesnake Quinn came to The City to rescue their daughter, Marya. The girl was kidnaped during an unprovoked attack on Crow City by High Lord Boston Quinn. He believed that the Enforcers, acting as his private army, would protect him from any sort of retaliation. But his daughter, Elli, grew up in The City exploring the tunnels that ran beneath Founder's Quarter. She and Emerson were able to sneak in and use a juice-hacker-made simulation app to end the control Lord Quinn had on the Middles. Emerson locked everyone's Interface and brought the high lord back to face his crimes against the people of Crow City. When he initiated a simulation which called all the citizens of The City into a grand hall and Emerson told them they were free, Alice was among them. She found herself there, alone with the rest of the citizens, but she had been in her simulation for so long she couldn't process what was happening.

Being snatched from normal reality to a simulation was disorienting enough, but jumping from one whole body sim to another could put a person into shock. Some inhabitants simply fainted. Others stopped breathing. Alice was able to stay conscious, but just barely.

During Emerson and Elli Quinn's announcement, she called Aver, but her Spirit Guide did not appear. Aver told her that if she ever left the sim, her character would be lost. The people and places would only exist in Alice's memory. She hardly heard Emerson's announcement. Her senses were dull as if her head was stuffed with cotton. By the end of the meeting, she realized what must have happened.

When the sim ended, Alice was cast into a nothing space. She was not alarmed, at first. All Interface users become used to the glitches and delays inherent in a completely digital environment. Nothing space was one of the more common delays the user experienced when switching from one server to another, though Interface transitions were supposed to be seamless. Opening trouble tickets always got a boilerplate response about how there was no such thing as *nothing space,* and therefore nothing could be done about it because it didn't exist. But everybody knew it did, and any Interface user with a year's experience had already experienced it.

Nothing space was exactly that: Nothing. You knew you were some-place, and you could think about it, but there was nothing there. No feeling, no sound, no light. You could see something in the dark, but it was just the shadow of empty space. Your imagination could conjure monsters in that dark if you weren't careful. It was the blank page of imagination.

Alice waited. She couldn't mark the passing of time; it went on and on. She knew panic wouldn't do her any good, but she still had to remind herself that it would end.

A strange thing happened to Alice. As she relaxed, her life scrolled out in her mind like a film strip of important moments. She was touched by what she saw, although the emotions did not overwhelm her. She found herself watching the reel of her life with Peter and her children. It made her happy.

She realized that her body might be dead and wondered if this was what death was like. It didn't scare her. She figured that if any part of her was gone, it must not have been the most important part since she was still able to think. The thought made her want to laugh. Like all the pieces of the puzzle finally fit and she could see the simplicity of it.

Suddenly, the lights came up, and she found herself in her body. She had to squint, but it was too bright to see.

Chandler said, "Hello, Alice." He lowered the intensity and adjusted the contrast. The room came into focus. She was sitting across from Chandler Estes in a handmade elk-skin chair in the main room of his home. A towering stone fireplace containing a small fire burned at their feet; the occasional knot popped and threw embers onto the worn, wide plank floor.

She was in the Chandler Cube.

When the old man came into focus, Alice said, "Hi." She felt secure and warm. "Who are *you,* and *where* am I?" She smiled and said, "Sorry. It's been a weird day."

"No problem." He stepped to her and bade her stand so they could hug. He said, "I'm Chandler Estes, Emerson Lloyde's granddad. It might be a little harder to explain the *where.*"

◆

"But how did I get here?" Alice was pacing now. Chandler had given her a cup of sassafras tea.

He said, "Well, I'm just part of a simulation myself, so I can't be sure. But I expect that when Emerson called his meeting and freed everyone, you were pulled out of that 2024 Los Angeles server you'd been living in. And when Emerson disconnected from The City's network, you somehow replicated into The Black Mariah's processors. It's one of the only quantum computers in use that I ever heard of. The other was built by Lord Bragg, but he was banished because of it. Nelson Bragg was quite a character. A real genius. He would have given High Lord Quinn a run. That's probably why he disappeared back when I was still living in The City. That's close to fifty years ago now."

Her voice rose. "What you are saying is that my life with Peter and my children is gone, erased. And my body. What happened to my body?"

Chandler looked sorrowful, but he said nothing. He didn't have any precise answers for her. "If there is a way to recover your avatars on the other system, I will. But I need to talk to Emerson." He held her shoulders, looked into her blue eyes, and said, "I can tell you one thing for sure. You were only in that simulation a short time. Time expanded inside of its processes. I've never seen anything like it."

"How do you know that?"

Chandler said, "I detected you in the server by accident. Before I figured out how to wake you up, if that's an accurate word for your consciousness bloom, I found a huge store of code that must have somehow come over with you. I've been analyzing it for a while. There are logs. I think I might be able to reboot the LA 2024 server."

"What? But wait. Didn't I just get here?"

"Ah, no, dear." Chandler took on that sorrowful look again. Like a dog who'd made a mess, and now he had to fess up.

"How long have I been in stasis?"

"Oh, not *that* long."

"How long?!"

"A year, maybe?"

◆ ◆

"I'm so confused." Alice sat down.

Chandler said, "It's not so bad."

"What?"

"Living in a simulation. I have a lot of free time. I can teach you to program. You can write your own boundaries."

"It's dizzying, that's all. Here I sit, only digitally alive in one simulated reality while I pine for the life I had in another simulated reality, all the while not much concerned that my real, actual, *LIVING* body is either dead or in a coma somewhere." She stared at him for a long minute and said, "I actually feel more alive than I ever have before."

Chandler handed her a copper flask and said, "Red corn hooch. The best I've ever made."

She took a sip and said, "Haa," and choked. "But it's smooth." She cleared her throat. "You have a still in here?"

Chandler said, "No, of course not. I programmed this whiskey."

She nodded, took another sip, and said, "So, what have you been able to figure out?" She handed back the flask.

"When Bragg created the LA 2024 server, he believed that it was a viable way to start a revolution. I'm guessing his plan was what got him banished. He thought that if enough people could experience a lifetime of healing inside the sim, they would be forever changed. And further, he targeted the ones who could not adapt to the new order, the ones who had the most resistance to the sort of control that High Lord Quinn ended up using. He reasoned that the people who were healed of their traumas would be like the true believers and would act as seeds of dissent in the general populations. With enough of them, the system would be forced to change."

Alice was looking around the room, obviously distracted. "Do you believe my body might still be alive out there?"

Chandler refilled her cup. He said, "Anything is possible. I'll mention it to Emerson the next time he opens the Cube. We'll crack that program. Bragg thought he was a better programmer than anyone. His arrogance was his blind spot. When we see Ana next, she'll open it right away. The girl has a real gift."

◆ ◆

At that moment, Ana was being marched through a temperate rainforest. Her hands were zip-tied behind her back. The soldier behind her poked a short-range crossbow into her spine. A cable around her neck connected to the soldier's belt. If Ana put a strain on it, the soldier would deliver a 5,000-volt shock through it. Ana had already discovered this the hard way.

The Chandler Cube was in the cloaked, Black Mariah shuttle. Emerson had it locked in a storage bin in in his cabin. Emerson and Saą were 160 kilometers north in the toxic lands, tracking Elli Rattlesnake Quinn and her daughter, Marya. Chandler and Alice were alone in the simulation. They spent their time getting to know each other.

ACKNOWLEDGMENTS

There are many, both living and passed on, who have supported the creation of our work. And while we would like to thank each personally, instead, this time, we dedicate this book to Goddard College, without which, we would not be who we have become. May Goddard live on in our hearts, minds and accomplishments.

Goddard College 1938 – 2024

Contact the author and learn more at **rkhillhouse.com**.
1280 Lexington Ave Front 2 #1288 New York, NY 10028

ABOUT R. K. HILLHOUSE

R.K. Hillhouse is an amalgam of Ron Heacock, MFA & Karen Mary Walasek, PhD

Ron spent many years as a performing songwriter and has shared the stage with such notable artists as Alan Ginsberg and Pete Seeger. His work has been published in Connotation, PaperTape, The LIMN Literary & Arts Journal, Cease Cows, Far Enough East, Rawboned, and Aphotic Realm. He earned his MFA and his MFA IA, as well as an MA in publishing at Goddard College and is pursuing the completion of a Masters in sustainability and social innovation at Prescott College. His collection of short stories, Hey, This is it, I'm Going to Die, was published in 2014.

Karen's relationship with the more than human world interweaves throughout her creative, practical and scholarly life. A Polish American shepherd, feltmaker, midwife, mother, grandmother, pisankarka and scholar, she received an MFA in creative writing & interdisciplinary arts from Goddard College and earned her PhD in Sustainability Education at Prescott College in May 2024, incorporating a Slavic econarrative with cultural reclamation and matriarchal land connections. She co-writes with husband Ron Heacock under the alias, R. K. Hillhouse. Hillhouse Farms operated a writers' retreat that nurtured working writers for seven years prior to 2008. It is now a family homestead where the team gets to fully nurture the growth of their own creative works and research.